In An... [barcode: S0-AWM-130]

IS "THE VOICE ... TODAY'S POSTMODERN
THRILLER GENERATION"
(*The Providence Journal,* RI) . . .

His explosive bestsellers featuring Mitch Rapp are
"FANTASTIC" (Glenn Beck) . . . "JUST FABULOUS"
(Rush Limbaugh) . . . "COMPLEX, CHILLING, AND
SATISFYING" (*The Plain Dealer,* Cleveland)

Fans of Vince Flynn's Mitch Rapp thrillers will be
held captive by this electrifying #1 *New York Times*
bestseller. . . . Behind the steely gaze of the nation's
ultimate hero is a young man primed to become an
AMERICAN ASSASSIN

"A bold and brawny tale that never wavers or lets up. . . .
Flynn has never been better."

—*The Providence Journal* (RI)

"Rapp is still the best CIA-trained human weapon this
side of Jason Bourne."

—*Contra Costa Times* (CA)

"Another terrific read."

—*The Toronto Sun*

PURSUIT OF HONOR

"A fast-paced page-turner . . . you won't want to put it
down. . . . Informative and insightful. . . . If you have
never read Vince Flynn and are upset about the current
political situation regarding homeland and national security, this book is highly recommended."

—Blackfive.com

Also by Vince Flynn

AMERICAN ASSASSIN

A THRILLER

VINCE FLYNN

Pocket Books

New York   London   Toronto   Sydney   New Delhi

Pocket Books
A Division of Simon & Schuster, Inc.
1230 Avenue of the Americas
New York, NY 10020

This book is a work of fiction. Names, characters, places, and incidents either are products of the author's imagination or are used fictitiously. Any resemblance to actual events or locales or persons, living or dead, is entirely coincidental.

Copyright © 2010 by Vince Flynn

First Pocket Books paperback edition September 2011

POCKET and colophon are registered trademarks of Simon & Schuster, Inc.

For information about special discounts for bulk purchases, please contact Simon & Schuster Special Sales at 1-866-506-1949 or business@simonandschuster.com.

The Simon & Schuster Speakers Bureau can bring authors to your live event. For more information or to book an event contact the Simon & Schuster Speakers Bureau at 1-866-248-3049 or visit our website at www.simonspeakers.com.

Cover design by Richard Yoo

Manufactured in the United States of America

10 9 8 7 6 5 4 3 2 1

ISBN 978-1-4165-9519-9
ISBN 978-1-4391-0051-6 (ebook)

*To the victims of the
Pan Am Lockerbie terrorist attack
and their families*

ACKNOWLEDGMENTS

WRITING is by necessity a solitary process. Fortunately, my wife, a beautiful, stoic Scandinavian from Northern Minnesota, understands this. Lysa, you are an amazing partner. Every year you bear the brunt of these deadlines. Even when I am physically around, I am mentally elsewhere . . . trying to figure out the twists and turns of the story. I can never say thank you enough.

Publishing, on the other hand, has very little to do with solitude. It is a dynamic, exciting industry where things can go wrong, or right, at countless junctures. I am extremely lucky to be surrounded by some of the best people in the business. From Sloan Harris and Kristyn Keene at ICM, to Emily Bestler, Sarah Branham, Kate Cetrulo, Jeanne Lee, Al Madocs, David Brown, and Judith Curr at Atria, to Louise Burke and Anthony Ziccardi at Pocket Books, to Michael Selleck and Carolyn Reidy at Simon & Schuster, and the entire sales force . . . you are all top-notch. For twelve straight publications, most of it during the most tumultuous times the industry has ever seen, you have managed to make each launch better than the previous.

To Lorenzo DiBonaventura and Nick Wechsler for continuing to push the boulder up the hill—I do not know how you do it. To my friend Rob Richer, who helped give me the flavor of Beirut in the early nineties, to Ed Schoppman for facilitating the hardware, to Dr. Jodi Bakkegard for straightening me out, and to all those who choose to remain in the shadows, thank you. To those whom I may have forgotten—my sincere apologies.

And last, to you, the reader. I have wanted to tell this story for fifteen years. How did Mitch Rapp become Mitch Rapp? Crafting this novel has been one of the greatest thrills of my writing career. Thank you for your support and enjoy the read.

AMERICAN ASSASSIN

PRELUDE

BEIRUT, LEBANON

M ITCH Rapp stared at his reflection in the dusty, cracked mirror and questioned his sanity. There was no shaking, or sweaty palms. He wasn't nervous. It was just a cold, calculated assessment of his abilities and his odds for success. He went over the plan once more from start to finish, and again concluded it was likely that he would be severely beaten, tortured, and possibly killed, but even in the face of such prospects, he couldn't bring himself to walk away, which brought him right smack dab back to that part about his mental health. What kind of man willingly chose to do such a thing? Rapp thought about it for a long moment and then decided someone else would have to answer that question.

While everyone else seemed content to sit on their hands, it was not in Rapp's nature to do so. Two of his colleagues had been grabbed from the streets of Beirut by a nasty little outfit called Islamic Jihad. They were a tentacle of Hezbollah that specialized in kidnapping, torture, and suicide bombings. The jihadis had, without question, already begun the interrogation of their new prisoners. They would expose the men to unthinkable pain, and they would begin to peel back each layer of the onion until they got what they wanted.

That was the savage truth, and if his colleagues could delude themselves into thinking otherwise, it just meant they had consciously or unconsciously gravitated toward convenient conclusions. After a day of watching the very people who said they would handle the situation do nothing, Rapp decided to look for a solution on his own. The bureaucrats and foreign service types back in Washington might be content with letting things take their natural course, but Rapp was not. He'd been through too much to allow his cover to be blown, and beyond that there was that nagging little thing about honor and the warrior's code. He'd been through the wringer with these guys. One he respected, admired, and liked. The other he respected, admired, and hated. The pull for him to do something, anything to save them was strong. The gang back in Washington might be able to simply write off losing the faceless operatives as a cost of war, but to the guys who were in trenches it was a little more personal. Warriors don't like leaving their own to die at the hands of the enemy, because secretly, they all know they might be in the same position one day, and they sure as hell hope their country will do everything in their power to get them back.

Rapp eyed his fractured reflection; his thick, uncombed head of black hair and beard, his bronzed olive skin and his eyes, so dark that they were almost black. He could walk among the enemy without attracting so much as a suspicious glance, but that would all change if he didn't do something. He thought of his training and everything he'd sacrificed. The entire operation would be exposed, and that meant his career in the field would be over. He'd be stuffed behind some desk back in Washington where he'd rot for the next twenty-five years. He'd wake up each morning and go to bed each night with the nagging thought that he should have done something—anything. And ultimately he would emasculate himself by questioning the size of his balls for as long as he lived. Rapp shuddered at the thought. He might be a little crazy, but he'd read enough Greek tragedies to understand that a life filled with that kind of recrimination would eventually lead him to the psych ward. *No*, he thought, *I'd rather go down swinging.*

He nodded to himself and took a deep breath before walking over to the window. Rapp gently pulled back the tattered curtain and looked down at the street. The two foot soldiers from Islamic Jihad were still positioned across the street keeping an eye on things. Rapp had dropped a few hints around the neighborhood about what he was up to, and they had shown up barely an hour after he had pressed his seventh hundred-dollar bill into the willing hand of a local merchant. Rapp had considered killing one lackey and interrogating the other, but knew word would spread so fast that his colleagues would be either moved or killed before he could act on whatever intel he could gather. Rapp shook his head. This was it. There was only one avenue open to him, and there was no sense in delaying what had to be done.

He quickly scrawled a note and left it on the small desk in the corner. He gathered his sunglasses, the map, and a large wad of cash and headed for the door. The elevator was broken so he walked the four flights to the lobby. The new man behind the front desk looked nervous as all hell, which Rapp took as a sign that someone had talked to him. He continued out the front door into the blazing daylight and held his map above his head to block the sun while he looked up and down the street. Looking out from behind the sunglasses, he pretended not to notice the duo from Islamic Jihad. With his face buried in the map, he turned to the right and started heading east.

Within half a block, Rapp's nervous system began sending his brain alarms, each more frantic than the previous one. It took every ounce of control to override his training and millions of years of basic survival instincts that were embedded like code into the human brain. Up ahead, the familiar black car was parked across the street. Rapp ignored the man behind the wheel and turned down a narrow side street. Just thirty paces ahead a rough-looking man was stationed in front of a shop. His left leg was straight and firmly planted on the pavement and the other bent up behind him and placed against the side of the building. His big frame was resting against the building while he took a long drag off his cigarette. There was something vaguely familiar about him, right down to the dusty black pants and the white dress shirt with the sweat-stained armpits.

The street was otherwise empty. The survivors of the bloody civil war could smell trouble, and they had wisely decided to stay indoors until the morning's sideshow was concluded. The footfalls from behind were echoing like heavy shoes on the stone floor of an empty cathedral. Rapp could hear the pace of his pursuers quicken. A car engine revved, no doubt the black BMW he'd already spotted. With every step Rapp could feel them closing in from behind. His brain ran through scenarios with increasing rapidity, looking for any way out of the impending disaster.

They were close now. Rapp could feel them. The big fellow up ahead threw his cigarette to the ground and pushed himself away from the building with a little more spring than Rapp would have guessed him capable of. He filed that away. The man smiled at him and produced a leather truncheon from his pocket. Rapp dropped the map in feigned surprise and turned to flee. The two men were exactly where he expected them to be, guns drawn, one pointed at Rapp's head, the other at his chest.

The sedan skidded to a stop just to his right, the trunk and front passenger door swinging open. Rapp knew what was next. He closed his eyes and clenched his jaw as the truncheon cracked him across the back of the head. Rapp stumbled forward and willingly fell into the arms of the two men with pistols. He let his legs go limp, and the men struggled with his weight. He felt the arms of the big man wrap around his chest and yank him upright. His 9mm Beretta was pulled from the back of his waistband and he was dragged the short distance to the car's trunk. Rapp landed headfirst with a thud. The rest of his body was folded in on top of him, and then the trunk was slammed shut.

The engine roared and the rear tires bit through a layer of sand and dirt until they found asphalt. Rapp was thrown back as the vehicle shot away. He slowly cracked open his eyes, and as expected, he found himself enveloped in darkness. His head was throbbing a bit from the blow, but not too badly. There was no fear on his face or doubt in his mind, though. Just a smile on his lips as he thought of his plan. The seeds of disinformation that he had spread over the past day had drawn them in just as he'd hoped. His captors had no idea of the true intent of the man they now had in their possession, and more important, no idea of the violence and mayhem he was about to visit upon them.

PART I

CHAPTER 1

SOUTHERN VIRGINIA
(ONE YEAR EARLIER)

MITCH Rapp removed the blindfold from his face and raised his seat back. The brown Ford Taurus sedan rocked its way down a rutted gravel road, twin plumes of dust corkscrewing into the hot August air. The blindfold was a precaution in case he failed, which Rapp had no intention of doing. He stared out the window at the thick wall of pines that bracketed the lane. Even with the bright sun he could see no more than thirty feet into the dark maze of trees and underbrush. As a child he'd always found the woods to be an inviting place, but on this particular afternoon it had a decidedly more ominous feel.

A foreboding premonition hijacked his thoughts and sent his mind careening into a place that he did not want to go. At least not this afternoon. Still, a frown creased his brow as Rapp wondered how many men had died in this particular forest, and he wasn't thinking of the men who had fought in the Civil War all those years earlier. No, he thought, trying to be completely honest with himself. Death was too open-ended a word for it. It left the possibility that some accident had befallen the person, and that was a convenient way to skirt the seriousness of what he was getting himself into. *Executed* was a far more accurate word. The men he was thinking of had been marched into these very woods, shot in the back of the head, and dumped into freshly dug holes never to be heard from again. That was the world that Rapp was about to enter, and he was utterly and completely at peace with his decision.

Still, a sliver of doubt sliced through the curtains of his mind and caused a flash of hesitation. Rapp wrestled with it for a moment, and then stuffed it back into the deepest recesses of his brain. Now was not the time for second thoughts. He'd been over this, around it, and under it. He'd studied it from every conceivable angle since the day the mysterious woman had walked into his life. In a strange way, he knew where it was all headed from almost the first moment she'd looked at him with those discerning, penetrating eyes.

He had been waiting for someone to show up, though Rapp had never told her that. Or that the only way he could cope with the pain of losing the love of his life was to plot his revenge. That every single night before he went to sleep he thought of the network of faceless men who had plotted to bring down Pan Am Flight 103, that he saw himself on this very journey, headed to a remote place not dissimilar from the woods he now found himself in. It was all logical to him. Enemies needed to be killed, and Rapp was more than willing to become the person who would do that killing. He knew what was about to happen. He was to be trained, honed and forged into an ultimate precision weapon, and then he would begin to hunt them down. Every last one of the faceless men who had conspired to kill all those innocent civilians on that cold December night.

The car began to slow and Rapp looked up to see a rusted cattle gate with a heavy chain and padlock. His dark brow furrowed with suspicion.

The woman driving the vehicle glanced sideways at him and said, "You were expecting something a little more high-tech perhaps."

Rapp nodded silently.

Irene Kennedy put the car in park and said, "Appearances can be very deceiving." She opened her door and stepped from the vehicle. As she walked to the gate she listened. A moment later she heard the click of the passenger door, and she smiled. Without an ounce of training he had made the right decision. From their very first meeting it was apparent he was different. She had audited every detail of his life and watched him from afar for several months. Kennedy was exceedingly good at her job. She was methodical, organized, and patient. She also had a photographic memory.

Kennedy had grown up in the business. Her father had worked for the State Department, and the vast majority of her education had taken place overseas in countries where an American was not always welcome. Vigilance was a part of her daily routine from the age of five. While other parents worried about their kids' wandering out into the street and getting hit by a car, Kennedy's parents worried about her finding a bomb under their car. It was drilled into her to always be aware of her surroundings.

When Kennedy finally introduced herself to Rapp, he studied her for a long second and then asked why she had been following him. At the time Rapp was only twenty-two, with no formal training. If Kennedy had a weakness it was with improvisation. She liked things plotted out well in advance, and being so thorough, she had gone in assuming the novice would have no idea that she had been running surveillance on him. She had recruited dozens of people and this was a first. Kennedy was caught off guard to the point of stammering for an answer. The recruit was supposed to be the one struggling to understand what was going on. Rapp's recognizing her was not part of the script.

Later, in her motel room outside Syracuse, she retraced her every move over the past eight months and tried to figure out where she had slipped. After three hours and seventeen pages of notes, she still couldn't pinpoint her mistake. With frustration, and grudging admiration, she had concluded that Rapp had extremely acute situational awareness. She moved his file to the top of her stack and made a bold decision. Rather than use the normal people, she contacted a firm run by some retired spooks. They were old friends of her father's, who specialized in handling jobs without creating a paper trail. She asked them to take an objective look at Rapp, just in case she had missed something. Two weeks later they came back with a summary that sent chills up Kennedy's spine.

Kennedy took that report straight to her boss, Thomas Stansfield. Midway through reading the file he suspected what she was up to. When he finished, he slowly closed the two-inch-thick biography of the young Mitch Rapp and made her plead her case. She was concise and to the point, but still Stansfield pointed out the potential pitfalls and obvious dangers of leapfrogging the initial phase of training. She countered perfectly. The game was changing. He had said it himself many times. They could not sit back and play defense, and in this ever more interconnected world they needed a weapon more surgical than any guided bomb or cruise missile. Having spent many years in the field himself, Stansfield also knew this person would have to be uniquely autonomous. Someone who conveniently had no official record.

Kennedy ticked off eight additional reasons why she felt this young man was the perfect candidate. Her logic was sound, but beyond that there was the simple fact that they had to begin somewhere. By Stansfield's reckoning this was an endeavor they should have started a good five years earlier, so it was with a heavy sigh and a leap of faith that he decided to proceed. He told Kennedy to forgo the normal training and take him to the only man they knew who was crazy enough to try to mold a green recruit into what they needed. If Rapp could survive six months of schooling at the hands of Stan Hurley, he might indeed be the weapon they were looking for. Before she left, Stansfield told her to eliminate any connection: Every last file, surveillance photo, and recording that could ever tie them to Rapp was to be destroyed.

Kennedy pulled the car through the gate and asked Rapp to close and lock it behind them. Rapp did as he was asked and then got back in the car. One hundred yards later Kennedy slowed the vehicle to a crawl and maneuvered diagonally in an effort to avoid a large pothole.

"Why no security on the perimeter?" Rapp asked.

"The high-tech systems . . . more often than not . . . they draw too much unwanted attention. They also give a lot of false alarms, which in turn requires a lot of manpower. That's not what this place is about."

"What about dogs?" Rapp asked.

She liked the way he was thinking. As if on cue, two hounds came galloping around the bend. The dogs charged straight at the vehicle. Kennedy stopped and waited for them to get out of her way. A moment later, after baring their teeth, they turned and bolted back in the direction they'd just come from.

Kennedy took her foot off the brake and proceeded up the lane. "This man," Kennedy said. "The one who will be training you."

"The crazy little guy who is going to try to kill me," Rapp said without smiling.

"I didn't say he was going to try to kill you . . . I said he is going to try to make you think he's trying to kill you."

"Very comforting," Rapp said sarcastically. "Why do you keep bringing him up?"

"I want you to be prepared."

Rapp thought about that for a moment and said, "I am, or at least as prepared as you can be for something like this."

She considered that for a moment. "The physical part is assumed. We know you're in good shape, and that's important, but I want you to know that you will be pushed in ways you never imagined. It's a game. One that's designed to make you quit. Your greatest asset will be mental discipline, not physical strength."

Rapp disagreed with her but kept his mouth shut and his face a mask of neutrality. To be the best required equal doses of both. He knew the game. He'd been through plenty of grueling football and lacrosse practices in the humid August heat of Virginia, and back then it was only a simple desire to play that kept him going. Now his motivation to succeed was much deeper. Far more personal.

"Just try to remember . . . none of it is personal," Kennedy said.

Rapp smiled inwardly. That's where you're wrong, he thought. It's all personal. When he responded, however, he was compliant. "I know," Rapp said in an easy tone. "What about these other guys?" If there was one thing that made him a little nervous it was this. The other recruits had been down here for two days. Rapp didn't like getting a late start. They would have already begun the bonding process and were likely to resent his showing up late. He didn't understand the delay, but she wasn't exactly forthright with information.

"There are six of them." Kennedy scrolled through the photos in her mind's eye. She had read their jackets. They all had military experience and shared, at least on paper, many of Rapp's qualities. They were all dark-featured, athletic, capable of violence, or at least not afraid of it, and they had all to one degree or another passed the extensive psychological exams. They had all showed a facility for foreign languages. In terms of a sense of right and wrong, they all hovered near that critical six o'clock position on the mental health pie chart. That thin line that separated law enforcement officers from career criminals.

Around the next bend the landscape opened up before them. A freshly mowed lawn roughly the size of a football field ran along both sides of the lane all the way to a white barn and two-story house with a wraparound porch. This was not what Rapp had expected. The place looked like a rural postcard complete with a set of rocking chairs on the big white porch.

A man appeared from inside the house. He was holding a cup of coffee in one hand and a cigarette in the other. Rapp watched him move across the porch. The man swiveled his head to the left and then right in a casual manner. Most people would have missed it, but Rapp's senses had been opened to the reality that the world was divided between those who were part of the herd and those who liked to hunt. The man was checking his flanks. He stopped at the top of the porch steps and looked down at them from behind a pair of aviator sunglasses. Rapp smiled ever so slightly at the realization that this was the man who was going to try to break him. It was a challenge he had been looking forward to for some time.

CHAPTER 2

RAPP looked through the bug-splattered windshield at the ballbuster he'd been warned about. Even from across the yard he could see the displeased look on the guy's face. He had medium-length brown hair swept to the right and a full Tom Selleck mustache. He was in a pair of faded olive shorts that were a little on the small side and a white V-neck T-shirt. As the car came to a stop Rapp noted the faded black combat boots and white tube socks that were pulled all the way up to his knees. His skin was a leathery, dark brown and all of it, even his cheeks, seemed tightly wound with muscles and tendons. Rapp wondered about the eyes that were conveniently concealed behind a pair of sunglasses. He thought about his plan, and he figured he'd find out soon enough.

"How old is he?" Rapp asked.

"Not sure," Kennedy said as she put the car

in park. "He's older than he looks, though, but I wouldn't bring it up. He doesn't like talking about his age." She unbuckled her seat belt. "Wait here for a moment."

Kennedy exited the vehicle and walked casually across the gravel driveway. She was wearing black dress slacks and a white blouse. Due to the heat and the fact that they were more than a hundred miles from headquarters, she'd left her suit jacket in the backseat. A 9mm Beretta pistol was on her right hip, more to avoid a tongue-lashing from the man she was about to face than from any real fear that she'd have to use it. She looked up at the man on the porch and brushed a loose strand of her auburn hair behind her ear. Stopping at the base of the porch steps she said, "Uncle Stan, you don't look too excited to see me."

Stan Hurley glanced down at Kennedy and felt a twinge of guilt. This little beauty could jerk his emotions around in ways very few could. He'd known Irene longer than she'd known herself. He'd watched her grow up, bought her Christmas presents from strange exotic places, and spent more holidays with the Kennedys than without them. And then a little less than a decade ago, all the joy had drained from their lives when a delivery van packed with over two thousand pounds of explosives pulled up to the U.S. embassy in Beirut. Sixty-three people perished, including Kennedy's father. Hurley had been away screwing one of his sources and had narrowly dodged the bullet. The CIA had lost eight valuable people that April day and they had been playing catch-up ever since.

Hurley was well aware that he had almost no control over his temper, so it was his habit to keep things brief when he was upset and talking with someone he liked. He said simply, "Afternoon, Irene."

Kennedy had been expecting and dreading this moment for some months. Normally Hurley would have greeted her with a warm hug and asked her how her mother was, but not this afternoon. She'd done an end around on him, and Stan Hurley did not like people going over his head for approval on something this serious. The chill in his mood was obvious, but still she pressed on, asking, "How are you feeling?"

Hurley ignored her question and pointedly asked, "Who's in the car?"

"New recruit. Thomas told me he filled you in." Kennedy was referring to their boss.

Hurley's eyes were shielded by the polarized lenses of his aviators. His head slowly swiveled away from the car toward Kennedy. "Yes, he told me what you were up to," he said with obvious disapproval.

Kennedy defensively folded her arms across her chest and said, "You don't endorse my decision."

"Absolutely not."

"Why?"

"I don't run a damn Boy Scout camp."

"Never said you did, Stan," Kennedy said in a biting tone.

"Then why the hell are you wasting my time sending me some titty-boy college puke who doesn't know the difference between a gun and a rifle?"

The normally stoic Kennedy allowed a bit of irritation to show. She was well aware of the special hold she had over Hurley, and a look of disapproval on her part was far more potent than a direct attack.

Hurley looked down at her and could see she was unhappy with him. He didn't like that one bit. It was the same with his own daughters. If one of his boys had so much as looked at him sideways he would have knocked him on his ass, but the girls had the ability to get past all his defenses. Get inside him and create doubt. Still, on this issue, he knew he was right, so he held his ground. "Don't make this personal, Irene. I've been at this a long time, and I know what I'm doing. I don't need you going over my head and then coming down here and dumpin' some untested rookie in my lap."

Kennedy stood sphinxlike, refusing to yield her position.

Hurley took a drag from his cigarette and said, "I think you should save us all the headache and get back in your car and take him back to wherever you found him."

Kennedy was surprised by the genuine resentment she felt. She'd been working on this for more than a year. Her analysis and her instincts told her Rapp was just the man they were looking for, yet here she was being dismissed like some complete neophyte who had no understanding of what they were trying to accomplish. Kennedy slowly climbed the porch steps and squared off with Hurley.

The veteran backed up a bit, obviously uncomfortable with someone whom he wouldn't dare lay a hand on entering his personal space. "I got a lot of work to take care of this afternoon, Irene, so the sooner you get back in the car, the better off we'll all be."

Kennedy squared her shoulders and in a tight voice asked, "Uncle Stan, have I ever disrespected you?"

"That's not what this is—"

"It's exactly what it's about. What have I done to you that has caused you to hold me in such low regard?" She inched closer.

Hurley's feet began to shuffle. His face twisted into a scowl. "You know I think the world of you."

"Then why do you treat me as if I'm still a teenager?"

"I don't think you're incompetent."

"You just think I should stick to analysis and leave the recruiting and training to you."

He cleared his throat and said, "I think that's a fair statement."

Kennedy put her hands on her hips and stuck out her chin. "Do me a favor and take off your sunglasses."

The request caught Hurley off guard. "Why?"

"Because I know your Achilles' heel, and I want to see your womanizing eyes when I tell you what someone should have told you a long time ago."

Hurley cracked a smile in an attempt to brush her off, but she told him again to take his glasses off. Hurley reluctantly did so.

"I respect you," Kennedy said, "in fact I might trust you more with my life than anyone in this world. You are unquestionably the best man to whip these operatives into shape . . . but there's one problem."

"What's that?"

"You're myopic."

"Really?"

"Yep. I'm not sure you really understand the type of person we're looking for."

Hurley scoffed as if the idea was preposterous.

"That's right, and you're too stubborn to see it."

"I suppose you think the Special Operations Group just showed up one day. Who do you think trained all those guys? Who do you think selected them? Who do you think turned them into the efficient, badass killing machines that they are?"

"You did, and you know that's not what I'm talking about. I'm talking about our third objective."

Hurley frowned. She knew right where to hit him. He quietly wondered if Stansfield had put her up to this and said, "You think this shit's easy? You want to take over running this little operation?"

Kennedy shook her head and smiled in amazement. "You know, for a tough guy, you're awfully thin-skinned. You sound like one of those damn desk jockeys back at Langley who run their section as if they were some Third World dictator."

She might as well have hit him in the gut with a two-by-four. Hurley stood there speechless.

"You've created a cult of personality," Kennedy continued. "Every single recruit is you twenty to thirty years ago."

"And what's wrong with that?"

"Nothing, if you're talking about our first two objectives." Kennedy held up one finger. "Training operatives with the skills to get down and dirty if they have to and," she held up a second finger, "creating a highly mobile tactical assault team, but when it comes to the third," she shook her head, "we're still at the starting gate."

Hurley didn't like hearing this, but he was not some unaware idiot. He knew what he'd been tasked to do, and he was acutely aware that he had so far failed to make any progress on the most delicate of the three programs. Still, it wasn't in him to cede the point so easily. "I can teach anyone how to kill. That's easy. You point the weapon, you pull the trigger, and assuming you can aim . . . bam, a piece of lead enters the target's body, hits a vital organ, and it's done. If you've got big enough balls I can teach you to slide a knife through a guy's armpit and pop his heart like a balloon. Fuck . . . I can show you a thousand ways to punch someone's ticket. I can teach you battlefield techniques until I'm blue in the face . . ."

"But?" Kennedy asked, prodding him in the direction she knew he was headed.

"Turning a man into what we're looking for," Hurley stopped and shook his head, "it just ain't that easy."

Kennedy sighed. This was the opening she was looking for. Touching Hurley's arm she said, "I'm not saying it is, which is why you have to start trusting the rest of us to do our jobs. I have brought you a gift, Stan. You don't realize it right now because you think a guy has to go through boot camp before he's ready to have a run at your selection process, and normally I would agree with you, but this is different. You're just going to have to let go of some of your control issues for a bit. What I have in that car is exactly what you've been looking for, Stan. No bad habits that'll take you months to undo. None of that stiff military discipline that makes all these guys stand out like a sore thumb when we dump them into an urban setting."

Hurley glanced at the car.

"He's off the charts on all of our tests," Kennedy added. "And he's yours for the shaping."

With a deep frown Hurley studied what little he could see of this raw lump of coal that Kennedy was about to dump in his lap.

"That is," Kennedy said, "if you can swallow your pride and admit that the little girl you used to bounce on your knee is all grown up and just might be better at spotting talent than you."

Checkmate, Hurley thought to himself. *I'm stuck with this puke. At least for a few days until I can figure out how to make him quit.* "Fine," he said with a defeated tone. "But no special favors. He pulls his weight just like everyone else or he's gone."

"I don't expect any favors, but," Kennedy said, pointing a finger at his face, "I am going to be very upset if I find out you singled him out and gave him some of your famous extra love and attention."

Hurley digested her words and then gave her a curt nod. "Fine . . . I'll do it your way, but trust me, if I so much as get a whiff of weakness—"

"I know . . . I know," she said, robbing him of the final word. "You'll make him wish he'd never met you." Kennedy had pushed it as far as she was willing for the moment. Rapp would simply have to show the crotchety old bastard what she already knew. "I have to head over to the Farm to take care of something. I'll be back for dinner." She turned to head back to the car and over her shoulder she yelled, "And he'd better look no worse for the wear than the other six, or you're going to have one very unhappy niece on your hands."

CHAPTER 3

RAPP watched Kennedy drive away, his heavy, oversized lacrosse duffel bag hanging at his side. The scene was a bit surreal. It brought back memories of being dropped off at summer camp when he was nine and watching his mom drive off. Just like today, he had gone of his own free will, but this time there were no tears in his eyes. Back then he'd been a boy afraid of the unknown. Today he was a twenty-three-year-old man ready to take on the world.

As the car drove down the lane, Rapp could feel the weight of his decision. A door was closing. He had picked one path over another and this one was undoubtedly the one less traveled. It was overgrown and more treacherous than his imagination could do justice to, but then again his youthful self felt invincible and was filled with schemes to cheat death. He would undoubtedly be pushed to quit, but he was confident that would not happen. He'd never quit anything in his life, and he'd never wanted anything anywhere near as bad as he wanted this. Rapp knew the score. He knew how his chain would be yanked and jerked every which way and he would be forced to endure all of it. The prize at the end was what it was all about, though, and he was willing to endure all of it for his chance.

Rapp could feel the man's eyes on him. He let his heavy bag fall to the ground and watched him come closer. The man with the 'stache and the sunglasses blocked his view of the long driveway. Rapp instantly smelled the acid mix of coffee and cigarettes on his breath. He wanted to take a step back, but didn't want to appear to be backing down, so he stayed put and breathed through his mouth.

"Take a good look at that car," Hurley said sourly.

Rapp tilted his head to the side and watched the sedan disappear around the corner.

"She ain't coming back," Hurley added in a taunting voice.

Rapp nodded in agreement.

"Eyes front and center," Hurley snapped.

Rapp stared at his own reflection in the polarized lenses and remained silent.

"I don't know what kind of fucking bullshit you pulled on her. I don't know how you managed to con her into thinking you had what it takes to make it through my selection process, but I can promise you that every day you're here, you will curse her a thousand times for walking into your life. But you better do it silently, because if I hear you utter one single unkind word about her, I will make you feel pain you never thought possible. Do you understand me?"

"Yes."

"Yes!" Hurley barked. "Do I look like one of your faggot college professors?"

"No," Rapp said without twitching.

"No," Hurley howled with a veiny throat. "You call me sir when you talk to me, or I'll stick my boot so far up your ass you'll be chewing leather."

A fleck of spit hit Rapp in the face, but he ignored it. He'd figured something like this would happen. He'd already taken a look around and hadn't seen any others, so this was probably his best chance. "Sir, permission to speak?"

"I should have figured," Hurley said with a sigh. He placed his hands on his hips and said, "All right, Ivy League. I'll give you this one chance to say your piece. I can only pray you're going to tell me this was a bad idea and you'd like to go home. And I've got no problem with that," he added quickly. "Hell, I'll drive you myself."

Rapp grinned and shook his head.

"Shiiiiit!" Hurley drew out the word as he shook his head in disgust. "You actually think you can do this?"

"I do, sir."

"So you're really going to waste my time."

"It appears so, sir. Although, if I may . . . I suggest we speed things up a bit."

"Speed things up?" Hurley asked.

"Yes, sir. My guess is once you step in the ring with a man you can probably figure out inside about twenty seconds if a guy has enough talent to make it through your selection process."

Hurley nodded. "That's right."

"I don't want to waste your time, so I say we find out if I have the goods."

Hurley smiled for the first time. "You want to take a run at me?"

"Yes, sir . . . so we can speed things up."

Hurley laughed. "You think you can take me?"

"From what I've heard . . . not a chance in hell."

"Then why are you in such a hurry to get your ass kicked?"

"I figure you'll do it sooner or later. I'd rather do it sooner."

"And why's that?"

"So we can get on with the important stuff."

"And what would that be?"

"Like you teaching me how to kill terrorists."

This was a first. Hurley took a step back and studied the new recruit. He was six-one and looked to be in perfect shape, but at twenty-three that was expected. He had thick, jet-black hair and dark bronzed skin. He had the right look. Hurley sensed the first glimmer of what Kennedy had alluded to. More amused than worried, Hurley nodded his consent and said, "All right. We'll have a go at it. You see that barn over there?"

Rapp nodded.

"There's an open cot in there. It's yours for as long as you can last. Throw your crap in the footlocker and put on a pair of shorts and a T-shirt. If you're not ready and standing in the middle of the mat in two minutes I'm sending you home."

Rapp took it as an order. He grabbed his bag and took off at a trot for the barn. Hurley watched him duck inside, noted the time on his digital watch, and walked back to the porch, where he set down his coffee mug on the edge of the glossy white floorboards. Without so much as glancing over his shoulder he unzipped his pants and began to urinate on the bushes.

CHAPTER 4

RAPP found the cot next to three bunk beds. It was standard military surplus. Not great, but a hell of a lot better than the floor. After stripping to his underwear, he opened his bag and pulled out a pair of shorts and a plain white T-shirt. Kennedy had told him to pack only generic clothing. She didn't want him wearing anything that could give one of the other men an idea where he came from. They were all under strict orders to not discuss each other's past. Rapp folded up his clothes, placed them in the footlocker, closed it, and set the bag on top. He would have unpacked the bag, but he heard his instructor approaching. Rapp took up his position in the middle of the well-worn wrestling mat and waited eagerly for his shot.

Hurley stopped near the entrance to the barn, took a long drag off his cigarette, and began to loosen up with a few side stretches and shoulder rolls. He was not expecting much of a fight, so after a quick calf stretch he took one last puff off his cigarette, stubbed it out against the sole of his boot, and entered the barn. The new recruit was standing in the middle of the mat wearing shorts and a T-shirt. Hurley gave him the once-over. He was fit, just like all the others, but there was a certain casual, relaxed posture that he found off-putting.

"Shoulders back! Eyes front and center!" Hurley shook his head and mumbled some incoherent words to himself. "I don't have time to babysit." He bent over and took off his boots and socks and set them neatly at a ninety-degree angle at the edge of the mat, socks folded on top. He took off his sunglasses and set them on top of the socks. Stepping onto the mat, he asked, "Rules?"

Rapp didn't flinch. "That's up to you, sir."

Hurley bent back, continuing his stretching, and said, "Since no one's here to monitor this little ass kickin' I suggest we keep it civilized. Stay away from the balls and the eyes, and no throat strikes."

"Choke holds?"

"Absolutely," Hurley grinned. "If you want it to end, all you have to do is tap out."

Rapp shook his head.

"Fair enough." Hurley caught his first glimmer of something he didn't like. There was no sign of tension on the kid's face. He looked as relaxed as a schmuck who was about to play a round of golf. Two possibilities presented themselves and Hurley liked neither. The first was that the recruit might not be the little mama's boy that he thought, and the second was that he might be too stupid to know he wasn't cut out for this line of work. Either way, he might have to waste more than one day of his valuable time trying to drum him out. Hurley was shaking his head and muttering to himself when he realized there was a third possibility—that the kid actually might have the goods.

The potential hazard made Hurley pause. He glanced at the young college kid and realized he knew surprisingly little about the man standing in the middle of the mat. The jacket he'd received from Stansfield was so sanitized that the pertinent details would have fit onto one page. Beyond the general physical description and test scores, every other piece of information had been redacted. The man was a blank slate. Hurley had no sense of his physical abilities and general bearing. He didn't even know if he was left- or right-handed. A frown creased Hurley's well-lined brow as he ran through some more scenarios.

Normally, when Hurley stepped onto the mat with a recruit, he already had the advantage of having read an extensive personnel file, as well as having watched him for several days. You could tell a lot about a man by observing him for a few days. He silently called himself a dumb-ass for not thinking of this sooner. There was no calling it off at this point. His bare feet were on the mat. If he called it off, it would be a sign of weakness.

Hurley set his apprehension aside and reminded himself that he'd bested every man he'd run through here. He moved forward with his normal swagger and a lopsided grin on his face. He stopped ten feet away and said, "Ready when you are."

Rapp nodded, dropped into a crouch, and made a slow move to his left.

Hurley began sliding to his right, looking for an angle of attack. He glimpsed his opening when his opponent made an aggressive head fake that was an obvious tell of what would follow. In that moment, Hurley decided to dispatch the kid quickly. He wasn't going to waste time with defensive blocks and holds. He was going to make this kid feel some real pain. Maybe bust a couple of his ribs. That way, even if he proved to be a stubborn fool, there'd be no hope of his keeping up with the others.

Hurley anticipated the punch, ducked into a crouch, and came in to deliver a blow to the kid's midsection. Right about the time he pivoted off his back foot and let loose his strike he realized something wasn't right. The kid was a lot faster than he had anticipated. The little shit had doubled back on his own weak fake and was now a good two feet to the right of where Hurley had thought he would be. It looked like he had been suckered. Hurley knew he was horribly out of position, and exposed, but he wasn't the least bit alarmed. He pulled back his punch and prepared to go back in again on a different angle of attack. He was in the process of delivering his second blow when he realized again that something was wrong. Hurley sensed more than saw the big left hook bearing down on his face. In the final split second before impact he braced himself by pulling in his chin and dropping his hips.

The crushing blow landed just above Hurley's right eye.

Punches are funny things in that each one is different. You've got uppercuts, hooks, jabs, roundhouses, haymakers, and rabbit punches, to name a few. If you've sparred enough, you've felt all of them, and you learn to recognize each one by feel almost the instant it lands. A little scorecard in your head quickly analyzes the blow, and there's a brief conversation that takes place between the part of the brain that analyzes the thousands of instantaneous signals that come flying in and the part of the brain whose job it is to make sure the brain stays online. Hurley had been doing this for years, and as a man whose job it was to judge talent and teach, he had grown very accustomed to giving instant feedback to the man whose ass he was kicking. On this occasion, however, he was too busy trying to stay on his feet, so he kept his mouth shut.

The punch hit him so squarely that Hurley actually went down to one knee for a split second. The turtle move had saved him from getting KOed. If his head had been exposed any further the force of the blow would have snapped his jaw around so quickly his equilibrium would have gone offline, and he'd be down for a nice long nap. The ringside announcer in Hurley's brain made him aware of two things in extremely quick succession. The first was that he hadn't been hit this hard in a long time, the second was that he'd better launch a counterattack, and do it quickly, or he was going to get his ass kicked.

Hurley pivoted from his back to his front foot and launched a flurry of combinations designed more to get this kid to back up than actually hit him. The first two were blocked and the next five found nothing more than air. Hurley realized the kid must have been a boxer and that meant he'd have to get him down on the mat and twist him into submission. No more punches. Before Hurley had a chance to regroup, he felt the leg sweep catch him perfectly in the ankle of his right foot, which happened to be bearing about 90 percent of his weight. What happened next was simple physics. The sweep took him out so cleanly that there was no hope of catching himself with his back leg, so Hurley went with it. He landed on his ass, tucked and rolled back and sprang onto his feet. The fact that the kid had just swept him was not lost on Hurley. Boxers did not know how to use leg sweeps. There was a split-second pause while Hurley looked across the mat at the new recruit and wondered if he'd been lied to about his lack of military training. The respite did not last long.

Once again Hurley found himself on the receiving end of a combination of well-placed punches. He had to get this kid down on the mat, or he really was going to get his ass kicked. He backed up quickly as if retreating for his life. The kid followed him, and when he launched his next attack Hurley dropped down and slid in. He grabbed the lead leg and stuck his shoulder into the kid's groin, while pulling and lifting at the same time. The kid tried to drop his hips but Hurley had too good a hold. Hurley was about to topple him when a double-fisted hammer strike landed between his shoulder blades. The blow was so solid Hurley nearly let go, but something told him if he did, he would lose, so he hung on for dear life and finally toppled the kid.

Hurley was on top of him. He found a wrist and jammed his thumb into the pressure point while maneuvering the rest of his body into position for an arm bar. He rolled off and delivered a scissor kick to the throat of his opponent that under the rules was not exactly fair, but neither was their business. The kick barely missed, but Hurley had his opponent's wrist in both hands now and was ready to lean back and cantilever the kid's damn arm until he hyperextended the elbow. Before he could lock in the move, though, the kid did something that Hurley did not think possible.

Rapp had somehow reversed into the hold and was now on top of Hurley, who still had a good grip on his wrist. Hurley's head, however, was now firmly locked between Rapp's knees. Rapp hooked his ankles together and began to close his knees like a vise crushing a coconut.

Hurley jabbed his thumb as deeply into the wrist of his opponent as he could, but it didn't get him to back off a bit. He could feel the early stages of a blackout coming on and scrambled for a way out. He released his left hand from the wrist hold and grabbed a handful of the kid's thick black hair. Instead of letting go, though, the kid squeezed his knees even harder. White lights were dancing at the periphery of his vision. Hurley couldn't believe he just had his ass handed to him by some college puke.

Still, he did not stop looking for a way out, and with the darkness closing in, he found his answer sitting only a few inches in front of his face. He vaguely remembered a brief discussion about rules before they had started but that wasn't important right now. Making sure he didn't lose was what was important. In a last-ditch effort to avoid calamity, Hurley released his opponent's wrist and lashed out with his now free hand. He found the kid's gonads and with every last ounce of strength he clamped down and began to squeeze.

CHAPTER 5

KENNEDY returned to the lake house just after six in the evening. She was tired, hungry, and not in the mood for another confrontation with Hurley, but there were certain developments that needed to be discussed. One of the unforeseen and increasingly difficult aspects of her job was the inability to communicate freely with her colleagues. Foreign intelligence agencies that operated in Washington were always a threat, but no longer her biggest concern. Now she had to worry about her own government and a new generation of journalists who wanted to break the next Watergate, Pentagon Papers, or Iran Contra scandal. Combined, they had ended hundreds of careers and done untold damage to national security. It was the new sport in Washington to pound on the very agencies tasked with keeping America safe. Surprisingly, Kennedy was fairly ambivalent about it. As her mentor Thomas Stansfield had told her many times, "Great spies don't complain about the rules, they find ways around them."

She parked the car in front of the house and climbed the porch steps, dreading the thought of going another round with Hurley. Kennedy opened the screen door and entered. The rooms to her left and right were empty, so she went down the center hall to the kitchen. Her feet stopped where the hardwood floor transitioned to linoleum. Sitting at the kitchen table was a bruised and battered Stan Hurley. He had a drink filled with ice and Maker's Mark pressed against a fat lip and a bag of ice held against his swollen right eye. Leaning against the counter directly across from him was Troy Tschida, a thirty-two-year-old former Green Beret and Hurley's right-hand man. Tschida tried but failed to suppress his amusement over his boss's battered physical appearance.

"You think this is funny?" Hurley snarled.

"Absolutely not," Tschida said with dramatic, false sincerity.

"You prick. Wait till I stick your ass in the ring with him. You won't be laughing after he lands a couple punches."

"What happened?" Kennedy asked, genuinely not sure what they were talking about.

Hurley hadn't seen her enter, because the bag of ice was covering his right eye, and he didn't hear her because his ears were still ringing. He turned his head and removed the bag of ice to reveal an eye that was so swollen it was almost entirely closed. The skin above the eye was a shiny bulbous red.

"What happened," Hurley said in a voice rising with anger, "was that fucking Trojan horse you dumped in front of my house this afternoon."

It clicked and Kennedy thought of Rapp. "You're saying my recruit did this to you?"

"Don't fucking play games with me. I am in no mood." Hurley slammed his glass down on the table and grabbed the bottle of bourbon. He filled it to the brim.

"I have no idea what you're talking about," Kennedy said sincerely.

Hurley took a big gulp and said, "My ass. He's your recruit. You give me some cut-and-paste fuckin' jacket on the guy that reads like a ransom note. I know nothing about him. He's here less than a minute and he up and suggests we find out if he has the right stuff." Hurley stopped to take another drink and then in a falsetto voice designed to mimic Rapp said, "Let's speed things up, and find out if I have what it takes to do this."

"My recruit did that to you?" asked Kennedy, still not entirely sure what the man was talking about.

Hurley slammed his glass down again. This time brown liquid sloshed over the lip of the glass. "Yes, God dammit! And don't stand there and act like this is a surprise to you." He pointed an accusatory finger at her. "You planned it. You set me up."

"I have no idea what you're talking about." Kennedy shook her head and asked, "Are you trying to say my recruit bested you?"

"Damn close." Hurley turned his attention to his drink and mumbled to himself.

"Your boy had him beat," Tschida interjected with a smile, "but Stan here broke the rules and put the kid's balls in a vise."

"You think this shit is funny?" Hurley barked.

Tschida smiled and nodded.

Hurley looked like he was going to launch his glass across the room at him, and then at the last minute decided to use the bag of ice.

Tschida stuck out his right hand and caught the bag with ease. "Don't be a baby. After all the asses you've kicked around here, it's about time you got a little taste."

"My problem," Hurley shot back, "is getting ambushed by this young woman here. Someone I helped raise, by the way." Hurley turned his one good eye back on Kennedy. "No military experience, my ass. Where did you find this kid?"

Kennedy was still in a bit of shock. She herself had seen Hurley tie NFL-sized linebackers into pretzels. Nowhere in her research had she found anything that would lead her to believe Rapp was capable of going toe to toe with Stan Hurley. "Stan, you need to trust me. I had no idea he could best you."

"He didn't best me! He almost did."

"Yeah, but you cheated," Tschida said, taking perverse pleasure in the torment he was causing Hurley. "So, technically, he beat you."

It took every last bit of restraint to not throw his glass at the gloating Tschida. Hurley turned his attention back to Kennedy and asked, "What are you up to? Why in hell would you try to sucker me like this?"

"Just calm down for a minute, Stan. I am telling you right now, we found nothing in our research that said he was capable of this." Kennedy gestured at Hurley's battered face. "It was my sincere hope that someday he would be able to do this . . . but not this soon."

"Then your research sucks. You don't learn how to fight like this in your basement. Someone has to teach you."

Kennedy admitted, "He's been going to a martial arts studio for the past year."

"That would have been nice to know," Hurley fired back.

"Stan, you have been bitching up a storm that this guy is a waste of time because he hasn't had Special Forces training. You think a year of training in a strip mall is equal to what the army puts guys through?"

"That depends on the instructor."

"And the student," Tschida added.

Kennedy folded her arms and thought long and hard before she spoke. "There is one other possibility."

"What's that?"

"I know you don't like to talk about your age, but is it possible that you've lost a step."

Tschida started laughing so hard his big barrel chest was rising and falling with each chuckle.

Hurley was seething. "I'm going to put your

ass in the ring with him, first thing in the morning. We'll see how funny you think this is then."

Tschida stopped laughing.

Kennedy pulled up a chair and sat at the table across from Hurley. "Please tell me what happened."

"You're not jerking my chain?"

Kennedy shook her head.

"You weren't trying to pull a fast one on me? Set me up?"

She shook her head again and said, "No. In fact I was worried that he would be on the receiving end of a beating. Not the other way around."

Even through his anger- and bourbon-induced haze, Hurley was starting to grasp that Kennedy was telling the truth. "Where did you find this guy?"

Kennedy gave him a look that he instantly understood.

"Shithead," Hurley said to Tschida, "go check on those clowns, and if they're screwing around bust 'em out and make 'em snap off a hundred up-downs."

"Got it." Tschida moved out, all business.

As soon as the screen door slammed, Hurley looked at Kennedy and said, "Who is he?"

She couldn't keep him in the dark forever, but she would have preferred to wait a few more days. Setting her apprehension aside she said, "His name is Mitch Rapp."

CHAPTER 6

RAPP lay on his cot, his head propped up on a lumpy pillow and a bag of frozen peas on his groin. Dinner had been served buffet style on a folding table at the far end of the barn. His appetite wasn't really there, but he forced himself to eat. There were seven of them plus two instructors, and among them, they polished off a giant pot of spaghetti, a plate full of rolls, and all the salad and corn on the cob they could stomach. The men were tired, hot, and ragged, but they stuffed their faces all the same and washed it down with pitchers of ice water and cold milk. Rapp had spent the last five years eating at a training table and knew how it worked. Tough drills in heat like this didn't exactly spur the desire to eat. It had the opposite effect, but you had to ignore it and shovel down the food. The physiology was pretty straightforward. They would be burning five-thousand-plus calories a day, and that meant either they had to eat a ton of food or they would begin to lose weight. With his frame and current weight, Rapp could lose ten pounds, but anything beyond that and he would open himself up to injury and illness.

Rapp tossed the copy of *Time* magazine on the floor and adjusted the bag of frozen peas. One of the instructors had pulled him aside as he was clearing his plate and told him he wanted him to get on his back and start icing. He then gave him strict orders to report any blood in his urine. Rapp simply nodded and took the bag of peas. After his sparring match and before dinner he'd had a few hours to reflect on what had happened while one of the instructors led him through a tough circuit of calisthenics and then a ten-mile run through the woods. Rapp made it seem like he was struggling, but he wasn't. Especially with the running. He could last all day if he had to, but he didn't want to show these guys too much too soon. Besides, give a teacher the choice between a straight-A student who has all the answers and an earnest one who gets better over time, and they'll pick the earnest one every time.

Rapp was still trying to absorb what lesson there was to learn from his earlier throwdown with the man whose name he still did not know. He was not happy that the man had changed his own rules in the middle of a fight, but there wasn't a lot he could do about it now. He had to focus on how it would affect things going forward. It was important to know how far he could push it, and if these instructors weren't going to abide by the rules, they could hardly expect him to do so.

Rapp's first chance to meet the other men was after his run. They were at the pull-up bars behind the barn doing four sets of twenty-five. In addition to the mean old bastard running the place, there were three more instructors. Just as his recruiter had told him, no one was to use his real name or discuss any personal information. The first two instructors were easy to keep straight. The short skinny one was called Sergeant Smith and the tall skinny one was called Sergeant Jones. They would start their days with Smith and end with Jones.

Rapp had to do two sets of twenty-five with a thirty-second rest between so he could catch up with the other recruits. After each man had polished off a full one hundred pull-ups Sergeant Smith went nuts. He lined them up and paced back and forth dumping disdain on them.

"One of you faggots doesn't think he needs to do a full pull-up," the instructor started. "Thinks he can go halfway down and not quite all the way up. Well, I don't like anything done half-assed so you ladies get to start over."

Then the invective really started to fly as he called into question their manhood, honor, intelligence, and lineage. Rapp noted that he treated them as a group rather than singling out the supposed offender, who he wasn't so sure even existed. He'd watched the other men, and none of them seemed to be slacking off. The sergeant was simply moving the goal line in hopes that one of them would grow sick of the games and quit. As he looked around, though, he didn't see that happening. The other six were hard individuals.

"Four more sets on the quick. Let's go!" the sergeant barked. "And do 'em right this time, or I'll send you ladies on a nice long run and you can forget about dinner."

There were two bars, so the men lined up and started over. Rapp was waiting for his turn when one of the other recruits poked him hard in the kidney. Rapp turned around and took inventory of the man who had jabbed him and was now cussing him out in a voice only the two of them could hear. The man looked like one of those professional rugby players from Europe. He had a heavy brow made heavier by a single black eyebrow that traveled laterally from one temple to the other. His eyes were coal-black and wide-set, but his most prominent features were a hook nose that looked to have been broken at least twice and a dimple in the middle of his pronounced chin. Rapp thought of two things almost instantly. The first was that it would be a waste of effort to try to knock him out with a punch to the head. The guy's neck was as thick as the average man's thigh. The second was that he didn't fit in. At least as far as Rapp understood the intent of what they were up to. The man's features were so distinctive as to make him almost impossible to forget. He looked more like an enforcer than a stealth operative.

"Do 'em right this time, shithead," the big man said testily.

Rapp was sweaty, dirty, hot as hell, and not used

to taking crap from anyone. He had done his pull-ups correctly. If anyone could be accused of not doing them all the way it would be the very man who was in his face. Rapp was tempted to set the tone and knock the guy on his ass, but he figured there would be plenty of time for that later. He turned back around without responding and stepped to the line.

"That's right," the big man said, "be a smart boy and keep your mouth shut. Just fucking do 'em right this time."

The rest of the afternoon proceeded without incident and they were allowed to jump into the lake to cool down before dinner. Rapp steered clear of Victor but kept an eye on him. He had learned that was the big man's name. Or at least the name he'd been given. Since they were forbidden to use their real names, the instructors gave each of them a fake first name. Rapp's was Irving, which they had already shortened to Irv. The other five guys were Fred, Roy, Glenn, Bill and Dick.

They all seemed decent enough and pretty much kept their heads down and their eyes alert. There were a lot of knowing glances and silent communication. Since they were forbidden to talk about their past, there was no mention of military service or the units they had served in. This created an interesting situation for Rapp. The instructors more than likely knew he'd never served in the military, but the other recruits had no idea.

It created a weird dynamic when you dumped a group of guys in a situation where they were forbidden to talk about their pasts. It pretty much killed small talk, so little was said during dinner. Rapp retired to his cot so he could ice his groin and was staring up at the slow, churning revolutions of the ceiling fan that hung from the rafters directly above him. He was thinking about the match, going through it move by move wondering what he could have done differently, when Victor appeared next to his cot.

"What's your name?" he asked in a hushed voice.

Rapp glanced over to the door where one of the instructors was giving orders to one of the other guys.

"Irv."

"No, dumb-ass." He shook his head. "I mean your real name."

Rapp was starting to think he didn't like Victor. He'd been warned by his recruiter repeatedly that talking about your personal life was grounds for immediate dismissal from the program. Just ten minutes earlier, while they were eating, the instructors had reminded them of this again. Rapp impassively looked up and said, "Didn't you hear what the instructors told us?"

A lopsided grin fell across the other man's face. "That's just a bunch of BS. It's a game. They're just trying to fuck with us." He glanced over his shoulder to make sure no one was close enough to hear and said, "Come on . . . where you from?"

"What's your angle?"

"Huh?"

"What are you up to?"

"Just trying to get to know the guys . . . that's all."

"Try not to take this the wrong way, but it's none of your business who I am or where I'm from."

"Is that so?" His face flushed a bit and his jaw tightened. "I'll tell you something. I don't need you telling me what is and isn't my business."

Rapp didn't like his predicament. He was on his back and vulnerable, but he didn't want Victor to think he was easily intimidated. "It's not me telling you," he said in a casual voice, "it's them." Rapp looked over at the instructor by the door.

The instructor finished whatever he was saying and left. It was just the seven recruits now.

Victor started laughing. "There goes your mother. Looks like your ass is mine."

Rapp decided lying down was no longer the best position to be in. He quickly swung his legs off the cot and stood. In a conversational tone that was loud enough for the others to hear, he said, "What's your problem, Victor?"

"You're my problem."

"I gathered that," Rapp said from the other side of the cot, "but could you be a little more specific. Maybe it's something I could fix."

"I doubt it," the bigger man said with disdain. "You look soft to me. Like you don't belong here."

"Well . . . why don't we find out." Rapp gestured to the wrestling mat.

Victor laughed as if the idea was preposterous. "You don't stand a chance."

Rapp nodded as if to say maybe, maybe not, and walked over to the edge of the mat. "I'm sorry about your mother, Victor."

"What did you just say?" Victor asked.

"I said," Rapp half yelled, "I'm sorry about your mom."

"You'd better watch yourself!" Victor's eyes had taken on a wild glare.

"Or what?" Rapp asked.

The other five guys all dropped what they were doing to see what was going on.

"You gonna take a swing at me, Victor?" Rapp egged the big man on. He was ready to end this thing right now. "What's wrong . . . your mom the neighborhood slut when you were growing up . . . she didn't hold you enough when you were little? She let every guy she met suck on her tit except you?"

"You got a big mouth," Victor snarled, barely able to contain his rage.

"Just trying to figure out what's wrong with you, Victor. You been shooting your mouth off all day. Acting like a world-class prick. We're all getting sick of it."

"I'm going to kick your ass!" Victor howled as he hopped from one foot to the other like a boxer.

Rapp didn't say a word. He moved to the middle of the mat and motioned for Victor to join him.

Victor started whooping and hollering as he danced circles around Rapp. He was throwing shadow punches and explaining in detail what he was going to do to Rapp, when suddenly one of the instructors reappeared in the doorway.

"What in hell are you ladies doing?"

Victor fell silent, but it was too late.

"That's it, you dumb-asses. If you've got enough energy to fight then you've got enough energy to run. You've got sixty seconds to muster your worthless asses outside on the line. Put your running gear on and move it!"

Everyone sprang into action, and while they were putting on their gear the other five men made their displeasure known through a mix of looks and verbal complaints. Rapp did not respond, while Victor seemed to relish it. He turned the taunts back on the other men and invited any of them to take a shot at him just as soon as one of them grew a set of balls. Rapp put on his shoes and sprinted for the door. He was the first one on the line, and while he waited for the others, it occurred to him that something wasn't right. If this program was so secretive and elite, what in hell was a loudmouth like Victor doing here?

CHAPTER 7

CAMP PERRY, VIRGINIA

TOM Lewis took the call on the secure line. He listened patiently to the person on the other end relay a seemingly benign message about a meeting that was to take place in Washington, D.C., the following afternoon. To anyone with the ability to breach the secure system, which of course included the internal security people back in Langley, the conversation would have seemed so ordinary as to not warrant a second thought. In the third sentence, however, an adverb was used that caused his right eyebrow to shoot up a quarter inch. Lewis thanked the person on the other end and said they would talk at the meeting the next day.

The clinical psychologist slowly placed the phone back in its cradle and tapped his pen on a generic desk blotter. Everything in the office was generic; all standard-issue government furniture, the kind that was purchased in massive quantities every year by the behemoth federal government. The desk, bookcase, and credenza were all made from particleboard coated with a thin plastic veneer that was supposed to look like wood, but didn't. The chairs were black plastic with coarse charcoal fabric seats that could render a pair of dress pants useless in just nine months. Lewis was amazed at how ubiquitous this type of furniture had become in Washington, which in turn led him to the conclusion that the maker of this substandard furniture was more than likely headquartered in the home district of the chairman of the House Appropriations Committee.

Lewis detested such poor craftsmanship, but nonetheless made no attempt to add a personal touch to this office. His private office was in the District and every square inch of it had been meticulously decorated. With what he charged for an hour of therapy he could not only afford the fine trappings, but even more, his clients expected it. In a rather short period of time he had built up a very profitable practice. His patient list was a virtual who's who of Washington's power elite. Lobbyists, lawyers, and CEOs made up the bulk of his business. He treated only a smattering of politicians, but dozens of women who were married to powerful senators and congressmen came to see him every week and poured their hearts and minds out. If he were unscrupulous he'd be able to use that information to his benefit, but he had never been tempted.

The thirty-six-year-old Lewis had both the passion and the natural inclination for his work. He had obtained an undergraduate degree in economics and math from Pomona College and a graduate degree in clinical psychology from the University of Pennsylvania. The latter was paid for by the government, which required him to serve four years in the army upon graduating. That stint in the army more than anything was what pulled Lewis into this current situation, in a windowless, crappy office on a base that very few people even knew existed. It seemed he had a knack for spotting mental deficiencies, which when he was in the army was something that greatly interested at least one flag officer and a couple of colonels down at Fort Bragg. He'd spent three years helping the Joint Special Operations Command tighten up their selection process and develop a new system for game theory.

Lewis took a moment to collect his thoughts and figure out how the call would affect his evening. The camp had a bachelors' quarters of sorts for the various employees and consultants who traveled back and forth to D.C. When a new class was on the post he normally stayed one or two nights a week so he could observe how they interacted. He had planned on staying the evening and spending some time with one of the recruits who was showing some troublesome signs, but the phone call was more pressing.

Lewis looked down at his World War II Elgin A-11 U.S. military watch. His father had given it to him on his deathbed three years earlier. Lewis had replaced the worn strap and kept the watch in near-perfect shape. It was seven-fourteen in the evening.

Nothing on his desk was that urgent, and besides, it was a perfect evening to get out on the open road and clear his mind. He collected the two open files and spun his chair around to face a gray metal safe, which was already open. Lewis placed the files in the proper slot, closed the safe, and spun the dial. He left the office door open, as there was nothing other than the contents of the safe that needed to be protected.

His motorcycle was parked in the first space in front of the building. Lewis took off his sport coat and tie and carefully folded and placed them on the seat. He unlocked one of the saddlebags of the BMW 1200 motorcycle and retrieved a gray and black leather riding jacket and pair of chaps. He never rode his bike without them. Even with the thermometer pushing ninety degrees. Imprinted on his brain was the road rash a friend had received when he'd been forced to lay his bike down on a hot California afternoon. The jacket and tie were placed in the saddlebag and he put on his gray helmet. The motorcycle hummed to life and Lewis climbed on. Sixty seconds later he tipped his visor at the sentry standing post at the main gate and blew past him. A minute after that he was rocketing up the entrance ramp onto Interstate 64 and on his way north. The drive would take a bit more than an hour, which Lewis didn't mind in the least.

No phones, no one knocking on his door wanting him to listen to his problems. Lewis was finding it increasingly difficult to find the time to clear his mind and focus on the task at hand. A big green sign informed him how many miles he had to travel to reach Richmond, but he barely noticed. He was already thinking of their new recruit. That had to be why she had called. Lewis set the cruise control at 70 mph, adjusted himself on the seat, and checked his mirrors. He considered how much work he had put into this one candidate. The man was as close to perfect as anyone they'd come across in the almost two years he'd been working on the program. Lewis leaned into a turn and wondered if it was possible for Hurley to run the kid out in one afternoon. Unfortunately, he knew the answer to that question, because he'd seen him do it on more than one occasion.

CHAPTER 8

LAKE ANNA, VIRGINIA

IT was a moonless night sky and all but a few of the exterior lights were off so as to not attract bugs. The mutts had just finished their run and another hundred up-downs and a few more exercises designed to fatigue little-used muscles and maybe get one or more of them to quit so they could get down to the serious stuff. Unfortunately, all seven were now filing into the barn in a manner not much different than that of cows returning from a day grazing in the pasture. Their heads were down, their pace was slow, and their footing unsure, and fortunately the arguing was over. The only thing they could think about at the moment was sleep.

Hurley took a sip of bourbon and looked out across the lawn. Despite the fact that it was his seventh in the past three hours, he was not drunk. When it came to booze, and a lot of other things, the spook had the constitution of a man three times his size. Tonight, however, his normally unshakable confidence was a little wobbly. Hurley was feeling a nagging indecision that to the average person was a daily occurrence, but to a headstrong, decisive man like him was rare. The shiner on his eye and his throbbing headache were nothing more than a nagging physical symptom. A few more glasses of Maker's Mark and they would be thoroughly dulled.

The problem was between his ears—a crack in his psyche that had put him in a rarely visited but increasingly familiar place. It was gnawing at the back of his head, trying to crawl into his brain stem and take him down. The signs were all there: tight chest, quick breath, a sudden desire to get the hell out of Dodge and go somewhere, anywhere but here. For a man who was used to being in control, used to being right all the time, it was the most unwelcome feeling he could imagine. He'd rather get kicked in the head until he was knocked unconscious than try to wrestle with this crap.

The fix, Hurley knew, involved something he still wasn't used to. He'd spent years burying his problems, patching them, hiding them under anything he could find. His job was too important, there were too many enemies to confront and not enough men willing to do it. There was too much to do, the stakes were too high for him to sit around and feel sorry for himself. He was after all a product of the Cold War. While the children of the sixties cut loose and got in touch, Hurley cut throats and got as out of touch with his feelings as was possible. He darted around Europe in the late fifties and early sixties and then Southeast Asia in the midsixties. The seventies brought him to South America, the early eighties to Central America, and then finally, for the biggest shit show of all, he landed in the Middle East. The entire thing was a gigantic multidimensional chess match with the Soviets, a continuation of what had happened at the end of World War I and then the aftermath of World War II.

Getting in touch with his thoughts or feelings, or whatever they were, was not something Hurley relished. There was right and there was wrong, and in between an abyss filled with society's whiners, people who had inherited the luxury of safety and freedom, while having done nothing to earn it. He had never heard these opinions pass the lips of his mother or father. They didn't have to. He was born during the Depression, but they had lived through it. They'd moved from Chicago to Bowling Green, Kentucky, with their five kids, to escape the long food lines and massive unemployment of the inner city. Hurley had come of age not knowing any better. His lot in life seemed just as good as the next kid's. He'd taken that stoic demeanor and joined the army. After serving his stint, he enrolled at Virginia Tech on the GI Bill and graduated with decent marks. That final spring a man from the federal government who was extremely interested in his military record asked him if he'd like to see the world. Asked him if he'd like to make a difference. Hurley bit.

Officially, he'd spent the last twenty-one years darting in and out of war-torn countries and doing his part to create a few wars, too. Unofficially, it had been longer than that. He'd been on the very edge of the conflict between the Soviets and America and had no illusions about which side was the more noble of the two. All a person had to do was spend a little time in Berlin to understand the effects of communism and capitalism. Talk about a tale of two cities, East Berlin and West Berlin were living, breathing examples. Posters for the governments who had run them since the end of World War II. One side was a vivid Kodachrome film and the other a grainy old black-and-white pile of crap.

Hurley had never been more proud than when that damn wall came tumbling down. He'd spilled his own blood in the battle and had lost a few friends and more sources than he could count or wanted to remember, but they'd won. Unfortunately, there wasn't a lot of time to enjoy their victory. Hurley and a few others already had their eyes on the jihadists. He'd come across them when he was helping bleed the Soviet Union of cash, equipment, manpower, and eventually the will to continue its despotic experiment. It had been in the Khyber Pass, and at first he saw nothing that made him nervous. These people wanted their land back and the Soviets out. The problem started with the religious zealots who were being shipped in from Saudi Arabia, Yemen, and a handful of other crappy little countries.

Hurley loved to swear, drink, and chase women, which put him on a collision course with the puritan, fun-sucking, Wahhabi jihadists from Saudi Arabia. He almost instantly developed a special dislike for them, but didn't understand back then that they would want to spread their jihad beyond the jerkwater mountains of Southwest Asia. That came later, when he started to see them meddling in the affairs of the Palestinians. It was starting all over again. The Soviets had been contained and beaten, and now this new enemy was out pushing its agenda. Hurley had a bad feeling about where it was headed, and on top of that, for the first time in his life he felt tired. This threat was not going away, and he suddenly wasn't sure he could find, let alone train, the next batch of kids who would be needed to meet the threat. He needed help. Unfortunately, asking for help was not something Hurley was good at.

He heard one of the dogs bark and then the sound of a motorcycle drifted through the pines. It was not the rumble of an American-made motorcycle, rather the purr of a Japanese or German bike. Hurley breathed a small sigh that was part relief, part resignation. It was the doc. He realized Kennedy must have called him.

A single beam of light slashed through the trees and a moment later the motorcycle coasted round the corner. The bike was so quiet, Hurley could hear the tires on the gravel driveway. The bike rolled its way up to the house and the rider eased the kickstand into the down position and then killed the engine. After retrieving a flat piece of wood from one of the molded saddlebags, he put it under the kickstand and then took off his helmet.

Thomas Lewis ran a hand through his shaggy blond hair and looked up at Hurley. He immediately noticed the swelling over the eye, but he was more concerned with a look on the man's face that he had only recently grown to understand. "Tough day?"

Hurley tried to laugh it off. "No easy days in this line of work. You know that."

Lewis nodded. He knew all too well the toll that their business could inflict on a person, and not just the body. The physical injuries were fairly straight-forward. They could either be mended or not. The assaults on the mind and soul were an entirely different matter.

CHAPTER 9

BEIRUT, LEBANON

THE battered, dusty Peugeot slowed to a crawl. The driver leaned out over the steering wheel and looked left and then right down the length of Hamra Street. His friend in the passenger seat did the same, but in a more halfhearted fashion. There was no stoplight, nor was there a stop sign, but habits formed during war died hard. Samir was the youngest of four brothers. Three of them had died in the civil war that had destroyed this once-beautiful city. His closest brother, only thirteen months his senior, had been killed by an RPG while crossing this very intersection. To the Westerners who covered the bloody civil war, Hamra Street was better known as the Green Line. Ali and his friends called it no-man's-land.

It was the street that divided East and West Beirut and, to a certain degree, the Muslims from the Christians, or more accurately the Shiite Muslims from the Maronite Christians. There were neighborhoods on each side of the line where you could find pockets of Sunnis, Armenians, Greek Orthodox, and Druze. Some of these outposts were more exposed than others, and they had all but disappeared during the lengthy and savage civil war, while a few of the more entrenched ones were now rebuilding. The civil war in many respects resembled the mob warfare of Chicago in the 1920s, but with much bigger guns.

With the war officially over for almost two years, virtually every part of the city was showing signs of life. The Christians to the east were rebuilding at a blistering pace, and the Muslims to the west were struggling to keep pace. Construction cranes dotted the skyline, and you were now more likely to get killed by a dump truck or a bulldozer than by a sniper. At least in certain areas. Hamra Street was not one of those areas. The buildings were still gutted shells, perfectly suited for a sniper to lie in wait.

Samir scanned the building across the street to his left while his friend Ali, who was sitting next to him, did the same thing to their right.

"Still cautious," the man in the backseat said in a coarse voice.

Samir looked sheepishly in the rearview mirror. "Sorry."

Assef Sayyed nodded and took another drag from his cigarette. He remembered that Samir's brother had been killed not far from here. A lot of good men had been killed along this godforsaken stretch of road. Sayyed, however, did not make small talk with his men. Such familiarity led to their getting ideas. Ideas were not good. They only needed to follow orders. He also had no desire to get too close to the all-but-disposable men who worked for him. It was far easier to mourn the loss of someone you didn't know well than the loss of a close friend.

Once Samir received the go-ahead from Ali, he gunned the engine and tore across the broad street, over the abandoned trolley tracks, and into a canyon of half-demolished buildings on the other side. A year or two earlier he would have never dreamed of taking this shortcut. The car continued for two blocks, dodging piles of rubble, and then hung a sharp left turn. Building by building, block by block, things got better. The first sign was that the roads were clear of debris. Scaffolding and cement mixers were the next positive sign, and then finally they came upon a row of buildings that actually had windows, although the stone facades were pockmarked from artillery shells and small-arms fire.

Two young men stood in front of a roadblock, AK-47 assault rifles at the ready. Samir slowed the car to a stop and looked at the young face of the man who was pointing the barrel of his rifle at his head. They were all young these days, or old, but there were very few in between. An entire generation had either fled the country or been killed. Samir jerked his thumb toward the backseat and watched the guard's eyes open wide as he recognized the ruthless Assef Sayyed. The young man gave a quick bow of respect, and then ordered his colleague to move the barricade.

The block was sealed at both ends. Some had started to question the manpower and effort that went into this, but all Sayyed had to do was flash them one of his withering stares and they were silenced. The Syrian intelligence colonel was of the mind that this peace was more of a lull in the fighting, and the second they let their guard down they would pay for it dearly. He continually advised the other militias to reconstitute, to find new recruits and to train them diligently, and to use this lull in the fighting to stockpile arms and ammunition. With each passing month it was becoming increasingly difficult to convince them to direct their resources to the next battle. To the men under his command, however, there was no questioning his orders. Sayyed had made certain of that by putting a bullet through the forehead of one of his aides at a staff meeting just two months earlier.

Sayyed tossed his cigarette in the gutter and entered the office building. Extension cords ran along the floor and the wall to bring power to various levels. The place had been functional for just two weeks, and Sayyed did not plan to use it for more than another few days at the most. The greatest vulnerability for his side was a complete lack of air power. If some dog in Israel found out where he was, he could have jets scrambled and dropping bombs on him in less than twenty minutes.

He took the stairs down to the basement level. The smell of raw sewage was an instant reminder that the city was still suffering the ills of almost fifteen years of fighting. Two men were in the hallway standing next to a kerosene lamp. They were still without power in the basement. Without having to be told, the men moved away from the door. The older of the two snapped off a distinctly British salute.

"Colonel, it is good to see you."

Sayyed ignored the greeting. "Where is Colonel Jalil?"

The man jerked his head toward the door. "He is inside with the prisoner."

Sayyed motioned for him to open the door.

The guard extended his hand. In it was a black hood. "To hide your identity."

Sayyed gave him a disdainful look, and the man put the hood away and opened the door. A man sat naked in the middle of the room tied to a metal chair. One man was standing beside him, another in front. Both were wearing black hoods. Sayyed entered the room and walked directly to the prisoner. He grabbed him by his hair and yanked his head up so he could see his face. Sayyed stood there searching the man's features for half a minute. So far he only had a trickle of dried blood on his upper lip. Other than that he looked untouched.

"Who are you?" Sayyed asked.

"My name is Nihad Wassouf."

Sayyed stared at him for a long time and finally said, "I think you are a liar. In fact I think you are a Jew."

"No!" the man protested vehemently. "I am a Syrian."

"I doubt that."

"I would not lie about such a thing. Check with the names I have given you."

Sayyed was already doing just that, but this man seemed like a rat to him, and those lazy fools back in Damascus could be tricked. Without warning, Sayyed walked over to a small cart. A variety of tools were lying on the surface. His hands danced from one to the next. He did not want to do anything that would require medical attention at this point. Finally, he settled on a pair of pliers. Sayyed walked back to the man and held the pliers in front of him. "I am not as nice, nor am I as patient as these two men. I will ask you only one more time . . . what is your real name?"

The man stammered for a second and then said, "Nihad Wassouf."

Sayyed reached out and straightened the prisoner's forefinger on his left hand. He clamped the pliers down on the quarter inch of nail that extended beyond the tip of the finger and rocked it back and forth a few times. The prisoner began to squirm. A line of crimson blood appeared at the edge of the nail bed. "Tell me your real name."

"I already have . . . I swear."

"Why are you looking for the American?"

"I was sent here to negotiate his release."

"By who?"

"His company."

"I think you are lying."

"No . . . I am not. Call my friends in Damascus. They will vouch for me."

"I do not believe you."

"Please. I am only a messenger. They are willing to pay a great sum of money."

"What if you are a spy?"

"I am not."

"Liar!" And with that Sayyed tore the man's fingernail completely out of its bed.

CHAPTER 10

LAKE ANNA, VIRGINIA

THE doctor peeled off his leather riding gear and stood on the porch listening to Hurley recount the afternoon's events. He did so as passively as possible, even though his concern grew on several fronts. Interrupting, he'd learned with Hurley, was a bad approach. It was best to let him get it all out. Questions or comments could be perceived as a personal attack, which in turn would elicit a spirited counterattack, all of which the doctor knew was very counterproductive.

Lewis had met the spook five years earlier. The Department of Defense had shipped his ODA team off to Pakistan to help the black ops boys from Langley who were trying to train and equip the mujahedeen in the treacherous border region between Pakistan and Afghanistan. Hurley, in his typical gruff manner, had expressed his amusement that the vaunted Green Berets were now attaching shrinks to their units. He wondered if Lewis was similar to the political commissars who were attached to Red Army units, which was not exactly a compliment, since the communist officers were political appointees and in charge of Communist Party morale among the troops. They were also known to ship off to Siberia anyone who did not show absolute devotion to the party. They were feared and despised by their own men.

Lewis had read clean through the rough bravado of Hurley, and rather than take offense, he laughed along. As the weeks passed, however, Hurley began to consult the shrink with increasing frequency. Hurley soon learned the good doctor was a valuable asset to have around. Lewis, he found out, had a gift. He could read people. The doctor was a walking, talking polygraph.

When Hurley was finished giving the afternoon's play-by-play he did not stop to hear the doctor's opinion or let him ask questions. He moved headlong into what he thought needed to be done. "I want you to sit down with him and run him through the wringer. Clear your calendar for the rest of the week if you have to. I want to know what the deal is with this kid. He's hiding something and I want to know what it is."

As was his habit, Lewis pursed his lips and stared off into the distance while he thought about other possibilities. He respected, liked, and felt a sense of loyalty to Hurley, but he was not exactly a well-balanced, mentally healthy adult male. Kennedy, on the other hand, was possibly one of the most measured and thoughtful humans he'd ever had the pleasure of working with. Before he did anything he wanted to hear her side of the story.

"I'll clear my schedule for tomorrow," Lewis said, agreeing without really agreeing. "Let's head inside. I'm starving and I need to use the bathroom."

After Lewis had relieved himself and washed his face, they found Kennedy at the kitchen table reading a file and picking at a plate of noodles. Lewis looked at the uninspired pasta and frowned. One of his passions was cuisine, and it pained him to watch his colleagues put so little effort into something so important. Without saying a word he began searching the cupboards for something, anything that he could use to create a passable meal. Kennedy and Hurley shared a brief smile.

Lewis stuck his nose into the refrigerator, and without bothering to turn around, said, "Stan, would you be so kind as to fetch a bottle of wine from the basement? A Chateau Dominique would be fine." He took out a package of chicken and closed the door. Moving to the sink he paused for a brief moment and then said, "You might as well grab two." When Hurley was gone, Lewis looked over his shoulder at Kennedy and motioned for her to join him at the sink.

"So," he said, "Stan's not exactly thrilled with your new recruit."

"He's not the easiest man to please."

Lewis turned on the water and began to rinse the chicken. With a wry smile he said, "He thinks you set him up."

Kennedy rolled her eyes.

"This is the one you told me about? The kid from Syracuse?"

"Yes."

Lewis splayed the chicken open and let the water run through the crevices. "You never said anything about his fighting abilities."

Kennedy sheepishly shrugged her shoulders and said, "I didn't know he had them."

"That's a pretty big thing to miss." Lewis glanced up at her. "I'm not judging."

"I'm not proud that I missed it, but in the end isn't it a good thing?"

"Maybe . . . maybe not."

Kennedy explained what she knew about Rapp, which admittedly wasn't a great deal, but she pointed out yet again that a blank slate was not necessarily a bad thing. That they could mold him into the man they needed. She finished her verbal report as Hurley made it back up from the basement. Lewis asked her to prepare a small salad while he went to work boiling noodles and slicing up the chicken and preparing a creamy white sauce. Hurley was left to open the red wine.

While Lewis put the finishing touches on the main dish, Hurley and Kennedy started up again. They volleyed back and forth, each one putting forth his or her version of what had happened and how the other one had screwed up. Like any good shrink, Lewis was a good listener, and he played his part. It helped that these two were rarely boring. Hurley was a once-in-a-lifetime patient, the kind of man who was so outrageously entertaining that you sometimes felt you should pay him rather than the other way around. Sure, there was a flourish of exaggeration here and there, but Lewis had witnessed several of his exploits firsthand and knew the stories to be for the most part accurate.

Kennedy was very different. There was no cussing, or anger, or animated hand gestures accompanied by thespianlike facial contortions. There was just a calm, analytical, intellectual way about her that put you at ease. Her answers were never rushed and almost always thoughtful. She did not participate in personal verbal attacks or attempt to sway opinion by exaggeration. Wildly different in almost every way, they did share a few qualities that served to exacerbate the situation. Both were deeply suspicious of everyone they encountered and did not find it easy to admit they were wrong. On top of that, their long history and familiarity served to bring both the best and worst qualities to the surface in a very raw way. Lewis would never admit this to them, but it had become one of his great clinical joys watching these two argue: It was verbal combat at an Olympian level.

The table was set, the wine poured, and the food dished up. Kennedy picked at her salad while Hurley and Lewis devoured both the salad and the chicken and tomato fettuccine. Lewis ate in near silence while he watched the two joust. He interrupted on three occasions, but only for clarification. When he'd cleaned his plate and poured himself a second glass of wine, he pushed his chair back and was ready to give them his take on the matter. One of the things they had decided at the formation of the group was that they wanted Lewis to have full operational input. Hurley was in charge, but there was some apprehension in Washington over his cowboy attitude. Hurley, to his credit, understood that he had certain weaknesses. Rather than cop an attitude about Lewis's role expanding beyond weeding out the whackjobs, Hurley had told him, "I don't want any bullshit, PC, shrink stuff. You're paid to voice your opinions. Not give me an endless stream of what-ifs."

With that in mind Lewis put his glass down and said, "Two mistakes were made and you both know what they were."

Kennedy nodded, while Hurley said, "I can think of one. Her not doing her due diligence. What's the second one?"

"You can't think of a single thing you did wrong today?" Lewis asked.

"I'm not perfect, but this one's not my fault." Hurley pointed at Kennedy. "I am busier than shit trying to see which one of these boys has the right stuff. I'm not responsible for the turds she dumps in my lap."

Lewis was suddenly resigned to the fact that he would have to box Hurley in a little tighter. Clearing his throat, he said, "We're left with two options. Either this kid is really good or you're losing a step." Lewis took a drink and asked, "Which one is it?"

Hurley's jaw tightened. "I haven't lost a step!" In a slightly embarrassed voice he added, "I just underestimated him, that's all."

"And that's what worries me the most," Lewis said in an accusatory tone.

"Don't worry . . . I won't let it happen again."

"I'm afraid that's not good enough."

Hurley lit a cigarette and casually said, "Let's not make this into something bigger than it needs to be."

"Bullshit!" Lewis said with genuine fury.

"Come on . . ." Hurley said, trying to shrug the whole thing off.

"Don't 'come on' me—you fucked up today, and you fucked up big-time."

Kennedy leaned back, her eyes wide, unable to hide her surprise at Lewis's strong condemnation.

"Let's not overreact," Hurley said easily, trying to take some of the heat out of the conversation.

"Overreact." Lewis leaned forward. "I'm not sure it would be possible to overreact to this situation, and what is really bothering me is that you know it, but you're too pigheaded to admit it."

"It's not the end of the world."

Lewis's indignation was growing with each denial. "You're supposed to be infallible. These guys are supposed to fear you, loathe you, hate your fucking guts, but the one thing they are never supposed to do is lay a shiner on you." Lewis pointed at Hurley's swollen eye. "And they definitely aren't supposed to beat you . . . especially not five minutes after they've walked through the gate."

"He didn't beat me," Hurley growled.

"Well . . . that's debatable. From what I've heard

he had you beat and the only way you got out of it was by cheating."

"Yeah . . . well, life's not fair."

"At this stage, Stan, these guys are like young pups. You know that. When we lay down the rules we can't break them. It sends the wrong signal."

Hurley leaned back and stubbornly folded his arms across his chest. "I was suckered into this thing."

"I'm not sure you were, but for a moment, I'll go along with you." Lewis paused briefly and then said, "You're not supposed to get suckered. You're supposed to run these dogs until they're so tired they can barely stand. You're supposed to watch them go after each other . . . get a sense of what they're capable of, and then you're supposed to bring them into that barn and smack them down, just like when you and I went through boot camp. This is delicate work, God dammit, and you know it. There's a reason why we do things the way we do them, and your ego has no place in the decision process."

"My ego has nothing to do with this," Hurley shot back with a sour look on his face. "I just let my guard down. That's all."

"No," Lewis shook his head, "I'm inclined to agree with Irene on this one. You still see her as a little girl, and you don't give her the credit she deserves. She shows up with this new recruit and because he doesn't fit into your little box of where these recruits are supposed to come from, you decided to skip steps one, two, and three, kick his ass, and send him packing." Lewis sat back, took a drink of wine, and then in a calmer voice asked, "Does it mean anything to you that Thomas signed off on this?" Lewis was referring to the deputy director of operations.

Embarrassed, Hurley said, "I didn't think of that."

"Do you understand the situation you've created?"

Hurley didn't react at first and then very slowly he began to nod.

Kennedy was feeling better about her position, but she wasn't entirely sure what they were talking about and asked Lewis, "What do you mean by situation?"

"These things have a way of spinning out of control," Lewis said. "One recruit has some success putting a shiner on an instructor and all of the sudden the rest of them think that maybe they can take a shot. That these guys are human. Throw in the fact that Stan here had to cheat to avoid losing, and we now have a potentially dangerous situation."

"How so?" Kennedy asked.

"Do you think it's in our best interest to train your boy, send him off, and have him decide that when things get tough, the rules don't really matter?"

Kennedy now saw the point.

"Fuck," Hurley mumbled to himself. "What do you want me to do?"

"You're going to get the hell out of here for about five days. I want you to heal up. You let me and the others run these guys down . . . I'll get a better sense of this Rapp kid and his full potential."

"And then?"

"You come back here and you head into the barn with him and you beat him fair and square."

"And if he can't beat him?" Kennedy asked.

Lewis and Hurley shared a look. They were in uncharted waters. Lewis finally looked at Kennedy and said, "That would be a nice problem to have."

CHAPTER 11

THE first night didn't go so well, at least as far as sleep was concerned. Victor had kept all of them up telling outrageous stories of his sexual conquests, each one more graphic and bizarre than the already twisted story he'd just finished. After an hour or so he ran out of steam and called them all a bunch of faggots for not reciprocating. Victor then proceeded to launch into a symphony of unabated flatulence for a quarter of an hour before eventually falling into a deep, snorting slumber.

Rapp placed his pillow over his head and tried to block out the noise, but it didn't work. It was in those much-needed, sleepless hours just after midnight that Rapp began to explore the idea of getting rid of Victor. At first he considered getting up and throttling the idiot, right then and there, but knew it would only result in further punishment from the instructors and disdain from his fellow recruits.

Still, the thought of spending the next six months with the lout was something that presented a very real problem. A guy like Victor could easily drag someone down with him, and Rapp had an undeniable feeling that the two men were on a collision course. And not one of those collisions that could be avoided if one or both of them changed their behavior. It was inevitable. It was the kind you needed to brace yourself for. Either drop your hips, lower your shoulders, and make the other guy feel more pain than you, or he would do the same to you and you were toast.

There was something undeniably odd about the man. The idea of his participating in a covert op was preposterous. If he could ever walk among the enemy undetected it would be a miracle. Rapp wanted this new vocation with every fiber of his body, although he was smart enough to know that saying he would never quit and actually never quitting were two very different things. He also knew he would be tested in ways he'd never imagined. He'd be pushed to the full extent of his physical and mental abilities, and it was likely that at some point, when he was really in the hurt bag, that pang of doubt would creep into his mind. Could Victor create a climate in which, at his lowest point, he might consider quitting?

Rapp didn't want to find out. Somewhere in the middle of the night, as he was lying on his back watching bats dart around the rafters of the barn and listening to the snorting Victor, Rapp decided the moron would need to quit, and if he didn't do it on his own, and do it quickly, Rapp would have to find a way to subtly nudge him in the right direction.

They were up before the sun. Two of the instructors came in and cursed, yanked, kicked, and slapped them out of bed. Luckily for Rapp, he was half awake and heard the door open. His feet were on the floor before the DI could dump him out of his cot. He'd guessed this was how the morning would start, but the yelling was nonetheless unsettling. In between the barking and smacking, Rapp tried to make out exactly what it was that he was supposed to do. Somewhere in the middle of it he heard the words *line* and *PT*. He threw on his workout gear and running shoes and was out the door like a shot. The lawn was covered with a thick morning dew and the sun was only a gray veil in the east. They weren't allowed watches and there were no clocks in the barn, so Rapp guessed that it was somewhere in the vicinity of 5:00 A.M. The air temp had to be in the midseventies and the humidity was pasty. It would be another hot one.

As Rapp came to a stop on the line he was aware that he was the first and only one out the door. He figured to start with, there were certain things where it was smart to be first and others where it wasn't. Getting out of bed and getting on the line was an area to be first. Hand-to-hand combat and fighting drills he would never hold back on, but the endurance stuff like running and PT he would. He needed to stay healthy and hold some things in reserve. These guys didn't need to know he could run like the wind.

As he waited for the others, he caught a whiff of coffee and turned to look at the house. There, standing on the porch, was a new face, a blond-haired guy who looked to be in his midthirties. The man was staring intently at Rapp. Rapp returned the stare and even at a distance of several hundred feet noted the blue eyes. The guy was in a pair of jeans and a T-shirt. He was leaning against one of the porch columns sipping his coffee and making no effort to conceal his interest in Rapp. There was something different about the guy. Rapp could tell he was in shape, but he was way more relaxed than the other DIs who were marching around and that sadistic little cuss who'd tried to neuter him.

One by one the guys trickled out of the barn and fell in. Victor was last, which was becoming a common theme. Sergeant Smith was walking quickly beside him giving him an earful in a hushed voice. They had all been warned that there would be no yelling on the line. This wasn't the only place on the lake, and voices carried across the water. Inside the barn with the door closed, however, the decibel level went through the roof. Victor fell in at the far end from Rapp.

Sergeant Smith stepped out in front of the seven recruits and with a clenched jaw said, "You puds better get your shit together, or I'm gonna start knocking some heads. I've seen Cub Scouts do better than this. This is damn sloppy. It shouldn't never take you morons more than sixty seconds to get your ass out of bed, dressed, and on the line. When you go to bed, you make sure your shit is ready. You lay it out on your footlocker so it's ready to go. We start PT at five every morning."

Rapp watched the DI's eyes shift to the opposite end of the line. He leaned forward and saw Victor had his arm raised.

"Sarge, when are we supposed to take a piss? I gotta go so bad I'm about to drown."

Sergeant Smith walked over to Victor and got in his face. "Maybe if you had gotten your lazy ass out of bed when I told you to, you would have had time to piss." He stepped back and looked down the line. "We're going to do a quick warm-up. As much as I hate you idiots, the powers that be don't want you ladies getting hurt until they see if you've got some potential. I have tried to dissuade them, as you are the biggest collection of shitlickers I've seen come through here in some time."

"Sarge, I gotta go real bad," Victor whined.

"Then piss yourself, you big idiot." His head snapped to the group. "If you can't take care of your business and get out here in sixty seconds, I'm going to have to treat you like a bunch of toddlers . . . so go ahead and piss yourself, Victor. The rest of you who need to go I suggest you wait until we head out for our run. You can pull over on the trail and take care of business. Now drop and give me fifty, and if I see any of you pussies cheating we'll start over."

They did the fifty push-ups, followed by one hundred sit-ups, fifty up-downs, and then a few minutes of scissor kicks and a couple of stretches, and then Sergeant Smith led them into the woods. Eight of them in a nice neat line, with Victor trailing. Rapp guessed they were moving at just under a six-minute pace. He could keep a five-minute pace for ten miles, so he was feeling good. They finished the five-mile run and found themselves standing in front of an obstacle course in the middle of the woods. The place looked like a relic from an abandoned Renaissance festival. Sergeant Smith had his stopwatch out and was clocking them.

Rapp positioned himself fifth in line, carefully placing one man between himself and Victor. He wanted to see how these other four guys navigated the course, guessing that they'd all done it when they'd gone through boot camp. His idea kind of fell apart when Sergeant Smith started sending guys at thirty-second intervals. The course started with a low wall. It was a ten-foot-tall wooden, moss-laden wall with two telephone poles stuck in the ground in front of it. The first telephone pole stuck out of the ground about a foot and a half and was four feet in front of the wall. The next telephone pole was two feet in front of the wall and stuck out of the ground three feet.

Rapp watched as the first recruit headed for the wall, picking up speed. Right before the telephone poles he did a quick stutter step and then as nimbly as you could imagine, he placed his left foot on the first and shorter telephone pole, using it as a step. His right foot then landed on the second telephone pole and he launched himself up and onto the wall, grabbing the top with both hands and pinning his knee to the wall just a few feet from the top. It was like a controlled collision. The recruit was up and over, dropping to the soft ground on the other side.

The second guy did it the same way, and the third tried something slightly different that involved doing a pull-up. After the low wall was a forty-foot dash to a fifteen-foot-high wall with ropes hanging on the face. There was nothing fancy about this one. You just grabbed the rope, put your feet on the wall, and walked your way up. Next in line was barbed wire. Again, pretty straightforward. Dive under, keep your butt down, and do an infantry crawl to the other end. After that was a forty-foot cargo net strung between two towering pines. Beyond that was a set of logs set up in a zigzag pattern about three feet off the ground. They acted as a sort of footbridge to test your balance.

Rapp didn't have a chance to see what came after the balance logs because it was his turn to start. He quickly dried the palms of his hands on his shorts, and then when Sergeant Smith gave him the signal, he ran toward the short wall, mimicked the exact steps of the first recruit, and threw himself up and at the top of the wall. He caught it, pulled himself up and over, and landed with ease on the other side. The second, taller wall was easy enough to navigate, and the barbed wire was about as primal as it got. If a guy couldn't grasp the simplicity of crawling he should just quit and go home. The cargo net proved to be the first real challenge. About a third of the way up Rapp realized there was too much slack in the middle so he moved over to the side. After that it was easier. The balance logs were a breeze, the tires were nothing, and the transfer ropes were playground 101.

Then he came across something that looked like a set of uneven parallel bars, like the kind female gymnasts use. He paused, not sure how to attack the two horizontal telephone poles, and then almost on cue, one of the DIs was right there barking orders at him. Telling him what to do, and to do it quickly. Based on what the DI was telling him, it sounded like a great way to break a rib, but Rapp could see no other way, so he launched himself into the first pole and then the second and then it was more tires and a thing called the Burma bridge. After that there were more logs, ropes, and walls to negotiate and a sprint to the finish.

When Rapp crossed the line Sergeant Smith was staring at his stopwatch and shaking his head. He glanced at Rapp, contempt on his face, and said, "You suck."

Rapp was doubled over with his hands on his knees, acting more tired than he was. He wanted to smile but didn't. He couldn't have done that badly. The guy in the number-six position had yet to finish. Rapp turned to see how the last two were doing. At the edge of the course, about fifty yards back, he saw the blond-haired guy he'd seen on the porch earlier in the morning. The man was standing at the edge of the woods staring straight at him, again making no effort to conceal his interest.

CHAPTER 12

LANGLEY, VIRGINIA

KENNEDY parked in the east lot and entered the Headquarters Building at exactly eight-oh-three. She'd used the hour-and-a-half drive up from Lake Anna to try to prioritize her ever-increasing list of responsibilities, both official and unofficial. Much of her job was off the books, and that meant no notes and no files. She had to keep it all organized in her own mind, and every time she came back to HQ she needed to have her story straight. When the elevator doors parted on the sixth floor one of her bosses was waiting with a deeply concerned look on his face.

Max Powers nudged her back into the elevator and said, "Problem."

Powers was the Near East Division chief. It had taken Kennedy a while to get used to his style. Powers was famous for speaking in one-word sentences.

His colleagues who had worked with him over the years called him Musket Max.

Kennedy stepped back and asked, "What's wrong?" Her immediate fear, as it was almost every time she entered the building, was that her black ops program had been uncovered.

"Beirut," Powers said, offering nothing more.

Beirut could mean a lot of things, but on this hot August morning Kennedy was aware of one thing in particular. "John?"

"Yep."

"Crap," Kennedy mumbled under her breath. John Cummins was one of their deep-cover operatives who had snuck into Lebanon three days earlier. An American businessman who worked for a data storage company had been kidnapped the previous week. This company, it turned out, was run by a Texan with big contacts in D.C. The owner was old-school, former army, and over the past thirty years he had freely and enthusiastically kept the CIA and the Pentagon abreast of all the info he and his people happened to pick up in their international dealings. A lot of very important people in town owed him, and he decided now was the time to call in a few of his IOUs.

The Pentagon had zero assets in the region and the CIA wasn't much better. They were still trying to recover from the kidnapping, torture, and death of their Beirut station chief half a decade earlier. Langley did, however, have assets in Jordan, Syria, and Israel. Cummins, who had lived in Syria for the past three years, was the best bet. He'd built up some great contacts by passing himself off as a counterfeiter of U.S. currency and smuggler of American-made goods that were embargoed in the region.

From the jump Kennedy argued against using him. He was by far their most valuable asset inside Syria, and Beirut, although safer than it had been in the eighties, was still pretty much the Wild West of the Middle East. If anything went wrong Cummins would be lost. Someone with a much bigger title had overruled her, however.

"How bad?" Kennedy asked.

"Bad."

The doors opened on the seventh floor and Kennedy followed Powers down the hall to the office of Thomas Stansfield, the deputy director of operations. The door was open and the two of them breezed through the outer office, past Stansfield's assistant, and into the main office. Powers closed the soundproof door. Kennedy looked at the silver-haired Stansfield, who was sitting behind his massive desk, his glasses in one hand and the phone in the other. Stansfield was probably the most respected and feared man in the building and possibly the entire town. Since they were on the same team, Kennedy respected but did not fear the old spy.

Stansfield cut the person on the other end off, said good-bye, and placed the phone back in its cradle. Looking up at Powers, he asked, "Any further word?"

Powers shook his head.

"How did it happen?" Kennedy asked.

"He was leaving his hotel on Rue Monot for a

lunch meeting," Stansfield said. "He never showed. He missed his check-in this afternoon and I placed a call to my opposite in Israel. Mossad did some quiet checking." Stansfield shook his head. "A shopkeeper saw someone fitting Cummins's description being forced into the trunk of a car shortly before noon today."

Kennedy felt her stomach twist into a wrenching knot. She liked Cummins. They knew all too well how this would play out. The torture would have commenced almost immediately, and depending on how Cummins held up, death was the likely outcome.

"I remember you voiced your opposition to this," Stansfield said, "but know there are certain things that even I wasn't told."

"Such as?"

The ops boss shook his head, letting her know he wasn't allowed to talk about it. "The important thing now is that Schnoz's Syrian contacts back his cover story. If they don't step up to the plate for him, this will end badly." Cummins was half Armenian and half Jewish and had a nose to make a Roman emperor jealous; hence his unofficial cover name was Schnoz.

"Double down," Powers chimed in. "Get the Texas boy on a plane with a couple suitcases filled with cash."

"It's a possibility that I already floated with the White House. They're getting nervous, though, and for good reason."

"They should be," Kennedy said. "They just

burned one of our most valuable assets trying to do a personal favor that as far as I can tell has nothing to do with national security."

"Bingo," Powers said.

Stansfield was quiet for a moment. "I have a back channel I can use with the CEO. He wants this employee back, and I think when I explain to him what happened to our man, he'll offer to pay for both. It should help cement the idea that Schnoz was working as a freelancer."

"It better happen quick," Kennedy said. "We never know how long someone will be able to hold out. If they break Schnoz . . ." She stopped talking and shuddered at the thought of the damage that would be done.

"I know," Stansfield sighed.

"Rescue op?" Powers asked.

Stansfield looked slightly embarrassed. "Not going to happen. We knew it going in. Beirut is still radioactive."

"What if we get some good intel?" Kennedy asked.

"That's a big what-if."

"But if we do," Kennedy pressed her point, "we need assets in place."

Stansfield sadly shook his head.

"Corner office or Sixteen Hundred?" Powers asked.

Kennedy understood the shorthand question to mean, was it the director of the CIA who was freezing them out or the White House?

"White House," Stansfield replied.

"Our friends at the Institute." Powers offered it as a suggestion. "They're in the loop?"

Stansfield tapped the leather ink blotter on his desk while he considered the Israeli option. The Institute was the slang Powers used to refer to the Institute for Intelligence, or as they were better known, Mossad.

"I'm told they knew before we did."

"Maybe let them handle the cowboy stuff . . . if it comes to that."

The fact that it had not occurred to him to have Mossad handle the rescue spoke volumes about the complicated relationship. "If something concrete comes our way I'll consider it, but . . ."

"You don't want to owe them the farm," Powers said.

"That's right. They would more than likely demand something that I'm either unwilling or unable to give them."

"May I say something, sir?" Kennedy asked.

Stansfield wasn't sure he wanted to hear it, but he knew he needed to let his people vent. He nodded.

"This problem is never going to go away until we send these guys a very serious message."

"I assume you mean the kidnapping?"

"Yes."

"I told the director the same thing five minutes before you walked in the door, but it seems we lack the political will, at the moment, to take a more aggressive approach."

"Pussies," Powers muttered, and then looked at Kennedy and said, "Sorry."

"No need to apologize." She paused and then decided this was the right time to push her agenda. "You know what this means?"

"No."

"It's yet another example of why we need to get Orion up and running. How in hell can we expect our assets to operate in this environment? It's bad enough that we won't get tough with these guys . . . it's inexcusable that we won't even consider a rescue op. He's one of our own, for Christ's sake!"

Stansfield was not surprised that she'd brought it up. He would have done the same thing if he was in her place, but during a crisis like this it was a common mistake to hurry things that needed time. "I want this to happen as badly as you do, Irene, but it can't be rushed. If we send a bunch of half-baked assets into the field, we'll end up spending all our energy trying to pull them out of the fire. Trust me . . . I saw it firsthand back in Berlin. Just try to be patient for a few more months. If a couple of these guys can prove that they have the stuff, I'll green-light it, and support you every step of the way."

Kennedy took it as a promise but couldn't get her mind off Cummins and what he was enduring. Her thoughts for some unknown reason turned to Rapp. She hoped he was the one. The weapon they could turn loose on these murderous zealots.

CHAPTER 13

LAKE ANNA, VIRGINIA

THEY each ran the obstacle course three more times and then double-timed it back to the barn for breakfast. They stuffed their faces with eggs and pancakes, then were given thirty minutes to digest their food and make sure their bunks were squared away. Rapp was somewhat relieved that Victor used this time to pester someone else. Then it was off to the pistol range, which was a two-mile hike back into the woods. It was not a leisurely hike, however. They were given twelve minutes to get to the range and were told that anyone who was late could pack his bags. Rapp was starting to get the idea that they would be doing a lot of running, which was fine by him. He kept a pace or two off the lead and made it look as if he was struggling to keep up, but he wasn't.

The range was adjacent to the obstacle course. It was twelve feet wide and one hundred feet long, and was as bare-bones as you could get. Basically a tractor had scooped out a ten-foot-deep trench that ran between a row of pines. It was lined with old car tires and covered with camouflage netting, which in addition to the tree branches made the light pretty weak. There were three shooting stations made out of pressure-treated plywood and lumber. Silhouette targets were already hung at twenty feet and silenced 9mm Beretta 92Fs were loaded and ready to be fired. The first three guys stepped up, and when Sergeant Smith ordered them to commence firing all three methodically emptied their rounds into the paper targets.

Rapp swallowed hard when they were done. The first two guys punched soup-can-sized holes through the chests of the black silhouettes. The third target had a nice neat hole about the size of a silver dollar in the center of the face. There was not a stray shot among the three. Rapp was impressed, but the thing that really surprised him was the reaction of Sergeant Smith. The instructor had a smile on his face.

Sergeant Smith stood beside the last shooter and said, "Normally I don't like you SEALs, but goddamn! They sure do teach you boys how to shoot." He gave the recruit a rough slap on the back and ordered the next three up. The results were similar— at least as far as the first two were concerned. They had both punched nice neat holes in the chests of their targets. Rapp's target, however, looked a little rough.

Rapp lowered the pistol and took in his handiwork. He'd only started shooting a few months earlier, and without any actual training from an instructor, the results were lacking. The target looked like a piece of Swiss cheese, with holes from the chest all the way down to the groin. He set the heavy Beretta down on the flat plywood surface and grimaced as the instructors fell in, one on each shoulder.

"Definitely not a SEAL," Sergeant Smith said.

"Nope," Sergeant Jones replied. "Not a D Boy either. Might be a gangbanger, though. That's how those little fuckers shoot. Just spray it all over the place and hope they hit a vital organ."

"Definitely not the way we do things around here," Sergeant Smith said.

"Son," the taller of the two said, "where the fuck did you learn how to shoot?"

Rapp cleared his throat and admitted, "I don't know how to shoot, Sergeant."

"You mean you've tried and suck, or you've never been taught?"

"Never been taught, Sergeant."

There was an uncomfortable pause while the two instructors tried to figure out what to do. Unfortunately, Victor took the opportunity to throw in one of his asinine comments. "He shoots like a girl."

Underneath Rapp's bronzed skin his cheeks flushed. He had known that, due to his lack of training, shooting would be one of his weaknesses. Still, it embarrassed him that the others were so much better. Rapp looked to Sergeant Smith and asked, "Any pointers?"

The shorter man looked up at Rapp and regarded him for a moment before nodding and saying, "Let's see you do it again." Sergeant Smith handed him a fresh magazine.

Sergeant Jones yelled, "All right, Victor, you jackass. Get up here and show us what you can do."

The other five stood back and watched in silence while two fresh targets were put up. Sergeant Smith stood at Rapp's side and quietly issued instructions. He watched Rapp squeeze off one shot and then reached in to adjust his grip, elbow position, and feet. With each shot the instructor issued corrections and the grouping of shots grew tighter. This time the holes were still loose, but at least all of them were in the chest area, as opposed to all over the entire target.

Rapp heard someone giggle and he looked over at Victor's target. The clown had shot eyes and a nose in the target and five more shots made a downturned mouth. The remainder of the shots were concentrated in the groin area.

"Victor," Sergeant Jones said, "what in hell are you doing?"

"Long-term strategic planning, Sarge."

"I doubt your pea-sized brain could attempt any such thing."

"Population control," Victor said, spitting a gob of chew on the ground. "Shoot the nuts off all the hajis and no more baby terrorists. Twenty years from now we declare victory. Brilliant, if I say so myself."

Sergeant Jones put his hands on his hips. "Put

the weapon down, Victor, and step back." The big man did so, and then Sergeant Jones continued in a disappointed voice, "Since all of you appear to be decent shots and Victor here thinks this is a joke, we're going to head back over to the O course where I'm going to run all of you until at least one of you pukes. Our earnest, yet respectful virgin will stay here with Sergeant Smith and attempt to learn the basics of pistol shooting." The big sergeant eyed the group and when no one moved he said, "Well, I guess you ladies would like to do some push-ups first." In a gruff voice he shouted, "Assume the position."

All six men dropped to the ground and got into the plank position. They were told to start and no one said a word except Victor, who continued to complain as they counted out their punishment.

While they worked through their push-ups Sergeant Smith began instructing Rapp on the finer points of marksmanship. Rapp listened intently, digesting every word. Sergeant Smith told Rapp to aim for the head this time. He slammed a fresh magazine into the hilt and hit the slide release.

"When you have a fresh magazine in and hit the slide release, a round is automatically chambered." The sergeant offered Rapp the weapon and said, "The hammer's back. So she's hot. Not every gun is like that, but that's how the Berettas work. Also that red dot right there . . . red means dead. So don't point it at anything you're not going to shoot at and always keep that finger off the trigger until you're ready to fire. Got it?"

Rapp nodded.

"All right, show me that stance. Keep those feet just so. You're a lefty, so put your right foot a few inches in front of your left. Create the power triangle with your arms and place that dot right in the center of the head. Some guys get all hung up on breathing in versus exhaling, but I don't want you to think about that crap. You're going to need to learn to shoot on the run, so breathing in or out ain't going to work. The main thing right now is how you squeeze that trigger. Notice how I didn't say pull. Don't pull it. Squeeze it straight back and put a round right through the middle of the head this time."

Rapp did everything he was told and the bullet spat from the end of the suppressor. The muzzle jumped and when it came back down Rapp was staring at a perfectly placed shot.

"Do it again," Sergeant Smith ordered.

Rapp squeezed the trigger and the bullet struck the target half an inch to the right of the first one.

"Again."

The third shot bridged the first and second. Rapp fell into a rhythm. He didn't rush it, but he didn't take too much time either. It took him less than twenty seconds to empty the rest of the magazine, and when he was done all of the rounds were within a six-inch circle—a jagged hole punched through the face of the paper target. Rapp breathed a sigh of relief.

Sergeant Smith clapped him on the shoulder and said, "You're coachable, kid. Nice work. Let's try this a few more times."

Rapp was in the midst of reloading the weapon when by chance he turned his head and looked over his left shoulder. About sixty feet away, in the shadows of a big pine, a man was watching them. With the poor light Rapp couldn't be certain who it was, but he thought it might be the guy he'd seen on the porch earlier in the morning. Rapp turned back to Sergeant Smith and was about to ask him who he was when he thought better of it. It would be a mistake to confuse a little one-on-one instruction with friendship.

CHAPTER 14

D R. Lewis walked into the office, offered a faint smile to his visitor, and closed the door behind him. He'd been watching the new recruit intently for the past three days. At twenty-three he was the youngest project they had attempted to run through the program, and from what he'd seen the last few days the man showed a great deal of promise. Before sitting, Lewis glanced down at the notepad and pen sitting in the middle of the desk. Next to them sat a file with Rapp's name written in large black letters. It was impossible to miss and intentionally so. They knew surprisingly little about the man, but then again how much could you really know about someone this young—this untested? If he listened to the irascible Hurley, inexperience was a curse, and if he listened to the more pragmatic Kennedy, it was a blessing. Lewis didn't know who was right, but he had grown tired of listening to them bicker.

Moving behind the desk, Lewis sat in the worn leather and wood desk chair and leaned back. The chair emitted a metal squeak. The doctor ignored it and moved his eyes from the subject to the contents sitting on his desk. There were many tools in his trade—little tricks that could be used to test the people he was assigned to evaluate. Some were subtle, others more overt, but all were designed to help him get a better glimpse into the minds of the men they were recruiting. The file on the desk had been a test. Lewis had spent the last five minutes in the basement watching the recruit via a concealed camera. Rapp had sat sphinxlike in the chair. He had glanced at the file only once and then adopted a relaxed posture that spoke of boredom. Lewis didn't know him well enough to gauge whether it was sincere, but there was something about this Mitch Rapp fellow that suggested great possibilities. There was a casualness on the surface that helped mask something far more complex.

Lewis considered reaching for the notepad and pen. It was a way of establishing authority, and creating stress for the subject. Making him feel the pressure of possibly giving incorrect answers. Lewis decided against it. From what he'd witnessed over the last three days, it was highly unlikely that the ploy would fluster this one. Nothing else had so far.

Going on a hunch, Lewis clasped his hands behind his head and casually asked, "You know what you're getting yourself into?"

Rapp looked at him with his dark brown eyes

and shrugged as if to say it wasn't worth acknowledging the obvious.

"I don't read minds," Lewis said, only half serious. "I'm going to need you to verbalize your answers."

"Hopefully, you're going to turn me into a weapon . . . a killer."

Lewis considered the straightforward answer and then said, "Not me specifically, but in essence, yes, that is what we are going to do."

Rapp gave a slight nod as if that was just fine with him and continued to look right back into the bright blue eyes of the man who had been watching him from a safe distance.

"Do you have any reservations?"

"Not really."

Lewis placed his palm on the desk, and after staring at the back of his hand for a long moment said, "It would be normal if you did."

Rapp cracked a thin smile. "I suppose it would."

"So do you have any reservations?"

It was a pretty vague question, and Rapp didn't like vague. "In terms of what?"

"This is a big commitment. Most of your friends are probably taking jobs with Kodak or Xerox."

More than a few of them were, but Rapp simply nodded.

Lewis noted that Rapp was not jumping out of his chair trying to please him with earnest answers. Nor was he displaying the open disrespect that many of the candidates would employ as a defense mechanism. He was striking the perfect balance.

Lewis decided to skip his standard twenty minutes of preamble and get to the heart of the matter. "Have you ever wondered what it's like to kill a man?"

Rapp nodded. He had spent more time wondering about it than he would ever admit to this guy, or anybody else.

"Do you think that's healthy?"

This time Rapp let out a small laugh.

Lewis noted the classic deflection technique, but didn't want to seem judgmental, so he smiled along with Rapp. "What's so funny?"

"I can answer your question six ways, and depending on your mood, you might find all of the answers acceptable, or none of them."

"How do you mean?"

"It's all in the context."

"Context is important," Lewis agreed. "Give me an example."

Rapp thought about it for a moment and then said, "If I'm lying awake at night thinking about killing the guy who broke into my car and ripped me off, it's probably safe to say that I have some anger issues, and a poor grasp of what constitutes just punishment." Rapp put his tanned arm over the back of the chair and looked out the window for a second, wondering how much he should admit. "But if I lie awake at night thinking about sticking a knife through the eye socket of a terrorist who's killed a couple hundred innocent civilians," Rapp shrugged, "I think that's probably not so far out there."

Lewis appreciated the blunt answer. Wanting a

deeper reaction, he asked, "Do you miss your girl-friend?"

Rapp gave Lewis a disappointed look and shook his head.

"What's wrong? Did I say something that of-fended you?"

"No . . . not really . . ."

"From the look on your face it would appear that I did."

"I volunteered for this, but I hate playing all these games."

"Games?" Lewis asked with an arched brow.

"You're a shrink, right?" Rapp didn't give him a chance to answer. "You've been watching me for the past three days. I've noticed that you seem to be paying a lot of attention to me. More so than the others. You choose your words carefully, and you've undoubtedly read that file that's sitting on your desk. You know why I'm here."

Lewis hid his surprise that Rapp had guessed his profession. "It's my job to ask questions."

"But why would you ask if I miss her? Don't you think that's pretty obvious?"

"So that's why you're here?"

"I'm not here because I miss her. I miss my father, who died when I was thirteen. I miss my grandparents, and someday I'll miss my mom when she dies, and maybe if I get to know you, I'll miss you, too. That's part of life. I'm here for a very obvi-ous reason. One that I'm sure you're already aware of."

Lewis noted how he had taken charge of the

conversation, but was willing to let this play out. "Revenge?"

"I prefer retribution, but it all depends on the definition you choose."

Lewis was pleased that he'd made the distinction. He was intimately familiar with the difference between the two words. "I'd like to hear your definition."

"Revenge is more wild, less calculated . . . deeply personal."

"And retribution?"

Rapp thought about it for a moment and then answered in a very clear voice. "Retribution is a punishment that is morally right and fully deserved."

"And the men who conspired to bring down Pan Am 103?"

Rapp leaned forward, placing his elbows on his knees, and said, "Every last one of them deserves to die."

Lewis looked at the file on the desk and asked, "You're Catholic?"

"Yes."

"So how do you square this with your Lord? Your idea of retribution doesn't exactly conform to the turn-the-other-cheek preaching of Jesus Christ."

"Nice try." Rapp grinned.

"How do you mean?"

"I'll tell you a little secret about me. I'm not the most patient guy. I have a lot to learn, and I'm eager to learn it, so when you start to hit me with selective theology you might get my back up a bit."

"Selective?" Lewis asked.

"Yeah. I've never understood the intellectual dishonesty of people who say the Bible is the word of God and then choose to pull verses only from the New Testament, for example. Turning the other cheek is one of their favorites, and they use it, while ignoring a dozen Old Testament verses and a few New Testament verses that say the men who brought down that plane deserve to die."

Lewis conceded with a nod. "So, if it comes to it . . . you don't think you'd have a problem taking another man's life?"

"That depends."

"On what?"

"Who the guy is, and more important, what he's guilty of."

CHAPTER 15

WHEN the sun rose for the fifth day they were one man short. It was Dick. Rapp didn't know the guy's real name, much less where he was from or where he was going, so it was hard to feel too bad when the guy stepped out of formation during a grueling set of up-downs in the hot afternoon sun. He simply approached one of the instructors, announced his intention, and the two men shook hands. Just like that the guy was done. Free of the pain, the sweating, the burning muscles, the tired eyes, and the battered ego. It all seemed too easy, and that's what scared the crap out of Rapp.

It made him briefly wonder if he was capable of pussing out. All it would take was a down moment. A bad spell, a cold, or a fever or another sleepless night. One misstep and he could be the one shaking hands and packing his bag. While falling asleep that night, Rapp focused on the positive. There was one man fewer to compete with. They kept saying it wasn't a competition, but Rapp wasn't so sure. If it wasn't a competition, why did they count or clock everything they did? The image of the fellow recruit bowing out after five days put Rapp on guard against a moment of personal weakness. It refocused him by showing just how rapidly this journey could come to a very unsatisfying end.

Rapp awoke tired but ready to push ahead. He was the first one on the line and was stretching his neck and shoulders waiting for the others when he noticed the two instructors having what looked like an unpleasant conversation. When everyone was finally on the line, Sergeant Jones stepped forward and with a disappointed look on his face said, "One of you screwed up real bad last night."

Rapp began racking his brain trying to think of any mistakes he'd made.

"We have rules for a reason. At this point you don't need to understand these rules, you just need to follow them." He paused to look each of them in the eye. "You have all been repeatedly warned to not divulge any personal information. Now . . . we're realistic enough to understand that you boys will discover certain things about each other. Some of you have a slight accent, so it's pretty easy to figure out what part of the country you come from. As far as prior military experience, we haven't busted your balls over debating the healthy rivalry between the services, but last night, someone crossed the line." He stopped and looked at the ground. In a disappointed voice he said, "The one thing you are never supposed to do is tell someone your real name."

Rapp heard someone farther down the line mumble something under his breath, but he couldn't tell who it was, and considering the mood of the two instructors, he didn't dare look.

"You are all smart enough to know this, and you were all warned what would happen if you slipped up on this one. This isn't a fucking summer camp. This is serious shit," Sergeant Jones said in a disappointed voice. He looked to the far end of the line and said, "Bill, pack your shit. You're gone."

The man they called Bill, whom Rapp had pegged as the hot-shooting Navy SEAL from Texas, took one step forward and shook his head at the harsh punishment he'd just received. He looked as if he was going to say something and then caught himself. Sergeant Jones started moving and told Bill to follow him back to the barn. Sergeant Smith stepped in to lead them in PT, but before he could start Bill turned back to the group.

"Victor, you're a real asshole. I told you I didn't want to talk, but you just wouldn't leave it alone." Looking at Sergeant Jones, he asked, "Why isn't he getting the boot as well?"

"Keep moving. We'll talk about it in the barn."

"This is bullshit. He told me who he was and where he was from. Same as me," Bill complained.

Victor laughed. "I gave you a fake name, you stupid hick."

"Why the hell would you do that?" one of the guys farther down the line asked Victor.

"Asshole," someone else grumbled.

"You guys should all be thanking me," Victor said in an easy voice. "One less guy to worry about."

Sergeant Smith silenced all of them with a growling order to assume the position. "The next one of you who opens his piehole is gone. Now push 'em out."

Rapp dropped his chest down to the dewy grass and pushed straight up, quietly counting out each push-up as he went. He'd done so many in the past five days that they were becoming second nature—almost like breathing. Somewhere past number forty and before number fifty, Rapp began feeling some serious ill will toward Victor. If only the big jackass would stumble and break an ankle. He was too risky to have around. For the rest of the morning, as they ran from one thing to the next, Rapp couldn't shake the feeling that he and Victor were on a collision course. With Dick quitting and Bill getting the boot, that meant two fewer people to run interference. Victor could focus more of his time on pestering Rapp.

The long run was actually nice, since Victor was the slowest of the group. They were spared his running mouth. When breakfast rolled around they all gave him the cold shoulder. It didn't matter to Victor, though. He stayed chatty, continuing to dole out insults and the occasional wise-ass comment that the instructors seemed to take better than they should have. They spent an hour on the obstacle course and another hour on the pistol range before heading back in for lunch. The attitude among the recruits was decidedly sour. It was as if they had a traitor in their midst. After lunch they went over field-stripping various handguns, and then it was announced that they were heading into the barn for a little hand-to-hand combat.

For Rapp it was his first time back on the mat since the day he'd arrived. He had wondered where the mean old cuss had gone, and had almost asked Sergeant Smith, but the guy wasn't exactly keen on sharing information. Jones and Smith paired the men up. Since there were five, someone had to be the odd man out and it turned out to be Rapp. The rules were simple: no blows to the head or groin. Choke holds were encouraged, but they warned the men to be careful not to crush anyone's larynx. If you wanted out all you had to do was tap the mat. Right before they started the blond-haired shrink quietly slipped into the barn.

The first two men up were Roy and Glenn. Rapp hadn't figured out where either of them was from, and wasn't about to ask. Like all of them, the two men were dark-featured, with black hair, brown eyes, and tan skin. Roy was five-ten and Glenn was perhaps an inch taller. Rapp guessed they were both around twenty-seven. He was not overly impressed with their fighting styles. They both used standard judo techniques. Lots of holds and throws, but nothing that could be used to incapacitate an enemy in one quick flurry. Technically, they were sound, and they were both tough enough, and in good enough shape, to draw out a lengthy, tiring, boring match.

After about four minutes they ended up in a

sweaty tangle in the middle of the mat and Sergeant Smith stepped in. Victor and Fred were up next. Fred was six feet tall and about 175 pounds, and had done a really good job of keeping to himself. He finished in the top three on every run, handled the obstacle course with ease, and was the top marksman after Bill. Victor, at six-two and 220 pounds, was by far the biggest of the group. His neck was nearly as thick as his thighs, which meant, as Rapp had noticed when he met him, that he would be really hard to knock out with a shot to the head. From all of the talking he'd done, Rapp half expected to see the second coming of Muhammad Ali.

Victor bounded across the mat, shadowboxing as he went. "You ready to get your ass kicked, Freddy?"

Fred said nothing. He walked to the center of the mat in his bare feet and took up his fighting stance. Rapp pegged him for a wrestler by the way he moved. Victor was such an oversized peacock that it was impossible to tell what he was capable of. Most guys his size were not boxers, but he did move pretty well on his feet. Sergeant Smith dropped his hand and the two men charged at each other. Fred went low just as Rapp expected him to. Victor tried to sidestep him, but his right leg got looped by his opponent. Fred hooked onto Victor's knee and pulled it tight to his chest. He stayed low and kept driving with his legs, trying to tip the bigger man over. Victor hopped back on his left leg and started delivering punches to Fred's back. The first few were misplaced and lacked power. Rapp watched Victor lose his balance and begin to go down. He changed his tactic and smacked Fred in the back of the head with a closed-fist punch. Fred appeared to slow for a split second, but he didn't lose his grip.

Victor went down and rolled immediately onto his stomach. He flared his arms and legs out so he couldn't be flipped. Fred scrambled over the top of him and shot his right arm under Victor's neck. He wrenched the bigger man's head back and placed his left forearm across the back of Victor's head. The hold was commonly known as the sleeper hold, and if it wasn't broken in short order it performed as advertised. Victor got hold of a couple of Fred's fingers and twisted with everything he had while turning in to the man. Victor used his strength to reverse out of it. At first it looked as if he was getting the upper hand, and then Rapp saw what Fred was up to. He had allowed Victor to think he was initiating the move, but in truth it was Fred's idea. Once on his back, Fred wrapped his legs around Victor's waist and clamped down with a vicious scissor lock. Victor only made things worse by trying to pull himself up and away.

As Rapp had learned the hard way, the best way to get out of that hold was with a well-placed elbow to the inner thigh. Earlier in the summer, his instructor had put him in the same scissor lock and made him pay dearly. By pulling away you stretched out the torso, which allowed the person initiating the hold to clamp down even tighter. Then you emptied your lungs to take in a big breath, and the person squeezed even tighter. The next thing you knew you were desperately in need of oxygen, writhing in pain and genuinely concerned that you were about to end up with a broken rib or two.

Victor made that mistake, and it was obvious by the worried look in his eyes that he knew he was in trouble. He swung hard, trying to hit Fred in the solar plexus, but the blow was blocked. Next he tried to twist away, which only allowed Fred to tighten his hold a few more notches. Victor's face was beet red. Rapp knew it would last only a few more seconds, and he was silently hoping to hear a few ribs pop between now and then. It looked as if Victor was going to quit. He started to wave his left hand, and then just as Fred relaxed a touch, Victor brought his big right fist smashing down. The blow hit Fred square in the face. His head bounced off the mat, and he released his legs. Then blood began to pour from his misshapen nose.

Rapp took a step forward, ready to kick Victor in the head. He was on the verge of delivering the blow when Sergeant Smith stepped onto the mat and began barking orders. Rapp took a step back and watched as Victor rolled off Fred, flopped onto his back, and began laughing.

CHAPTER 16

SERGEANT Jones was attending to Fred's broken nose. Roy and Glenn were talking quietly and shooting Victor daggers. Rapp looked to the door and noticed the shrink studying him. Twice now, Rapp had seen the rules of engagement broken, and so far, there had been no punishment handed out. Not that the old codger could be punished, but Victor was one of them, and if he could get away with it then Rapp could as well. It got Rapp thinking that maybe it was time to bend the rules a little bit. While he was working out the details of what he wanted to do, Sergeant Smith ordered him onto the mat and then pointed at Glenn.

"I would rather fight Victor," Rapp said.

"Well, you're not running the show around here," Smith snapped.

"He's doing you a favor," Victor said, still out

of breath. "A little pussy like you wouldn't last five seconds against me."

Rapp stayed calm, but there was something unmistakably ominous just beneath the surface. "Let's find out," he said evenly.

"Suicide," Victor retorted.

"I think you're afraid."

"Shut up, all of you," Sergeant Smith said. "Glenn, get your ass on the mat."

Rapp moved to his left, cutting off Glenn. He stayed facing the wiry instructor and said, "I'm confused. Do rules matter around here, or does Victor get to do as he pleases?"

"We have rules, dammit! Now get in the middle of the mat and shut up."

"No disrespect, Sarge, but this is bullshit. How are we supposed to trust each other . . . how are we supposed to trust you when he keeps doing whatever the hell he wants without getting punished?"

"You think there's any rules out there," Victor laughed, "in the real world? Hell no!"

"But in here . . . we should just let you do whatever you want?"

"Sarge," Victor said as he got to his feet, "I got this one. Don't worry. I can take care of this little college puke with one arm tied behind my back."

Sergeant Smith looked as if he was about to lose it, but the blond-haired shrink stepped in and said, "Sergeant, I think we should allow Victor and Irving to have a go at it."

The sergeant's head snapped around. Rapp noticed a brief exchange of thoughts between the men before the sergeant retreated. "All right," he grumbled, "both of you, center of the mat, square off, and on my mark you start."

"Do we bother with rules this time, or should I assume Victor will break them?" Rapp asked, stone-faced.

"The head and neck are off limits, dammit!"

"I appreciate the effort, Sarge, but I'd prefer no restrictions," Rapp said.

"I don't care what you prefer. I make the rules."

Rapp hesitated. He wanted clarification on this point, and he'd rather not have to worry about Victor cheating. "And if Victor accidentally punches me in the face?"

"God dammit!" the sergeant boomed. "This isn't a debate club. Do you ladies want to go for a nice long run?"

Rapp silently moved to the center of the mat, satisfied that he had made his point, but nonetheless wary that Victor would do whatever it took to win. A strategy was already forming in his head. Victor had shown that he was a fairly one-dimensional fighter. Against the uninitiated he could probably hold his own on the mat, but boxing was his preference. That was plain enough to see.

Victor was all smiles as he slapped one fist into the fleshy palm of the other. "I'm gonna kick your ass, you little puke."

Rapp brought his fists up close to his face like a boxer, elbows in tight. "And if you can't, Victor?"

"Oh! . . . there's no doubt. You're going down."

Rapp drew him in. He feigned that he was out

of position and allowed Victor to initiate the first salvo. Two slow left jabs were launched straight for Rapp's face. Rapp blocked them with his right hand and then ducked under a big hook that would have knocked him off his feet if it had connected. Rapp noted that three punches had been thrown by Victor and all three had been directed at his supposedly off-limits head, and more important, Sergeant Smith didn't seem to care that Victor was breaking the rules yet again. That would make things easier for Rapp. He changed directions and bobbed back to his left as Victor threw two hard right jabs. The first one Rapp dodged and the second one hit him in the left shoulder. The blow was solid, but Rapp played it up, intentionally stumbling to his right as if he were in trouble. Victor took the bait and charged in, his left hand trying to push Rapp's hands out of the way so he could deliver a knockout blow with his right.

As Victor brought his fist up by his right ear, Rapp sprang forward with such quickness that he caught Victor completely off guard. He grabbed the bigger man's left wrist with his right hand and threw up his left arm to block the coming punch. Rapp launched himself at Victor, his head arching back and then whipping forward. His hard forehead slammed into the soft cartilage of Victor's nose, making a sickening crushing sound. Before Victor could counter, Rapp wrapped his hands around the back of the big man's neck, pulling him down and in. Rapp delivered two harsh knee strikes to the big man's sternum before releasing him. Victor staggered back, blood pouring from his nose, gasping for air.

"Sorry about that, Victor," Rapp said, egging him on. "I didn't mean to break your nose."

"I'm going to fucking kill you," Victor screamed.

Rapp simply motioned for Victor to bring it on.

The big man charged. Rapp expected the bull rush. He feinted to his right and then back to his left, and as Victor lumbered by, he hit him with a punch to the kidney, which stood him up. Victor pivoted to meet the next blow, and rather than gain distance, Rapp engaged, moving in and wrapping his left hand around the back of Victor's neck and his right hand around Victor's biceps. Victor reared his head back and was prepared to deliver a head butt of his own, but before he could strike, Rapp did something that none of them expected. He jumped up in the air, swung his left leg under Victor's right armpit and then his right leg around Victor's neck as he allowed himself to fall to the mat. Rapp was now upside down hanging on to Victor's left arm and pulling him down on top of him. Rapp raised his hips, and the pressure toppled Victor to the mat. Rapp had him in a version of the same arm bar that he had put the mean old cuss in on the first day, except that Rapp wasn't looking for submission this time.

Rapp grabbed Victor's wrist with both hands. He twisted and pulled the arm until the elbow socket was on top of his right hip bone, and then he raised his hips while pulling down as hard as he could with his hands. Rapp did not stop, even when

Victor started to scream. The entire thing took just under two seconds. There was a loud pop, and then Rapp released the arm, which was now bent at a very unnatural angle.

Rapp got to his feet and looked down at Victor. The man was moaning, his entire body rigid with pain. Rapp didn't smile or gloat. There was a touch of guilt over what he'd just done, but Victor was a bully and a jerk. Fred was sitting at the edge of the mat with cotton shoved up his nostrils and an ice pack on his nose. Fred nodded to Rapp and flashed him the thumbs-up. Roy and Glenn wandered over, each man quietly congratulating him for solving their problem. Sergeant Smith was too busy attending to Victor, who was flopping around writhing in pain. Rapp had no idea whether he was in trouble. He looked over at the shrink, who was watching him intently. The man's lips were pursed in thought as if he appeared to have drawn some conclusion about Rapp. The only problem was, Rapp couldn't tell if it was admiration or disappointment.

CHAPTER 17

LEWIS made the calls late in the afternoon, after he'd had an hour to put his thoughts and observations down on paper. As darkness approached, they descended one by one on the house by the lake in southern Virginia. Kennedy was the first to arrive, then Deputy Director of Operations Stansfield, and finally Hurley. Stansfield's bodyguards remained on the porch. They were two of his most trusted and knew to be very selective about what they saw, and more important, about what they remembered. Stansfield suggested in his typical quiet way that they all adjourn to the basement. It was not a suggestion. It was an order.

The four of them walked downstairs and proceeded to a free-standing room that sat in the middle of the basement. It served as the surveillance/communications shack for the property. The inside walls and ceiling were covered with an egg-carton-gray foam that absorbed sound. A bank of monitors and two listening stations occupied the wall on the right, and an oval conference table for six sat in the middle. When everyone was seated, Stansfield closed the soundproof door and threw the bolt.

The number-three man at Langley took the chair at the head of the table and loosened his tie. He looked the length of the short table and said, "Doctor."

Lewis was leaning back in his chair, his hands steepled in front of his face. "We've had an interesting development."

"I'd say so," Hurley interrupted, unable to contain himself. "I heard one of my instructors is out of commission for six months. Three titanium pins in his arm. For Christ's sake. He was one of my best." Hurley held up the appropriate number of fingers to punctuate his point. "Three pins."

The doctor's bright blue eyes locked in on Hurley with the kind of all-knowing stare that could be flashed only by a spouse or a therapist. The message was clear. *I know you better than you do yourself. Shut up and let me speak.*

"Sorry," Hurley apologized halfheartedly.

"Irene's recruit has proven himself quite capable." Lewis directed his comments at Stansfield. "You heard what he did to Stan earlier in the week?"

"No." Stansfield turned his inquisitive gaze on Hurley. "The bruising on your face . . . that was caused by this Rapp fellow?"

The swelling was down, and the bright red bruising had turned dark purple with a yellow tinge.

Hurley shrugged his shoulders. "I made a mistake. It won't happen again."

"You got thumped by a college kid with no military experience," Kennedy said. "I still can't get over it."

Lewis interceded before Hurley could blow his lid. Looking at Stansfield, he said, "Let me give you the narrative." Lewis explained in detail what had transpired during the opening minutes of Rapp's arrival at the complex. Hurley tried to interrupt twice, but Lewis shut him down with an open palm. Stansfield, for his part, listened in total silence. Kennedy had nothing new to add and knew how Stansfield hated too many people talking, so she kept her information to herself. In situations like this, Hurley was more than capable of scuttling his own ship.

"Now to Victor," Lewis said, turning his gaze from Stansfield to Hurley. "I have made it very clear from the outset that I am not onboard with your methods of deception."

"I know you have," Hurley said, "and in your theoretical world I'm sure your points have merit, but this is where the rubber meets the road. I don't have all day to dick around with these kids. I need to know who has the goods, and the sooner I find out the better."

"And using your system, how many men have you found thus far?" Kennedy asked, unable to resist.

"My concerns," Lewis said forcefully, "are centered on building a relationship of trust, and if we introduce deceit into the training—"

"It's not training," Hurley said with a scowl. "This is selection, and besides, this is what we do for a living. We deceive people. If these kids don't understand that, they have no business signing up with us."

"There is a major difference between deceiving each other and deceiving our enemy. Again, strong relationships are built on trust. We can work on the deception part later."

"This is bullshit," Hurley said defensively. "You two come and go as you please, but I'm the guy down here twenty-four-seven playing nursemaid. I don't pretend to know how to do your jobs . . . do me a favor and stop trying to pretend you know how to do mine."

"You are so thin-skinned," Kennedy said with a tone of open contempt.

"Yeah, well, young lady, this is serious shit. It ain't amateur hour. We recruit our candidates from the best of the best and that means Special Forces and Spec Ops guys. It doesn't mean some amateur who doesn't know the right end of a rifle from his ass or how to navigate his way through the woods in the dead of night or a thousand other things."

"Are terrorists living in the woods these days?" Kennedy asked, making it clear she was mocking him. "The last time I checked they were urban dwellers, so I'm not so sure knowing how to start a fire with a knife and belt buckle qualifies you to hunt terrorists."

"Don't talk to me about training. You have no idea what it takes to turn these guys into killers."

"Apparently, you don't either."

"Well, at least I know how to recruit, which is more than I can say for you."

"And what exactly is that supposed to mean?"

"It means you didn't do your job. I did a little reconnaissance of my own the past few days. Do you know where your boy spent the last few months?"

"He was staying at his mother's house in McLean."

"Yeah, and spending his days hanging out at a dojo in Arlington."

"And what, pray tell, would be wrong with that? I told him he would need to be in shape, and it would be a good idea to start taking some judo classes."

"Yeah, well . . . I spoke to his sensei."

"You did what?" Kennedy was irked that he had gone behind her back.

"I went in and had a conversation with his sensei. After going a round with him on the mat, I could tell something wasn't right."

Kennedy looked to Stansfield for help. "He had no right to do that. It's my recruit. I have worked almost two years on bringing him in, and I haven't left a single trail. No one in his life knows that we're interested in him."

"And they still don't," Hurley said dismissively.

"Really . . . how in hell did you introduce yourself?"

"I told him I was a trainer from Richmond. Said I went a round with this young kid named Rapp and was very impressed. I wanted to ask his sensei what he thought."

"And?" Lewis asked, suddenly very interested.

"The kid doesn't pass the smell test. His sensei says he came in three months ago and claimed he had almost no experience. Within a month and a half he had throttled everybody in the dojo except the sensei."

"Brazilian jujitsu?" Lewis asked.

"Yeah . . . how'd you know?"

"I saw him take Victor down today. The style is hard to miss."

"So he comes in here and almost bests me and then he snaps Victor's elbow . . . I'm telling you, the kid isn't who he says he is."

Stansfield's patience was wearing thin. "Be more specific."

"I'm not sure, but it doesn't feel right."

"What . . . you think he's a plant . . . a spy?" Kennedy asked in a mocking tone.

"I'm not sure. I'm just telling you he doesn't pass the smell test. You can't get that good that quick."

Kennedy looked at Stansfield. "Let's cut to the chase. He doesn't like him because he's my recruit." She sat back and folded her arms across her chest. "He's a misogynist."

"I don't like him because I don't know who the hell he is. We need to know everything there is to know about these guys before we bring them in. That's why military experience is a must. That way we know exactly what they've been doing for a minimum of four years."

"And how is that working out for us, Stan?" Kennedy shot back. "We don't have a single operative in the pipeline, and we've been at this for almost two years."

"I am well aware that I have failed to produce. Painfully fucking aware, but that doesn't mean I'm going to rush things and have something this important blow up in our faces."

Lewis, in a neutral tone, asked, "Stan, what is your problem with Rapp?"

He took a while to answer and finally said, "I can't put my finger on it. It's more of a feeling. A bad feeling."

"Do you know what I think it is?" Kennedy asked. "Two things. First . . . I think you have major control issues. You can't stand the fact that you weren't involved in recruiting him. And second . . . you feel threatened."

"What?" Hurley's face was twisted into a mask of confusion.

"He's you. He's the man you were forty years ago, and it scares the crap out of you."

Hurley shook his head dismissively. "That's bullshit."

"Really . . . well, I can say the same thing about your gut feeling. It's bullshit. What, do you think the PLO planted him in a D.C. suburb twenty-three years ago, raised him Catholic, and sent him off to Syracuse to play lacrosse? Or do you think it was the KGB before the Soviet Union collapsed and now he's a rogue deep-cover operative? Ridiculous." Kennedy dismissed the ludicrous idea with a flip of her right hand. "You're clutching at straws."

No one moved or spoke for five seconds, while

Kennedy's stinging remarks set in. Lewis finally said, "She has a point." He pushed back his chair and stood. "I'd like to show you something. I sat down and talked with him before all of you arrived. I think you will find this very interesting." Lewis approached the surveillance control board and pressed a few buttons. A black-and-white image of Rapp appeared on the screen. He was sitting in the office on the first floor. Lewis's voice came over the speakers. He was offscreen to the right.

"That was unfortunate, what happened this afternoon."

Rapp sat still for a few seconds and then nodded.

"Do you feel bad at all about what you did to Victor?"

It took him a long time to answer, and then he said, "We're all big boys here."

"So you feel no remorse?"

"I wish it hadn't happened, but Victor isn't exactly the nicest guy."

"I see. Is it possible that you intentionally broke his arm?"

"*Intentionally* is a strong word. We were sparring and one thing led to another."

"The thing that led to the other was you snapping his arm before he could tap out."

"I'm not sure he would have tapped out."

"You could be kicked out for what happened."

"Why?"

"Sergeant Smith thinks you intentionally broke Victor's arm."

"I don't see how that would be fair. No one said anything about what holds we could use or not use. We were supposed to stay away from the head and the groin. That was it."

"If you intentionally broke another recruit's arm that would be grounds for dismissal."

Rapp looked at the floor for a long moment and then said, "I don't like playing all these games."

"Games?"

"Yeah . . . games."

"How do you mean games?"

"You know what I'm talking about."

"I'm not sure I do."

"That file on your desk the other day." Rapp pointed to the clear surface. "The file with my name on it."

"What about it?"

"You were testing me."

"Really?"

"Yes," Rapp said in an easy tone. "I've seen the way you monitor what's going on around here. You study everything." Rapp gestured at the desk. "You're not the kind of guy who leaves sensitive files lying around unless there's a reason. I'm sure this place is wired for video and sound." Rapp motioned toward the bookshelf and then the overhead light. "When you asked to see me a few days ago and I was left sitting in here by myself for fifteen minutes, you were probably sitting up in the attic or down in the basement watching me. Testing me to see if I would open the file and read what was in it."

Lewis could be heard clearing his throat and

then saying, "Even if that were true, I don't see it excuses your breaking Victor's arm."

"I never said it excused anything. What I said is that you are playing games with us. You leave files lying around, tell us one set of rules and then let Victor break them. You were in the barn, how was it okay for Victor to punch Fred in the face?"

"We will deal with that separately. This is about what you did."

"I saw the way you reacted when Victor punched Fred in the nose." Rapp paused and looked down at his hands. "Do you know what I think . . . I think Victor doesn't fit in."

"How so?"

"Based on what I've seen since I've been here, there are just two logical conclusions where Victor is concerned. Either Victor is a recruit just like the rest of us or he's part of your evaluation process."

"Part of the process?"

"He works for you guys. He's one of the instructors."

"And why would we do that?"

"So you could get a closer look at us. You put Victor in with us, and his job is to tempt us into making mistakes. Ask us who we are and where we're from. Try to get guys to screw up so you can get rid of the guys who don't have the discipline."

"Interesting."

"Either way it isn't good. If I understand this program correctly, Victor is not the kind of guy you're looking for. So if he is a recruit, and you guys can't see that, I'm not sure I want to work for people who can't grasp the obvious."

"And if he is one of the instructors?"

"It's a pretty fucked-up way to train disciplined men."

"Let's assume you're correct for a second. Knowing all of that . . . you decided to break his arm."

Rapp shook his head. "I had my suspicions before, but I wasn't sure. After I broke his arm, I saw the way you and the other instructors reacted, and I pretty much knew he was one of you."

There was a good five seconds of silence and then Lewis asked, "Do you think you have a good moral compass?"

Rapp let out a small laugh. "Here we go with your vague questions."

"I know, but please try to answer this one."

"You mean do I understand the difference between right and wrong?"

"Yes."

Rapp hesitated. "I would say pretty much yes."

"But?"

"Here . . . at this place . . . it seems like that line keeps getting moved."

"Can you give me an example."

"That angry old cuss . . . the one my recruiter warned me about . . . well, I'm not here five minutes and the two of us end up in the barn . . . He's telling me to quit and save all of us the effort. I tell him no and suggest we should find out if I have what it takes. He very clearly tells me that the head and groin are off limits while we spar. We lock horns and twenty seconds into it I have him beat. He was about two seconds from blacking out when he grabbed my nuts and practically turned me into a eunuch. He never said anything to me about it. In fact I haven't seen him since. Then you have Victor running around here breaking every rule he wants while the instructors are all over the rest of us. Again, we go in to spar today and the instructors clearly tell us the head and groin are off limits, and what does Victor do . . . Fred is within seconds of beating him and Victor punches him square in the face. I saw the look on your face, but the other two didn't say boo. It's screwy. I don't know how you expect the rest of us to follow any rules. And here I sit . . . technically I didn't do anything wrong, and I'm being threatened with the boot."

"I didn't threaten you."

"You said Sergeant Smith thinks I should get the boot. I'd say that's a threat."

Lewis hit the stop button and turned to face Hurley. With arms folded, he said, "That was one of the more difficult sessions I've conducted. Do you know why?"

Hurley shook his head.

"Because I agreed with virtually everything he said."

CHAPTER 18

STANSFIELD stood at the end of the dock, looked up at the moon, and ran through the list of transgressions. Although he didn't show it, and he never did, he was livid with what was going on down here. He had allowed Hurley far too much latitude, and while much of his anger was directed at the snake eater, more of it was directed back at himself. How had he not seen the signs earlier? This place, this operation, all of it was his responsibility. Kennedy had tried to warn him as respectfully as she could, but his days were filled with a hundred other pressing issues of national security. And he had a blind spot when it came to Hurley. Especially on the operational side of things. He'd known Stan longer than anyone at the company. He knew his long list of talents, and his short but potent list of faults.

There'd been a few bumps over the years, occasions when Hurley had let him down, but even the great Ted Williams struck out every now and then. They had met in Budapest in the summer of 1956 just as everything was heating up in the unwilling Soviet satellite. Stansfield was in his thirties and was quickly rising through the ranks of the fledgling CIA, while Hurley was in his early twenties, fresh out of training and thirsting for a fight. Stansfield saw firsthand in the run-up to the Hungarian Revolution that Hurley had a real aptitude for mayhem. He was talented, and wild, and a lot of other things, some good and some bad. But one thing was undeniable. He knew how to get at the enemy. Engage them, upset them, bloody them, and somehow make it back with nothing more than a few bumps. In the espionage business it was easy to fall into a safe daily pattern. Begin the day at your apartment, head to the embassy for work, a local café for lunch, back to the embassy, maybe a cocktail party at another embassy in the evening, a stop at a local café for a nightcap, and then back to your apartment. You could safely move about a foreign capital without ever risking your job or your life. Not Hurley. When he landed in a new place he headed straight for the rough part of town. Got to know the prostitutes, the barkeeps, and most important, the black-marketeers who despised their communist overlords. Hurley fed him daily reports about the rising contempt among the citizenry and proved himself to be a first-class field operative. He became Stansfield's indispensable man.

Tonight, however, Stansfield was having his doubts. Budapest had been a long time ago. Sooner or later all skills diminished. The obvious transition was to move him behind a desk, but that would be like asking a racehorse to pull a plow. It would kill him. Stansfield looked back up at the house. He had silently left the meeting and walked down to the lake on his own. A simple hand gesture was enough to tell his bodyguards to wait at the top of the small hill. Hurley would know to come find him. He did not have to be asked.

Stansfield could tell his old colleague was well aware that he had disappointed him. He was as down as he'd seen him in many years, and it could have been because of a variety of factors. At the top of the list was probably that shiner on his face. Stansfield had to bite down on the right side of his tongue when he'd found out that Kennedy's recruit had been the one who'd painted him. Hurley's fighting abilities were unmatched by any man he'd ever encountered. His tolerance for pain, his quickness, his mean streak, his Homeric ability to find the weakness of another man, no matter how big or strong, had become the stuff of legend at Langley.

Looking back on it now, Stansfield could see where the mistakes had been made. He had allowed Hurley to create a cult of personality down here. His own little fiefdom of Special Operations shooters. All of them were extremely talented and useful, but as a group they had the ability to create a toxic stew of contempt for anyone who had not walked in their shoes. Even Doctor Lewis, a snake eater himself, had voiced concern. Kennedy had repeatedly attempted to nudge him in the right direction. She had the gift—the ability to glimpse where it was all headed. She knew they needed to adapt, change course and tactics, and she had been trying to get Stansfield's attention. The problem was, as the deputy director of operations, he was in charge of it all. Every valuable operative they had in every major city all over the globe and all of the support people who went with them. Virtually all of it was compartmentalized in some way, and a good portion of it wasn't even put to paper. It was a never-ending chess game that was played in his head every day, all day long.

Stansfield heard the soft footfalls on the stairs coming down to the lake. He turned and made out the image of Hurley in the moonlight. The platform swayed as he stepped onto the L-shaped dock. Hurley approached his boss without a word and pulled out a pack of Camels. He offered his old friend one, knowing that he liked to reacquaint himself with his old habit when he was away from his wife. The two men stood facing the lake, looking up at the starry night sky, puffing on their cigarettes for nearly a minute before Hurley finally spoke.

"I fucked up."

Stansfield gave no reply. Just a simple nod of agreement.

"Maybe it's time I call it quits."

Stansfield turned his head a few degrees to look at Hurley and said, "I will tolerate a lot of things from you, but self-pity is not one of them. You've never been a quitter and you're not going to start now."

"I got my ass beat by a college puke."

"You got your healthy ego bruised is what happened."

"You don't understand. It should have never happened. I still can't explain *how* it happened. I'm not getting any younger, but even on an off day I'm still better than ninety-nine point nine percent of the guys out there."

"I know math was never your strong suit, but the answer is pretty obvious."

"What the hell is that supposed to mean?"

"If you can beat ninety-nine point nine percent of the guys out there and he bested you that means he's in the point one percent."

Hurley shook his head. "I don't see how it's possible. Not enough training."

"You don't see it, because you don't want to. I did a little checking on my own. Irene's find is an exceptionally gifted athlete. He's considered a bit of a freak of nature in the world of lacrosse. Did you know he's considered to be one of the greatest college lacrosse players of all time?"

"What in hell does that have to do with fighting?"

"A great athlete can learn almost anything, and do it a lot quicker than an average athlete," Stansfield said firmly. "Your big problem, though, is that you allowed your personal disdain for anyone who hasn't worn the uniform to cloud your judgment."

"Still—"

"Still nothing," Stansfield cut him off. "The boy is a three-time All-American and national champ. You got thumped by a world-class athlete."

"Who has no real training."

"You yourself said he's been taking classes."

"Rolling around some mat at a strip mall is not training."

Stansfield let out a tired sigh. It was his way of releasing pressure so he didn't blow. Some people you could gently tap with a finishing hammer a few times and they would get the point. Not Hurley, though. You had to hit the man square in the forehead with a sledgehammer repeatedly to get your point across.

"Sorry," Hurley said meekly. "I'm still having a hard time buying this kid's story."

"You are possibly the most stubborn person I have ever met, and that's saying a lot. You have used that to your advantage many times, but it has also gotten you into a fair amount of trouble, and before you get all sensitive on me, this is coming from the guy who had to get you out of all that trouble over the years. I've called in a lot of favors to pull your ass out of the fire. So hear me when I tell you that this issue is moot. The kid beat you, and quite honestly I don't care how he did it, or where he learned how to do it. The fact is, he did it, and that makes him a very desirable recruit."

Hurley finally got it. "What do you want me to do?"

"Fix it."

"How do I fix it if I'm not even sure where I fucked up?"

"Stop being so conveniently modest. You know where you made mistakes . . . It's just not in your nature to confront them, so dig a little harder and they'll turn up. And by the way, I made a few mistakes of my own. Ultimately, you are my responsibility." Stansfield glanced back up at the house. "That last hour in there was one of the most embarrassing of my career."

Hurley was too embarrassed himself to speak.

"We're supposed to know better," Stansfield continued. "We're the veterans, and we just had two kids point out something that we both should have caught. There was a day when I knew better. To put it mildly, you are an organizational nightmare. You belong in the field. I think this," Stansfield held his arms out and motioned at the nature around them, "lulled me into thinking that you were in fact in the field, but you're not. You're too corralled down here."

"Then let me go active again," Hurley said in an almost pleading voice.

Stansfield mulled the thought over while taking one last puff. There were any number of sayings that could be applied to the espionage trade, but few were as appropriate as the phrase "nothing ventured, nothing gained." At some point you had to jump into the game. Stansfield had grown weary of receiving secure cables telling him that another one of his assets had been picked off by these radical Islamists. It was time to start hitting back.

"Stan, these Islamists aren't going away."

"I've been telling you that for ten years."

"Looking at the big picture, they've been a minor irritation until now, but I sense something bigger. They are organizing and morphing and spreading like a virus."

"You can thank the damn Saudis and the Iranians for that."

That was true, Stansfield thought. Very few people understood the bloody rivalry between the Sunnis and the Shias. Each sect was growing more radical—more violent. They couldn't wait any longer. Stansfield lowered his voice. "Stan, in six months' time, I want you operational. Stop trying to run these kids down like it's a Special Forces selection process. Irene's right, I don't really care if they can survive in the forest for a week with nothing more than a fingernail clipper. I want them ready for urban operations. I'm going to task Doc to you full-time. Listen to him. He knows what he's doing."

"Okay . . . and after six months?" Hurley asked with a bit of optimism in his voice.

"I'm going to turn you loose. We need to hit these guys back. At a bare minimum I want them lying awake at night worried that they might be next. I want you to scare the shit out of them."

Hurley smiled in anticipation. "I know just what to do."

"Good . . . and one last thing. You're almost sixty. This is a young kid's game. Especially your side of the business. Our days are numbered. We need to start trusting these kids more. In another ten years they're going to take over, and we'll probably be dead."

Hurley smiled. "I'm not going down without a fight."

CHAPTER 19

BEIRUT, LEBANON

SAYYED mopped his brow with a rag. The front of his white T-shirt was splattered with the blood of the man who had just confessed to myriad sins. The basement was warm and damp, and he'd been at it for most of the day. He couldn't remember the last time he'd had to work so hard to get a man to talk. He was thirsty and hungry, but both needs would have to wait. They were gathered upstairs, nervously waiting to hear what he'd discovered.

Sayyed dropped the pliers on the metal cart. The device bounced and fell open, the serrated clamps releasing a bloody fingernail. There were eight total, strewn about the stainless-steel surface, sticky and gooey with blood and tissue. Sayyed admired his work for a second. Every man was different. For some, the mere threat of physical pain was enough to get them to admit their deception. Others, like this Jewish pig, took a little more work.

He'd employed many different methods to get at the truth, but he preferred fingernails and toenails for the simple reason that there were twenty of them. And they grew back.

Sayyed had seen torture practiced in a wide variety of forms. Most sessions were brutish and conducted without forethought or planning. Slapping and kicking was the most common method, but employed against a man who had been desensitized to such things, it was more often than not useless. There were stabbing and slicing and shooting, and although they worked, they also required medical care if you were going to continue to interrogate the individual. There was degradation, such as shoving a man's head into a bucket full of human excrement, sticking things in orifices where they didn't belong, and a long list of things Sayyed found distasteful. Electrocution was the only other form that Sayyed would use. It was extremely effective and clean. Its only downside was the potential for heart failure and long-term brain and nerve damage. Sayyed liked to spend time with his subjects. To truly debrief a prisoner took months.

Sayyed could never understand why people would so casually throw away such a valuable commodity. Killing a subject after he admitted to his lies was foolish. As an interrogator you had barely scratched the surface. An admission of guilt was just that and often nothing more. The truly valuable information lay buried in the subject's brain and needed to be slowly and carefully coaxed to the surface. And to do that you needed time.

Sayyed wiped his hands on a blood-smeared towel and said to one of the guards, "Clean the wounds and bandage the fingers. I don't want him getting an infection."

He put on his black dress shirt and left the interrogation room. He continued past the guards and up one flight of stairs. There were a dozen men milling about the lobby. Most were in plain clothes, a few wore fatigues, but all were armed with rifles and sidearms. Sayyed continued up another flight of stairs to the second floor, where he found more armed men milling about the hallway.

He frowned at the sight of them. The presence of so many men was bound to draw attention. His colleagues were far too one-dimensional. They were still thinking of their struggle as a ground battle between vying factions. Car bombs, snipers, and assaults must always be taken into account, but the bigger threat at the moment was the jets flown by Jews and the Americans. These men had not walked here, which meant there were far too many cars parked in front of the building. Sayyed traveled with a light contingent of bodyguards for this very reason. Three or four were usually more than enough. The others were either too paranoid, too proud, or too stupid to see the folly of traveling in such large motorcades.

Eight guards were standing in the hallway outside the office at the back of the building. Sayyed approached one of the more recognizable faces and said, "I pray for the sake of our struggle that no more than six vehicles are parked in front of this building."

The man looked in the direction of the street and without answering took off at a trot.

Sayyed was pleased that at least one of these morons knew how to take orders. He opened the door to the office and found four faces instead of the three he had expected. Mustapha Badredeen, the leader of Islamic Jihad, was at the head of the table. To his right was the leader of Islamic Jihad's paramilitary wing, Imad Mughniyah, and then Colonel Amir Jalil of the Iranian Quds Force. He was Iran's liaison between Islamic Jihad and Hezbollah. The last man, Abu Radih, was not welcome, at least not as far as Sayyed was concerned. He was the representative for Fatah, the extremely unreliable band of men who claimed to speak on behalf of the approximately five hundred thousand Palestinians living in Lebanon. In Sayyed's conservative opinion, they were nothing more than a gang of organized mobsters who stumbled from one confrontation to the next leaving a trail of havoc in their wake. They were only good for two things: to use as a buffer against the Jews to the south or as cannon fodder against the Christian militias to the east.

"Well?" Colonel Jalil asked.

Sayyed ignored the Iranian and turned instead to Mustapha Badredeen. "CIA."

"I knew it!" Radih said, excitedly.

Sayyed glanced at the imbecile who had created the problem and said, "You knew no such thing."

"I did so," Radih said defensively.

"How could you have possibly known? What

evidence did you have in your possession that pointed to the fact that this man was CIA?"

"I have my sources."

Sayyed laughed at him. It was an empty claim and everyone in the room knew it. "And the businessman you kidnapped last week, what has he told you?"

"He admitted that he is an American agent."

Sayyed was dubious of the claim, but the fool had just painted himself into a corner. "In that case I will need you to turn him over to me."

Radih realized his mistake. "Well . . . he has admitted to a lot of things. My men are not done interrogating him."

Sayyed stared at him with a look that told everyone in the room that he didn't believe a word of it.

"I will give you a report in a few days," Radih said.

Sayyed dismissed him with a look of contempt and addressed the other men. "The man downstairs is an employee for the CIA who has spent the better part of the last four years in Damascus. My government will want to assess the damage he has caused. To do that thoroughly, I will need Radih to transfer his hostage to me. I'm afraid this point is not negotiable."

"But he is my hostage," Radih said, half yelling. "It was my operation."

"An operation that was not approved."

Radih ignored the point and said, "He is extremely valuable. He has told us his company will pay a large sum to get him back."

"Not if he is an American agent." Sayyed shook his head sadly and scratched his thick black beard. "As we know all too well, the Americans do not negotiate for hostages. Especially the CIA." Pointing at the ceiling he added, "They are far more likely to track him down and drop a bomb on all of us."

The other men shared nervous looks. "The other American, the one you grabbed in front of his hotel last week," Badredeen said to the Fatah leader, "he has told you implicitly that he is an agent?"

"It is my suspicion," Radih said, thankful for the breathing room.

"What was he doing in Beirut?"

"He works for one of their big telecommunications companies."

Radih blathered on about his prisoner, but Sayyed was only half listening. The CIA man in the basement had verified the fact that the other man was a legitimate businessman, but Sayyed did not feel like coming to the aid of the twit from Fatah. He would know for certain only after spending months interrogating the men. Sayyed looked at Mughniyah and said, "Some men are very good liars. It takes a skilled hand to discern the truth from these Americans."

Mughniyah nodded and spoke for the first time. "I don't like the coincidence. We should turn him over to Sayyed. He will get to the bottom of it."

Sayyed was quietly pleased. Mughniyah had a reputation for killing those who crossed him. Radih would not want to defy him.

"The entire thing gives me great concern," the Iranian chimed in.

Sayyed could barely stand the man. He was a self-proclaimed intellectual who was part of the rabble who had helped bring down the shah and bring about the Islamic Revolution of Iran.

"It cannot be a good sign that the Americans are back," Jalil said, as he caressed his bottom lip with the forefinger of his right hand. "Nothing good can come from them poking around in our business."

"I will find out what they are up to," Sayyed said confidently.

The three men exchanged looks, ignoring Radih, who was growing more agitated by the second. Badredeen spoke for the group. Turning to Radih he said, "Please transfer your hostage to Sayyed as soon as is possible."

"That means tonight," Sayyed said, not wanting to give the man an inch.

"That is impossible," Radih said, as if they were asking him to fly to the moon. "This man is too valuable. I am more than capable of finding out his true identity." With a casual flip of his hand he said, "I will give all of you a report within a few days."

"That will not work." Sayyed held his ground. "I want him tonight."

"I will not give him to you. He is my prisoner."

Mughniyah leaned forward in his chair and glared at the representative from Fatah. The temperature seemed to drop a few degrees. "I don't remember your seeking our permission to conduct this operation in the first place."

"And when was the last time any of you came to me to ask permission to launch an operation?"

With an icy voice Mughniyah said, "I do not need your permission."

"That hardly seems fair."

"You are invited to these meetings as a courtesy . . . nothing else."

"The rest of you have taken hostages for years and have profited greatly while the rockets of retaliation rained down on my people and I did not complain to you. Now all I am asking is that I be allowed to share in the spoils of war. You have not allowed me to partner on any of your other business ventures, so I must take what is rightfully mine." With a look of sadness he added, "I have given nothing but loyalty and this is how you treat me."

Mughniyah threw his arms up in frustration. He looked at Badredeen and Jalil. "Talk some sense into him before I shoot him."

Sayyed didn't let it show, but he was enjoying every minute of this.

Badredeen sighed heavily and said, "This is only temporary. Hand the man over to Sayyed. He is without question the best man to do the job. When he is done, if the man is in fact a businessman, he will turn him back over to you and you can then negotiate a ransom. That is fair."

Radih shifted nervously in his chair. He did not want to give up the man, but he could not defy these four. Any one of them could have him killed before the sun rose again. He could see what Sayyed was up to. The hostage could be worth as much as several million dollars if he did in fact work for the telecommunications company, and once the man was out of his hands, he would be lucky to get half of the ransom. Still, half was better than being dead. With great reluctance he said, "Fine," and then glancing sideways at Sayyed, he added, "you can interrogate him at my camp."

Sayyed laughed. "Nice try."

"Why not?"

"Because I said so. I do not need to explain such things to you."

"He is being unreasonable," Radih said to the other three.

Before they could answer, Sayyed said, "I need to inform Damascus of this situation, and I need to continue my discussion with the American agent. I expect Radih to have his prisoner here by ten o'clock tonight so I can get to the bottom of this, and I suggest you all leave as quickly as possible." He glanced at the ceiling. "The four of us," he said, intentionally leaving Radih out, "are far too tempting a target, and with the American in the basement, who knows what they are up to these days. They may have other spies in the area." Moving toward the door, he said with absolute finality, "I will have more answers for you tomorrow."

PART II

CHAPTER 20

ISTANBUL, TURKEY

OF all the changes Rapp had to make over the six months of his training, adjusting to the solitude had been the most challenging. As he became increasingly immersed in his new trade, he drifted further and further away from his friends. The big change was not that he did not see them as much. It was a mental detachment. With each new level of training they had less in common. His new life was far from social.

Rapp's childhood had been fairly normal. He'd grown up in a nice upper-middle-class suburb of Washington, D.C., and pretty much stayed out of trouble. He did well in school, although some subjects, like French, were far easier than math and science. He excelled at every sport, which guaranteed a certain level of acceptance among his peers. There had been just one setback, and it was a pretty big one.

When Rapp was thirteen, his father dropped dead of a massive heart attack. It was a heavy blow, but Rapp didn't go into a complete free fall, nor did he retreat into a shell. The truth was his dad wasn't around much. He was a workaholic who golfed on the weekends. He was in no way a bad father. He was fair and honest with his two boys, and as far as Rapp could tell he had been faithful to his mother and treated her with the respect she deserved. It was neither bad nor good, it just was.

Rapp had a tight group of friends in the neighborhood, and his father had been wise enough to take out the right amount of life insurance, so very little on the home front changed. The awkward moments came at the sports banquets where he was the only one without a father, and the holidays when the memories of his father inevitably bubbled to the surface, but through it all he was more concerned about his little brother and mother.

There was one area where it definitely changed him. He wanted stability in his personal relationships. His friends became more important than ever. Not that they hadn't been before, it was just that he had never had to think about it. All he had to do was walk out his front door, get on his bike, and within a block or two he couldn't help but stumble onto a basketball or stickball game. More than anything, though, his father's death taught him that the clock was ticking. Everyone was going to die. Some a lot sooner than others, but in the end there was no avoiding it, and since he wasn't a Hindu, he pretty much figured he'd better make the best of his one shot. This drove him with amazing intensity and focus on the fields and courts of his youth.

And then there was Mary. Rapp met her when he was sixteen. He was playing baseball and she was running track. He didn't know if it was love at first sight, because he hadn't a clue what love was, but it was unlike anything he'd ever experienced. It was like every great emotion he'd ever felt all rolled into one euphoric wave and it scared the crap out of him, because he instantly knew he was not in control. Fortunately, she was, and she had the sense and stability to not jerk him around too much. Her father was a captain in the navy and a huge lacrosse fan. With three daughters of his own, he enthusiastically attended Rapp's lacrosse matches. Rapp and Mary dated all through high school and then headed off to Syracuse together, where Mary ran track and eventually landed in the Newhouse School of Public Communications. Her ambitious plan was to become a sports announcer. On a chilly December night in 1988 Mary was returning home from a semester abroad when her plane was blown out of the sky, killing 259 passengers and crew and 11 more innocent souls on the ground in Lockerbie, Scotland. The terrorist attack that became known as Pan Am Lockerbie hit Rapp like a hammer blow.

They had planned their entire life together. They'd discussed kids, ambitions, and fears, but never once did they think that one of them would be taken. If he'd made it through the death of his father relatively intact, the opposite was true this time. He crumbled. He was already home for Christmas break and planning on picking Mary up at Dulles after she'd connected through JFK. Strangely enough, when he received the news he never questioned it, never challenged it, never asked for proof. The downing of the plane was all over the news and there was no doubt that she was on it. She'd called him from Heathrow right before she'd boarded.

He was a wreck for the first week. He refused to see a soul, including Mary's parents, and then on the morning of her funeral he emerged from the basement shaved and wearing a suit and tie. His mother and his brother, Steven, accompanied him to the funeral, where he sat stone-faced in a state of bewildered shock. Midway through the service, though, something happened. The shock, the pain, the agonizing self-pity over the fact that he would never see her again, never hold her, never smell her, the list went on, and on, and on like some pounding surf that threatened to drown him.

Sitting in that pew that morning, listening to all of the crying, witnessing all of the pain and loss, made him want to make a break for it. He did not want to share his heartache with these people. None of them knew her the way he did. It was his dreams that had been dashed. His life that had been turned upside down and wrecked. Self-pity was something he had never experienced before, and it sickened him.

Rapp took his pathetic self-absorbed emotion and shoved it as far down in his gut as it would go, and he plugged it with the first and only thing he had available—anger. That anger slowly metastasized into a suit of armor. For the first time since the news had hit him, he saw a way out. A faint light at the far end of the cavern. He wasn't sure what it was, but he knew he had to head toward it. It was the only thing that offered him hope. The rest of these people could sit around and feel sorry for themselves and each other, but not him. He wanted to hurt someone. He wanted to make someone pay. He didn't know for certain that he would achieve his goal, but he knew with absolute certainty that he wanted to kill the men who were responsible for bringing down that plane. Rapp didn't know if it was right or wrong, and he didn't care. All he knew was that the anger kept the pain at bay.

Rapp and Hurley had developed a hate-hate relationship. The shrink had told him it didn't really matter as long as they were united in their hatred for the enemy. It had been a strange six months, and looking back on the journey, Rapp was amazed that he'd made it through without any serious injury. He was young enough going in to be fearless, but coming out on the other end, looking back at what he'd been through, was another story. It was a little like being told not to look down while on the high wire. You just take it one step at a time, and when you get to the other side, and reality sets in, you think you must have been off your rocker to ever try it in the first place.

Rapp could point to a specific date and time when the physical hell and mental abuse had all but vanished. It was replaced by eighteen-hour days that were structured to the minute and more academic than grueling. There were still long runs and lots of push-ups and pull-ups, but they were designed to keep them in peak shape, not to try to get them to quit. The low point was the day after he'd broken Victor's arm.

For the first week they were rousted at five every morning. Rapp didn't need an alarm. He was on his feet as soon as the door was opened, but on the morning after the incident with Victor, Rapp found himself thrown from his cot and rolling across the dusty floor. After landing with a thud, he came up swinging. It was still dark and his muscles were tight and he never saw the blow that came out of the darkness. It hit him in the solar plexus, and as Rapp doubled over from the first strike another punch hammered his left eye. Rapp hit the floor and lay there gulping for air like a largemouth bass flopping around on a dock.

The lights suddenly came on, and with them the insults came raining down from the mouth of the mean old cuss. He stood over Rapp, his fists clenched, a look of smug satisfaction on his face. If Rapp had had a gun at that moment he would more than likely have killed the man. The four remaining recruits were ordered outside and for the next four hours were forced to endure unimaginable tortures. One man collapsed from exhaustion and another simply quit. It was now down to just Rapp and Fred. That was when the bastard turned all of his attention on Rapp. By noon they were down to one. It was an unwarranted slap to the back of the head that did Rapp in. As calmly as possible, he turned to face the old man and told him, "If you ever slap me again, I'm going to put you in the hospital."

The old man ordered Rapp into the barn and they went at it again. This time Rapp lost fair and square. Or so he thought at first. As he lay there on the mat, bloodied and exhausted, he realized what had happened. The old man didn't think he could take him fair and square, so he ran Rapp into the ground first. He dumped him from his cot at 4:00 A.M. and spent the next eight hours wearing him down and tenderizing him. Rapp never had a chance. The old prick had made it personal, and in Rapp's mind that did not reflect well on the organization he thought he was joining. The whole thing was starting to look and smell like a shit show. Rapp got to his feet, told the old bastard exactly what he thought of him, and quit.

Rapp packed his stuff and was almost to the gate when the shrink caught up with him. He tried to talk Rapp out of quitting and when that didn't work he outright asked him to stay. Rapp still didn't budge, so Lewis put all the cards on the table. He formally introduced himself and admitted that Victor was in fact one of the instructors. He explained that he had vigorously protested using him to infiltrate the recruits. Rapp asked him for the old cuss's name, but Lewis refused. "If you stay and make it through the rest of the training you will find out who he is, but short of that, I cannot oblige you."

When Rapp held his ground, Lewis told him only that the old man was not the most likable guy, but he assured Rapp that he was exceedingly good at his craft. He assured Rapp that the nonsense was over and that from this moment forward they would be focusing on tradecraft. Rapp still wavered. He simply couldn't see how it was possible for the old cuss to change his behavior. Lewis, sensing Rapp's indecision, said, "You're one of the best I've ever seen. We could really use you. In a way that might explain why he's so hard on you."

Rapp finally relented. It was down to just him and Fred. They still began every day with a workout, but the rest of the time was spent either in the classroom, in the barn, on the pistol range, or on field exercises to Richmond and then to Atlanta. They employed their skills against random targets—unwitting businessmen. They followed them, surveilled their every move, and looked for the right opportunity to dispatch them. Everything was analyzed and critiqued by Lewis and the old man.

While at the lake house they were allowed to speak only Arabic. They honed their fighting skills with virtually every conceivable weapon. They focused on knives and guns for the most part, but they were also taught to inventory every room they entered for objects that could be used to defend or kill. A day didn't go by where the old cuss didn't remind them of the endgame—he was turning them into killers. They studied physiology until they had an intimate understanding of the best ways to either dispatch or incapacitate an opponent. They became expert marksmen with a variety of pistols, shooting with both left and right hands. They were taught escape and evasion techniques, explosives, and the tricks of the countersurveillance trade.

As a final step, Rapp and Fred were told that if anything went wrong they were on their own. Embassies and consulates were off limits. The United States government didn't know they existed and it sure as hell wasn't going to claim them if they landed in hot water. The mean old cuss asked them if they accepted this. If they didn't, they could walk away right now, no questions asked. After only brief consideration, both men said they fully understood the need for plausible deniability. They were in.

Hurley then formally introduced himself and told Rapp and Fred they were now free to reveal to each other their real identities. Rapp and Fred had already done this several months earlier, but they went through the motions as if it were the first time. After that they were forced to memorize a lengthy list of addresses and phone numbers across Europe and the Middle East. A day did not pass without Hurley's reminding them that the United States government had no knowledge of their existence. If they were caught doing something illegal in a foreign country they were on their own. There would be no cavalry or diplomatic effort to gain their release. As often as Hurley brought it up, Rapp did not dwell on it, for the simple reason that he did not plan on getting caught.

CHAPTER 21

As planned, Rapp was the first one to arrive in the former capital city of the Byzantine Empire. He'd been given a long list of orders, and one of them was to stay away from the safe house until it was dark. It was February and the temperature was in the midfifties. Rapp took the tram to the Beyoglu District, found a men's room, retrieved a few objects from his luggage, and then deposited the suitcase in a locker and set about exploring the area, which he'd already memorized by map. He was immediately taken by the scope of the city, as well as its rich history. He'd traveled to London and Paris previously, and Istanbul rivaled them in every way. The images of London and Paris were well known throughout the Western world, but Istanbul, far more rich in history, had in a way been forgotten by people in Europe and America.

After stopping for a quick bite at a café, Rapp

made his way toward the Galata neighborhood, where their target lived. Hurley had given him specific orders to stay clear of both the target's apartment and his office. Rapp had not made a conscious decision to defy the order; it more or less just happened. As he turned onto Bankalar Daddesi, or Banks Street, he couldn't help but walk past the target's place of work along with several hundred other people who crowded the sidewalk. Rapp passed on the opposite side of the street and noted the bank guard standing next to the front door. With that done, he decided he might as well take a look at the man's apartment, which was six-tenths of a mile from the office. It was on a tree-lined street that reminded Rapp of a much smaller version of the Boulevard Montmartre in Paris. It was a wealthy enclave, and as in all such enclaves in cities the world over, the occupants were protected from the riffraff by security guards, ornate fences, and iron bars on the first-floor windows. At first glance, neither the office nor the apartment looked like the ideal place to strike.

When the sun finally set, Rapp found his way to the two-bedroom flat via a back alley. He went by once without stopping to check and see if there were any surprises and then circled back. In the poor light he threaded the worn key into the lock and held his breath. The first attempt did not work. Rapp jiggled the key a bit and then tried again. This time the dead bolt released. He stepped into the room, barely breathing, and closed the door behind him. He stood statuelike, all of his senses on high alert. This apartment was the only definitive link to him in the entire city of twelve million people. Hurley had warned him that this was the second-most-dangerous moment when conducting an operation. Rapp asked him what was the most dangerous, and the old man had replied with a devilish smile, "When you engage the target."

After dropping his bag, he locked the door and found the wall switch. Two small wall sconces cast a yellow light over the room. He fished a large rubber doorstop from his suitcase and wedged it under the door. He couldn't help but smile to himself as he thought of Hurley's rules. The man even had rules about how to go to the bathroom. Some of them, like the rubber doorstop, made complete sense, while others, like which stall to choose, and why, seemed a bit much. Rapp checked the windows next. They had bars, which were padlocked. There was only one way in and out—the door he'd just come through. That was not the best situation should the police come looking for them. Rapp made sure the shades were pulled tight on the two garden-level windows that faced the alley and then he went straight for the bedroom.

At the bottom of the armoire, under an extra blanket and pillow, he found what he was looking for. Rapp placed the tattered leather suitcase on the bed, dialed in the combinations, and popped the clasps. Inside was a shrink-wrapped file, a small arsenal of pistols, silencers, ammunition, knives, and a surveillance kit. Rapp snapped on a pair of latex gloves and retrieved a Beretta 92F from the foam cutout. He checked the slide, the chamber, the firing pin, and then the trigger. The gun had been cleaned by a pro. After screwing a silencer to the end, he took one of the fifteen-round magazines and inserted it, chambered a round, and checked the safety.

Rapp then set about doing a complete examination of the apartment. He retrieved the electric razor from his shaving kit, pressed two buttons, waited for the light to blink. The shaver was actually a scanning device used to detect bugs. Hurley had explained that the flat had been rented by a freelancer, which in this case was code for a retired Agency employee. The man was to sanitize and stock the flat, but Rapp had been ordered to go over the entire place again from top to bottom just to make sure. It took him the better part of an hour to go over the entire apartment.

When the jet lag finally caught up with him, Rapp was too tired to make anything to eat, so he took a quick shower and then tore the shrink wrap from the file. He had been given a full briefing on Hamdi Sharif back in the States, but this file, he was told, would be far more target-specific. The target was fifty-eight years old. He was a Turkish national, and according to press clippings, had made his money in real estate. What the clippings left out was that the majority of his wealth had come from supplying arms to various regimes throughout the Middle East and Southwest Asia. British, French, and American intelligence agencies all had his number, but Sharif was in bed with the Russians, which made him a bit of a sticky situation. None of the allies wanted to risk upsetting the Russians, so they tolerated him.

Rapp frowned as he reviewed the section on Sharif's ties with the tangled web of former Soviet generals and Ivan-come-lately millionaire businessmen. All but a few were thugs and Mafiosi, and the legitimate businessmen were being dropped and squeezed out of their holdings on a weekly basis. Russia had become the Wild West, and the sheriff was in on the fix. The KGB brutes had new business cards, but other than that, not much had changed. The allies, for some reason, couldn't see that the more they turned a blind eye the more brazen these men were becoming. Rapp could give a rat's ass about the Russians and who they used to peddle their arms, so long as those arms didn't end up in the laps of terrorists. Unfortunately for Sharif, that was precisely what he had been doing, and in ever-increasing shipments.

Most of the file was a summary of what Rapp already knew, such as his ties to Hezbollah, but there were a few new snippets about a Marxist outfit called Dev Sol. In the past year the group had targeted the overseas offices of fifteen U.S. corporations in Istanbul. The bombs were all military grade, and the Brits were saying Sharif's outfit had supplied the goods. Sharif was a Muslim and an ardent supporter of Hezbollah, Hamas, and Fatah. How he had ended up in business with a bunch of leftist, God-hating communists was a real head-scratcher. The file didn't draw any conclusions, just gave the facts. Rapp was left to venture guesses on his own. He supposed it was money first, and then the old saying—my enemy's enemy is my friend.

The Dev Sol wrinkle gave Rapp pause, however. He got the sense that this might be about more than just Pan Am Lockerbie, or at least that certain important people stateside don't care so much when innocent civilians get killed, but by God, if the day-to-day operations of a couple of Fortune 500 companies were disrupted, it was time to send a message. Those corporations contributed a lot of money to the coffers of important politicians in Washington. The more Rapp thought about it, the more he realized it didn't matter. It was like Sharif supporting Dev Sol. As long as he and the corporations were going after the same enemy, it didn't much matter.

Rapp finished the file and stuffed it under the mattress. He lay there for a long moment with his eyes open thinking about the detailed report. It was written in English, but it had not been written by an American. The choice of words was distinctive and the sentence structure more formal. Rapp concluded the Brits had put the report together, and that they had taken a long, hard look at solving the Sharif problem. They had conducted careful surveillance on the arms dealer. His daily routine was detailed down to the minute. The report didn't say how long they had watched him, but he got the impression it was for several weeks. Rapp remembered that the shrink back at the lake house had told him you could discern patterns in almost any person's life. In reading Sharif's file, those patterns jumped off the page. And one in particular was almost impossible to ignore. Rapp's mind began to wander down a path that he should have steered clear of, but he found it impossible to resist.

After a few minutes he set the alarm on his watch, turned off the bedside lamp, glanced at the loaded pistol, closed his eyes, and began to drift away. Hurley's orders couldn't have been more clear, but it would be two more days before he arrived in the city. Rapp began to imagine how he would do it. The act of his first kill played out in his mind like a movie. As he drifted off to sleep, he decided he would go for a nice long run in the morning. And he would break another one of Hurley's rules.

CHAPTER 22

RAPP awoke rested and went through the motions of his morning routine without coming to grips with what he had for the most part already decided. He shaved, drank a glass of orange juice, and mixed some granola and yogurt into a small bowl. He read the file again while eating. He started with the summary and worked his way back to see if he'd missed anything. After reading it a second time he was even more convinced that it had been prepared by the Brits, which led to a very obvious question. Why had they decided not to act? It could have been as simple as Hurley, or someone at Langley, offering to solve the problem for them.

Rapp had been trying to decipher the organizational structure of the team that was centered on the Lake Anna house for some time now. There had to be more people involved than the handful of operatives he'd met. After Rapp had proved himself worthy of joining their endeavor, the veil of secrecy was lifted a notch. His recruiter gave him her real name, although he had no way of knowing if it in fact was her real name. Irene Kennedy was the only person in the small group who actually worked at Langley. According to her, everyone else was a contractor. Rapp asked the obvious question: "What am I?"

Kennedy thought about it for a second and said, "Does it matter to you?"

"Maybe."

"Technically you don't work for the CIA."

"But I work for you."

"That's correct. The important thing is that you have no record of ever working for the federal government, and we'd like to keep it that way."

Rapp thought long and hard about what he was about to say. "So I'm a hired gun."

Kennedy's squinting eyes showed that she wasn't exactly in love with the label. Rapp surprised her even more by what he said next.

"How about assassin?"

She frowned. "No."

"By my estimate, I've fired around twenty thousand rounds of ammunition since arriving here."

"And you've become quite the marksman."

"And what's the point of all of this training? To keep shooting paper targets . . . or to eventually sink a bullet into a target's head?"

"You know the answer."

He did. "Remember the first time we met?"

She nodded.

"You told me there are people in Washington

who think that we need to take a more aggressive approach with these terrorists."

"Yes."

"But they don't have the courage to say so publicly."

"It would be foolish for them to do so. We live in a civilized society. They would be thrown out of office."

"And a civilized society would never condone assassination, even in instances where it involved national security."

"Not unless we were at war, and even then it would be tricky."

Rapp digested that for a moment and then said, "I'm not into semantics. Private contractor, hired gun, operative . . ." he shook his head, "killer . . . The point of all of this is to go out, find the enemy, and put a bullet in his head. Right?"

"I suppose that is an accurate definition. I suppose the answer is yes."

"So I'm an assassin."

"Not yet," she offered with a sly smile. "You haven't killed anyone."

Rapp looked in the mirror at his reflection and wondered if he really knew himself. The college athlete looked back at him with the innocence of youth. The public face in no way jibed with the thoughts of retribution that filled his head. Inside he was a much older man. A jaded, hard man who was now a trained killer. He thought again of his conversation with Kennedy and his new profession. He was ready. Eager really, but not in a reckless way. More methodical perhaps than at any time in his life. He asked himself again if he should proceed with his plan. The answer came back a resounding yes.

Rapp secured the silenced Beretta in a shoulder holster and covered it with a lightweight blue and silver reversible running jacket. He stuffed one of the surveillance kits into a fanny pack and strapped the pack to his waist. He put a dark blue Nike baseball hat on his head and checked himself in the full-length mirror on the inside door of the armoire. There was a slight bulge under his right arm where the 9mm was holstered. As a last measure he grabbed a white towel from the bathroom and looped it around the back of his neck. He stuffed the ends inside the running jacket, zipped it up, and checked himself in the mirror. The bulge was no longer noticeable. Rapp lowered the zipper, turned to the side and stuck his left hand inside the jacket. He gripped the Beretta and attempted to aim the weapon. The silencer caught on the jacket. He tried again, this time partially drawing the weapon, but keeping it hidden inside the jacket. He found it worked best if he raised his right arm as if he were checking the time on his wristwatch. Rapp practiced the move fifty more times until he was completely comfortable with it. Finally, he checked the alley and then left the apartment, locking the door behind him. He decided to skip stretching before the run. No sense in giving the neighbors time to observe him.

Whenever possible, reconnaissance is best done on foot. A satellite can't give you the smells and sounds of a neighborhood, and it can't see what might be lurking behind a window or under the awning of an apartment building. A car isn't bad, but then again cars usually travel at fairly high speeds, placing them in the area of concern for a few seconds at most. Often they were the only choice, but in this situation, walking the neighborhood was the best option. Or in Rapp's case, running it.

He took off at a trot. From studying the file, Rapp knew there was a park a block down the street from Sharif's apartment. The previous night he'd found a low wall that offered a decent vantage point where he could stretch and keep an eye on Sharif's building without drawing too much attention to himself. It was a mile and a half to the park. After one mile Rapp stopped at a public phone and punched in an international calling card number using the knuckle of his forefinger. When he heard the dial tone he punched in the number for the phone service. Five seconds later he heard the prerecorded greeting. At the beep he left a coded message in Arabic that told Hurley everything was proceeding according to plan, which technically was the case, but probably not for much longer.

Rapp carefully placed the phone back in the cradle and took off for the park. He circled the entire area twice and saw nothing that would lead him to believe that there was any surveillance. There were a few doormen who were out sweeping, a couple of early morning exercisers, and some people walking their dogs, but no police. Rapp entered the park at seven-forty-one and settled in by the wall. He started stretching his calves; first his right for thirty seconds and then his left. He'd positioned himself so that he had a clear view of the front of Sharif's apartment building. There was no wind and Rapp guessed the temperature was in the high fifties. According to the Brits, Sharif's apartment was one of two on the fifth floor. It was a big place, totaling forty-five hundred square feet. His mother, his wife, and one of his daughters lived with him.

Rapp started on his calisthenics and kept track of the people entering and leaving his corner of the park. Every minute or so a pedestrian passed just outside the park. None of them paid him an ounce of attention. It was the same the world over. Most of these people had been sound asleep thirty minutes ago and they were now off to start their daily grind. They would be lucky if they were fully awake by the time they reached their offices.

Rapp did fifty push-ups, followed by fifty sit-ups, and then stretched some more. At eight he checked the apartment door and his pulse quickened just a touch. At eight-oh-five he frowned and started to doubt the accuracy of the surveillance report. Then at eight-oh-seven the apartment building's doorman stepped outside and held the door open for a plump man and a little brown Dachshund. The man was wearing sunglasses and a long black trench coat. He had his collar turned up against the morning chill. The sunglasses, coat, and dog all matched the photos from the surveillance report. It was Sharif.

Rapp glanced at the open park bench about

eighty feet to his left and started doing more sit-ups. Every time he rose, he could look over the wall and see Sharif moving closer with his dog. Every time he lowered himself to the ground he thought of his orders. The plan was for Rapp to arrive two days early and conduct countersurveillance to make sure they weren't being watched. He would then call the service and flash them the all-clear. Hurley and Richards would arrive on the third day and they would begin direct surveillance on the target for a minimum of five days. If all went well, they would then make their move.

Rapp let out a slight grunt even though the sit-ups were easy. Sharif was almost to the bench. Rapp lowered himself to the ground and rested for a second. The entire operation seemed far too complicated. Far too many moving parts, as his college coach liked to say. Too many places where something could go wrong. Rapp began another set of twenty-five sit-ups. Sharif was just arriving at the bench. The man bent over, undid the dog's leash, and tossed a small blue ball into a grassy area. The little brown sausage took off after it. When Rapp came up the next time, Sharif had a mobile phone out and was punching in a number. Kennedy had played a tape to Rapp and Richards two weeks earlier on which Sharif implicated himself in a number of illegal dealings with known terrorist organizations. Rapp asked her where she got the intel, and she politely told him it was classified information. Rapp guessed it came from these morning chats on his mobile phone.

Rapp did another sit-up and thought of Dr. Lewis, the shrink. The man must have asked him in every conceivable way how he thought he would cope with taking another human life. Rapp had answered that question so many times he finally said to the shrink, "Well . . . I guess I won't know until I kill someone."

"That's right," Rapp muttered to himself. The whole idea behind the Orion Team was that it would have a small footprint. It would cut through all the bureaucratic BS and get things done in a more expeditious manner. And of course deniability was paramount. Rapp finished the set of twenty-five and lay flat on his back for sixty seconds, playing the entire thing out in his mind's eye. The longer they were on the ground in Istanbul lurking around Sharif's apartment and office, the greater the chance they'd be noticed. He didn't like that one bit. He also didn't like the idea of dragging this thing out when the solution was so obvious. He thought of how mad Hurley would be and dismissed the thought almost immediately. The man was always mad about something.

Rapp thought of the past three years. All the sleepless nights when he had yearned for the opportunity to meet just one of the men behind the downing of Pan Am 103. When he had imagined down to the most minute detail what he would do to them. And now he had the man who had supplied the plastic explosives and military-grade fuse and detonator sitting in his sights. He'd waited long enough. When the best course of action was staring you in the face you should take it. Rapp hopped to his feet and did a couple of side bends before walking over to a tree. He stretched one thigh and then the other, stealing a glance at Sharif as he did so. The man was too busy yapping on the phone to notice Rapp.

Rapp did a few more stretches and took a quick inventory of his surroundings. He counted four people within two hundred feet. The closest had just passed by on the sidewalk. Rapp waited to give the woman a good head start and then stepped out from behind the tree. His feet fell silently on the dirt jogging path that ran in front of Sharif's bench. He unzipped his jacket a foot and slid his left hand inside. His thumb found the safety. He flipped it up. Rapp then pulled his hand out of his jacket and kept moving toward the target, who had yet to notice him. Twenty feet away Rapp's pulse was as steady as it had ever been. His eyes narrowed a bit and he took in a deep breath. He could hear the man clearly now. It was the same voice he'd heard on the tape Kennedy had played for him. He was talking about an extremely valuable shipment.

Rapp never flinched, never wavered for a second. He was only ten feet away when Sharif finally looked up. Rapp gave him a friendly nod and then raised his right wrist to look at his watch. A split second later his left hand slid between the folds of his jacket and found the grip of the Beretta. He swung the gun up, the holster acting as a sling, the blue fabric of his running jacket bulging just slightly.

Rapp's finger was prepared to squeeze the trigger when he changed his mind. He wanted to look into Sharif's eyes. He wanted to confront the man. The two men locked eyes for a second. Rapp smiled at him, and then changed directions, took two steps, and casually sat down on the bench next to the arms dealer. Rapp leaned forward and jabbed the end of the silencer into Sharif's ribs.

A look of panic washed over the Turk's face. His mouth was agape, the mobile phone held in his right hand a half foot from his face. A man's voice could be heard squawking from the tiny speaker. Rapp elevated the silencer a few inches and squeezed the trigger. The bullet pierced the fabric of the running jacket, leaving a small hole, and then a millisecond later it shattered the cell phone. Sharif let out a yelp, dropped what was left of the phone, and clutched his bloody hand.

Rapp jabbed the silencer firmly into the man's ribs and in a menacing voice said, "How do you sleep at night?"

"What?" Sharif asked in total confusion.

"You heard me, you piece of shit. How do you sleep at night? Do you think of all the innocent people you've helped kill? Do you think of their faces?" Rapp poked him hard with the silencer. "Do you think of their final seconds . . . how they react when a bomb goes off in the cargo hold of a 747 at thirty-one thousand feet?" Rapp saw the recognition and then fear in the man's eyes.

"I don't know what you're—"

"Shut up," Rapp commanded. "I know who you are, and I have no desire to listen to your lies."

"But—"

This time Rapp jabbed the silencer so hard into the man's ribs that Sharif let out a small cry. "I only want to know one thing," Rapp said. "Do you ever think about them? Have you ever felt an ounce of guilt over all the people you've helped kill?"

Sharif shook his head slowly and parted his lips to speak.

Rapp didn't want to hear his lies. He squeezed the trigger and sent a bullet into Sharif's chest. The Turk grunted and clutched his chest with both hands. Rapp stood, lifted his right arm again, as if he were checking the time, and squeezed the trigger three times in quick succession. The bullets spat from the end of the silencer, all three of them striking the arms dealer in the nose. The hollow-tipped rounds were designed to pancake on impact and triple in size. A pink mist exploded from the back of Sharif's head. A good portion of the man's brain was now in the bushes behind the bench. Rapp flipped the safety into the up position and moved off down the path without even the slightest bit of remorse.

CHAPTER 23

LANGLEY, VIRGINIA

THE Counter Terrorism Center was tucked away in the basement of the Old Headquarters Building at CIA. It was underfunded, understaffed, under decorated, underground, and pretty much isolated from all the major players in the building by both geography and attitude. Eight diligent souls worked there, and that was counting an overworked administrative assistant and Irene Kennedy, who was loosely attached to the group as an expert on all things Arab and Islamic.

Kennedy had spent her youth moving from one diplomatic post to the next, all of them in the Middle East and all of them save one in Arabic-speaking countries. Her father had diplomatic credentials but in fact worked for the CIA. Kennedy was reviewing a particularly bad translation that had been kicked downstairs by someone on the intel side of the building. The translation was so poorly done that Kennedy finally sat back and looked at her colleague Andrew Swanson. The tall, blond-haired Dartmouth grad was leaning against the wall of her cubicle tugging at his curly hair. He'd been up all night trying to make sense of the intercept.

"You keep pulling your hair like that and you'll go bald," Kennedy said without looking up.

Swanson pulled his hand away and tried to stand still. After a half minute he couldn't take it any longer and said, "The thing doesn't make any sense."

"That's because the translation is wrong." Kennedy scratched a few more notes in the margin.

"I knew it."

Kennedy closed the folder and tapped it with her pen. "I'm going to need the tape."

Swanson groaned in frustration. "Shit."

She looked at the designation on the folder. "What's the problem?"

"It's frickin' NSA."

"I see that."

"I'll be lucky if I get the tape before the Fourth of July."

Kennedy grabbed a Post-it note and wrote down a name and number. She stuck it to the front of the folder and handed the whole thing back to Swanson. "Call Kathy. Tell her I said she owes me and ask if she can messenger the tape over this afternoon."

"And if she tells me to get in line like everyone else?"

Kennedy's phone rang. She looked at the small, rectangular, monochrome screen and saw that it was Stansfield's extension. "She won't. I promise. Now run along and bug someone else. I need to take this." Kennedy grabbed the handset and said, "Good morning, sir."

"Good morning. Would you please come up-stairs. There's something we need to discuss."

Kennedy instantly recognized the touch of in-tensity in her boss's voice. The average person would not have noticed, but she knew him so well that she was instantly alert. "I'll be right up." She hung up her phone, locked her desk, and started for the door. On the elevator ride up she reviewed the various op-erations that she was currently running or involved in. There were fourteen active operations that she was associated with to one degree or another. It could be any one of them, or something entirely new. She really hoped it wasn't anything new. She didn't know if her marriage could take much more of her job. She barely saw her husband as it was.

Kennedy passed through Stansfield's outer of-fice. His assistant Meg was on the phone and mo-tioned for her to go in. Kennedy entered and closed the door behind her. Stansfield was standing at the map table behind his desk reviewing a document. The corner office was devoid of any personal touch, with the exception of a family portrait of his wife and kids that he kept on his desk, and even that faced away from visitors. As Langley's top spy, he was very cognizant of those who collected infor-mation and ferreted out secrets. Kennedy had done some digging three years earlier and came up with a long list of medals, citations, ribbons, and awards that Stansfield had received dating back to World War II. Not a single one of them was displayed, either here or at home. Thomas Stansfield was an intensely private man.

"Please sit," he said without turning around. "There's tea on the table. Help yourself."

Kennedy went to the leather couch, opened the bamboo box, and selected a green tea. After tearing open the package she dropped the bag in a cup and filled it with steaming hot water. Stansfield crossed the office, a piece of paper in hand. He sat in the chair to Kennedy's right, slid the sheet of paper across the cherry-inlaid coffee table, and clasped his hands in front of him.

Kennedy stopped dunking the tea bag and looked at the very top edge of the sheet. As someone who was on the operations side of the business, she was intimately familiar with what she was looking at. It was a secure cable. These sheets came in all day long from U.S. Embassies and Consulates the world over. They were sent using some of the most secure and classified encryption software mathematicians could design. The designation across the top told her not only the sensitivity of the information but where it had originated. This particular piece of paper had come from the U.S. Consulate in Istanbul. Kennedy swallowed hard as her eyes raced through the body of text. Hamdi Sharif was dead. Gunned down in a park across the street from his house.

"Is my memory failing me," Stansfield said, "or was I misinformed about the operational timetable?"

Kennedy read the cable again and went over the dates in her head. Finally, she looked up at her boss and said, "To the best of my knowledge Stan and Richards aren't even in the country."

"Where are they?"

"Greece."

Stansfield sat back and ran his right hand over his black-and-blue-striped tie. "Where is Rapp?"

"In-country."

He thought about that for a second. "When did he arrive?"

"Yesterday afternoon."

"You're sure."

She nodded. "He checked in last night and then again this morning."

"His time or ours?"

"It would have been around midnight our time."

Stansfield looked out the window for a moment and then removed his black glasses. He set them on his lap and rubbed his eyes. Jumping to conclusions wouldn't do him any good. Anything, of course, was possible when it came to a character like Sharif. He had made more than a few enemies over the years, but the notion that two separate camps had decided to go after him at the exact same time was a tough one to swallow.

Before Stansfield could say what was on his mind, his office door burst open. Max Powers, the Near East chief, strolled in without offering an apology. "Big news."

"What now?" Stansfield asked.

"Our favorite arms dealer is no longer with us."

Out of the corner of his eye Stansfield saw Kennedy withdraw the secure cable and fold it in half. "Which arms dealer would you be referring to?"

"Sharif, that fat Turk," Powers said with a satisfied grin. "Someone blew his head off in Istanbul this morning."

"His entire head?" Kennedy asked, taking the comment literally.

"The back of it at least." Powers placed the palm of his right hand on the back of his head and tapped his bald spot several times. "I have a good source who works for Turkish NIO. Says someone plugged him up close. One in the heart and they're not sure how many in the face, but more than one. Right here." Powers tapped the space at the top of his nose between his eyes. "Tight grouping. Very professional. Blew the back of his head off."

NIO was Turkey's National Intelligence Organization. "Do they have any idea who carried it out?" Kennedy asked.

"Not a clue, but the rumor mill is already working overtime."

"Candidates?" Stansfield asked.

"Usual suspects . . . Jews, Frogs, Iranians, Iraqis, Syrians, and us, of course."

"Russians?"

"My guy said they were thick as thieves. Also said he got a call from your old friend at KGB."

"You mean SVR," Kennedy reminded him of the Russian Intelligence service's new name.

"Yeah, but, he referred to them as KGB. Same assholes as before. Just a new name."

"What did Mikhail want?" Stansfield asked, referring to Mikhail Ivanov, the deputy director of Directorate S, perhaps the most ruthless outfit in the espionage business.

"Not happy," Powers said with an emphatic shake of his head. "I guess he made some pretty heavy demands."

"Such as."

"He wants to know who did it, and he expects full cooperation. Said he's going to make life very hard for anyone who doesn't cooperate fully. Pushy bastard."

"Any witnesses?" Kennedy asked.

"Not one," Powers said with a grin. He looked at his watch. "The Turk's been dead for five hours. It looks like it was professional. Five hours means the guy who pulled the trigger is long gone. They're screwed."

"Guy?" Kennedy asked.

Powers shrugged. "Just my guess. No offense, but it's pretty much an exclusively all-men's club."

Kennedy smiled to let him know she wasn't offended.

Stansfield asked, "Your source . . . he's good?"

"Great. Very dialed in."

"Loyalties?"

"To the almighty dollar, but he prefers to do business with people he likes. We can trust him."

"Keep me posted. I want to know what Mikhail is up to. If he starts swinging his velvet hammer, we might be able to win over a few more hearts in Ankara."

"Good idea."

"Anything else?"

"I'll have my gang put together a full workup for you."

"Thank you." Stansfield looked to the door, letting Powers know he wanted to get back to his meeting with Kennedy.

As soon as the Near East chief was gone, Kennedy was on her feet. She made a beeline for Stansfield's desk and grabbed the handset of his secure phone. She started punching in numbers, pausing for prompts and then hitting more numbers. After an interminable twenty seconds she accessed the voicemail. Kennedy listened intently to Rapp's brief coded message and then slowly hung up the phone.

Stansfield twirled his glasses in his right hand and asked, "Well?"

Kennedy nodded, cleared her throat, and said in near disbelief, "It was him."

CHAPTER 24

THE handsome young man loosened his tie and nudged his bag toward the Customs desk at John F. Kennedy Airport. He casually yet carefully studied the face of every officer who was checking passports and clearing people through Customs. He had a U.S. passport and thus was spared the more stringent and crowded queues that were serving foreigners seeking to visit the United States. He chose this particular line, not because it looked like the fastest, but because the officer manning it looked to be the oldest and most uninterested of the six currently on duty. When it was his turn he stepped to the elevated desk and slid his passport across the cheap blue laminate surface.

The officer, a fifty-some-year-old gray-haired man, gave him a serious look and then glanced at the passport. He was all business. In a voice devoid of real interest he asked, "Did you have a good trip, Mike?"

The man gave a relaxed shrug and said, "Business."

"What do you do?"

"Computer software. Workforce management stuff."

The man asked a few more standard questions before getting back to his second one. "Workforce management . . . what's that?"

"Sorry . . . scheduling software. They tell me workforce management sounds more cutting-edge."

The officer let out a small laugh while he applied the appropriate stamps. He closed the passport, slid it back across the surface, and said, "Have a nice day."

"Thanks, you too." The software salesman headed for the main door and a connection to one of the domestic terminals. He was just another man in a blue suit, white shirt, and burgundy tie trying to earn a living. Other than the fact that he was tanned and fit, there was nothing that made him stand out. He found a stall in the men's room outside the Delta ticketing desk. He carefully pulled back the magnetized liner on his black Travelpro carry-on bag. He deposited the passport for Mike Kruse along with a wallet stuffed with matching credit cards, a Maryland driver's license, a bent and tattered UVA college ID, and a brand-new Blockbuster card.

He extracted a thin money clip with just one credit card, a Virginia driver's license, and eight hundred dollars in cash. After closing the suitcase, he left the men's room and proceeded directly to the Delta ticket counter, where a very enthusiastic young woman with a Southern accent asked how she could be of service.

"I'd like to purchase a ticket on your next flight to Dulles." He placed his driver's license on the counter.

The woman was already pecking away at her keyboard. She nodded at her screen and then looked at the license. "Well, Mr. Rapp, we have a flight that leaves in one hour and forty-eight minutes."

She went on to give Rapp the time of arrival and cost of the ticket plus tax. He simply smiled and slid four hundred-dollar bills across the counter. Three minutes later he was on his way with his change and ticket. He'd spent the last three days traveling across Europe pretending to be someone else. He was relieved to be back on U.S. soil, but was not naive enough to think that his problems were over.

He'd taken a roundabout way back to the flat after he'd executed Sharif, and he'd forced himself to run at a much slower pace than he was used to. A man running a sub-five-minute mile in any city of that size would look as if he were running away from something. Back at the flat, Rapp snapped on the latex gloves and wiped down and disassembled the Beretta. He placed the magazine, slide, and frame back in the worn leather suitcase along with the surveillance kit. He locked the case and put it back in the armoire under the pillow and blankets. The barrel and firing pin were tightly rolled up inside the running jacket and placed in a brown grocer's bag. The rest of the clothes that he'd worn to the park, including his shoes, were placed in a second grocer's bag.

Rapp took a fast shower and put on his suit. After taking two minutes to walk through the flat and make sure he wasn't missing anything, he stuffed the two paper bags in his black duffel and attached the duffel to the top of his black, wheeled carry-on suitcase. Forty-one minutes after executing Sharif, Rapp locked the apartment and headed for the tram. The closest stop was three blocks away and Rapp had two major decisions to make.

The first was to find the right place to dispose of the two brown bags and to do it quickly. The second decision involved getting out of the country. Three different plans had been researched. The first was to simply fly out of the country, the second was to take the train, and the third was to rent a car. Rapp did not like the car rental as an option unless it was to be used to drive to Ankara, eight hours away, where he would leave it at the airport and grab a flight. Using the car to cross the border would create a different set of problems that he wanted to avoid. It put a name in a system that the police could trace. It would be a fake name, of course, but even the false identities that they had manufactured were to be protected. Heading straight for Istanbul's airport would be the faster way out of the country, but it would also involve standing in close proximity to a large number of police, who he didn't think had a description of him, but he couldn't be sure.

A half block from the tram stop he ducked into

a bakery and purchased a coffee, newspaper, and breakfast roll. He paid in liras and took the coffee black and in a to-go cup. Outside he removed the lid, blew on the hot coffee, and watched a nearby public garbage can. He had enough credits left on his tram card that he didn't need to worry about buying a new ticket. The digital readout above the stop told him he had two minutes before the right tram arrived. Rapp put the lid back on his coffee and partially opened the black duffel bag. He extracted the more damning of the two paper bags and stuffed it under his left arm.

The hum of the approaching tram caused everyone to look, and that was when Rapp moved. He headed toward the flock of passengers who were waiting to board, pausing for a split second near the garbage can. He released the suitcase, grabbed the bag and stuffed it in the big circular receptacle. The tram stopped, the throng moved forward in unison, and ten seconds later they were all on their way to Sirkeci Station.

When they pulled into the grand old home of the Orient Express, Rapp searched the crowd for police officers who were showing unusual signs of alertness. There were none to be seen, which he took as a good omen. He exited the train and went straight to the nearest kiosk. Rapp had the departure times for Greece and Bulgaria memorized and knew that the express trains for both countries left in the evening. Hanging around the busy transportation hub for the rest of the day just to grab an express train was foolish. It was better to start working his way toward the border. A train was leaving for Alpullu in fifteen minutes. Rapp bought his ticket and made a quick stop at a bank of pay phones. He punched in the long series of numbers and then, in Arabic, left the coded message that would tell Richards and Hurley to not bother coming to Istanbul. Then, threading his way through the busiest part of the terminal, he slid past a trash bin and got rid of the second paper bag that contained his running gear.

After that he found the right platform, boarded his train, and took his seat. He pretended to read the newspaper, while keeping a close eye on the platform. When the train finally pulled out of the station, Rapp relaxed a touch with the comforting thought that he was putting distance between himself and the crime. Distance, he had been taught by Hurley, was your greatest ally and your number-one objective after taking someone out. As the train rolled through some of Istanbul's less desirable neighborhoods, he thought of Hurley. The man would lose it when he retrieved the message.

Rapp spent the rest of the afternoon hopping westbound trains until he crossed the Greek border at two in the afternoon. The Greeks and Turks did not have good relations, diplomatic or otherwise, so for all intents and purposes he was safe. He was sick of riding in trains and listening to other people yammer, so he decided to rent a car. It would be returned at the Macedonia International Airport in Thessaloniki, and as long as he didn't kill anyone in Greece, no one would care that an American by the name of Mike Kruse had rented a crappy little red, four-cylinder Fiat.

Rapp pointed the tin can south and headed for the coast. As he neared the ocean he cracked the window and smelled salt air. The landscape before him didn't look anything like the travel brochures he'd thumbed through back at the rental agency. The city of Alexandroupolis lay before him, an industrial fishing village with a few archeological sites of significance. Istanbul it was not. It was gray and brown and dirty and dead and it didn't affect his mood one bit. Rapp was not the kind of person who allowed geography or climate to depress him—as long as he didn't have to stay in one place too long. He rolled through Alexandroupolis just before sunset and continued up the coast for another fifteen kilometers until he found a small light blue seaside hotel. It was off season so the place was not busy and the rate was cheap. Rapp wheeled his bag straight into the reception area, which also doubled as the bar and dining room.

A heavyset, older gentleman waved to Rapp from behind the bar. Rapp walked over and the two of them worked out the details in broken English. The proprietor then held up a bottle of liquor and asked Rapp if he would like a drink. Rapp wondered for a brief second what Hurley and Richards were doing in Athens, and then decided that a drink was a great idea. He ordered a beer. The barkeep placed a bottle of Mythos in front of him along with a full bottle of ouzo and two shot glasses. He filled both glasses and slid one closer to Rapp. It was the beginning of a long night.

Three beers, and as many shots, into the evening, Rapp looked at the house phone and considered calling Hurley at his hotel. He dismissed the idea as a bad one and ordered some dinner. Fortunately, two college kids from England showed up and the bartender now had to divide his attention among the three of them. Four beers and a few more shots later, Rapp looked up and caught a reflection of himself in the mirror. It was at that exact moment that he realized a killer was staring back at him. He studied the reflection for a long moment and then held up a shot glass filled with ouzo. He toasted the man in the mirror and went to bed. He did not awaken until almost noon the next day.

CHAPTER 25

VIENNA, VIRGINIA

THE world headquarters for International Software Logistics, Inc., or ISL, was located in a new office park on Kingsley Road. The campus, as the developers called it, consisted of five buildings. They were all made of brown brick and reflective glass. Three of the buildings were strictly office space while the other two were a mix of office and industrial. The developers were an LLC out of the Bahamas who had quietly set aside the southernmost building for Software Logistics. It was at the far end of the office park and it backed up to a ravine. Nice and private. The building had twenty-two thousand square feet of space. The front quarter was built out with a reception area, six offices, a conference room, an area for cubicles, a break room, and a bathroom. The warehouse occupied the remainder of the space and for the most part sat vacant. There were plans, however, to do some expansion.

Stansfield looked at the building through the windshield of a Dodge Caravan and suppressed his concern. These front companies were laborious to set up. The LLC he was part of had directed legitimate funds into the development of this piece of land. The other owners were like-minded men of his era who had made millions and now in that final season of their lives were suddenly very concerned with where their country was headed. All five of them had fought in World War II under the command of Wild Bill Donovan, who ran the Office of Strategic Services. After the war they went on to have successful careers in defense, politics, finance, and in Stansfield's case, espionage. He went to great lengths to make sure they were protected should the Orion Team ever be exposed. But they all understood that if you were going to run an effective clandestine operation you actually had to lock horns with the enemy and possibly get your hands very dirty.

Kennedy told him she could handle the meeting, but he had his doubts. It wasn't that he didn't think her capable. While it was perfectly fine to send people off with messages, words had a funny way of being interpreted differently by different people, often in a way that gave them the outcome they were seeking. And there was a very real chance that his old friend would steamroll her. Even so, his desk was full and he did not want to go through the deceptions it would take to actually get to the meeting.

Kennedy left his office and Stansfield began to

systematically move through the stacks on his desk and map table that required his close attention. As the afternoon ticked away he periodically found himself staring out the window thinking about the new recruit. There was something about this Rapp fellow. He hadn't seen any of his people this fired up about anything in a long time. The kid was either a diamond in the rough or a disaster waiting to happen, depending on who you listened to. Kennedy was possibly biased by the fact that he was her find and Hurley was surly on a good day and an intolerable bastard on a bad day, so it was hard to see who was right. Lewis was steady, analytical, and unfortunately had no desire to run things. He had no doubt that Kennedy was right for the job, but she needed a few more years under her belt before she would be ready.

Stansfield stewed over their personalities for a good five minutes and then decided he needed to go to the meeting. The outcome was preordained. Hurley had never liked this Rapp fellow, and while Kennedy and Lewis were formidable, Hurley would wear them down with his bombastic, stubborn ways. And in truth, it was his call. As the person in charge of field ops he needed to be able to trust his men without question. Stansfield became stuck on the team concept for a second. Through all of the bickering and managing of egos, they had lost sight of one very important fact—the new recruit had not only succeeded, but had done so on his own. He arrived in Istanbul and less than twenty-four hours later he had successfully removed a very nasty thorn in America's side. There were a number of allies who would be cheering Sharif's death as well, and Stansfield hoped that at least one of them would be blamed. As much as Stansfield would love to take the credit for the assassination of Istanbul's merchant of death, he couldn't. The Orion Team needed complete anonymity or they risked investigation and exposure, which would in short order render them useless. That was why these new recruits could have no link whatsoever to Langley.

But what was the sense of any of it if you didn't engage the enemy and make him bleed? Stansfield had to be cautious with his hopes, though. How much of this was wishful thinking? He had yet to meet the young man. Who was to say this Rapp fellow wasn't in reality an uncontrollable asset who would eventually blow up in his face? Lewis didn't think so, and that was worth something, but still Stansfield realized he needed to meet this fellow and find out for himself what he was made of. If he was as good as some of them were saying it would be a tragedy to throw him away.

Stansfield asked his security detail to prepare for the vehicular version of a shell game. Langley kept a number of nondescript, windowless vans in the motor pool for just this type of thing. As the Operations boss, Stansfield did not have to inform anyone of his needs. His security detail only had to show up and take what was available. The detail had access to extra license plates and a variety of magnetized decals to help facilitate the deception. At seven-oh-four they left the back service gate at

Langley in a white van with the Red Carpet Linen Service logo on the sides.

They headed for Tyson's Corner and once inside the busy parking structure, Stansfield was moved to a Ford Taurus. Fifteen minutes later, he found himself standing alone, under a tree next to the main entrance of George Mason University. The Dodge minivan was parked across the street. Stansfield waited for five minutes and then the vehicle flashed its brights. After climbing into the backseat he handed Joe, head of his security detail, a piece of paper with an address on it. The driver memorized the address and handed the paper back to his boss. He briefly consulted his road atlas and then put the car in drive. Five minutes later they were at the office park.

"Joe," Stansfield said, leaning forward, "take us around back. There's a call box and a code for the door."

When they reached the back of the building Stansfield got out and punched in the code. He trusted Joe, but the fewer people who had the numbers, the tighter the circle remained. Stansfield motioned for Joe to pull in and then pressed the big red button to close the door. Four cars and a motorcycle were already parked inside. To the right, shelves, like the kind you'd find in a library, jutted out from the near wall. They were filled with software titles that were legitimately being shipped overseas. To the left were pallets and boxes and then a sea of darkness.

Stansfield headed for the offices and asked Joe to stay with the car. There was a cipher lock on the door. He punched in the four-digit code, leaned into the door, and was immediately aware of loud shouts coming from just ahead.

Stansfield frowned and wondered first and foremost why the conference room hadn't been soundproofed. He also wondered why these supposed professionals were incapable of keeping their tempers in check. As he stepped into the room, he almost didn't notice the man sitting at the break table reading a magazine.

"They've been at it like that for almost an hour."

Stansfield recognized the face instantly. "Mr. Rapp, I presume."

CHAPTER 26

RAPP didn't know who the man was, but there was something about him that instantly garnered respect. The gray hair, charcoal suit, shiny wing tips, discerning eyes, and the fact that he'd just walked unannounced into the secure building told him he was standing before someone who more than likely had an office on one of the top floors at Langley. After he gave him the once-over, he couldn't help but think the man reminded him of a more slender version of Spencer Tracy. Rapp decided he'd better stand. He offered his hand and said, "Yes. And you are . . . ?"

Stansfield gave him a grandfatherly smile. "George."

Rapp studied him with suspicion. "That's not your real name, is it?"

"No," Stansfield said.

After a moment Rapp said, "Any chance you're the guy running this show?"

Stansfield gave him a relaxed smile. "When you get to my age you better be running something, or it's time to retire. Please sit." He motioned with his right hand toward the chair Rapp had been sitting in. Rapp returned to his seat. Stansfield smelled coffee and found a pot on the counter. He helped himself. "Would you like some?"

"No thanks."

After joining him at the break table, Stansfield blew on his coffee and said, "I hear you've been making waves again."

Rapp wasn't sure how much he should say, so he shrugged his shoulders and kept his mouth shut.

"Would you care to walk me through your decision?"

"What decision would that be?"

"Why you decided to act on your own in Istanbul?"

Rapp's dark eyes narrowed. He studied the old man for a few seconds. He was in enough hot water for breaking their damn rules. He wasn't about to break another. "I'm afraid I don't know what you're talking about."

Stansfield grinned. "I'm afraid you do."

"I'm at a bit of a disadvantage. If you're who I think you are, you know I can't discuss any of this with someone unless they give me the green light." Rapp jerked his head toward the conference room door.

"Good point. You don't know me, and that's for good reason, but I know you."

Rapp gave him a dubious look that changed

into a humble one as the silver-haired man recited his life story, including date of birth, Social Security number, parents' names, a long list of athletic accomplishments, and his relative strengths and weaknesses. It wasn't until the last part, though, that Rapp began to feel vulnerable.

"Three days ago you used a 9mm Beretta pistol to execute a man at point-blank range. Here and here." Stansfield touched his heart and then tapped the bridge of his dark glasses. He looked at the door to the conference room and said, "You have one avid supporter, another who thinks you have great potential, and one very forceful detractor. They are in there deciding your fate right now. If you want to continue on your current career path, I am more than likely your best hope. So if you have anything you'd like to say, now is the time to do it."

That this man knew so many details about his life and was able to recite them, chapter and verse, without a single note, told Rapp all he needed to know. "You seem to have most of the facts." He carefully turned the question back on George by saying, "I'm sure you've formed some opinions."

Stansfield sat back and crossed his left leg over his right. "I'm hearing conflicting stories. That is why I decided to meet you in person."

"What are the conflicting stories?"

"You appear to be a man who is possibly uniquely suited for this line of work. You also appear to have a hard time following rules, and that, young man, can be a dangerous thing."

Rapp nodded. It was becoming apparent that

Spencer Tracy's little brother really was the guy who ran this entire show, which meant he needed to get him in his corner, and do it before Hurley sank him once and for all. "Sir, would I be totally off the mark if I guessed that at some point in your career you spent some time in the field?"

Stansfield grinned but did not answer the question.

"And when you were in the field, did things always go as planned?"

Stansfield saw instantly where he was headed. "There's a big difference between adapting and disregarding orders."

Rapp nodded and was sullen for a split second. That was exactly what Hurley had screamed at him, with a few colorful words thrown in to boot. If Doc Lewis hadn't been there, Rapp was pretty certain they would have come to blows.

"To be fair," Stansfield continued, "I use great caution when I evaluate a decision that someone has made while operating in a high-stress environment."

The man's choice of words gave Rapp pause. He considered them carefully and then said, "High-stress?"

"Yes."

"I'm not sure I'd call it high-stress, sir."

Stansfield's eyes sparkled with amusement. "You snuck into a foreign country using a false identity, killed a man at close range, and then made it out of the country all on your own. You didn't find any of that stressful?"

"The getting-out part . . . maybe a little, but really only getting out of Istanbul. After that the odds of getting caught were pretty low."

"Why did you decide to act on your own?"

"I didn't go to Istanbul thinking that I would handle the job on my own. It happened. It evolved. I saw the opportunity and I took it."

"What do you mean you saw the opportunity?" Stansfield was keenly interested in the young man's next words.

"I read the surveillance briefing that the Brits gave us . . ."

Stansfield held up his hand and stopped him. "Who told you the Brits gave us that report?"

"No one."

"Then why did you say the Brits gave it to us?"

Rapp shrugged as if to say it was obvious. "I could tell by the way it was written."

Stansfield nodded for him to continue and made a mental note to revisit the subject later.

"I read the report and there it was . . . it jumped right off the page."

"There what was?"

"The opportunity. The report said that the target took his dog to the park every morning. He sat on a park bench and talked on his cell phone while he threw a ball to his little dog." Rapp turned his palms up and said, "How does it get any easier than that? No bodyguards to deal with, no drivers or armor-plated cars, no security cameras . . . very few witnesses, and the few who are around are busy living their own lives."

"And it didn't occur to you to pass this information on to Stan?"

"It did, but it also seemed like it was too good to pass up."

"If you'd brought it to Stan, you wouldn't have been passing it up."

"You're not serious."

"Completely."

"If I had brought my idea to Stan he would have called me a moron and told me to shut my mouth."

The young recruit was probably right. "Stan is very good at this type of thing. This is not his first dance."

"So I've been told," Rapp said, unimpressed.

"You have some problems with Hurley, I hear."

"Who doesn't?"

The point was more accurate than not. "Still . . . he has a lengthy resume."

"I'm sure he does, but the entire thing was more complicated than it needed to be. The whole idea here is that we are supposed to get in, get it done, and get out without anyone noticing we were there. If we'd stuck with Stan's plan, we would have followed the guy around for five days and come to the same conclusion that was right there in the Brit report, and our odds of screwing up somewhere . . . being noticed . . . would have increased fivefold at least."

He was probably right, but Stansfield didn't tell him so. He would have to deal with Hurley later. "When did you read the report?"

"When I got to the safe house."

"That first night."

"Yes."

"And you decided that night that you would handle it on your own?"

"No . . . I saw the possibility, that was all."

"And when you decided to go to the park armed the next morning?"

"I thought there was a chance. I wanted to see with my own eyes and then decide."

"But when you left the safe house you were prepared to kill him if the opportunity presented itself?"

Rapp hesitated and then admitted the truth. "Yes."

Stansfield took a sip of the coffee and slowly set the mug on the table. "Any other reason why you chose to act on your own?"

"How do you mean?"

Stansfield gave him a knowing grin. "I was your age once . . . a long time ago. I was asked to do certain things for my country, and until I actually did them, I wasn't sure I had it in me."

Rapp looked down and studied the pattern in the gray-and-black carpeting. It was not in his character to be this open with someone he'd just met, especially on a subject like this, but there was something about this guy that made it difficult to be anything but forthright. "I wanted to kill him," he finally said.

"Revenge?"

Rapp shrugged his shoulders in a noncommittal way.

"Remember . . . we recruited you for a reason. I know what you went through. I know how you were affected by Pan Am Lockerbie."

"Revenge, justice . . . I don't know. I just know when I left for the park that morning I wasn't sure, and then as soon as I laid eyes on him I wanted to kill the bastard. I was sick of all the planning and talking. It made no sense that it had to be so complicated."

Stansfield took off his glasses and looked at Rapp with his gray-blue eyes. "Any other reason that may have pushed you over the edge?"

Rapp looked at the carpeting again. He hadn't even admitted the next part to himself. At least not fully. Without looking up he said in a soft voice, "I was afraid I wouldn't have the guts to do it."

With the understanding of someone who had walked the same path, Stansfield gave him a sympathetic nod. It had been a long time since Stansfield had killed a man, but he remembered the doubt that gnawed at him until he pulled that trigger for the first time. "How do you feel now?"

"How do you mean?"

"Now that you have taken a human life?"

Rapp gave a nervous laugh and checked his watch. "Do you have a few hours?"

"You know laughter is often a defense mechanism used to deflect."

Rapp thought of Doc Lewis. "I've heard that somewhere else recently."

"This isn't a good time to deflect."

Rapp noticed the concern on the old man's

lined face. He fidgeted with his hands and then said, "This isn't exactly a topic I'm used to discussing."

"No . . . you're right about that." Stansfield himself had never spoken to a soul about the men he had killed. It simply wasn't his way. There were others, though, whom he had worked with over the years, who were quite different in that regard. Some spoke with an intensity that was more academic, as if they were simply trying to perfect their craft for the sake of perfection. Others took a more lighthearted or twisted approach to their play-by-play analysis of how they had killed a man. The best ones, Stansfield had always felt, were the ones who kept it to themselves.

"This is very important," Stansfield said. "How are you up here?" The old man tapped his temple.

"I think I'm fine."

"No problem sleeping?"

"No, in fact I've slept better than I have in years."

"Good. I want you to understand something very important. Hamdi Sharif chose to get into the arms business, and he knowingly sold weapons to terrorist groups that were going to use those weapons to kill innocent civilians."

"I know."

"I am every bit as responsible as you for his death."

Rapp frowned and gave him a look that said he wasn't quite buying it.

Stansfield had expected that. "Who do you think sent you on that operation?"

"I don't know."

"I did. I was the judge and the jury. You were merely the executioner. Never forget that." He spoke with intensity for the first time in the entire conversation. He was almost pleading for Rapp to grasp the gravity of what he was saying.

Finally Rapp nodded, even though he wasn't sure he fully grasped the man's meaning.

Stansfield stood and said, "Why don't you go home now?"

"What about their decision?"

"Don't worry. I'll smooth things out. Just try not to cause any problems for the next few months."

CHAPTER 27

T HANK God," Lewis announced upon seeing Stansfield enter the room. "I can't spend another minute trying to talk sense into these two."

With pure disappointment, Stansfield glared down the length of the table, first at Hurley, who was on the left, and then at Kennedy, who was directly across from him. They were both on their feet. "Sit," he commanded. Kennedy sat. Hurley remained standing. "The first person who raises his voice is being sent to Yemen for the rest of his career."

"You can't send me anywhere," Hurley snarled.

Stansfield directed his full attention to Hurley and communicated his resolve with an icy stare that silently communicated the fact that he could do a lot worse than sending his ungrateful ass to Yemen. Of the three, Hurley was the only one who had seen this look before. It had been nearly three decades ago but Hurley still remembered that his stupidity had almost cost him his life, and if it hadn't been for Stansfield's magnanimous attitude he would have died that day. Hurley slowly sank to his seat.

"Have I failed you two so poorly that it has come to this?" Stansfield said in a calm but disappointed voice. "You scream at each other like children trying to bully their way to victory." He cocked his head in Kennedy's direction. "I expect far more from you. What did I tell you about losing control of your emotions?"

"That it's a weakness."

"Correct. And how has it worked for you this evening . . . screaming at one of the most hotheaded men in all of our nation's capital? Did your logic become more clear? Did your points carry more weight? Did you somehow persuade him to see things your way by shrieking at him like some wild banshee?"

Kennedy shook her head, her embarrassment complete.

Stansfield turned his icy gaze on Hurley. "And you . . . are you happy that you have succeeded in getting young Irene to finally sink to your depths?"

"That's bullshit. She's a grown woman. She can fight her own battles. I resent the fact that every time she doesn't like what I'm doing she goes running to you." Hurley pointed at him. "You know the rules as well as I do. I'm in charge in the field. What I say goes. I'm God and that too-smart-for-his-own-good college punk wandered so far off the reservation he's lucky I don't put a bullet in his head."

"That's our litmus test these days? When an operator doesn't follow orders to the letter, we put a bullet in his head?"

"You know what I mean. He went way beyond his operational parameters. He basically threw them out and flew off the handle."

"And succeeded. Let's not forget that part."

"Shit," Hurley scoffed at the point. "Even a blind squirrel finds a nut once in a blue moon."

"This is how you would like to argue with me . . . by mixing squirrel and moon metaphors?"

"You know I'm right."

"You are partially right, and you have also become an intolerable bully whom I'm not so sure I can keep around."

"Say the word and I'll resign. I'm sick of this bullshit."

"And then what will you do, Stan?" The deputy director of operations leaned over and placed his hands on the table. "Become a full-blown alcoholic. Another bitter, discarded spy who closes himself off from an ungrateful citizenry. You're already halfway there. You drink too much. You smoke too much. You piss and moan like some miserable woman who's mad at her husband because she's no longer young and beautiful. And there's the meat of the problem, isn't it, Stan?"

"What's the meat of the problem?"

"I think you may have heard this before. He reminds you of yourself."

"Who? The college puke?"

Stansfield nodded slowly. "And he might be better than you. That's what really scares you."

"That's bullshit."

Stansfield should have seen it sooner. He stood up abruptly and said, "So, your recommendation is that I cut him loose?"

"Absolutely. He's too much of a loose cannon. Sooner or later he's going to cause you a lot of problems."

"And who do you have to replace him?"

Hurley waffled. "A couple of decent candidates."

Stansfield looked to Lewis, who was at the head of the table. "Doctor?"

Lewis shook his head. "Neither of them have his skill set. Even if we worked with them for a year I don't think they could match him."

"That's not true," Hurley said, while looking as if he'd just taken a bite out of a lemon.

"Irene?" Stansfield asked.

She didn't speak. Just shook her head.

Stansfield pondered the situation for a moment and then said, "Here is my problem. We are flying blind in Lebanon and Syria. The director and the president overruled me and sent Cummins in to negotiate for the release of that Texas businessman." Stansfield stopped speaking for a second. He couldn't get over the stupidity of that decision and all of the damage that had been done after Cummins himself had been taken hostage. "Our assets have been getting picked off one by one for the past six months. Our network, that we worked so carefully to rebuild, is now in shambles. This situation has to be turned around, and I need men in the field to do it. I need shooters on the ground. We've all spent enough time over there to know that weakness breeds contempt. That stops today. I want these guys looking over their shoulders wondering if they're next. I want the leadership of Islamic Jihad and Hezbollah afraid to pop their heads out of their holes for fear that they might get those heads blown off. I want them on notice that if they're going to grab one of our assets who is negotiating in good faith and torture him for months on end . . . dammit, we are going to come after them like crazed sons of bitches." He turned his attention back to Hurley. "I don't want to lose you, but I need this kid. He's too good to just throw away. He knows how to take the initiative."

"Initiative? That's what you want to call it?"

"Oh, for Christ's sake, Stan, could you please get hold of your ego and hypocrisy and listen to me. This is bigger than you. We have a gaping hole in our operational abilities. A big nasty neighborhood in the Middle East that is breeding terrorists like rabbits, and we have nothing. I need to get back in there."

"You're calling me a hypocrite?"

"You have an extremely convenient short-term memory. Tell me, Stan, how many times in your first two years did you get yourself into trouble by ignoring orders or running off and launching your own operations?"

"It was a different time back then. We were given far more latitude."

"And you still got in trouble." Stansfield shook

his head as if trying to reconcile an irreconcilable thought. "Does the truth matter to you at all, or do you just want to go round and round all night until you wear everyone down? You don't remember all the times I had to go to bat for you and bail your ungrateful butt out of trouble, and now you're coming down on this new kid as if you were some saint."

Hurley started to speak, but Stansfield cut him off. "I'm not done. If the kid had screwed up, we wouldn't be having this conversation. He'd be gone. But he didn't screw up, did he? He made all the right decisions. He took care of our problem and didn't leave a speck of evidence and made it back here all on his own. He's a natural and you want to throw him away."

Hurley stubbornly shook his head.

Stansfield was done arguing with him. "Irene," he said, turning his attention to Kennedy, "what about running him on his own? Break him off from the team. Let Stan and Richards work together."

Hurley didn't hear Kennedy's answer because he was too busy reliving all the various times he'd landed in hot water with a station chief or someone back at Langley. There were too many to even begin counting. That was part of the reason why Stansfield and Charlie White had set him up as a freelancer almost twenty years ago. He'd worn out his welcome at every embassy from Helsinki to Pretoria. Simply put, he wasn't good at following rules, so White and Stansfield had removed him from the system. They had gone to bat for him against Leslie Peterson, that Ivy League prick who wanted to gut the Clandestine

Service and replace it with satellites. He liked to say, "Satellites don't get caught breaking into embassies." Yeah, well, satellites can't seduce an ambassador's secretary into working for the CIA or kill a man. At least not yet anyway. Hurley grudgingly saw the plain truth—that he was an ingrate.

"I can work with him," Hurley announced. "And if I can't, I'll turn him back over to Irene, and she can run him."

Stansfield was speechless for a moment. Kennedy and Lewis were thunderstruck.

"Don't look so surprised," Hurley grumbled. "No one hates these fuckers more than I do."

CHAPTER 28

MOSCOW, RUSSIA

SAYYED stood just inside the glass doors. He looked through the frosted window as a gust of wind whipped up a cloud of dirty snow. It moved like a ghost through the dark night and caused a shiver to run up his already frigid backside. He did not like Moscow, had never liked Moscow, and would never like Moscow. Not in summer and definitely not in winter. His warm Mediterranean blood found it to be perhaps the most inhospitable place he had ever visited. He could practically feel his skin cracking.

With voyeuristic awe, he watched an abnormally round woman waddle by. She was wrapped from head to toe in the dark fur of some animal he couldn't quite pinpoint. Why did these people live here? He would endure a hundred civil wars if he could avoid ever coming here again. A vehicle entered his field of vision from the left. The handler reached out and touched his elbow. He gestured to the waiting SUV and grunted the way big Russian men do.

Sayyed was fairly certain he'd smelled vodka on the man's breath when he'd met him at the gate. That was another thing about these Russians, they all drank too much. Sayyed was not the kind of Muslim who ran around telling everyone what they could or couldn't do. He enjoyed a glass of wine from time to time, but never in excess. They would want him to drink tonight. He knew it. He didn't want to drink and he didn't want to go outside, but he had no choice. He had been summoned, and his bosses in Damascus had eagerly offered him up. With great effort he clutched his long black coat around his neck and stepped into the cold Moscow night.

The bite of the cold wind snatched at his ears and cheeks. His eyes filled with tears, and he could have sworn the hair in his nose had turned to icicles in under a second. He opened his mouth narrowly to catch a breath, but his teeth ached from the subzero temperature, so he lowered his head and shuffled toward the car. He'd learned that the hard way on the last trip. You never ran on a Moscow sidewalk in winter. No matter how cold it was. You shuffled. Half skating. Half walking.

It wasn't until he was in the backseat that he realized he was sitting in a brand-new Range Rover. Apparently capitalism had been very good to the SVR, the KGB's bastard offspring. The man who had fetched him from the gate tossed Sayyed's suitcase in back and jumped in the front passenger seat.

"I take it you don't like the cold?" a voice asked in decent yet accented English.

Sayyed had his head shoved so far down into his jacket that he hadn't noticed the diminutive man sitting next to him. "How do you people live here?"

The man smiled, popped a shiny cigarette case, and offered one to his guest. Sayyed grabbed one. Anything that would provide a scintilla of warmth was to be taken advantage of. After he'd taken a few long drags and had stopped shivering, Sayyed sat back and said, "I do not think we have met before."

"No, we have not. I am Nikolai Shvets."

Sayyed offered his hand, "I am Assef."

"I know," the boyish-looking man replied with a smile.

"I take it you work for Mikhail?"

"Yes. The deputy director is a very busy man. He will be joining us later."

That was fine by Sayyed. Mikhail Ivanov, the deputy director of Directorate S, was not someone he looked forward to dealing with. Sayyed had done everything in his power to get out of the trip, and then to delay it when he was told he had no choice. Two days ago Ivanov had called his boss at the General Security Directorate in Damascus and told General Hammoud he would consider it a personal insult if Assef Sayyed was not in Moscow by week's end. The last the general had heard, the meeting had already been scheduled. He was not a happy man, and he made sure Sayyed understood just how unhappy he was.

"The deputy director is very much looking forward to speaking with you. He has been talking about it for some time."

Sayyed couldn't pretend happiness over seeing the old spider, so he said, "It's too bad you did not travel to Damascus. It is very nice there this time of year."

"I would imagine." The man glanced over his shoulder and looked out the back window. "Your Mediterranean blood is too thin for our Moscow winters."

The boy man made idle conversation as they worked their way around one of the ring roads that circled the big metropolis. Sayyed barely glanced out the window even though it was his habit to be constantly alert for surveillance. It wouldn't matter in this iceberg of a city at this time of night. Streetlights and headlights were amplified by the white snow, blinding him every time he tried to see where they were. This truly was a miserable place. No wonder communism had failed. How could any form of government succeed if everyone was depressed?

They finally stopped in front of a hotel in the heart of old Moscow. A doorman in a massive black fur hat and red wool coat with two rows of shiny brass buttons yanked open the door, and Sayyed felt a blast of cold air hit his ankles. With a second doorman shuffling along with him, he walked through the front door of the hotel and did not stop. Cold air was still whistling through the doors and he wanted to get as far away from it as possible. Eight steps into the lobby he found himself drawn in the direction of heat and then finally spied a roaring fire on the far side of the lobby. He actually smiled and shuffled over, his brain not realizing the lobby was ice free.

"What do you think?"

Sayyed parked his backside directly in front of the flames. He took in the opulent lobby and nodded. It was much nicer than the dump he had stayed in the last time he was here. "Very nice."

"It has just reopened. It is Hotel Baltschug. Very historic. Very expensive." Shvets left out the fact that his boss owned a piece of the hotel. He owned a piece of most things in Moscow these days. At least the nice things. A group of Russian, Austrian, and Swiss businessmen had purchased the hotel just after the collapse and had tried to renovate. After a year of getting turned down for permits and dealing with theft and workers not showing up, one of the Russians went to Ivanov for help. The problems disappeared almost overnight. All they had to do in return was sign over 10 percent of the hotel.

Sayyed did not want to leave the fire, but he had to get ready for dinner. He was finally convinced to move when they informed him that his room had two fireplaces that were both lit and waiting for him. The room was as nice as the lobby, with gilded plaster and hand-painted murals on the ceiling, tapestries on the walls, and a commanding view of the Kremlin and Red Square. It was fit for a pasha.

That was when it hit him. Ivanov the spider never did anything nice unless he wanted something in return, and he was being extremely nice. Sayyed took a steaming-hot shower and wondered what the man was after. He'd heard stories lately that the SVR was worse than the KGB. That once they sank their talons into you, they owned you for the rest of your life. He suddenly longed for the bombed-out rubble of Beirut. There, he was a lion. Here, he could end up being someone's lunch.

CHAPTER 29

SAYYED had just one wool suit. It was black and was worn for special occasions. He was wearing it tonight because it was his warmest suit, and also because to a man like Ivanov, appearances were exceedingly important. He lectured his people about taking care of themselves and was known for firing people who put on too much weight or women who wore too much or too little makeup. Sayyed had carefully trimmed his beard and slicked his black hair back behind his ears. At forty, he was still in decent shape, or at least he wasn't out of shape. The black suit and white shirt and tie helped hide those few extra pounds he'd put on over the last couple of years.

As he walked toward the restaurant he immediately picked out the men from Ivanov's security detail. There were four in the lobby, one by the front door, one by the elevators, and two bracketing the entrance to the restaurant. The boy man suddenly appeared from behind a large plant. His cigarette was hanging from the side of his mouth and he was smiling. Sayyed had been in such a rush to avoid the cold earlier that he had failed to notice that Nikolai was extremely handsome. More pretty, really. In kind of a movie star way. There were none of the usual rough edges that were standard with the lackeys in the Russian state security services. His skin was fair, his eyes a greenish blue, and his hair a light enough brown that he would probably be blond if he lived in a warmer climate.

"Your room is nice . . . Yes?" Shvets asked.

"Very."

Shvets popped his cigarette case with one hand and offered one to his guest. Sayyed took one, as well as a light.

"Director Ivanov is waiting for you at your table. I hope you are hungry."

"Yes. Very much so."

"It is the cold weather. Please follow me."

The restaurant was decorated in deep reds and sparkling golds, most of it in velvet. It was typical Russian. Heavy-handed and desperate to impress. This backwater behemoth knew nothing of understated class. Sayyed was no snob, but he was proud of where he came from. The Ottoman Empire had lasted for more than six hundred years. After fewer than one hundred years these brutes had gone from one of two superpowers to a mob state.

A haze of blue-gray smoke hung in the air. Every table was occupied. There were easily several hundred people in the restaurant, and they all appeared to be in various states of inebriation. It occurred to Sayyed, for the first time, that the Russians were loud people. Especially when they laughed. Sayyed didn't recognize any faces, but he guessed they were all very important. That was the Russian way. Even during the height of the great workers' paradise, the ruling elite had lived an opulent life, separate from the workers. They enjoyed luxuries that the little people never dreamed of.

Two towering men stood watch near a booth in the back corner. Red velvet curtains were pulled open and fastened with tasseled ropes to marble columns. Sayyed glimpsed Ivanov sitting between two young beauties. The man was nearing sixty and was showing no signs of slowing down. He was a consumer of all things that interested him. In a way he was the perfect man to run an intelligence service, assuming his interests were in line with those of the state.

Sayyed had been told that Ivanov's power had grown significantly in recent years. In the days of the Politburo, the black market was tolerated but never flaunted. During the transfer from centrally controlled markets and government plans to pseudocapitalism, no one was better positioned to take advantage of the new wealth than the men at the KGB. They had the guns, the enforcers, and the spycraft to break, blackmail, or frame any man who did not welcome them to the buffet. And Ivanov had an insatiable appetite.

Ivanov saw him coming and yelled his name. He

tried to stand but was stuck between the two girls, so he gave up and sat back down. "Assef, it is good to see you." The Russian threw out a large hand with rings on the forefinger and pinky.

"And you, too, Mikhail," Sayyed lied. He reached across the table and clasped Ivanov's hand.

"If you had turned me down one more time I was going to send my men after you," Ivanov said with a hearty laugh, although his eyes weren't smiling.

Sayyed laughed and tried to play along. The comment was without a doubt meant for him to remember. And keep remembering every time Ivanov called on him. Sayyed so badly wanted this evening to end, and it had only just begun.

Ivanov ordered an expensive bottle of Bordeaux and introduced Sayyed to the girls. The blonde one was Alisa and the redhead was Svetlana. The redhead was suddenly very interested in the spy from Syria. That was how Ivanov had introduced him—as a spy, of all things. The Russians might have found the moniker intriguing, but to Sayyed it was an insult, one of many he was sure he would be forced to endure on this cold winter evening.

More wine was ordered, along with plate after plate of food. Sayyed was full by the time the main course was served. Ivanov steered the conversation away from anything serious, and Svetlana steered her hands toward Sayyed's groin. Sayyed had no illusions about his ability to woo women. He was handsome enough, but not enough to garner the attention of a twenty-year-old runway model. Ivanov had undoubtedly ordered her to take care of him.

Sayyed wondered if she would be beaten after he turned her down.

When the plates were cleared, Ivanov nudged Alisa out of the booth and ordered Svetlana to follow. He told the girls to go to the bar and order dessert. As they walked away, he slapped each girl on the ass. They turned around, one giving him a dirty look, the other pouting. Ivanov laughed at them and watched them hold hands all the way to the bar, and then as if a switch had been flicked, he turned all business. After whispering something in one of his bodyguards' ears, he plopped back into the booth and moved around so that he was sitting a mere foot from Sayyed. The drapes were pulled shut, and they were alone.

"You have been avoiding me."

He'd said it with a crooked smile, but that menacing glint in his eye was back. Sayyed deflected by saying, "I do not enjoy travel, and the cold weather is something my body is not used to. I meant no offense."

"Ah . . . I know what you mean. In the summer I find Damascus to be unbearable. But don't worry, I wasn't offended," Ivanov said, lying to himself more than Sayyed. "I just wish it hadn't taken this long. We have many important things to discuss."

"Yes, I know," Sayyed said, trying to be agreeable.

Ivanov took a gulp of wine and asked, "How long have we known each other?"

"A long time," Sayyed said, looking into his own glass. "Twelve years, I think."

"Thirteen, actually. And we have fucked with the Americans like no one else." Ivanov made a fist and shook it. "Every time they have tried to stick their nose in your business, we have sent them running away like a scared dog."

"That is true," Sayyed said, making no mention of all the times the Russians had stuck their long snouts into his business.

"And now they are back again."

Sayyed was still looking at the expensive French wine in his glass. He could feel Ivanov watching him with intensity. He shrugged and said, "Not really."

"That is not what I have heard."

"What have you heard?"

"I have heard you captured one of Langley's deep-cover operatives."

Sayyed's mind was swimming with thoughts of murder. The idiots in Damascus, no doubt, had passed the information to the Russian. Did anyone in his government know how to keep a secret? Knowing he was trapped, he said, "We caught one of them snooping around. I'm not sure he was an agent of any particular importance."

Ivanov smiled. "I think you are being modest."

Sayyed didn't know how to answer so he took a drink of wine.

"I am told this man worked in their Directorate of Operations. That he reported directly to Deputy Director Stansfield. That he worked in Berlin and Moscow for a time."

Someone in Damascus really did have a big mouth. "As you know from experience, these men are trained to lie. I cannot say with any certainty that his claims are truthful."

"They usually try to understate their importance, not overstate it."

That was true. "The important thing is that we have bloodied them yet again, and as you know, they do not have the stomach for this kind of thing."

Ivanov gave him a dubious look. "I'm not so sure these days."

Sayyed was. "Do not worry yourself with such little fish."

"This might be a bigger fish than you think," Ivanov said, with a hint of inside knowledge.

"What have you heard?"

"Things . . . rumors here and there. Nothing concrete, but I've been in this business long enough to smell a rat."

"What things?"

"Hamdi Sharif."

Sayyed thought of the recently deceased arms dealer. "Yes. I knew him well."

"Who do you think killed him?"

Sayyed had heard two rumors. "Mossad more than likely, but there was something else I picked up."

"What?"

Sayyed was not afraid to repeat the rumor. A man like Ivanov would take it as a compliment. "That he was stealing from you and you had him killed."

Ivanov looked at him with unblinking focus, but did not respond.

"If that was the case," Sayyed said, "then that was your right."

Ivanov shook his head. "If he was stealing from me I would have known, and I would have killed him. But he was not stealing from me."

"So it was the Jews."

"No . . . I don't think so."

"Who then?"

Ivanov sat brooding for a half minute and finally said, "I would like to speak to the American rat you are keeping in that basement in Beirut."

He had not told a soul in Damascus where he was keeping the CIA man, which meant either that Ivanov had obtained the information from one of Sayyed's supposed allies or that it was a good guess. Whichever was the case, he would need to move the American as soon as he got back. "You are more than welcome to speak to him. You are welcome in Beirut anytime. You know that."

Ivanov began shaking his head at the mention of Beirut. "I cannot. There are far too many things happening here in Moscow. Things that need my urgent attention."

Sayyed tried to deflect by saying, "So you think the Americans are trying to get back in the game?"

"I don't think so, I know so."

Sayyed looked skeptical. "How?"

"Because Thomas Stansfield is finally in charge of their clandestine activities."

"You think one man is capable of turning that mess around? They don't have the stomach to get back into Lebanon. This man I caught . . ."

Ivanov pounded his fist on the table, cutting him off. "Let me tell you something about Thomas Stansfield. I had to go up against him early in my career. The man plots on more levels than you or I are capable of comprehending. He is a master of deception operations. He gets you running around like a dog chasing your tail." Ivanov circled his hand around his wineglass faster and faster. "You become obsessed with traitors in your midst and you forget to do your job. You see shadows everywhere you turn, and you become completely defensive, and that is just one facet of the man. There is another side, where he is more Russian than American."

Sayyed had no idea what he meant. "More Russian than American?"

"He is the last of a breed of Americans who knew how to be every bit as dirty as the dirtiest enemy. Don't let his grandfatherly image deceive you. The man is a street fighter with a big set of Russian balls."

Sayyed wasn't sure why the man's balls were Russian. Beyond that, he thought Ivanov was overreacting. "The Americans haven't bitten back in years," Sayyed scoffed.

"I know, and that was because we had the CIA in a box and Stansfield didn't have the power. But he is in charge of their clandestine service now, and I'm telling you he is going to stick his nose in our business, and we can't allow that to happen. Trust me. If he gets so much as a toehold, we will be in for the fight of our lives."

Sayyed still wasn't convinced.

Ivanov leaned forward, then grabbed the Syrian's hand. "I am asking you this one time. I will only ask it once. Will you give me the American, so I can find out what he knows? I know your Iranian friends want him, but I will make sure you are compensated."

This was why Sayyed did not want to come to this godless frozen city. There was nothing in it for him, especially since he was not done dissecting the mind of Agent John Cummins. Unfortunately, there was no way out. If he did not bend to Ivanov's wishes, he might not make it out of the country in one piece. With a heavy sigh he told Ivanov that he could have the American.

CHAPTER 30

HAMBURG, GERMANY

THE Hamburg operation was significant for a number of reasons, not the least of which was that certain people began to take notice. A single murder can be an accident or an aberration. Two murders in as many weeks, separated by time, but connected by relationships, is a tough one to swallow for people whose job it is to be paranoid. The second reason it was significant was that Rapp finally realized Stan Hurley was extremely good at what he did. Hurley had given them five days to get their affairs in order. They were going on the road and would not be coming back to the States for several months.

The old clandestine officer announced with a gleam in his eye, "We've been kicked out of the office by management. They don't want to see us back in Washington until we have some results to show for all the money and time that's been spent on your sorry asses."

Rapp was not given all the details, but he got the distinct impression that Langley was upset about something. Hurley's attitude had changed even before they left the States. They were to engage the enemy and make them bleed, and the prospect of finally getting back in the game had transformed Hurley. This time Rapp and Richards went in together. Or at least their flights arrived the same afternoon. Rapp arrived second. He saw Richards waiting for him on the other side of Customs. Rapp was carrying an American passport on this trip, and he handed it to a nice-looking older gentleman, who flipped through the pages with German efficiency. The backpack, jeans, and beat-up wool coat must have been enough to tell the man he was not here on business, because he didn't ask that standard question, "business or pleasure." He applied the proper stamps and slid the passport back. Not a glance or a question. Rapp laughed to himself. If only it was always this easy.

The two men shook hands and made their way to ground transportation, where they took a cab to the harbor promenade or Landungsbrücken, as it was known to the locals. A big cruise ship was coming into port. Tourists lined the sidewalk gawking at the massive ship that looked completely out of place so close to all the old brick buildings. Rapp and Richards did not gawk. They were on the move toward the warehouse district, where Hurley was waiting for them.

They passed a prostitute working the riverfront. Richards turned to Rapp and said, "Isn't this where the Beatles got their start?"

Rapp cracked a small smile. He liked Richards. The guy was quirky in a normal way. They were in Hamburg to kill a man and Richards wanted to talk about the Beatles. "Never heard that," Rapp said.

"Pretty sure they did. They played some strip club for something like two months straight." Rapp didn't say anything. "I'd like to see it while we're here."

Rapp cocked his head and gave Richards a long look before he couldn't help himself and started laughing.

"What?" Richards asked.

Rapp lowered his voice and said, "We're here to kill a man, and you want to go hang out at some strip club where the Beatles played thirty years ago?"

"What's wrong with that? That we do what we do for a living doesn't mean we can't do what normal people do?"

Richards had a much easier time transitioning between their two worlds. "You have a point. I can't wait to see the look on Stan's face when you ask him."

"Ha . . . you watch. If it involves booze and strippers, my bet is he's all in."

"You're probably right."

The flat was located in one of the hundred-year-old warehouses that had been converted into condominiums near the river. It was damp and cold. A lot like London. Hurley informed them that the majority of the units in the building were as yet unsold. The one they were using was owned by an American company that had purchased it as an executive apartment. Rapp didn't concern himself with certain details beyond the target, but Richards was more curious. He tried to find out which American company the unit belonged to and if it was a former spook who let them use it. Hurley said if there was something he needed to know he'd tell him. "Otherwise . . . don't worry about it."

Rapp and Hurley hadn't exactly made peace. It was more of a truce. After the night he'd met George, or whatever his real name was, Rapp, Richards, and Hurley had gone back down to the lake house to begin prepping for the Hamburg operation. Hurley from time to time still looked at Rapp as if he were mentally retarded, but he had cut back on his yelling and cussing. Rapp took this as a sign of détente.

After five days Hurley asked Rapp to take a walk. "Have you gone over the last op in your head?"

"You mean Istanbul?"

"How many ops have you been on?" Hurley asked him with a wake-up expression on his face.

"Sorry," Rapp said. "Yeah . . . I've thought about it."

"Anything you would have done different?"

Rapp stared at the ground while they walked. "I'm not sure I know what you mean."

"The fact that you acted on your own is behind us. I already told you that. Part of my job is to make sure you get better. What I'm asking you is a tactical question. When you look back on what happened in the park that morning, once you decided to kill him, is there anything that you would have done different?"

"I don't know," Rapp answered honestly. "It all just kind of happened."

Hurley nodded, having been there before. "That's good and bad, kid. It might be that you're a natural at this. Ice in your veins, that kind of shit. Or . . . you got lucky. Only time will tell, but there's one thing you did that jumps out as being pretty stupid."

"What's that?" Rapp asked. Hurley had his full attention.

"I read the police report."

Rapp didn't know why he was surprised, but he was.

"The shot to the heart . . . it was point-blank. Literally. The report was conclusive. The muzzle of the weapon was in direct contact with Sharif's coat."

Rapp nodded. He was there. He remembered it well.

"Why would you do that?"

"Because I wanted to kill him."

Hurley stopped and faced him. "Kid, I've seen you shoot. You're not as good as me, but you're damn good and you keep getting better. You don't think you could have popped him from say ten feet?"

Rapp didn't answer.

"Why did you sit down next to him?"

"I'm not sure."

"Bullshit," Hurley said with a smile. "You allowed it to get personal, didn't you?"

Rapp thought back to that morning, not even a week ago. The feeling came back. That split-second decision to sit next to Sharif so he could look into his eyes. He slowly nodded. "Yeah . . . I guess I did."

Hurley's jaw tightened while he processed the admission. "I'm not going to stand here and tell you there haven't been times . . . times that I took a certain amount of joy in sending some of these scumbags to paradise . . . but you have to be really careful. Pick the right environment. Never in public like you did. He could have had a gun, somebody could have seen you sitting next to him . . . a lot of things could have gone wrong."

"I know."

"Remember, in public, the key is to look natural. That's why I showed you the shoulder holster technique. That's why we practice it. You look at your watch and no one thinks twice about it. You're a guy checking the time. You sit down on a park bench that close to another guy and someone might notice. Just enough to cause him to look twice, and that's all it might take. The next thing you know the carabinieri are chasing you down the street shooting at you." Hurley gave him a dead-serious look. "Trust me, I've been there." Hurley shuddered at the memory.

"What?" Rapp asked.

"You ever been to Venice?"

"Yeah."

"The canals." Hurley made a diving motion with his hands.

"You dove into one of those canals?" Rapp asked while recalling their putrid shade of green.

"And this was thirty years ago. They're a lot cleaner now than they were back then."

The condo was raw exposed brick with heavy timber beams secured to each other by sturdy iron brackets with big bolts. The floors were wide plank, more than likely pine, stained light to add a little brightness in contrast to the dark mud-red bricks. The furniture was utilitarian. Grays and blues. Wood and metal frames. Long sleek lines and the kind of fabrics that could be cleaned. Pure bachelor efficiency. It was a corner unit, so it had two small balconies, one off the master bedroom and another off the living room. There was a second bedroom and a loft space with a desk and pullout couch. When they arrived Hurley had everything prepared.

The dining-room table was covered with a sheet. Hurley carefully pulled it back to reveal what he'd pieced together in three short days. The target was a banker by the name of Hans Dorfman. He looked innocent enough, but then again, to Rapp, most bankers did. Dorfman's crime, as Hurley stated it, was that he'd decided to get into bed with the wrong people.

"You're probably wondering," Hurley asked, "why a well-educated man, who was raised a Christian, would decide to help a bunch of Islamic whack jobs wage terrorism."

Richards looked down at a black-and-white photo of the sixty-three-year-old banker and said, "Yep."

"Well, officially it's none of your goddamn business. When we're given an assignment it's not our place to question . . . right?"

Both Rapp and Richards gave halfhearted nods.

"Wrong," Hurley said. "I don't care what anyone tells you, HQ can fuck up and they can fuck up big-time. Beyond that, you'll run into the occasional yahoo who doesn't have a clue how things work in the real world. When you get a kill assignment, you'd better question it, and you'd better be damn careful. We don't do collateral damage. Women and children are strictly off limits."

Rapp had heard this countless times from Hurley and the other instructors. "But people make mistakes."

"They do," he agreed, "and the more difficult the job, the greater the chance that you'll make a mistake, but if you want to make it out of this one day with your soul intact, follow my advice on this. Question the assignments they give you. We're not blind—or robots."

Richards was still looking at the photo of the banker. "Stan, are you trying to tell us this guy isn't guilty?"

"This guy?" Hurley waved his right hand from one side of the table to the other. "Hell no. This Nazi piece of shit is guilty as hell. In fact, guys like this piss me off more than the ones who shoot back. This prick lives in his fancy house, takes two months off every year, goes to the nicest places, and sleeps like a fucking baby every night. He thinks it's no big deal that he helps these scumbags move their money around. No," he shook his head, "this is one of those times when I will enjoy pulling the trigger."

CHAPTER 31

HURLEY explained to them that the process wasn't so much about finding the best option as it was eliminating the bad ones. That is, if you had the time to go through all the alternatives. After two days together, Hurley made the decision and they both agreed. Sunday night was the perfect time to make their move, and it would happen at the house. It was located thirty-five minutes outside of Hamburg, a nice wooded one-acre lot. Rapp was pretty sure Hurley had known from the get-go that this would be the appointed hour, but he wanted some pushback. He wanted Rapp and Richards to tear into his plans and make sure there wasn't a better time to go after Dorfman. For two days that's pretty much all Rapp and Richards did.

For Rapp, one of the more enlightening exchanges happened when he asked the salty Hurley, "What about the dogs?"

"Dogs," Hurley said with a devilish smile, "are a double-edged sword. Take this fuck stick, for example." Hurley pointed to Dorfman's black-and-white photograph. Hurley had taken a black marker and drawn a Hitler mustache on him the night before. "He's an anal-retentive Nazi prick if I've ever seen one. Wants complete order in his life, so he gets two poodles . . . why?" He looked at Rapp and Richards.

"Because they don't shed," Richards answered.

"Exactly. Hans is a neat freak. Wants everything just so . . . wakes up the same time Monday through Friday, and Saturdays and Sundays he allows himself one extra hour of sack time. He thinks he's too smart for the religion his parents raised him on, so on Sundays instead of going to church, he reads two or three newspapers, studies his Value Lines or whatever it is that a German banker studies, and he takes his dogs for a walk along the river and comes back and takes a nap. He has pot roast, mashed potatoes, and green beans for dinner, watches some crappy TV on the couch, and then lets the dogs out one last time at ten o'clock and then it's lights out."

Richards looked at the surveillance info. "How do you know all these details? I don't see any of it here."

Hurley smiled. "This isn't my first banker."

Rapp set that thought aside for a second and asked, "But what about the dogs?"

"Oh, yeah. The dogs. The dogs run the show. They need to be let out four times a day. Every morning at seven on the dot, a couple more times during the day, and then one more time before they turn in. What does he have to do every time before he lets them out?"

"Turn the alarm off," Rapp answered.

"You two see any alarms at the lake house?"

"No," Rapp answered.

"That's because they can make you lazy. You ever see me lock my hounds up?"

"No."

"What good does a dog do you if he's locked in his kennel?"

"If he's a guard dog, not much."

"That's right." Hurley looked at Rapp and said, "I bet I can guess your next question. You think we should take him while he's walking the dogs by the river?"

"The thought occurred to me."

"There's three reasons why I would prefer to avoid that option. The first is that it's harder to control things in a public setting. Not to say we couldn't do it. We might get lucky and have no witnesses like you did in Istanbul, but that can't be guaranteed. But two and three are why the park won't work. I need to talk to him and a public park is hardly the place for the kind of conversation we're going to have."

This came as a complete surprise to Rapp and Richards. Richards asked, "Why?"

"I'll explain it later."

"What's the third reason?" Rapp asked.

"We can't let anyone know he's dead before 9:00 A.M. Monday."

"Why?" Richards asked.

Rapp answered for him. "He'll tell us when we're done."

The Dorfman file was shredded and burned late Saturday night. By Sunday morning the ashes were cool enough that they could be scooped into a bag and thrown down the garbage chute. They spent two hours that afternoon sanitizing the condo. If they had to come back they could, but Hurley wanted to avoid doing so if possible. At eight in the evening they packed the last of the gear into the trunk of the rented four-door Mercedes sedan and left.

Rapp was the wheel man for the evening. Hurley and Richards were going in. It occurred to him that he was being punished for taking the initiative in Istanbul, but what could he say? Someone had to stay with the car. On the drive down the E22 Hurley went over the plan one last time. Every minute or so, he threw a question at Rapp or Richards asking them how they would react if this or that thing did not go as planned. Traffic was almost nonexistent, so they made it in just thirty minutes.

It was a dark, cold, windy night with temperatures expected to dip near freezing. They were all dressed in jeans and dark coats. Hurley and Richards also had black watch caps on their heads. The neighbor behind Dorfman was a widow with cats, but no dogs. The plan was to access his property from her backyard. At nine they did a final radio check and then at nine-fifteen Rapp turned the silver Mercedes onto the winding country road. The dome light was set to off. Rapp downshifted and coasted to a near stop several hundred feet from the widower's house. Richards and Hurley stepped from the slowly moving vehicle, carefully nudged their doors closed, and then disappeared into the trees. Rapp continued. A little less than a minute later he turned onto Dorfman's street and did a slow drive-by. The house was set back from the street about seventy-five feet. The front of the house was dark, but faint lights could be seen beyond what they knew was the living room and dining room.

Rapp pressed the transmit button on the secure Motorola radio, "All's clear up front."

Hurley and Richards found their way through the overgrown property of Dorfman's neighbor with relative ease. This was not Hurley's first trip, and he didn't feel the slightest bit guilty for not telling the new recruits. They did not need to know everything. He had personally put together the surveillance package on Dorfman eight months earlier. The stuff about the dogs he knew from many years of experience, and as far as bankers being anal retentive, it was a fairly accurate statement. The stuff about Dorfman having left the church that his parents raised him in and being a Nazi prick, he'd learned by keeping an eye on the man for close to two years.

To run an effective organization you need money. Hurley and Kennedy had been working overtime trying to map out how these various groups moved their money around the globe, and they had decided Dorfman was the key. In this, the ultimate asymmetric war, where they could not use even a fraction of the might of the United States military, they needed to get creative. If they couldn't openly bomb the terrorist training camps in the Bekaa Valley, then maybe there was another way to hurt them.

Hurley and Richards took up position near the back door at nine-thirty. If they had missed him somehow, Hurley was prepared to cut the phone line and break in. That option presented two problems, however. If he busted the door in, the security system would be tripped, and although an alarm would not be received at the monitoring station, the house's siren would begin to wail and would likely arouse the attention of one of the neighbors. Dorfman also owned a pistol, a shotgun, and a rifle. That Dorfman might react quickly enough to stop the intruders was unlikely, but Hurley didn't like unlikely.

The back light, above the kitchen door, was turned on at ten-oh-one. Hurley was crouched closest to the door on one knee and Richards was right behind him. From where he was positioned, Hurley could hear the chimes on the keypad as the digits were entered. The door opened, and the two standard poodles bounded out the door and onto the patio. Hurley had to trust Richards to do his job and stay focused on his. He sprang from his position and put his shoulder into the door before it could be closed. He hit it with enough force that it bounced back and hit an unsuspecting Dorfman in the face.

Over his shoulder he heard the dogs begin to growl. He grabbed the door by the edge and, looking through the glass, came face-to-face with a stunned Dorfman. The growling had turned to barking and Hurley resisted the urge to turn around to see how close they were to taking a bite out of his ass. Instead he pulled the door toward him and then smashed it into Dorfman's face. There was a scramble of nails and paws on the brick patio and then the welcome sound of compressed air forcing a projectile down a muzzle. One shot and then a second, each followed by short yelps and then some whimpering. Hurley saw the light switches to his left. There were three of them. He raked his silencer down the wall, knocking all three into the off position and relegating them to semidarkness. Quickly, he slid through the door, partially closed it, and stuffed the silencer into the shocked and open mouth of Dorfman.

CHAPTER 32

THE Mercedes was the same color and model as the one Dorfman drove. Rapp cruised the neighborhood listening to Hurley and Richards with one ear and the police scanner with the other. His German was nonexistent, but as Hurley had pointed out, the only thing he needed to listen for was a car being dispatched to Dorfman's address. No car was dispatched, so Rapp pulled the rented Mercedes into the driveway and turned around in the small car park so it was facing out. Hurley reasoned that if any of the neighbors saw the car they would assume it was Herr Dorfman's.

Rapp walked around the side of the house to the backyard and helped Richards carry the second poodle down to the basement. A small dart with red fins was still stuck in the animal's rib cage. It rose and fell with the animal's heavy breathing. Rapp had been tempted to say something to Hurley two days earlier when he informed them that they were going to use a tranquilizer gun to take out the dogs, but he kept his mouth shut. He knew that Hurley loved his dogs, but still, they were going to kill a man tonight. From a big-picture standpoint, it didn't make a lot of sense to him. Hurley's way was going to take a little more effort and would not silence the dogs as quickly. Hurley knew what Rapp was thinking and noted that the surveillance report said that the dogs usually barked when they were let out of the house. Especially at night. It wasn't as if they were storming a terrorist stronghold. It was just a German couple in their fifties, so Rapp kept his tactical opinion to himself.

Rapp was now looking down at one of the Germans. Frau Dorfman was blindfolded, gagged, hog-tied, and shivering from fright. He glanced at the knots Richards had made. They were well done. Her wrists and ankles were bound and attached with a length of rope. The only reason Rapp knew anything about them was that his little brother had been fascinated by many things as a child, but knots and magic were the two that became his passion. After their father died, Rapp saw it as his duty to take an interest in Steven's various hobbies, even if they weren't his.

The basement had been finished as a rec room with a bar and a small pool table. Richards had been nice enough to deposit the big German woman on an area rug. Rapp saw a blanket on the back of the couch. He grabbed it and paused. On the wall behind the couch was a poster-sized photo of Dorfman and his two dogs. He was holding a trophy and the two dogs were licking his face. Rapp covered the woman with the blanket. It was going to be a long night for her, and an even longer morning, but unlike her husband, she would live. Rapp grabbed the phone next to the couch and yanked the cord from the wall. He quickly coiled the cord around the phone as Richards reappeared from the utility room flashing him the all-clear sign. They were not to speak a word in front of the woman. Rapp climbed the stairs to the first floor, turned off the basement lights, and closed the door.

Per the plan, all of the lights had been turned off on the main floor except for the single light over the kitchen sink, as was the Dorfmans' habit upon going to bed. Rapp walked through the formal living room, past Richards, who was keeping an eye on the front of the house. The French doors that led to the study were cracked an inch. Rapp pulled his black mask down to cover his face, entered, and closed the door behind him. Dorfman was on the floor in his light blue pajamas. His comb-over hair was all askew and his nose was bleeding. A leather reading chair had been tossed to the side and the rug pulled back to reveal a floor safe.

Dorfman looked up at Rapp with tears in his eyes. Again, Rapp didn't understand German beyond a hundred-odd words, but he could tell the whimpering idiot was asking about his dogs and not his wife. Rapp looked around the office and counted no fewer than ten photos of his dogs. There was one five-by-seven of the wife and two kids that had to be fifteen years old. Rapp counted seven trophies and a dozen-plus ribbons.

Dorfman was still desperately asking about his "Hunde." Rapp raised his silenced Beretta and said, "Shut up!"

Hurley squatted down on his haunches and tapped the dial of the safe with the tip of his silencer. His German was perfect. He ordered Dorfman to open the safe. Dorfman closed his eyes and shook his head. They spoke for another twenty seconds, and still he refused. Hurley looked up at Rapp and said, "Go get his wife."

Rapp shook his head.

Hurley frowned.

"Let me take a shot at this. What do you say I grab one of your dogs and put a bullet in his head?" Rapp saw the flicker of recognition in the banker's eyes. "That's right, you idiot. I'm going to get one of your dogs and bring him up here." Rapp reached into his coat and pulled out a tactical knife. He bent over and stuck the tip in front of Dorfman's face. "I'll do you one better. I'm going to lay your *hund* at your feet and then I'm going to cut out one of his eyes and force-feed it to you."

"*Nein . . . nein.*" Dorfman looked truly frightened.

"If you don't open the safe, I'm going to start with your pooch's eyes, and then his tongue, and then his nose, and then his ears, and if you still haven't opened it by then, I'm going to shove all of it down your throat, and then I'll start in on the second dog, and if that doesn't get you to do it, then I'll start in on you."

Dorfman closed his eyes as tight as he could and shook his head in defiance.

Patiently waiting for Dorfman to decide to open the safe wasn't in the cards. Rapp flipped the knife up in the air and caught it, reversing his hold. He then slammed the tip of it down into Dorfman's thigh. The banker's entire body went rigid with pain and he opened his mouth to scream. Hurley gave him a quick backhanded chop to the throat, successfully choking off the shriek of agony.

Ten seconds passed before Dorfman was calm enough to talk to. "Last chance. Open the safe," Rapp said.

Dorfman was now slobbering, muttering something, and shaking his head.

"Fine," Rapp said as he moved to the door. "We'll do it your way." Rapp went back into the basement, turned on the light, and stood over the two poodles and the wife. He wasn't sure which one to grab, so he picked the one on the left. Rapp cradled it in his arms and went back to the office. Richards opened the door for him. Rapp gently laid the pooch at his master's feet. The sight of his precious dog in the arms of the masked maniac sent Dorfman into a near-apoplectic state. Hurley slapped him hard and once again pointed at the safe. At least this time Dorfman didn't shake his head.

Rapp retrieved his knife and held the tip in front of the dog's face. "Left eye or right eye? You choose."

Dorfman was now bawling like a child, reaching out for his dog.

Rapp wasn't sure he had the stomach for this, but what the hell else were they going to do? He glanced at Hurley, whose dark eyes, alert with uncertainty, framed by his ski mask, seemed to be pleading with him to stop. Rapp got the impression that Hurley would rather torture the banker than harm the dog. Rapp cradled the dog's head in his arms and slowly started moving the blade toward the poodle's left eye. He was within a centimeter of piercing the outer layer when Dorfman finally relented. He literally threw himself onto the safe and began spinning the dial. Rapp waited until he'd entered the correct combination and then released the dog. Dorfman crawled to his dog and pulled him in, kissing him on the snout and the top of his head.

"What the fuck," Rapp muttered to himself, and then asked Dorfman, "You care more about that damn dog than you do your wife . . . don't you?" Dorfman either didn't hear him or chose to ignore the question. Rapp looked at Hurley, who was emptying the contents of the safe.

"I told you," Hurley said as he pulled out three objects and held them up for Rapp to see. "An SS dagger and insignia. Nazi prick."

"A poodle-loving Nazi who helps terrorists. Great." Rapp started to raise his gun but stopped. "Is it in there?"

Hurley held up some files, computer disks, and an external hard drive. "I think so." He leafed through the files quickly. "Yep . . . it's all here. Jackpot!"

"Dorfman," Rapp said as he pointed his gun at the banker's head. "I bet if those damn terrorists were running around killing dogs you would have thought twice about helping them."

"Please," Dorfman said, "I am just a businessman."

"Who helps terrorists move their money around so they can target and kill innocent civilians."

"I know nothing of such things."

"You're a liar."

"That's for certain," Hurley said as he stood with the bag full of files and disks. He placed the rug back over the closed safe and while moving the chair back said, "You have their names, their accounts." Hurley shook the bag. "You knew exactly who you were dealing with."

"I was doing my job . . . for the bank."

"Like a good Nazi." Hurley gave him a big smile and pointed the Beretta at Dorfman's head. "And I'm only doing my job." Hurley squeezed the trigger and sent a single bullet into Dorfman's brain. The man fell back against the hardwood floor with a thump that was louder than the gunshot. A puddle of blood began to seep out in all directions. Hurley looked at Rapp and said, "Let's get the fuck out of here. We need to be in Zurich by sunrise."

"What's in Zurich?"

"Same thing that's always in Zurich . . . money and assholes."

CHAPTER 33

MOSCOW, RUSSIA

IVANOV carefully lowered himself into his chair at SVR headquarters in the Yasenevo District of Moscow. Last night had been a wild one. He had closed a very lucrative business deal. A group of foreign investors were looking to pick up some natural gas contracts and were willing to give Ivanov a seven-figure retainer and a nice piece of the action if he could guarantee the acquisition. Now all Ivanov had to do was talk some sense into one of his countrymen who had already made a nice profit on the fields. And if he couldn't talk some sense into him he would have Shvets and a crew of his loyal officers pay the man a call and make him an offer he couldn't refuse. Ivanov smiled as he thought of his favorite movie, *The Godfather*. He would very much like to meet Francis Ford Coppola someday. The man had captured the essence of power perfectly.

That was what Russia was all about in the wake

of the collapse of the Soviet Union. The two systems were not, at the end of the day, all that different from each other. Both were corrupt to the core, and both systems served to line the pockets of the powerful. Under the old Soviet system, the inefficiencies were ridiculous. People who had no business holding a position of authority did so often, and their inability to make smart decisions doomed the communist experiment from the start. There was no motivation for the talented to rise to the top. In fact, it could be said that there was the opposite motivation. If you dared criticize the foolish systems put into place by some imbecile who held a post because he was the brother-in-law of an important official, you were more likely than not to get your meager pay cut. Everyone wallowed in that subaverage world except the lucky few.

Today things were dynamic. Money was to be made everywhere, and lots of it. Start-up companies were popping up at an incredible rate and foreign investors were lining up to get into the game. The game, though, was a treacherous one. Remnants of the Soviet system were still in place, sucking off the system and causing a huge drain on the efficiency of the new economy. And then there were the corrupt courts, police, and security services. It was *The Godfather,* the Wild West, and 1920s gangster America all rolled into one.

These bankers and businessmen could either wallow in that inefficiency and red tape for months, costing them valuable time and money, or they could come to Ivanov and he could make their problems go away. Unlike the army of Jew lawyers who had descended on the city, who claimed they knew what they were doing, Ivanov could actually follow through on those claims and deliver real results to his new partners. And they were always partners. Depending on the deal, Ivanov would sometimes lower his fee, but never his percentage. The 10 percent ownership stake was non-negotiable.

He was not alone in this, and that was yet another parallel to the Academy Award–winning movie. There were others in Moscow and across the vast country who were doing the same thing, although, Ivanov would argue, not as well. Ivanov was not shy about touting the importance of his role in this brave new world, and defended it as a natural extension of his state security job. Someone needed to keep track of all these foreign investors and make sure they weren't stealing the Motherland's natural resources. After all, he was far more deserving of the profits than some twenty-five-year-old business-school graduate. At least that was what he told himself.

Shvets entered the office looking far too rested and handsome, which had the effect of worsening Ivanov's mood.

"Good morning, sir." Shvets remained standing. He knew better than to take a seat unless he was ordered.

"Get me some water," Ivanov grumbled.

While Shvets poured a glass he asked, "You look like you stayed out all night. Would you like some aspirin as well?"

"Yes." He snapped his long tanned fingers to spur his assistant to move faster. He could feel his headache passing from one temple to the other and then swinging back, as if he were being scanned by an irritating beam. He downed the three pills and the water. For a split second he thought of adding vodka. It would definitely help with the headache, but it was too early to surrender. Shvets and the new breed would take it as a sign of weakness.

"I heard you got them to agree in principle to the partnership."

"Yes," Ivanov moaned.

"Would you like me to have Maxim bring the contracts over?"

"Yes . . . and so, I want to know when you are leaving for Beirut and who you're bringing with you."

"Tomorrow, and I'm bringing Alexei and Ivan."

Ivanov thought about that. Alexei and Ivan were two of his best. Former Spetsnaz, they'd fought with valor and distinction in Afghanistan but had gotten in trouble when their regiment's political officer had turned up with his throat cut one morning. They had more than likely done it. Political officers were notorious for being assholes, and in those final days of the USSR more than a few of them simply disappeared. Ivanov was always looking for men who were good with their hands, and these two were better than good. "Why Alexei and Ivan?"

"Because they're from Georgia and they look like they could be Lebanese."

That was true, but Ivanov didn't like having his two best gunmen leaving his side. In Moscow these days, the only thing you could count on was that sooner or later someone would try to take you out. It was just like the American mobsters. The vision of Sonny Corleone being mercilessly gunned down at the tollbooth, betrayed by his own brother-in-law, the snake, sent chills down Ivanov's back. He shuddered and then decided he would keep Alexei and Ivanov close. They were his Luca Brasi times two. "Take Oleg and Yakov."

Shvets frowned.

"Why can't you just follow my orders?"

In a calm voice, Shvets said, "When have I once failed to follow your orders?"

"You know what I mean. Your face. I am in no mood for it this morning." Ivanov lowered his big head into his hands and groaned.

"I might as well go by myself."

"That is a brilliant idea. Travel to the kidnapping capital of the Mediterranean by yourself so they can snatch you off the street and hold you for ransom. Brilliant!"

"Is it my fault that you stay out drinking and screwing until sunrise?"

"Don't start."

"I am half your age, and I can't keep up with you."

"You are half my size, too, so we're even."

"You need to slow down or there will be problems."

Ivanov's head snapped up. "Is that a threat?"

"No," Shvets said, shaking his head, with a pathetic disappointment in his boss. *Why must my loyalty always be questioned?* "I am talking about your health. You need to take some time off. Go someplace warm. Maybe come to Beirut with me."

"Beirut is a hellhole. It was once a great place . . . not anymore. You will see."

"I heard it's coming back."

"Ha," Ivanov laughed. "Not the part where you'll be going. The famous Green Line looks like Leningrad in 1941. It's a bombed-out shell. Our friends are trying to reconstitute it before the Christians take it over. It is not a nice place."

Before Shvets could respond there was a knock on the office door. It was Pavel Sokoll, one of Ivanov's deputies, who worked exclusively on state security financial matters. And if his ghostly complexion was any hint, he was not here to bring glad tidings. "Sir," Sokoll's voice cracked a touch. It did that when he was afraid he was going to upset Ivanov. "We have a problem."

"What kind of problem, God dammit?"

Sokoll started to explain, and then stopped, and then started again when he realized there was no good way to spin the bad news. "We have certain accounts that we use to move money overseas. For our various activities, that is."

"I'm not an idiot, Sokoll. We have accounts all over the place. Which ones are you talking about?"

"The ones in Zurich . . . specifically the ones"—he glanced at his notes—"at SBC." He closed the file and looked at his boss.

Ivanov glared at the pasty man. They had 138 accounts with the Swiss Bank Corporation. "Which accounts, dammit!"

Sokoll opened the file again. Rather than trying to read the numbers, which even he didn't understand, he reached across the desk and handed the paper to his boss.

Ivanov looked down at the list of accounts. There were six, and he was intimately familiar with whom they belonged to. "What am I supposed to learn from this? There is nothing. Just account numbers."

"Actually, sir"—Sokoll pointed nervously at the sheet—"on the far side those are the balances of each account."

Ivanov's eyes nearly popped out of his head. "This says these accounts are empty!"

"That's right, sir."

"How?" Ivanov yelled as he jumped to his feet.

"Swiss Interbank Clearing executed the order at nine-oh-one Zurich time this morning. The money was emptied out of these accounts electronically."

"I know how it works, you fucking moron, where did it go?"

"We don't know, sir."

Ivanov made a fist, as if he might come over the desk and bash his deputy over the head. "Well, find out!"

"We can't," Sokoll said, fearing for his life. "Once the money is gone, it is gone. There is no way to trace it. Swiss banking laws—"

"Shut up, you fool," Ivanov yelled. "I am well

aware of Swiss banking laws, and I don't give a shit. You'd better find a way around them or you are going to be either dead or looking for a job."

Sokoll bowed and left without saying another word.

The vodka was on the sidebar. It was always on the sidebar. Five different kinds. Ivanov could barely see, his head hurt so much, and he really didn't care which bottle he was grabbing, vodka was vodka at this point. He poured four fingers into a tall glass, sloshing a bit over the side. He took a huge gulp, clenched his teeth, and let the clean, clear liquid slide down his throat. No one was supposed to know about those accounts, let alone have the ability to drain them of their funds. This could seriously jeopardize his standing within not just the Security Service but the entire government as well. It could potentially destroy all of his investments. Without the power that came with his office, he would be worthless to his partners. The long list of enemies that he'd made over the years would think nothing of coming after him. His hand started to shake.

Shvets finally asked, "How much money?"

Ivanov had to take another drink to gain the courage to speak the number. "Twenty-six million dollars . . . roughly."

"And it belonged to . . . ?"

It took Ivanov a moment to answer. "Our friends in Beirut."

Shvets thought of the different militant terrorist groups. "Their money or ours?"

"Both . . ."

"Both?"

"Yes! Think of it as a joint venture."

"We invested money with those zealots?" Shvets asked, not bothering to hide his surprise.

"It's control, you idiot. I don't even know why I bother explaining sometimes. We put in money so we would have a say in how it was used. Think of it as foreign aid." It was more complicated than that, but Ivanov didn't have the time or clarity of mind to explain the complicated arrangement this morning. Or the fact that approximately ten million of it was KGB money that had been siphoned off over the years.

"Foreign aid to terrorists? Lovely."

"Stop with your judgments. You know nothing. They put money in the accounts as well. In fact, most of it was theirs." Ivanov had helped them find new revenue streams by peddling black market items such as drugs, guns, and porn. The drugs and guns were shipped all over the Middle East and North Africa and the porn was smuggled into Saudi Arabia.

"If the majority of the money was theirs, why did we have control of it?"

Ivanov gave an exasperated sigh as it occurred to him that he would have to go upstairs and tell the director. He tolerated these side business deals, but only to a point. This he would not like very much. In fact, there would be a great deal of suspicion that Ivanov had stolen the money for himself, if for no other reason than that they could all imagine themselves doing it.

Shvets repeated his question, and Ivanov said, "It was part of the deal. If they wanted our help, we wanted to know what they were doing with it, and we wanted them to put their own funds in as well." It was only a half truth, but Ivanov did not feel the need to go into details with one of his deputies.

"I'm assuming the twenty-six represents the bulk of their assets."

"Yes." Ivanov took another gulp. The vodka was starting to lubricate the gears in his brain. He began to make a list in his head of who he would need to talk to.

"Who had access to the account information and pass codes?"

"They did and I did. Any withdrawal of more than twenty-five thousand had to be authorized by each of us separately."

"So you had one pass code and they had the other?"

"Yes." Shvets was asking too many questions.

"Who had access to both sets of pass codes?"

"No one." The headache was starting to come back, although this time it was in his neck. He began rubbing the muscles with his left hand while he took another drink of vodka. "It was intentionally set up so that neither party would have both pass codes."

Shvets considered that for a moment and then said, "Someone had to have both codes. Someone at the bank. How else could the codes be verified and the money moved?"

Ivanov stopped rubbing his neck. Why hadn't

he come to the same conclusion sooner? "Dorf-man."

"Who?"

"The banker." Ivanov looked up Dorfman's office number and punched it in as fast as his fingers could move. It took more than two minutes, three people, and a string of threats to get an answer that told him things were not good. Dorfman had not shown up for work, and they had been unable to reach him. Ivanov hung up the phone and laid his head down on the desk.

Shvets opened the office door and asked the secretary to bring them coffee. He then walked over to the desk and took the glass of vodka. Ivanov tried to stop him.

"This is not helping," Shvets said in a paternal voice. "I am tied to you whether I like it or not, and if we are going to avoid being interrogated by our colleagues in the Federal Security Service, we need to clear your head and get you thinking straight."

Ivanov's entire body shuddered at the thought of the FSS goons dragging him into the basement of Lubyanka, the once-feared grand headquarters of the KGB. He knew all too well what went on in those prison cells in the basement, and he would kill himself before he ever allowed that to happen.

CHAPTER 34

SOUTHERN GERMANY

THE trip was uneventful, in the sense that they pointed the hood of the big Mercedes south and stopped only twice before reaching the Swiss-German border. For eight hours they cruised at an average speed of 120 kilometers an hour down the smooth, twisting autobahn. Near some of the larger towns they had to slow, and when they neared the mountains to the south the winding, rising road slowed their progress only slightly. They were thankful that there was no snow.

They skirted Hannover, Kassel, Frankfurt, Strasbourg, and a blur of other towns, while Hurley pored over the treasure trove of information he'd retrieved from the banker's safe. Richards fired up the laptop and used the decoding software to uplink the information on Dorfman's disks via the satellite phone. Kennedy had a team assembled in D.C. who were translating and filtering the information.

Richards was done sending the information by the time they reached Kassel. He slept for the next two hours. Rapp listened to the snippets of conversation coming from the backseat and wondered what the next move would be. Hurley liked to operate on a strictly need-to-know basis, and Rapp and Richards rarely needed to know, at least as far as Hurley was concerned.

Halfway through the trip, Hurley ordered Rapp to pull over and switch with Richards. They topped off the gas, used the men's room, and Hurley bought coffee and some snacks for him and Richards. Rapp didn't mind driving but Hurley was insistent. An hour or two of downtime was crucial. One never knew when things would get interesting. As was often the case, though, Hurley did not listen to his own advice and continued to work at a feverish pace. Rapp climbed into the backseat, and after a few minutes of silence he asked Hurley, "What are we doing?"

Uncharacteristically, Hurley laughed. "I'll explain before we cross the border. Right now I need to figure this shit out."

It occurred to Rapp that the man was punch-drunk, but he didn't dwell on it. Within minutes the hum of the tires rolling at high speed on the concrete surface of the autobahn sent Rapp into a trance. He rolled up his jacket, wedged it in between the door frame and his head, and fell asleep. For the next few hours he drifted in and out of sleep, the shrill ring of the satellite phone interrupting dreams of poodles, bad comb-over hairdos, and trussed-up, plump

German women. At one point he was drifting off to sleep and wondered what Frau Dorfman would do with the dogs now that her husband was not of this world. For some reason that made him think of the expanding pool of blood under Dorfman's head. How far had it stretched? Would it begin to dry in the arid winter air? How much blood was actually in a human head? One pint? Before he could decide on an amount he drifted off.

Hurley never slowed. He reviewed every document, every file, Post-it note, and receipt. He'd filled close to an entire notepad with the most pertinent information. At 5:00 A.M., they stopped at a roadside motel outside Freiburg and got two connecting rooms, where they cleaned up and changed into suits and ties for the border crossing. Hurley ordered them to pack their weapons in the hidden compartments inside their suitcases. By six they were back on the road with fresh coffee and rolls. And Hurley was ready to explain what they were doing. Unfortunately, he chose the wrong military campaign to illustrate his point.

"You two familiar with Sherman's march to the sea?"

Rapp was behind the wheel. Having been raised in northern Virginia, he didn't really consider himself a Southerner, but he was a proud Virginian, and that meant he knew his Civil War history. To a true Southerner like Richards, who had been raised in Covington, Georgia, the mere mention of William Tecumseh Sherman was enough to start a fight.

"Total war," Hurley said. "Just like Sherman. If

our enemy won't come out and meet us on the field of battle, we need to bring the war to their doorstep. We need to destroy their capacity to fight. We need to spook them into maneuvering in the open so we can crush them."

Rapp could see both men's faces in the rearview mirror. Hurley was oblivious to the revulsion on Richards's face.

"Are you trying to tell me," Richards said, "that we're Sherman?"

"I sure as hell hope so," said Hurley, in a state of near elation. "He won, didn't he?"

Rapp couldn't take it anymore and started laughing.

"What the hell's so funny?" Hurley asked.

When he got control of himself he said, "You're sitting next to one of Georgia's finest. It's like singing the praises of Andrew Jackson to a bunch of Indians."

"Oh," Hurley said as he realized his mistake. "No offense intended. We'll have to debate that one over beers one night. Sherman was a badass." Throwing him a bone, he added, "And Lee and Jackson were two battlefield geniuses. Can't deny that." Then he changed tactics and asked, "You've hunted birds, right?"

"Yeah."

"Why do you bring a dog into the field?"

"To get the birds up."

"Exactly," Hurley said. "These guys have done a damn good job keeping their heads down the past ten years while Langley's been focused on Cen-

tral America and avoiding those dickheads up on
Capitol Hill. I told you about our operative that
got snatched off the streets of Beirut a few months
back . . . well, that's not the first time that's happened. We got soft in the eighties and let these assholes get away with way too much shit." Glancing
at Rapp's face in the mirror, he said, "April of '83
our embassy gets hit . . . sixty-three people killed.
Langley lost eight of its best people that day, including our Near East director and station chief."
Hurley left out the fact that he had been in the city
that day. That he could have easily been one of the
victims. He also left out the fact that Kennedy's dad
was one of the men they'd lost. It was not his place
to share something so personal. If she wanted to
tell them one day, that was her business. "Our response . . . we send in the Marines. October of '83
the Marines and French forces get hit by a couple
of truck bombs. Two hundred and ninety-nine
men wasted, because a bunch of fucking diplomats conned the command element into thinking
too much security would send the wrong message. Mind you, not a single one of those dilettante
pricks ever spent a day in that godforsaken city.
Our response after the barracks bombing . . . we
say we're not going to leave, we drop a few bombs,
and we leave."

Hurley swore to himself. "And they get it in
their heads that they can fuck with us and get away
scot-free. March of '84 they grab my old buddy Bill
Buckley, our new station chief, Korean and Viet-
nam War vet. Amazing guy." Hurley looked out

the window for a moment with sadness in his eyes. "They tortured him for almost a year and a half. Flew him over to Tehran. The bastards taped it. I've seen parts." Hurley shook his head as if trying to get rid of a bad thought. "They sucked every last drop of information out of him, and then they sold it to the Russians and anyone else who was interested. Bill knew a lot of shit. The info they got from him did a boatload of damage. I can't even begin to tell you how many nights I've lain awake wondering how I would have handled it. They brought in a so-called expert. A Hezbollah shrink by the name of Aziz al-Abub. Trained by the Russians at the People's Friendship University. The names these assholes come up with just boggles the mind. Al-Abub pumped him full of drugs and poked and prodded. The word is he had two assistants who helped him. They turned it into a real science project. Bill's heart eventually gave out, but not before they extracted some of our most closely held secrets.

"One by one assets started to disappear. Highly placed sources in governments around the region and beyond, and how did we react? We didn't do jack shit, and the result was they became more emboldened. Qaddafi, that quack, then decides to plant a bomb in a disco in Berlin, and finally we decide to hit back and drop a few bombs on his head. Unfortunately, we missed, and then in July of '88 that cowboy captain of the *Vincennes* decides he's going to start racing all over the Strait of Hormuz chasing ten-thousand-dollar fiberglass gunboats with a half-billion-dollar Aegis guided missile cruiser."

Hurley had to stop and close his eyes as if he still couldn't believe that ugly piece of history.

Rapp finished it for him. "Iran Air Flight 655. Two hundred and ninety civilians."

"Yep," Hurley said, realizing that having lost his girlfriend later that same year, Rapp would know the story. "Not our proudest moment. I don't care what anyone tries to tell you, that one was our fault. Instead of owning up to it, and using it as an opportunity to show the Iranian people that we weren't out to get them, we denied the entire thing. Went so far as to blame it on them. Now, they weren't without fault, but that captain had two choppers on board to deal with those gunboats. The strength of the Aegis cruiser is distance. You don't close with the enemy to use your World War II–era guns. If there's really a threat, you back off and fire one of your missiles."

"And that's what led us to Pan Am Lockerbie," Rapp said.

Hurley nodded. "It's a little more complicated than that, but in a nutshell . . . yeah."

"So," Richards said, "we fit in how?"

"Let's just say some people in Washington have seen the error of their ways. This terrorism, especially the Islamic radical shit, has some people spooked, and it should. They saw what happened last time when we allowed someone like Buckley to get snatched without lifting a finger. It gives people the wrong idea. Now the Schnoz has been grabbed, and it's starting all over again. I'm not supposed to tell you guys this, but what the fuck . . . five of our sources have been killed in just the last few months. We've had to recall another dozen-plus. We're flying blind. And once again, by doing nothing, we've reinforced the idea that they can do whatever they want to us, and we won't lift a finger."

"And the stuff you've been working on all night. How does that fit in?" Rapp asked.

"Let's suppose for a second that you have five million dollars sitting in a Swiss bank account. That money represents years of extortion, drug and gun running, counterfeiting, and a host of illegal scams. You've worked yourself to the bone squirreling away this money. What would you do, if you woke up one morning and found out that account, your account, was empty?"

Rapp looked at the winding road and said, "I'd flip."

"You think you might pick up the phone and start demanding some answers?"

"Yeah."

"Damn right you would. Right now these pricks are sleeping soundly in their beds, thinking their money is safe in Switzerland. At some point in the next twenty-four hours they're going to find out that their ill-gotten gains have vanished, and they are going to pick up the phone and they are going to go absolutely apeshit. And when they do"—Hurley pointed skyward—"we will be listening."

CHAPTER 35

ZURICH, SWITZERLAND

As promised by Hurley, the border crossing was uneventful: dour, serious Anglos in nice suits, in a nice car, crossing from one efficient European country into an even more efficient European country. They continued to wind their way toward the banking capital of the world as the sun climbed in the sky and Hurley explained in more detail what they were up to. After another forty minutes they arrived on the outskirts of Zurich. Hurley told Rapp which exit to take, and where to turn. A few minutes later they pulled up to the gates of an estate.

"What's this, an embassy?" Rapp asked.

"No," Hurley said, smiling. "The home of an old friend."

The car had barely come to a stop when the heavy black-and-gold gate began to open. Rapp eased the sedan slowly up the crushed-rock drive. The garden beds were bare and the manicured arborvitae wrapped in burlap to protect them from the heavy, wet snows that were common this time of year. The place must have been magnificent in the summer. The house reminded him of some of the abodes of foreign ambassadors that dotted the countryside west of D.C. Hurley had him pull the car around the back, where one of six garage doors was open, the stall empty, anticipating their arrival.

Carl Ohlmeyer was waiting for them in his library. The man was tall, thin, and regal. At first glance, he was more British-looking than German, but his thick accent washed that thought from Rapp's mind almost as quickly as it had appeared. He was dressed impeccably in a three-piece suit. Hurley had given them the man's brief history. They had met in their twenties in Berlin. Ohlmeyer had been fortunate enough to survive World War II, but unfortunate in that his family farm was twenty-one miles east of Berlin rather than west. He had received his primary education at the hands of Jesuit priests, who had drilled into him the idea that God expected you to better yourself every day. Luke 12:28 was a big one: "For of those to whom much is given, much is required." Since Ohlmeyer was a gifted mathematician, much was expected of him. When he was sixteen the Russian tanks came down the same dirt road that the German tanks had gone down only a few years before, but going in the opposite direction, of course. And with them, they brought a cloud of death and destruction.

Two years later he enrolled as a freshman at the prestigious Humboldt University in the Russian-controlled sector of Berlin. Over the next three years he watched in silence as fellow students and professors were arrested by the Russian secret police and shipped off to Siberia to do hard time for daring to speak out against the tenets of communism. The once-grand university, which had educated statesmen like Bismarck, philosophers like Hegel, and physicists like Einstein, had become nothing more than a rotted-out shell.

Buildings that had been partially destroyed during the war sat untouched the entire time he was there. All the while in the West, the Americans, British, and French were busy rebuilding. Ohlmeyer saw communism for the sham that it was—a bunch of brutes who seized power in the name of the people, only to repress the very people they claimed to champion. Hurley recited for them Ohlmeyer's stalwart claim that *any form of government that required the repression, imprisonment, and execution of those who disagreed with it was certainly not a government of the people.*

But in those days following the war, when so many millions had been killed, people were in no mood for another fight. So Ohlmeyer kept quiet and bided his time, and then after he received his degree in economics, he fled to the American sector. A few years later, while he was working at a bank, he ran into a brash young American who hated the communists even more than he did. His name was Stanley Albertus Hurley, and they struck up a friendship that went far beyond a casual contempt for communism.

Ohlmeyer, upon seeing Hurley, dropped any pretense of formality and rushed out from behind his desk. He took Hurley's hand in both of his and began berating his friend in German. Hurley gave it right back. After a brief exchange, Ohlmeyer looked at the other two men and in English said, "Are these the two you told me about?"

Hurley nodded. "Yep, these are Mike and Pat."

"Yes . . . I'm sure you are." Ohlmeyer smiled and extended his hand, not believing their names were Mike and Pat for a second. "I can't tell you how exciting it is to meet you. Stan has told me you are two of the best he has seen in years." Ohlmeyer instantly read the looks of surprise on the faces of the two young men. With mock surprise of his own, he turned to Hurley and said, "Was I not supposed to say anything?"

Hurley looked far from enthused over his friend's talkativeness.

"You will have to excuse my old confidant," Ohlmeyer said, putting a hand on Hurley's shoulder. "He finds it extremely difficult to express feelings of admiration and warmth. That way he doesn't feel as bad when he beats you over the head."

Rapp and Richards started laughing. Hurley didn't.

"Please make yourself comfortable. There is coffee and tea and juice over there on the table and fresh rolls. If you require anything else, do not hesitate to ask. Stan and I have some work to do, but it shouldn't take too long, then I suggest all of you get some sleep. You will be staying for dinner tonight . . . no?" Ohlmeyer turned to Hurley for the answer.

"I hope."

"Nonsense. You are staying."

Hurley hated to commit to things. "I'd like to, but who knows what might pop up after this morning?"

"True, and I will have my plane ready to take you wherever you need to go tomorrow morning. You are staying for dinner. That is final. There is much we need to catch up on, and besides, I need to tell these two young men of our exploits."

"That might not be such a good idea."

"Nonsense." Ohlmeyer dismissed Hurley's concern as completely inconsequential. He looked down at the briefcase in Hurley's hand. With a devilish look he asked, "Did you bring the codes?"

"No . . . I drove all the way from Hamburg just so I could stare at your ugly mug. Of course I brought them."

Ohlmeyer started laughing heartily before turning to Rapp and Richards. "Have you ever met a grumpier man in your entire life?"

"Nope," Rapp said without hesitation, while Richards simply shook his head.

While Rapp and Richards retired to the other end of the forty-foot-long study to get some food, Ohlmeyer and Hurley were joined by two men whom Rapp guessed to be in their midforties. They looked like businessmen. Probably bankers. The four of them huddled around Ohlmeyer's massive desk while the silver-haired German issued explicit instructions in German. Forty minutes later the two men left, each carrying several pages of instructions.

At nine-oh-five they received the anticlimactic call that the seventeen accounts had been drained of all funds, but that was just the beginning. Over the next three hours the computers continued to execute transfers. Each account was divided into three new accounts and then split again by three, until there were 153 new accounts. The money had been flung far and wide, from offshore accounts in Cyprus, Malaysia, and Hong Kong, and across the Caribbean. Each transfer ate away at the balance as the various banks charged their fees, but Hurley didn't care. He was playing with someone else's money. The important thing was to leave a trail that would be impossible to untangle. With all the different jurisdictions and separate privacy laws, it would take an army of lawyers a lifetime to slash through the mess. By noon the number of accounts had shrunk to five with a net balance of $38 million.

CHAPTER 36

BEIRUT, LEBANON

SAYYED'S lungs and thighs ached as he climbed the crumbling concrete stairs. His week had gone from miserable to intolerable, starting with his trip to Moscow and ending with his superiors in Damascus issuing one of the most idiotic orders he had received in all of his professional career. With the cease-fire finally looking as if it was going to take hold, the cursed Maronites had decided to accelerate their land grab. Their focus, it appeared, was the historically important area known as Martyrs' Square in Beirut's Central District. Damascus ordered Sayyed to get to the square, plant his flag, and plant it as quickly as possible. Like some battlefield general who had been ordered to hold a piece of land at all costs and then given no support, Sayyed was left to sort out the how.

Fifteen years in this city had taught him the importance of keeping a healthy distance between himself and the other factions. Rifles and machine guns were nasty things, and placed in the hands of teenage boys they were extremely unpredictable. The idea of taking up one side of the square while the Maronites grabbed the other made his skin crawl. One errant shot, one young, crazy Eastern Catholic, who wanted to avenge the death of a brother or the rape of a sister, could plunge the entire city back into war. Orders, unfortunately, were orders, and as much as he would have liked to, he could not ignore them. So Sayyed sent Samir and Ali to choose an adequate building. And while he was contemplating how to fill it with enough men to deter the Maronites, he was struck with an ingenious solution.

Shvets would be coming from Moscow to collect the CIA agent in just a few days. That would leave him with the American businessman Zachary Austin. He was not an agent of any sort, Sayyed was sure of that. The only question that remained was how much they could get for him, and how that money would be split with that fool Abu Radih. The Fatah gunman had been crying like a little girl over the fact that he'd been forced to surrender the telecommunications executive. If Sayyed brought him in, it would be seen as a great gesture of maturity and goodwill by the others. And maybe he could negotiate it in such a way that he could get the Fatah rats to come hold the entire western end of the square.

The two had sat down over tea the previous afternoon. Radih had brought no fewer than twelve men—a ridiculous number for the current level of tension. Sayyed first explained the situation with the Maronites moving into Martyrs' Square. He was hoping that the emotionally charged piece of land would spur Radih to action, and he was not disappointed. The man was so eager to show his passion for the cause that he leaped at the chance to hold the western half of the square. Without so much as seeking a concession in return, he pledged fifty men to the operation.

The number surprised even Sayyed, and he was tempted to hold back his offer to hand over the American. Radih was an emotional fool to commit so much without gaining a single concession, but Sayyed had a problem. He couldn't very well hold the west side of the square and leave the two Americans in the basement of the office over on Hamra Street with only a few men guarding them. He had served three years in the army before joining the General Security Directorate, and he recalled something they'd told him in infantry school about consolidating your forces. It would be for only a few days, until the Russians could pick up the CIA spy. After that, Sayyed didn't really care what happened to the businessman, just so long as he got his share of the ransom.

Sayyed looked across the small bistro table and said, "I have finished interrogating the businessman from Texas."

"So is he a spy?" Radih asked.

"No. I am certain he is in fact a businessman."

"Good. Then I can commence negotiations for his release."

Sayyed did not speak. He waited for Radih to make him an offer—the same arrangement they'd had in the past.

"I will guarantee you 20 percent of the ransom."

Sayyed was tempted to ask for fifty. The others would likely back him, but he needed Radih's help with the Maronite problem. "I think thirty would be fair . . . considering everything else." Before Radih could counter, Sayyed said, "I will bring him to the new building tonight along with the other American. It can be your new command post for a few weeks." It was an honor Radih would never be able to refuse. He would be considered the vanguard in the struggle to reclaim the city from the Christians.

The building itself would have to eventually be destroyed. It listed at a five-degree angle toward the square and looked as if a strong wind might topple all seven stories into the street, but it was built out of sturdy concrete and would have to be blown up before it would fall. Of all the buildings that bordered the square it was perhaps the second-strongest position. Unfortunately, the Maronites had the best position, no more than three hundred feet directly across from them.

Radih had already made one mistake, and Sayyed blamed himself for it. The self-promoter had left his sprawling slums near the airport in a ten-vehicle convoy and arranged for the peasants to send him and his men off as if they were valiant Muslims on a mission to evict the Crusaders. Instead of a quiet arrival, they had pulled into the square flying the bright yellow Fatah flag. The chances for escalation were now ripe.

That was not Sayyed's preference. The last thing he needed with Shvets coming to pick up the CIA man was open conflict. The prisoners had arrived the previous evening, transferred in just two cars. The proper way. Very low-key. And then for the next few hours, men and supplies were slowly transferred over from the office on Hamra Street. They had successfully moved the bulk of their stuff without tipping their hand, and then in one fell swoop, with a gesture of egotistical grandeur, Radih had announced to the entire city that they were staking out their turf. While that might accomplish the short-term goals of Damascus, it also might plunge the city back into chaos.

As Sayyed reached the roof, he realized that it also might get him killed. He peered around the corner with his left eye and looked across the street. The Maronite building was one story taller, and with a glance he counted no fewer than five heads and three muzzles along the roof line. It had just been reported to him that they were filling sandbags and barricading the windows and doors on the first floor. Of course they were. That's what he would do, and was in fact doing. It would be really nice if they could get through this little standoff without a shot being fired, because if just one shot was fired, the entire square would erupt in a fusillade of lead projectiles. He'd seen it happen before. Literally thousands of rounds would be exchanged in minutes. He would have to remember to tell the men to keep their weapons on safe.

Sayyed found Samir around the other side of the blockhouse at the top of the building. It was the place most shielded from the position across the street. Samir handed Sayyed the satellite phone that Ivanov's effeminate deputy had given him before Sayyed left Moscow. "Hello," he said as he placed it to his ear.

"My friend, how are things?"

Sayyed frowned. It was Ivanov, and he sounded as if he was drunk. It was only midafternoon. "Fine," Sayyed said, as he stole a quick look around the corner. The sun had reflected off something across the street, and he got the horrible feeling it was the front end of a sniper's scope.

"How are things in your fine city?"

Sayyed pulled the phone away from his ear and looked at it with skepticism. Something was wrong with Ivanov. The man hated Beirut. He sighed and put the phone back to his ear. "A little tense at the moment, but nothing I can't handle."

"What is wrong?"

"Just a land grab by one of the other militias. It has created a bit of a standoff."

"Fellow Muslims?"

"No," Sayyed said, irritated by the implication. Ivanov liked to get drunk and lecture him on history. Specifically, that Muslims loved nothing more than to kill each other, and the only time they stopped killing each other was when they decided to kill Jews, Hindus, or Christians. "Maronites."

"Ah ... the wood ticks of the Middle East. Haven't you been trying to exterminate them for a thousand years?"

"What do you want?"

"My package," Ivanov said, slurring the words. "Is it ready? You haven't decided to negotiate with the Persians, have you?"

"I am standing by our deal. When can I expect it to be retrieved? I assume you are still sending someone."

"Yes ... although I am considering coming myself." There was a long pause and then, "You did offer ... didn't you?"

"Oh," Sayyed said, surprised that Ivanov was taking him up on his insincere offer. "Absolutely."

"Good. I will be there in three days. Maybe sooner."

"Fantastic," Sayyed lied. "I will have everything prepared. I must go now. There is something urgent I need to attend to. Please call if you need anything else." Sayyed punched the red button and disconnected the call. He looked around the desolate landscape, with its pancaked and shelled-out buildings, and wondered how he could ever play host to Ivanov in this pile of rubble.

Then as he turned to go down the stairs he came face-to-face with Imad Mughniyah, the coleader of Islamic Jihad. Mughniyah, not known for levity, looked as if he was ready to kill someone. "Imad," Sayyed said, "what is wrong?"

Mughniyah looked back into the stairwell and motioned for his two bodyguards to give him some privacy. "Who was that?" he said, looking at the phone. "I heard you talking."

"Ivanov."

"What did he want?"

"To insult me, I think, but I did not take the bait."

"Anything else?"

"He was going to send one of his men to pick up the spy. Now he's changed his mind and he's going to come himself."

"He just changed his mind . . . right now?"

"Yes," Sayyed said, wondering what all the questions were about. "What is wrong?"

Mughniyah again looked over his shoulder to make sure no one would hear him. In a raspy voice he said, "My bank accounts . . . in Switzerland . . . they are empty."

"What do you mean empty?"

"Empty . . . gone . . . nothing."

Sayyed knew there must have been a mistake. "Impossible."

"I have checked three times already. And it is not only the two Islamic Jihad accounts. My personal account you helped me set up is also empty." There was a hint of accusation in his words.

"This can't be. There has to be a mistake. Have you called Hamburg?"

Mughniyah nodded. "My cousin tried six different times today."

"Did he get hold of Dorfman?"

He shook his head. "Herr Dorfman is dead."

"Dead!"

"Killed in his own home last night."

Sayyed's knees felt weak. He was the one who had suggested Dorfman to Mughniyah and the others.

"You are the only one of us who knew this banker. You specifically said we would never regret investing our money with him."

Sayyed could see where this was going. They would need to blame someone, and he was the easiest target. "Are you sure he's dead?"

"As sure as I can be from here."

Sayyed didn't like the way the Islamic Jihad's heavy was looking at him. "We will get to the bottom of this. I promise you I had nothing to do with this. Come with me," Sayyed said, wanting to get off the roof lest Mughniyah decide to throw him off. "We'll go to my bank here in town. I'm sure there has been a mistake. I had money with him as well."

"Tell me again . . . what is the connection with Dorfman?"

Sayyed had already reached the first landing. He stopped dead in his tracks and looked at Mughniyah. "Ivanov introduced me to him six years ago."

"And he just called you and mentioned none of this?"

"Not a word."

"Fucking Russians . . . always scheming."

CHAPTER 37

ZURICH, SWITZERLAND

RAPP and Richards missed most of the excitement. With the time change and lack of sleep over the past few days, both of them took Ohlmeyer up on his offer of a room. Rapp had just enough energy in him to slip out of his suit and pull back the covers, but not enough to brush his teeth or anything else. He didn't even bother to close the curtains. He did a face plant on the big king-size bed and was out cold. He could do that sometimes. Just lie down on his stomach, close his eyes, and it was good night, Irene. The only problem came when he woke up. Lying on his face like that caused his sinuses to drain and blood to pool around his eyes.

His arms were pinned beneath him. He cracked one eye and thought of the ultimate yin and yang—life and death. He wondered if it was normal to think about it so much or if he should bring it up to Lewis when he made it back stateside. That was if he made it back. That thought brought a smile to his face. He had no idea why he found it amusing that someone might kill him, but he did. Probably because there was a better-than-even chance that whoever the man was, he had no idea the kind of fight he was in for. Rapp didn't discuss it with anyone, not even Lewis or Kennedy, but he was good at this kind of work and he was getting better.

At twenty-three he was already intimately familiar with death. There was his father and then Mary, and now less than a week ago he'd stared into the eyes of a man and pulled the trigger. And as life drained from the man's face, he had felt nothing. At least not guilt, or sorrow, or nerves. It was as if a calm had passed over him. And then last night, the bizarre home invasion of Herr Dorfman. When he'd signed on with Kennedy, he hadn't had that type of thing in mind. Killing a man in the manner that he'd killed Sharif, he'd dreamed of at least a thousand times. Dorfman, never. Never once had his fertile imagination predicted that he would see a man shot in the head while he clutched his prized poodle.

Without warning, or any real conscious decision, he jumped out of bed, assumed the position, and started doing push-ups. He thought of the old saying: If you're not busy living, you're dying. It felt good to be living. He ripped through fifty push-ups, flipped over, and did fifty sit-ups, and then decided he needed to take a run. He dug out his gear. It was four-thirty-seven in the afternoon. His running shoes were virtually brand-new, as the last pair had been stuffed in a garbage can in Istanbul. With a house this big, Rapp assumed they had to have a workout room. He was right. A staff member must have heard him coming down the stairs and met him in the foyer. He escorted Rapp back upstairs, down the hallway past his room to the far wing of the house. The room had windows on three sides, a treadmill, a bike, and a rowing machine, as well as a universal machine and some dumbbells.

Rapp got on the treadmill, picked the mountain course, and hit start. For the next thirty minutes the ramp rose and fell, and all the while he kept a six-minute pace. When the digital readout told him he'd run five miles, he punched the red stop button and jumped off, his chest heaving, sweat dripping from his face. He didn't even have enough left for a cool-down. As he stood hunched over, his hands on his knees, he wondered for a brief moment if he might vomit. And that was when she walked into the room. Rapp stood up straight, a pained look on his face, and tried to take in a full breath.

"Here you are," she said in near perfect English. "I have been looking all over for you."

Rapp could hardly conceal his surprise. Here, standing before him, was possibly the most attractive woman he'd ever laid eyes on, and she was looking for him. Still out of breath, he started to speak but stopped. The nausea came back and he decided rather quickly that he needed to open one of the windows or he really was going to vomit in front of this beauty. He held up a single finger and said, "Excuse me."

Rapp cranked one of the windows open and took in the fresh cold air. A couple of deep breaths later the nausea began to pass. "Sorry," he said as he turned back around. "I'm a little out of shape."

The blond beauty placed a hand on her hip and gave him an appraising look. "I don't see anything wrong with your shape."

Rapp laughed nervously and, not knowing how to respond, said, "You look great . . . too, I mean, you don't look like you need to work out . . . is what I mean." That's what came out of his mouth. Inside his brain he was screaming at himself. *You're a moron.*

"Thank you." She flashed him a perfect set of white teeth.

That was when Rapp noticed the dimple on her chin. Her overall looks had knocked him so off-kilter that he was just now getting around to categorizing her individual features: blue eyes, platinum blond hair pulled back in a high ponytail, prominent cheekbones, like some Nordic goddess. *Weren't these people all related somehow?* A tiny little upturned nose. The dimple on the chin, though, that had caught his attention for some reason.

"My grandfather sent me to find you."

That was where he had seen it. Herr Ohlmeyer had that same dimple, or cleft, or whatever it was that they called it. Somehow it looked much better on her. Rapp smiled and offered his hand, "I'm Mitch . . . I mean Mike." *Get ahold of yourself,* his brain screamed at him.

"Greta. Pleased to meet you."

The smile made him a bit wobbly in the knees. *Of course you are,* Rapp thought to himself. The image of Greta in pigtails and lederhosen with a white blouse and ample cleavage, holding a couple of beer steins, flashed across his mind. *What the hell is wrong with me?* He noticed her face muscles tighten a bit and then she looked down at their still-clasped hands. "Oh, I'm sorry," Rapp said as he released her hand. He hustled over to the shelf where the towels were and grabbed her one. Instead of giving it to her, he began mopping her hand. "I'm so sorry."

She laughed nervously and took the towel from him. "My grandfather wanted me to tell you, drinks are being served at six sharp in the library. Jacket and tie are required. His rules, not mine."

"Okay," Rapp replied, and then, feeling some irrational need to keep talking, he asked, "What are you wearing?"

She crinkled up her nose and said, "You are funny."

And then she was gone. In stunned silence Rapp watched her leave. He didn't know how it was possible, but she looked every bit as good from behind. She was in a pair of jeans that were tucked into brown leather riding boots. The door closed with a click that snapped Rapp out of his trance. He slapped himself in the head twice. "What are you, fifteen, you moron?"

He tried to finish the workout, but his mind wasn't in it, so he went back to his room, took a cold shower, and thought about Greta. Romance, companionship, call it whatever you want, it was not something he had put a lot of thought into since losing Mary. He'd had a few flings here and there, but they were purely physical. They all wanted to fix him. That was the problem. They knew who he was, and that he'd lost his high-school sweetheart in the attack that had so devastated Syracuse. Being the captain of a national championship lacrosse team, at a school that was crazy about the sport, virtually guaranteed that a certain number of women would end up in his lap. Unfortunately, they eventually wanted to talk about his feelings, about how he was coping with the loss and heartache. Nothing could have been more unappealing to him. His feelings, his personal agony, were no one else's business.

It had been almost four years now. Maybe that was what was going on. Time really was healing the wound. Or maybe it was Sharif and Dorfman. Maybe tossing their bodies down that big hollow pit in the back of his mind had helped stay the pain. Or maybe it was simply the fact that Greta was so stunning, she'd blinded him into forgetting his past for a moment. *No, that couldn't have been it. At least not all of it.* He'd met plenty of gorgeous women the past few years, and none of them had hit him with this kind of lightning bolt.

Rapp knotted his tie in the mirror and decided to leave the question there. It was a riddle. An unsolved problem, more than likely all the above, or some of the above. And what did it really matter? He'd felt something he hadn't felt in years and wasn't sure he would ever feel again. The spark of a crush, or love at first sight, he had no idea. He had a hard time buying the latter. More than likely it was simple lust. Two young, attractive people, their pheromones in overdrive. Was there a chance she felt the same thing? He recalled the look she'd given him as she gave him the once-over.

Staring at his reflection, he asked, "What does any of it matter? I'm leaving in the morning. Going on safari." Rapp cinched the Windsor knot just so and decided to enjoy the evening. He would forget about yesterday and tomorrow, the pain and the obligations, and just try to live like a normal person for one night.

CHAPTER 38

MOSCOW, RUSSIA

IVANOV placed the handset back in the cradle and reached for the glass of vodka. It was snatched from his grasp a split second before his hand got there. His fingers closed and found air. He blinked several times before looking up and seeing Shvets holding the glass. "Mine," was all he could manage to say.

Shvets wanted to tell him he spoke like a toddler when he was drunk, but it would do no good at this point. "What did he say?"

"He has no idea."

"You're sure?" Shvets should have listened on the extension. When his boss got like this he was extremely unreliable.

"What's there to be sure about?" He pushed himself away from his desk and leaned back in his high-back leather chair. "The man is a camel jockey. He is not smart enough to steal this money from us."

Shvets would have loved nothing more at this exact moment than to tell his alcoholic boss that Sayyed was smarter than him, but he'd seen him shoot people for such insolence. "I should go to Hamburg?"

"No. I need you here. Send Pavel."

Now, there was an idiot, Shvets thought. Pavel Sokoll was fine with numbers and balance sheets, but borderline retarded when it came to everything else in life. Sending him to Hamburg would get them nowhere. "We need answers, and I'm afraid sitting here will not get us any. Sending Pavel will only add to the confusion. You won't allow me to discuss this with anyone other than you or Pavel, so getting those answers is going to be very difficult."

"But I need you here."

"There will be no 'here' in a few days," he said with some force. "Once word gets out that the money is missing, the phone will start ringing and sooner or later it will be kicked upstairs, or worse, across town, and once that happens, they will pull you in."

"Us! You mean us!" he half screamed. "Your wagon is hitched to mine."

"Trust me, a minute doesn't pass that I don't think of it."

"And I have been good to you."

"Yes, you have," Shvets said halfheartedly.

"And I will continue to take care of you. We just need some answers."

"What we need is money," he said, trying to get Ivanov to see the fundamental problem. "Answers might lead us to the money, but we will not get those answers sitting here in Moscow."

"Stop speaking in riddles."

"Just let me go to Hamburg and see what I can find out. I will fly out tonight, and if all goes well, I'll be back on the first flight in the morning."

"And what am I going to do?"

Shvets's solution was suddenly very clear. "Go out and get drunk. Order up some women and go to Hotel Baltschug."

Ivanov frowned. He was in no mood to socialize.

"You must keep up appearances. You know how this town is. If rumors start that you are in trouble and no one sees you in public they will believe the rumors. If they see you out acting as if everything is normal they won't believe the rumors." Shvets was willing to say almost anything to convince him. Sitting here in this office was getting them nowhere. He'd seen his boss in these funks before. Usually only for a day or two. Always a pity party, but somehow the heaps of despair and recrimination eventually focused him, and he came out of it like a bear ready to charge. And when that happened, Shvets had better have a better understanding of what had happened, or he could end up being the casualty.

He suggested, "Bring Alexei and Ivan. They will make sure you are taken care of."

Yes, Ivanov thought. *My two Luca Brasis. No one would dare challenge me with them as my companions.* Ivanov felt better just thinking of his two loyal soldiers, and besides, some flesh might be the remedy for his dismal attitude. And he wanted a drink. "Fine," he relented, "but I want you to call me as soon as you hear something."

Shvets turned tentative. They'd done enough talking on the phones today, and in this new era of electronic surveillance, there was no telling who was listening. "I promise," he lied as he started for the door. "And remember . . . act like nothing has changed tonight."

CHAPTER 39

ZURICH, SWITZERLAND

RAPP entered the study a few minutes before six and found Hurley alone, a phone in his left hand and a drink in his right, staring out the French doors at the snow-capped mountains in the distance. Hurley glanced casually over his shoulder, the phone pressed against his left ear, to see who it was, and then went back to what he was doing. Rapp glided across the room, stepping from the hardwood floor onto a large Persian rug. The library was on two levels. The second floor consisted of a catwalk that accessed the stacks of books lining the four walls. There wasn't a dust jacket on a single book.

A large wood-paneled door to Rapp's left opened with a click. Herr Ohlmeyer appeared, a warm smile on his face. He held up one of his long fingers and silently motioned for Rapp to join him. Rapp glanced at Hurley to see if the man wanted to discuss anything, but he was still on the phone, so he followed Ohlmeyer into a much smaller windowless office.

Something about the room felt different. Off in some way. When Ohlmeyer closed the door, there was a click of finality and then near total silence. Only the faint hum of a CPU. Rapp became aware of his own breathing and then realized the room was soundproof. The floor was elevated a few inches, and the walls and ceiling were built-in and covered in fabric. Behind the desk with the triple screens was a bank of black-and-white security monitors three high and five across. In front of the desk was a small conference table maybe forty-eight inches across. It had four bland wood chairs. The room was such a stark contrast to the rest of the house that Rapp couldn't help but take notice.

Ohlmeyer could see the younger man's interest and said, "In my business one must take certain precautions." He pulled out one of the chairs, told Rapp to sit, and then grabbed a file from his desk. Placing it on the conference table, he said, "I admire what you are doing. This is not an easy life you have chosen."

Rapp nodded in a noncommittal way, but other than that did not respond.

"Do you have any regrets so far?"

Without hesitation, Rapp said, "No."

"No problems sleeping . . . no second thoughts?"

"I'm not a big sleeper."

Ohlmeyer smiled and scratched the dimple on his chin. "Your type rarely is."

"My type?"

"Yes. The hunter. It is imprinted in your genetic code. Almost everyone has it, dormant for thousands of years. In many there isn't enough of it left to do them any good. They spend their days in sedentary jobs that challenge them neither physically nor mentally. They do not have your abilities and your drive, of course."

Rapp supposed there was a good deal of truth in his words; he simply had not put a lot of time into thinking about it.

"I have some documents here," Ohlmeyer said as he tapped the file. "Stan knows about this, but he does not want to know the details."

"Details?" Rapp asked, wondering what Hurley was up to now.

"You are in a very dangerous line of work. You are but a small vessel in a harbor packed with giant supertankers. Those supertankers bump up against each other sometimes, causing little harm to themselves, but to you it is the end." He clapped his hands together, signifying the destruction of Rapp's boat. "In your work, you need a special kind of insurance, and do you know why?"

Rapp could hazard a guess but he got the idea Ohlmeyer would prefer to do the talking. "Not really."

"Because those supertankers don't really care about you. They may lament your misfortune, but only briefly. The tanker, the ego of the captain, all comes before you. Think of it as the ship of state, if you will. You are young, and if you are lucky your career will last for another four decades. During that time your handlers will come and go and the political winds of change will reverse directions more times than you will be able to count, and sooner or later it is likely that someone within your own government will begin to think of you as a problem. Ships of state do not like to be embarrassed, and if that means sinking a small vessel every once in a while . . . well, that is a price they are willing to pay."

Rapp had a bad feeling. He looked at the file and said, "What's that all about?"

"It is your insurance policy." Ohlmeyer opened the file and clipped to the first sheaf of documents was a Swiss passport. "Stan has assured me that your French is perfect."

Rapp nodded.

"And your Italian, German, and Arabic?"

"My Italian is good, my German is weak, and my Arabic is pretty good."

Ohlmeyer nodded. That matched with what Hurley had told him. "I have prepared three separate legends for you. Swiss"—he slid the set of documents out of the file, followed by two more. "French, and Italian. You will need to memorize everything in these files and, most important, you will need to visit Paris and Milan in the coming weeks."

"Why?"

"You now own a safety-deposit box in each city, and one in Zurich, but I will take care of that one for you. You will want to place certain things in these safety deposit boxes. Things that will help you survive should you need to go underground, as they say."

Rapp frowned. "Does Stan know about this?"

"It was his idea. Mine as well, but we did the same thing for him years ago." He slid over a blank sheet of paper with three names on it. The first two were French and the third was Italian. "Please practice signing each of these a few times before I have you sign the signature cards."

Rapp took the pen and began practicing the name Paul Girard. "Why isn't Stan handling this?"

"He does not want to know the details."

"Why?"

"Because every man in your profession needs a few secrets."

"Even from his own boss and government?"

"Especially from your boss and your government."

Rapp was wondering how he was going to keep all of these different aliases straight. Hurley had already given him two, and here were three more. He practiced a few times on the other names and then signed the cards.

"In each box," Ohlmeyer said, "will be twenty thousand dollars in cash, various documents, such as birth certificates, in case you lose the passport, and a matching set of credit cards and driver's license. As I said, you will want to add certain things to each box, but you should talk to Stan about that. There is also a numbered account here in Switzerland that I will be administering."

"A numbered account," Rapp said, barely able to conceal his surprise.

"Yes, Stan has requested that as well, and told

me that it is up to my discretion to release the funds."

Rapp was tempted to ask the size of the account, but instead said, "May I ask you a personal question?"

Ohlmeyer nodded, with a smile, as if he already knew the question.

"Why are you doing this . . . helping us?"

"We will discuss it over dinner tonight, but the short answer is that I believe in freedom."

"Freedom," Rapp said as he turned the word over in his mind for a second. "That's a pretty vague term."

"Not really, but if it helps you understand my motivation, you'll need to understand that I grew up in East Germany. I saw what the Soviets were really like."

Rapp's mind was filled with a menagerie of black-and-white atrocities, courtesy of the *World at War* shows he saw as a kid. "So you hate the Russians."

Ohlmeyer gave a little laugh and said, "Let's just say I believe in good guys and bad guys."

CHAPTER 40

HAMBURG, GERMANY

BY early afternoon they learned that Dorfman was dead. The news sent Ivanov into a fit of rage. He went on for a good five minutes, ranting that he had never trusted the man, which caused Shvets to silently ask himself why the fool had let a man he didn't trust handle such a large sum of money. After that, Ivanov, whose job and nature was to be paranoid, spewed out no fewer than a dozen conspiracy theories in as many minutes. He was convinced that Dorfman had gotten drunk and whispered secrets in the wrong person's ear. That this person had then decided to bump Dorfman off and take the money for himself. But then again, there were supposed to have been safeguards in place, so the criminals had to have had a certain level of sophistication.

Ivanov had a long list of enemies that he ran through. There was a Cuban general he'd screwed over in an information swap five years earlier. How that man could possibly fit into this scenario was beyond Shvets, but he'd asked for the list of possible suspects so he simply listened and let Ivanov purge the information from his vodka-soaked brain. There was a German industrialist whom he'd fleeced a year earlier, a Spanish tycoon as well, and then there were a host of Jews and Bolsheviks who had been out to get him for years. None of it appeared to be useful, but then again maybe it was.

Shvets took the information and boarded a Lufthansa flight to Hamburg. Before leaving he'd called their man at the consulate and told him to work his contacts with the local police and get him a copy of the crime scene report. When he arrived at five-thirty-six that evening, Petrov Sergeyevich was waiting for him, the report in hand. Shvets had met Petrov briefly a few years earlier. After a polite exchange, Shvets told him to drive him to the bank. He sat in the passenger seat and read the report. Herr Dorfman had been stabbed in the thigh and shot once in the head. His wife was found bound and gagged and locked in the basement. She reported two men wearing masks entering the house at approximately ten in the evening. She did not hear them speak and could not give police a description other than the fact that they were roughly the same size.

The dogs, strangely enough, were unharmed. One was locked in the basement with the wife and the other was found wandering around the first floor. At some point the latter dog stepped in the pool of blood by Dorfman's head and then tracked it around the first floor. There was no sign of forced entry and none of the neighbors had seen a thing. Shvets found it interesting that the wife and dogs were unharmed. That more than likely ruled out the vying factions in Moscow, although if Shvets was advising them, he would have tried just this thing to throw off a man like Ivanov. Whoever they were dealing with was very professional.

Shvets finished the report, closed it, and decided it was nearly useless. Anything was possible. Dorfman could have told someone about the money and that someone could have gotten the idea in his head to steal it. Twenty-six million dollars could do that to certain people. Shvets had thought about it himself. He had the skill set to make it work. It would have been so much easier if Dorfman had stolen the money and tried to disappear. They would have tracked him down. They always did. The fools habitually ran off to some beachside resort where they naively thought they would blend in with the locals and tourists.

They reached the bank shortly after six-thirty and Shvets weighed the benefits of having Sergeyevich accompany him into the building. He decided against it. There was no need for muscle. At least not yet, he hoped, and besides, the fewer who knew about Ivanov's vulnerable position the better. The bank was typical. Tall, covered in glass, and imposing, all meant to give the impression of stability and security. It was one of many things Shvets was counting on.

The armed guard who tried to stop him in the

lobby told him the bank was closed, but Shvets assured him that he did not wish to make a financial transaction. He was tempted to add that that was, of course, unless the guard could somehow refund the $26 million that had been stolen from Shvets's employer and associates, but Shvets was fairly certain that this man was incapable of making that happen, so he instead asked to see the head of security.

When the security guard hesitated, Shvets said, "Of course this has something to do with Herr Dorfman's death."

That changed things significantly, and in less than a minute Shvets had been escorted to the top floor, where he came face-to-face with another, much older security guard. Same white shirt with black epaulets and black pants. Shvets flashed his SVR credentials and told the man secrecy was of the utmost importance. He was then told that the bank president was extremely busy.

"No doubt meeting with the board of directors." The uncomfortable look on the man's face gave him the answer he was looking for. "I will wait no more than two minutes. Tell him now, and tell him that it involves Herr Dorfman. There are some very influential people in Russia who require some immediate answers."

Shvets sent the man off to deliver the message. Less than a minute later, the guard came back down the hall with a well-dressed man who looked as if he had been through a difficult day. The guard stood awkwardly nearby while the bank president said, "I am Herr Koenig. How may I help you?"

"I am Nikolai Shvets. I am with the Russian government." He again flashed his gilded badge and then, nodding toward the receptionist, said, "Is there a place where we can have a word in private?"

"Yes," the banker offered, nodding enthusiastically. "Please follow me."

Shvets was disappointed when they ducked into a glass-walled conference room instead of the man's office. There was nothing to learn from this bland space. No photos of loved ones. Not a single hint of personal information. He would have to ask Sergeyevich to look into the man's life for some leverage.

Koenig remained standing, obviously impatient to get back to the board. "What is it you wish to discuss?"

"I understand," Shvets said, "that Herr Dorfman had a very unfortunate evening last night."

The man nervously cleared his throat. "The police have advised me not to discuss matters surrounding the murder of Herr Dorfman."

"Would you like me to inform the police that $26 million of Mother Russia's money went missing this morning, or would you like me to go straight to the press with that announcement?" Shvets was well aware of his lie, but he could hardly tell the man the money belonged to various terrorist groups and the head of the SVR's feared Directorate S.

The banker's gray pallor deepened, and he steadied himself against the back of a nearby chair while he mouthed the number.

"I do not wish to go to either the police or the press, but that is up to you, Herr Koenig."

"What would you like to know?"

"How much money is missing?"

"Counting your twenty-six million . . . forty-seven. But none of the money was actually in our bank," Koenig said defensively. "In fact, we are trying to sort out what Hans has been up to for all these years."

"What do you mean the money was not in your bank?"

"The deposits were all in Swiss banks or off-shore accounts in the Caribbean and Far East."

"But Herr Dorfman managed the accounts in his official capacity as a vice president of this bank."

Koenig raised a cautionary finger. "We are not sure on that point. So far we have found no official records of any of these accounts in our system."

Shvets wasn't so sure he believed the man. "Up until a minute ago you were thinking your exposure was roughly twenty million. It has now more than doubled. What makes you think it won't double again before tomorrow?"

"I disagree with your use of the phrase 'your exposure.' As best we can tell, Herr Dorfman was in no way acting as an officer of this bank while he managed these various accounts."

"Herr Koenig," Shvets said with a sad laugh, "you and I both know that will not stand up. Those deposits may not have sat in your vault, but you had an officer of this bank who was managing on a daily basis a minimum of forty-seven million, and quite possibly more. This bank earned fees off that money . . ."

"But—"

"Please let me finish, Herr Koenig. I am not here to assign guilt. I am here to catch whoever took this money so we can get it back to its rightful owners."

Probably for the first time since midmorning, a touch of color returned to Koenig's face. "As there always is in these situations . . . a financial forensic investigation is under way."

"How long will it take to complete?"

"It could take some time."

"Please be honest with me. I am going to head back to Moscow tomorrow and the men I work for . . . they are not nice. They could never have a conversation like this. They would much prefer to strap you to a chair and attach things to your testicles, so I suggest you tell me what you know." Switching to a friendly tone, he added, "Then I can go back to them and tell them you are a reasonable man. Someone we can trust."

Koenig struggled with what he was about to say and then blurted it out. "I'm afraid we will never find that money."

"Why?"

The banker threw his arms out. "It has been spread to the wind. I have never seen anything like it in all my years. The initial round of transfers was executed via fax in three waves. They came from all over the world."

"Where?"

"Hong Kong, San Francisco, New York, London, Berlin, Paris, Istanbul, Moscow, New Delhi . . ."

"Moscow?"

"Yes."

"I would like to see the faxes."

The banker shook his head.

Shvets sighed, "Ohhhh . . . why must we do this the hard way? Herr Koenig, I know where the accounts were held. Your branch in Geneva. You are not as innocent as you would like me to believe. You will show me those faxes, and if you don't, some people will come visit you in the middle of the night and do to you what was done to Herr Dorfman."

Koenig swallowed hard. "I think I can make that concession."

"Good. Now why do you say we will never find the money?"

"My legal counsel has informed me that not a single bank that we transferred the money to today has consented to our request for information."

"Certainly there's a way."

"It would involve years of lawsuits, and even then you would be lucky to track down a fraction of the funds."

"Well, maybe you need to turn up the pressure." Koenig watched as his words seemed to have the opposite effect from the one he'd intended.

Koenig stiffened. "I should warn you that a faction of the board feels very strongly that this is dirty money."

"Dirty money?" Shvets asked, as if the accusation were an insult.

"There are rumors that Herr Dorfman was an agent for the East German Stasi before the wall fell."

"Rumors are bad things."

"And there is another rumor that he worked for your GRU as well. That he helped certain people launder money."

Shvets gave him a wicked grin. Dorfman had, in fact, been a spy for the KGB, not the GRU. "Where have you heard such things?"

"From people who know such things," Koenig answered cagily. "Would you like to talk to them?"

Shvets suddenly got the feeling that he'd lost the upper hand. He needed to say something to fluster Koenig. "Back to these banking laws for a moment. I assume these very same laws could be used to conceal gross incompetence of your branch in Geneva . . . or better yet, that one of Herr Dorfman's colleagues at the bank helped himself to millions of dollars that did not belong to him. Don't they say that most bank heists are inside jobs?"

"That is pure, unfounded speculation."

"As is your gossip about Herr Dorfman being a GRU spy." Checkmate.

Koenig squirmed for a moment and then offered, "Would you be willing to talk to the people who have sworn that Herr Dorfman was a spy?"

"Absolutely," he said, even though he had no such intention, "but I would like to see those faxes first. Especially the one that originated in Moscow."

Koenig studied him cautiously for a moment and then said, "I will have copies of the faxes made for you. Give me a minute." He left the room, glancing back over his shoulder with a frown.

Shvets paced while he waited. This was starting to look like a big mess. Once these thieves in suits confirmed that Dorfman had worked for the KGB, they would not be the slightest bit inclined to repay a single dollar. The Germans hated the Russians almost as much as the Russians hated the Germans.

Koenig came back a few minutes later. He had two other men with him this time, and Shvets knew the jig was up. Koenig handed over the stack of faxes. They were blank, except for the sending and receiving fax numbers. The man might as well have written "Fuck you" in large letters across the top sheet. Still, it was better than nothing.

CHAPTER 41

ZURICH, SWITZERLAND

THEY had drinks in the library, although Rapp thought of it more as shots like he had done back in college, except instead of a smelly bar in upstate New York he was in a mansion on the out-skirts of one of the most refined cities in the world. Herr Ohlmeyer did not believe in ruining fine spir-its with anything other than ice, so the liquor was served either up, on the rocks, or neat, which Rapp learned was basically naked, meaning nothing but the booze. Rapp chose a glass of sixteen-year-old Lagavulin single malt scotch and asked for it on the rocks. Ohlmeyer liked playing host and told Rapp it was a fine choice. Rapp took the glass, smiled, and said, "Thank you."

Greta had not made her entrance yet, so Rapp took the opportunity to corner Hurley, who was standing by the massive granite fireplace speaking with one of Ohlmeyer's two sons. He approached

Hurley from behind and tapped him on the shoulder. "We need to talk."

Hurley said something to Ohlmeyer's son in German that Rapp did not understand, and after he had walked away, Hurley turned to Rapp and asked, "What's up?"

Rapp jerked his head in the direction of the small soundproof office. "What was that all about?"

Hurley's jaw clenched as was his habit when he didn't want to talk about something. Reluctantly he said, "It's part of the deal. Don't worry. Just listen to Carl, he knows what he's doing."

"Does Irene know about it, or Spencer Tracy, that guy who I'm not supposed to know?" That was how Rapp referred to the man he had met briefly at the offices of International Software Logistics, the man who, he assumed, was running the show. The question caused the veins on Hurley's neck to bulge, which in turn caused Rapp to take a step back. That particular physical cue was often a precursor to Hurley's blowing his top.

Hurley felt the older Ohlmeyer's eyes on him and told himself to take a deep breath through his nose and exhale through his mouth. It was a trick Lewis had taught him. It helped him center himself. Ohlmeyer despised public outbursts. "Listen, kid . . . this is a tough business. There's certain things they don't need to know about, and quite frankly, don't want to know about."

Rapp considered that for a second before asking, "Can it get me in trouble?"

"Pretty much everything we do can get you in trouble with someone. This is about taking care of yourself. No one else needs to know about this other than Carl and his two boys."

Rapp took a sip of his scotch and was about to ask another question, but thought better of it. *Don't look a gift horse in the mouth.*

Hurley wished he could say more, but the kid would have to figure it out the hard way, as he himself had had to do back in the day. He took a big gulp of bourbon and thought about how much easier it would have been if someone had just pointed a few things out to him. Hurley changed his mind and decided to let it fly. "Kid . . . you're good, and that's no small thing coming from me. My job is to find faults and try to beat them out of you. At some point in this line of work . . . I don't care how good you are . . . I don't care how just your cause . . . sooner or later you're going to land yourself in a big pile of shit. It might be your fault, although more than likely, it'll be some asshole back stateside out to make a name for himself so he can advance his career. He'll put a target on your back, and trust me on this one, even though you're going to want to stand and fight, you need to run. Run and hide . . . lie low . . . wait for things to blow over."

"And then what?"

"You live to fight another day, or maybe you just disappear for good." Rapp frowned, and Hurley knew exactly what he was thinking. "We're not that different, kid. The idea of running away for good isn't in our veins, but it's nice to have options. You bide your time, you find out who it is who's out to get you, and then you go after them."

Rapp absorbed the advice and looked around the courtly library. "When are we shipping out?"

"Tomorrow morning. I was going to tell you guys later."

"Where to?"

"Back to the scene of the crime."

"Beirut?" Rapp whispered.

"Yep." Hurley held up his glass. "Although I might have a small job for you first."

"What kind of job?"

"We might have a lead on someone."

"Who?"

"I don't want to say yet."

"Come on!"

"Nope . . . no sense in getting your hopes up. Irene is flying over in the morning to brief us. If she's verified it, I will send you on a quick one-day detour, and then you can join up with us in Beirut."

"And the intel on Beirut?"

"It's good . . . really good. These guys have been singing like birds all day."

The men spent another thirty minutes in the library. Ohlmeyer took the time to introduce both of his sons to Rapp and Richards. The older one was August and the younger was Robert, and both were vice presidents at the bank and held positions on the board. The patriarch of the family assured the two young men that they could trust his sons, and Hurley seconded the opinion. Ohlmeyer knew that they would be leaving in the morning and suggested that they reconvene at the earliest possible time to work out the protocols and to make sure that each man understood the details of his various legends.

CHAPTER 42

SHORTLY before seven they moved from the library to a sitting room that was decorated in the French Baroque style. The white, carved flowers, leaves, and shells on the furniture and molding were in stark contrast to the deep natural woods of the library. Sitting on one of the room's four sofas was Greta. Next to her was an older woman whom Rapp took to be her grandmother, and thus Carl Ohlmeyer's wife.

Greta smiled at him from across the room. Rapp, in control of his faculties this time, flashed her a crooked grin and walked over, shaking his head. "Good evening, ladies." Rapp offered his hand again. This time it was dry. "Greta, you look lovely."

"Thank you, Mitch . . . I mean Mike."

Rapp laughed, "You're good."

"I'd like you to meet my grandmother, Elsa."

Rapp offered his hand. "Very nice to meet you,

Frau Ohlmeyer. You have a lovely home." Rapp thought he noticed something wrong with her eyes when she smiled. A certain disconnect. Her grip was also a bit weak, and he wondered if she might be ill.

Herr Ohlmeyer was suddenly at Rapp's side. "Michael, I see you have met Greta."

"Yes, we bumped into each other this afternoon."

"And my wife." Ohlmeyer placed a hand on her shoulder.

"Yes."

Looking back at his granddaughter, he said, "Greta is our pride and joy."

"I can see why. She is very sharp."

"Yes, and so far the only one of my grandchildren who has shown any interest in getting into the banking business."

For the next five minutes, Rapp got the family history. Carl and Elsa had two boys and two girls. One daughter was married and lived in London and the other was divorced and in Spain. August's and Robert's wives were currently on vacation with their sister-in-law at her Spanish villa. There were eleven grandchildren, of which Greta was the third-eldest. Elsa did not speak, although she did smile a few times. Richards, Hurley, and the two brothers were at the opposite end of the room, no doubt discussing matters of far greater importance, but Rapp didn't beat up on himself too badly. Standing this close to Greta was worth it. Every chance Rapp got he stole a look. Her high ponytail had been changed out for a loose clip in the back that made her look much more mature than when he'd met her earlier in the day. She was wearing a cobalt-blue silk blouse and a black skirt with gray tights. He thought Herr Ohlmeyer caught him at least once ogling her and he had no idea what Elsa was thinking. She just kept smiling at him with that faraway look in her eyes.

The Ohlmeyers were kind enough not to ask him any personal questions about his own family, as he would have been forced to tell them a lie. Herr Ohlmeyer decided it was time to sit for dinner. He asked for his wife's hand, but before she stood, she pulled her granddaughter close and whispered something in her ear. Greta giggled, while her grandmother pulled away and flashed Rapp an intriguing smile, before pulling her granddaughter close again. She whispered another few lines before finally taking her husband's hand and standing.

Elsa took a step toward Rapp, and to his surprise, she reached out and gently patted him on the cheek. She gave him a warm smile and then walked away without saying a word.

Rapp turned to Greta. "You have a very interesting grandmother."

Greta reached out and grabbed his arm, pulling him close and walking him toward the dining room, but in no rush to catch up with the others. "Granny Elsa is an amazing woman. Unfortunately, she is not well."

"What's wrong?" Rapp said, as his stomach did flips over Greta's touch.

"She has Alzheimer's."

"I'm sorry."

"No need to be sorry. These things happen. Such is life."

"I suppose," Rapp said, turning toward her. She smelled so good, he wanted to bury his face in her mane of shiny blond hair.

"She has no regrets. She led a very active life up until just a year ago. I am living here now and working at the bank. This way I can spend time with her . . . while she still remembers me."

"That's nice."

"We spend our evenings going through letters and photos. There is so much family history that only she knows. My grandfather is a brilliant man, but he has a hard time remembering the names of his own grandchildren."

"Not yours. You can tell, he thinks the world of you."

"Well . . . I work for him. I would hope he remembers my name."

As they entered the dining room, Rapp said, "Do you mind me asking what your grandmother whispered in your ear?"

Greta gave him a nervous laugh and rested her head against his shoulder before releasing his arm. "Maybe after a few drinks."

Rapp followed her like a puppy dog down the right side of the long table. There were chairs for twenty but they were only eight, so they clustered at the far end with Carl at the head of the table and Elsa to his left, followed by Greta and Rapp. Hurley was to Carl's right, followed by August, then Richards, and finally Robert.

The wineglasses were filled and conversations that had been going continued while new ones were started. Richards got Rapp's attention at one point and gave him a you-lucky-bastard shake of his head while darting his eyes at Greta. Rapp for his part struck up a rather boring conversation with Greta's uncle, who was sitting directly across from him. When Greta had finished her glass of wine Rapp leaned over and asked, "So can you tell me now?"

Greta slid her hand over and patted his thigh. "One more glass, I think." She held up her glass and one of the servants filled it. "So how does an all-American boy such as yourself end up in this nasty line of work?"

"We get recruited like any other profession."

"So your background is military?"

Rapp shook his head and smiled. "I'm a fine arts major with a minor in poetry."

Greta's face lit up in surprise for a moment and then she caught herself. "You are teasing me."

"Yes, I am."

"Why?" she asked playfully.

"Because you know I can't talk about my past . . . and I tend to tease people whom I like."

"So, you like me?" she said with an approving nod.

He didn't know why he decided to say it. Maybe it was the wine, maybe it was his newfound confidence that he was finally making a difference, that he was part of something important, but he did nonetheless. Rapp leaned in close so only she could hear and said, "I don't know what it is about you, but I've had a hard time thinking of anything but you, since we met this afternoon."

She smiled at him, her cheeks flushing just a touch. "You are different. Not so guarded."

Rapp laughed. "I'm probably the most guarded person you'll ever meet. Just not with you, for some reason."

"Is that good or bad?"

"I think it's good. At least it feels good." Rapp looked into her blue eyes. She was smiling back at him. He was about to really open up when Herr Ohlmeyer tapped his wineglass with his knife several times and stood. Ohlmeyer raised his glass and started giving a toast. Rapp turned his chair slightly so he could face him, and his right knee moved to within a few inches of Greta's thigh. Then her left hand slowly slid over from her lap and found his knee. From that moment on, Rapp didn't register a single word that came out of Herr Ohlmeyer's mouth. Nor did he hear anything Hurley said when he rose to make his toast.

The main course arrived. It was a braised beef of some sort, served with mushrooms, potatoes, gravy, and vegetables, the kind of meat-and-potatoes meal Rapp loved. There was only one problem. He had just stuffed a forkful of beef in his mouth when Greta leaned over and told him what her grandmother had whispered in her ear.

"My granny thinks you are extremely attractive. She told me I should sleep with you."

Rapp would have been fine if it had ended there, but it didn't. As he tried to swallow the meat Greta leaned over once more.

"She said that if I don't she will."

Rapp froze, his eyes bulged, and a piece of meat got stuck in the crossroads of his throat. His brain's autopilot kicked in and the hunk of meat came flying back up as fast as a major-league fastball. The only thing that saved it from pelting Richards in the face was Rapp's quick hands. A fit that started out as a cough morphed into eye-watering laughter. Greta smacked him on the back a few times and had to hold her napkin over her mouth to conceal her own laughter and amusement that she had set the chain of events in motion. Conversation ceased and all eyes settled on the young duo.

Greta saved them by announcing, "I am sorry." She dabbed at her eyes. "I told him a bad joke."

Rapp finally got hold of himself and everyone went back to their conversations. Rapp noticed Hurley giving him a few cautious looks, but other than that no one appeared to notice the flirting. Shortly after dessert was served, Elsa tapped Greta on the arm and told her she was tired. Everyone stood while the two women made their exit, and then Ohlmeyer suggested they retire to the library. Hurley disappeared into the small soundproof office, and it was Rapp's turn to talk with the two uncles. They gave Rapp a message service to call if he needed to contact them. He was never to call the office directly, especially if he was in trouble. Rapp kept looking over his shoulder, hoping to see Greta, but she did not return. About an hour into it the brothers thought they had made enough progress and agreed they would sit down again when Rapp came through town again in the coming weeks.

It was just before ten when the two brothers left. Rapp thanked Herr Ohlmeyer for an interesting evening and headed upstairs with one thing on his mind—Greta. He stood in the long hallway outside his room for a moment, loitering, hoping she would suddenly appear. He had no idea where her room was, but suspected that the guests were in this wing and the family's rooms were in the other wing of the house. After another fifteen seconds of standing there feeling stupid, he gave up and opened his door.

Rapp peeled off his suit coat and tie, draping both over the back of the desk chair. With the water running, he started brushing his teeth and unbuttoning his white dress shirt. He walked back into the bedroom and was dropping the dress shirt on top of the tie and coat when he thought he heard a sound at the door. He froze, hoping it was Greta. A few seconds later he heard the footsteps of someone walking away. He walked to the door and listened for a few seconds before checking the hallway. It was empty. Rapp closed the door and stood there resting his head against the door. After nearly a minute he decided he was acting like a fool. He twisted the lock from midnight to three and climbed into the big bed, wishing Greta was next to him.

He yawned and rubbed his eyes. He was tired after all. Rolling over, he extinguished the bedside lamp and thought about tomorrow. The side trip that Hurley had alluded to had his interest. He wondered who the target was, and if he'd had a direct role in the Pan Am attack. The happy thoughts of ending that type of man's life sent him drifting off toward sleep, and then suddenly there was a faint knock on the door.

Rapp threw back the blankets and rushed to the door. The knocking grew a bit louder. Rapp twisted the lock and opened the door a crack. The sight of Greta's blond hair put an instant smile on his face. She pushed through, not wanting to be discovered in the hall, closing the door behind her and locking it.

Rapp opened his mouth to speak, but she put a finger on his lips and a hand on his chest. She pushed him back toward the bed, and then, rising to her toes, she kissed him on the mouth. Rapp responded with a soft gasp and pulled her close, wrapping an arm around her waist. Hands started to roam and the kissing became intense, and then Rapp pulled her head back and rested his forehead against hers. He looked into her eyes, but before he could speak, she gave him a wicked smile and pushed him back onto the bed.

Rapp watched as Greta undid her robe, letting it fall to the floor. She was naked. He reached out for her, and she slowly climbed onto the bed. He pulled her close, kissing her neck and running a hand down her perfect, smooth, naked backside. A low rumble of approval passed his lips as he nibbled on her ear and then other parts. Holding her tight, he took control and rolled over. Rapp held her exquisite face in his hands and looked into her eyes. At that moment there was nothing beyond the here and now. There was no yesterday, or tomorrow. He hadn't felt this alive in years.

CHAPTER 43

BEIRUT, LEBANON

THEY were to meet two hours after sunrise. Sayyed asked Mughniyah why two hours, and he told him it was because the cowardly Americans attacked only with the cover of darkness and the Jewish dogs with the rising sun at their backs. Sayyed had seen the Jews attack at all hours of the day but he wasn't going to argue with Mughniyah, at least not considering his current mood.

Sayyed looked down at his little CIA guinea pig. The man was not doing well. None of the nails had grown back enough to use the pliers, so he'd been forced to drill a hole through one of the agent's nail beds to try to get him to respond to his questions. Instead the man had passed out. There were parameters in these situations, but they were only parameters. You could never tell when you had an outlier. On that note, Sayyed still wasn't sure about Cummins. Given the less than sanitary conditions, it was entirely possible that he was seriously ill. Aziz al-Abub had taught him how a subject could become sick to the point of the nervous system shutting down. Once that happened, the only thing you could do was nurse the subject back to health and then start over.

Unfortunately, Mughniyah and the others wanted answers that were simply not here. At least not in Cummins's head. They were distrustful of Ivanov and his constant plotting, but there was still a deep-seated hatred of the Americans and Jews, and they wanted to know if this man knew anything about their missing money. Beyond that there was a fundamental problem that they had overlooked, which was not unusual for the collective group. They were far too one-dimensional and always looked at a situation as if it were a street battle in Beirut. Attack, retreat, dig, and fight—this was the extent of their military repertoire. In the espionage business Sayyed had to analyze in three dimensions and project possible outcomes. This John Cummins was going to eventually end up in the hands of Ivanov, if for no other reason than that Ivanov was used to getting his way. Sayyed had to be very careful what type of questions he asked, with an eye to the fact that the subject would eventually inform Ivanov of what he'd been asked.

Sayyed would have to start the subject on a cycle of antibiotics. The others could talk all they wanted about not handing Cummins over, but Sayyed was done with him. There was nothing more to learn and he did not wish to be put in the middle of this fight. He wiped the small splotch of blood on the front of the white butcher's apron and wondered what he should tell Damascus. They would want to be fully briefed on the situation, but they did not have to deal with all of these crazy Palestinians.

That was the paradox of Lebanon in general and Beirut specifically. The Palestinians were supposed to be in Palestine, not Lebanon. The Palestinians had upset the balance that the Turks had kept for centuries. Their displacement by the Jews shattered the fragile peace and plunged the country into civil war. And now more than fifteen years later, that civil war was over and the Palestinians were growing cocksure. With relative peace, Damascus was losing its sway over how all these vying factions conducted themselves. Damascus, for its part, was slow to realize what was plain to see. The child was now an adult and did not appreciate, much less need, the consent of the parent. Fortunately for Sayyed, he was more like an uncle—a very nonjudgmental uncle. Especially this morning.

Sayyed knocked on the metal door and waited for it to be opened by the guard. He stepped into the hallway and closed the door behind him. Looking at the two guards, he said, "He will need medical attention. Pass the word to the others. I want him treated like a baby. No more kicking or punching."

The two men nodded and Sayyed moved off down the hallway, still struggling with what he should tell Damascus. He could hardly share the details of the past few days. The Swiss accounts that had been so carefully set up were now empty. Damascus had contributed zero to the accounts, but they were aware of their existence. They did not know, however, that Sayyed had set up an account for himself with the aid of Sharif and Ivanov. He took a cut of every arms shipment that came into the country by helping assure that the various Syrian factions would leave the merchants be. Damascus needed to be kept in the dark as long as possible.

He stopped in the small sandbagged lobby on the first floor. The door was completely blocked and the floor-to-ceiling windows on each side were now nothing but small portholes, just enough to allow a man to take up a rifle position. Oh, how he wished those pesky Maronites would go away. He climbed to the second story and followed the extension cords and phone lines to the makeshift command post. Once again the hallway was filled with armed men, but this time they did not upset Sayyed. He needed them to deter the Christians from doing anything stupid.

They were living in abject squalor. There was no running water, electricity, or phone service. The men were relieving themselves in the basement in random rooms and corners. No wonder Cummins was sick. Electricity and phone service would have to be brought in from three blocks away, via a series of patched cords and lines that had been spliced into the service of an apartment building.

The guards stepped aside so he could pass, and he entered the command post. The men were standing around a sheet of plywood that had been placed on top of two fifty-gallon oil drums—Mughniyah and Badredeen from Islamic Jihad; Jalil, who was Sayyed's Iranian counterpart; and Radih from Fatah. Each man had benefited handsomely from his association with the Turkish arms dealer and now they were once again paupers.

"Close the door," Mughniyah commanded.

Sayyed did so, and joined the men at the makeshift table.

"Well?" Mughniyah asked.

"Nothing."

"Nothing?" Radih asked, obviously dubious.

Sayyed looked at the little toad from Fatah and said, "I have been informed that some of your men have taken certain liberties with my prisoner over the past few days."

"Your prisoner?" Radih shouted. "He is my prisoner!"

"The prisoner," Sayyed said, "has been kicked and brutalized by your men and due to the lack of sanitary conditions from your men defecating all over the basement like a pack of wild dogs, it appears *the* prisoner is now ill."

Badredeen made a foul face and said, "Really . . . you should institute some basic hygiene. At least have the men go on the roof. The sun will take care of it for you."

"Do you want to walk up seven flights of stairs to go to the bathroom?" Radih asked.

"Enough," yelled an impatient Mughniyah. He looked from one end of the table to the other, making it clear to all that he was not in the mood for petty arguments. "Someone has stolen millions of dollars from us and you want to argue about where the men should shit?"

"I was only—"

"Silence!" Mughniyah screeched. With his fists clenched he turned on Radih. "I am sick of it . . . all of the complaining and fighting, the bickering, and for what . . . it gets us nowhere. Millions are gone, Sharif is dead, our banker is dead, and that vulture Ivanov is now talking about coming to Beirut for the first time in years. Am I the only one who finds this a bit disconcerting?"

"He told me he had nothing to do with Sharif's murder," Sayyed offered.

"And since when do you believe anything that comes out of a Russian's mouth?"

"I have no trust in the man, but on this point, he did seem to be upset that someone had killed Sharif."

"Maybe someone else did kill Sharif, and that was when Ivanov decided that with our Turkish friend gone it was the perfect time to take all of the money."

Sayyed considered that one for a moment. It was possible. Ivanov had proven many times that he could be ruthless.

"Add to that these damn Christians deciding to make a show of strength." Mughniyah gave a swift shake of his head. "I like none of it. Something is very wrong and we know far too little."

"Why would Ivanov want to visit Beirut?" Badredeen asked.

"Land."

All eyes fell on Colonel Jalil of the Iranian Quds Force. "Explain," Mughniyah ordered.

"There is a great deal of valuable land here in Beirut, and many are saying that with war finally behind us, there are huge sums of money to be made."

"Why can't these people leave us alone?" Mughniyah asked no one in particular.

"What about the Americans?" Radih asked. "We have one of their agents in this very building."

"Who was sent here to negotiate the release of the businessman you kidnapped." Sayyed's tone suggested what he thought of the idea.

"That is the story he has given you."

Sayyed turned his head to look at Radih. "You doubt my ability to get the truth out of people?"

"None of us are perfect."

"So you think the American is holding back on us? That his coming here is all part of a master plan by the Americans to take over Beirut?"

"I did not say that."

"You did, in so many words." Looking back toward the leaders of Islamic Jihad, he said, "We do not have enough information to know what is actually happening. It could be anyone at this point, but based on what we do know, we have to assume that Ivanov is the front runner."

"So what should we do?" Badredeen asked.

Sayyed thought about it for a moment and then said, "Let him come to Beirut. Keep our eyes and ears open and see what we can find out."

Mughniyah was scratching his beard thinking

about what had been said. "Beirut is our fortress. Spread the word to our people at the docks and the airport. I want to know of anything that looks suspicious. Americans, Russians, Jews . . . I don't care."

"And we should alert our allies," the Iranian said. "Everyone should be extra careful until we know exactly what is going on."

"I agree," Mughniyah said. "Quietly spread the word to our people in Europe. Especially anyone who has a connection to Sharif. Let them know of our concerns . . . that someone might be targeting us."

It was the right decision, but Sayyed needed to add something. "No mention of the money, though. At least not yet." One by one they all nodded as he knew they would. To a man, they were too proud to admit that they had been duped out of such a large sum of money.

CHAPTER 44

ZURICH, SWITZERLAND

THE Gulfstream 450 landed at Zurich International Airport and proceeded to the fueling pad rather than Customs. The flight plan stated that the plane was stopping for fuel before continuing to Kuwait. The truck was waiting, and while one of the men began to unwind the hose, a second man in blue coveralls approached the plane's fuselage, opened his hand, and slapped the side of the plane three times. A second later the hatch opened and the stairs lowered. The man bounded up the steps and hit the button to pull the stairs back up and close the hatch. He checked to make sure the cockpit door was closed and proceeded into the cabin.

Hurley took off the baseball cap and sat in one of the two open chairs across from Irene Kennedy. They were separated by a table. "Good morning." Hurley tapped the thick file that was sitting in front of the young counterterrorism analyst. "I assume that's for me."

Kennedy pulled the file closer to herself and said, "Before we get to this, there are a few things we need to discuss."

"Well, let's make it quick, because I have a schedule to keep, and we need to get you back up in the air before Customs comes poking around."

She nodded as if to say fine and then asked, "What was the final dollar amount?"

"For?"

"You know damn well what for."

"Oh . . . the thing." Hurley looked around the cabin as if he was trying to add it all up in his head. "I suppose somewhere in the neighborhood of . . ." Hurley flashed her a four with one hand and a five with the other. "Roughly, of course. A lot of it gets siphoned off along the way. Fees and whatnot."

"You're sure?" Kennedy asked, fairly confident that he was lying to her.

"Irene, to be frank, it's really none of your business. This is between Tom and me."

"Well, Thomas wanted me to ask you face-to-face, since you're so paranoid about using phones."

"He knows damn well why I don't use phones. The same reason he doesn't."

"True . . . but he still wants to know."

"Why?" Hurley asked.

"Because he thinks you're holding back on him."

Hurley laughed. Stansfield knew damn well Hurley would never give him an official accounting.

To handle all the black-bag stuff they threw his way, he had to have access to piles of cash. "Darling niece, I think you are either bending the truth or trying to bluff me. Which one is it?"

Kennedy studied him with a crooked frown, none too happy that he had figured out what she was up to. "A little of both, I suppose."

"And why are you trying to stick your pretty little nose where it doesn't belong?"

"Because someday, not too soon, I hope, you and Thomas are going to die and somebody will need to make sense of the tangled web you've left behind."

"If anything happens to me in the next few days, tell Thomas I said to visit our old friend from Berlin who now lives in Zurich. He'll have the answers you need."

Her bluff called, Kennedy grabbed a file sitting in the seat next to her. Unlike the bland manila one on the table, this one was gray. Kennedy placed it in front of Hurley and opened it to reveal a black-and-white photograph of a man exiting a car on an unknown city street. "Look familiar?"

Hurley glanced at the photo and lied. "Not really."

"This is Nikolai Shvets . . . Name ring a bell?"

"A soft bell. I have a lot of Russian names floating around in my head. It's hard to keep them all straight. Kind of like reading *War and Peace*."

"Sure," Kennedy replied, not buying a word of it. "Care to guess where this photo was taken?"

Hurley glanced at his watch. "We don't have

time to play Twenty Questions, young lady, so let's get on with it."

"Hamburg. A certain bank that drew a lot of interest yesterday. Any idea why one of Mikhail Ivanov's top deputies would show up yesterday, of all days?"

Hurley shook his head.

"He threatened the bank's president about some missing funds." Kennedy searched his face for some recognition. "And if your answer is still no, I won't bother playing you the tape of your old friend Ivanov talking to a certain terrorist that we've been looking for."

Hurley frowned. He didn't like being forced to answer this kind of question by someone so junior.

"Thomas told me," Kennedy said, "that you would be reluctant to talk about this, but nonetheless, I have been ordered to get an answer from you."

"What kind of answer?"

"How many people did you piss off yesterday, other than the ones we know about?"

"It was a thick file." Hurley shrugged. "Some accounts had names attached to them . . . others were just numbers."

"So your earlier estimate might be a little light?"

"Get to your point."

"It looks like you've pissed off some people in Moscow, and you know how they can be when they're upset. They don't play nice. If they get so much as an inkling that we were behind any of this . . ." She shook her head. "We'll be in serious trouble."

"So you want me to confirm what you don't want to hear?"

"I just want to know the facts so I can go back and brief Thomas. He needs to tell our embassy people, if they are in danger of reprisals, and anyone else who might get stuck in Ivanov's crosshairs."

Hurley swore under his breath and finally said, "Yes, I took some of the bastard's money, and with any luck it'll be the beginning of the end of him."

Kennedy took the news without comment and placed a small tape player between them. "Now . . . you will be very interested to hear this brief conversation."

Kennedy pressed play and the slurred voice of Mikhail Ivanov could be heard asking, *"My package . . . Is it ready? You haven't decided to negotiate with the Persians, have you?"*

"I am standing by our deal."

Kennedy pressed the stop button. "You recognize the first voice?"

Hurley nodded. "Ivanov."

"Correct. The second voice?"

"No."

"Colonel Assef Sayyed."

Hurley was impressed. "What the hell are they doing talking on an open line?"

"They weren't, but you didn't hear that from me."

"Then how'd you get it?"

"I can't say." Kennedy pressed play again.

"When can I expect it to be retrieved? I assume you are still sending someone."

"Yes . . . although I am considering coming my-self. . . . You did offer . . . didn't you."

"Absolutely."

"Good. I will be there in three days. Maybe sooner."

Kennedy hit stop. "There's more. Tapes of Iva-nov and Sayyed and others as well. You'll want to listen to all of them, but Thomas does not want you bringing the tapes into Beirut."

"Understood. Did you happen to pick up Badre-deen or Mughniyah?"

"Unfortunately, no, but we have a few others that I think will please you." Kennedy retrieved another folder from her briefcase and laid it before Hurley. "Tarik al Ismael."

"Music to my fucking ears. Please tell me you ID'd the prick."

"Hiding right under our noses a few kilometers down the road."

"Where?"

"He's been working at the UN office in Geneva. Attached to the Office for the Coordination of Hu-manitarian Affairs, if you can believe it. He lost a few pounds, cut his hair and beard, and ditched his contacts for eyeglasses. You have to admire his tradecraft." Kennedy fingered the old photo from his days when he was running operations for the Libyan intelligence service, and then the new photo. "It's a pretty good effort."

"You sure it's him?"

"Ninety percent on the photo and ninety-nine point nine on the voice ID. And he was calling about money missing from his account. If we hadn't had the big ears focused on these banks, I don't think we would have ever caught him."

Hurley thought of their conversation last night and frowned. "So you want to send Rapp after him?"

"Not just me. Ismael is near the top of Thomas's list."

"I don't know, Irene," Hurley said with obvious reluctance. "Ismael could bite back. He's not some fat arms dealer. He's a real killer."

"In a perfect world, Thomas would send all three of you after him, but we don't have that luxury right now."

"Why? Let's put Beirut off for a few days."

Like a Vegas dealer, Kennedy slid the gray file off to the side and moved the manila file front and center. "In the transcript, you heard Ivanov ask if his package was ready?"

"Yeah."

"He asked Sayyed if he was going to negotiate with the Persians instead . . ."

"Yeah."

"Remember what they did to Buckley?"

"Remember—I think about it all the time. I was just telling Mitch and Bobby Richards about him."

"Well, Thomas thinks the Schnoz is the package they are referring to."

Everything stopped. Hurley didn't so much as twitch for a good ten seconds. He'd known the Schnoz for close to twenty years and there was a running shopping list in his head of all the operations he'd been involved in. After a quick assessment of the potential damage, he leaned back and dropped the F bomb. Cummins had worked in Moscow before Damascus. If the Russians got their hands on him, they would be screwed in some of their most sensitive operations. He shook his head to get over the shock and said, "We can't let that happen."

"Thomas agrees. He has a source that says Schnoz is still alive. Emaciated and battered, but still alive."

"Shit."

"That's why he wants you and Richards to get to Beirut ASAP. As we discussed last night, Rapp will join up with you tomorrow or the next day. In the meantime, you two start poking around. If you can't find anything in forty-eight hours, Thomas wants you to use some of the new funds to negotiate for the Schnoz's release. Very quietly, though."

"Of course." Hurley was still trying to calculate the damage. "What about backup?"

"He's agreed to send a SOG team, but doesn't want to put them in-country until you have something solid."

"Understood." SOG stood for Special Operations Group. There was a good chance Hurley would know the men. "Air cover?"

"If you need it he'll get it. Last resort, though."

Before Hurley could comment, there was a banging on the side of the plane and he realized it was time to go. Kennedy passed him two files. "Those are for you. This one," she said as she handed him a third, "is for Mitch. Make sure he knows to destroy it before he makes contact with Ismael."

"Will do." Hurley stood. "Anything else?"

Kennedy joined him in the aisle. She didn't want him to go, but he was a good soldier, so there was no stopping him. So much of their shared sorrow revolved around that once-beautiful city on the eastern shore of the Mediterranean.

Hurley could see that she was concerned, and he knew why. He gave her a hug and said, "Don't worry. Everything will be fine."

"Yeah," she said, not really believing it herself and holding back the tears. "Beirut's still a nasty place." She stayed strong for him. There was no turning back now that he knew. The only thing to do was support him. She kissed him on the cheek and said, "Be careful."

CHAPTER 45

GENEVA, SWITZERLAND

WHEN it was all done Rapp would swear that he felt the zip of the bullet as it passed his left temple. It was that close. The only thing that saved him was the awkward movement that the Libyan made as he drew his pistol. The fake was weak. He looked over his left shoulder a bit too dramatically and then swung back to his right, drawing his gun, his long overcoat flaring like a matador's cape. The other reason Rapp didn't fall for it was that mean old cuss Stan Hurley. It was the first time Rapp could honestly say he was grateful for all the shit Hurley had heaped on him. All of that damn methodical, shitty training paid off in the split second it took Ismael to draw his gun and turn on him.

The fact that Rapp didn't want to kill the wrong man also contributed to the harsh reality that he was now cowering behind a Swiss mailbox, rounds of an undetermined caliber thudding into the metal receptacle at an alarming rate. And Hurley had been right, of course. He had told them that there were two ways to win a gunfight. Either land the first shot or find cover and conserve your ammunition. Hurley had put them in a situation so similar to this that it was now damn near calming to listen to his opponent mindlessly fire one shot after the next into a four-sided box of steel that had survived every change of season for the past fifty years.

Back in the woods of Virginia the idea was to find cover while Hurley fired live shots at you. And mind you, he didn't fire them safely over the horizon. He liked to hit things close to you. Not rocks or anything hard enough to cause a life-ending ricochet, but soft things like dirt, sandbags, and wood. The object of the lesson was to teach you what it felt like to be shot at, so you could keep your head when confronted with the real thing. As a bonus, you learned to count not just the number of rounds you fired, but the number of rounds your opponent fired as well. At first, the exercise was unnerving, but after a while, as with most things in life, you adapted and got the hang of it.

Rapp squatted, his back pressed firmly against the mailbox, and counted the number of shots, which had been eight so far. He was waiting for the inevitable calm in the storm. There was a problem, however. While Rapp's pistols were equipped with silencers, the Libyan's gun was not. Eight extremely loud gunshots had rung out in a city with one of the lowest murder rates in the entire industrialized world. It might as well have been an artillery barrage.

There was no telling how many extra magazines the Libyan had in his possession, but he doubted the man could match the seventy-two rounds Rapp carried. Rapp released the grip of his still-holstered Beretta and stabbed the big gray button on his Timex digital watch. Just as Hurley had taught him, it was set for stopwatch mode. The average response time for a police car in a city of this size was roughly three minutes. And that was assuming there wasn't one nearby. There were rules that were flexible, and there were rules that couldn't be broken, and killing a police officer was one of those unbreakable rules. Hurley had told them, "If you kill a cop I will kill you before they do."

The first eight shots had come in rapid succession. By the sound they were 9mm or maybe .40 caliber at the most. Rapp never heard where the first one landed after it flew past his head, but the second shot had blown out the driver's-side window of the white BMW parked a few feet away, which was now chirping and beeping like a car with Tourette's syndrome. The next six had hit the mailbox. Not a smart move unless he had a second gun, and he was closing on him. Rapp thought that unlikely. Ismael was spooked and on the run, which in itself bothered Rapp.

The drive from Zurich had been easy. Just under three hours, counting a quick stop to call the answering service and confirm that the target was at his place of work. The file was straightforward. They were monitoring the calls he made at work, they knew where he lived and the make and model of his car. Hurley gave Rapp specific instructions. Tail Ismael after work and follow him to his apartment. If he comes out for an errand or an evening stroll and there's an opportunity, take him. If not, wait until morning and shoot him while he's getting into his car. Rapp had followed the instructions to the letter, and when Ismael bowed out of his apartment at ten-oh-nine that evening, Rapp watched him round the corner and then pursued on foot.

A block later Rapp noticed that Ismael had a duffel bag slung over his left shoulder. It was at that point that the wheels started to turn in Rapp's head. He asked himself if it was normal to leave your apartment on a crisp winter night when you should be getting into bed. It wasn't unheard of for someone to head out after ten, but it was far from common. Especially on a Tuesday night. Throw in the overnight bag and you now had someone who might be running. That was pretty much what Rapp was thinking when Ismael pulled his lame matador move. That, and wondering if he could rush him at the next intersection, shoot him in the back of the head, and be in France before midnight.

Now, because he had failed to heed Hurley's warnings, he was crouched behind a mailbox, counting bullets and wondering if Ismael had one or two guns. One more shot thudded into the mailbox and then there was a two-second pause. Rapp stuck out his gloved hand to see if he could draw a shot. He pulled it back as a tenth bullet whistled harmlessly past. It sparked off the stone sidewalk and skipped down the street. Rapp thought he heard the clank of a slide locking in the open position, but he wasn't sure. A split second later he heard the heavy footsteps of someone running. That was it. He was either reloading or out.

Rapp drew the silenced Beretta from under his right arm and bolted between the two parked cars to his left. He stayed low, glancing over the roofs of the cars. He caught a glimpse of the Libyan as he took a left turn at the next corner. That put a smile on Rapp's face. *Run all you want,* he thought. The more distance we can put between us and those ten muzzle blasts the better.

Rapp rounded the corner wide and fast, trying to keep the parked cars between himself and Ismael. They were on the Left Bank, or Rive Gauche, and Ismael was headed toward the Rhone. They had just turned off a street that was purely residential and onto one that was a mix of retail and apartments. The shops were all closed and fortunately the sidewalk was deserted. Rapp stayed in the street and broke into a full sprint. Geneva, because it was wedged between two mountain ranges on one end and a lake on the other, was even more cramped than your standard European city. The streets were barely wide enough for two small cars to pass. An American SUV was out of the question.

Ismael was a good hundred feet in front of him. Not an easy shot standing still, let alone running and aiming at a moving target. Rapp kept the pistol at his side. Long black coat, black pants, black shoes, and a black gun. Black on black. Nothing to see. He was gaining on Ismael with every stride, staying low, the top of his head just barely visible over the roofs of the vehicles. And then Ismael saw him as Rapp passed from one car to the next. There was now no more than seventy feet of separation. Just over twenty yards. Either the man was really slow or Rapp was really fast, or probably both.

Sixty feet and closing was the best Rapp could figure when they locked eyes. Rapp started to raise his pistol to fire, but before he had it leveled, Ismael was swinging the bag around and then all hell broke loose. The bag exploded, spitting red-orange flashes on the dark street. Rapp turtled, dropping behind a nice piece of German steel. Counting shots was not an option with whatever it was in the overnight bag. The rate of fire told Rapp that it was probably an Uzi or a MAC-10. To the uninitiated, a gun was a gun, but in his new line of work, caliber was every bit as important as rate of fire. Since the Mercedes had no problem stopping the rounds, Rapp concluded it was a 9mm Uzi. If it had been the MAC-10 he would have felt the punch of the .45 caliber rounds as they penetrated the body and rattled around the interior of the car.

Rapp glanced at his watch as glass rained down on him from the blown-out windows. He could picture, in his mind's eye, the Libyan backing up as he laid down fire. The Uzi he was firing used either twenty-, thirty-two-, or forty-round magazines. The forty was unlikely because it probably wouldn't fit in the bag, and if it was twenty he would be done already, so that meant it was thirty-two rounds and he was almost out. And once Rapp heard the click it would be over. There was no way the guy could pull a weapon like that out of a bag and reload it before Rapp was on him.

The bullets stopped, the noise replaced by a half dozen car alarms that were now chirping and beeping and screeching and flashing. Rapp came up with his weapon this time, his finger on the trigger, ready to fire. Ismael was gone. Rapp caught a glimpse of him farther down the block and tore off, again staying in the street so he could use the cars for cover. The clock in his head was marking time as he pressed his advantage. He closed again to within sixty feet. Ismael looked over his shoulder, raised the bag, and let loose another burst. Rapp went into a crouch behind a car but kept moving. Rapp couldn't be sure if it was a four- or five-round burst, but it had stopped and Ismael was on the run again. Rapp, thinking the gun was out of bullets, or close to being out, ran tall now, more worried about speed than cover.

Ismael made it to the corner and turned left. Rapp stayed wide again, and when he cleared the corner, he came upon the unwelcome sight of Ismael standing there with his left arm wrenched around a woman's throat. Rapp didn't look at her. He didn't want to look at her. Old, young, fat, skinny, none of it mattered. Ismael's right hand was still in the duffel bag, gripping the Uzi, which might or might not be out of bullets. Ismael started screaming at him to drop his weapon or he would kill the woman. Rapp continued to close as he had been taught. His pistol was up, directly in front of his face, an extension of his left eye, which was attached to his brain, which was still counting the seconds and telling him to finish this and get the hell out of there.

The woman was now screaming, and for the first time Rapp noticed she had a small dog on a leash that was yipping and snapping at Ismael's legs. He had no doubt that Ismael would kill the woman, but what purpose would it serve? If Ismael had any bullets left in that gun he would turn it on Rapp right now and zip him with a nice burst to the chest. If he shot the woman, he was a dead man, and he didn't want to die, as he had proven very loudly over the last half minute. His only way out of this was to kill the man who had been chasing him. He was nicely shielded by the woman. All he had to do was swing the bag around and unload. Rapp stopped at twenty feet and decided that since Ismael hadn't taken aim at his chest, he was bluffing.

In the end, it was the dog that tilted things in Rapp's favor. Ismael wisely tried to create some distance between them by stepping back. What he didn't know, because he hadn't bothered to look down, was that the little yipping dog had run a couple of circles around them, and his leash had formed a nice little lasso around the Libyan's ankles. Ismael stumbled and jerked to his left to catch himself. For a brief second, the side of his head was clearly visible. Rapp was now only twenty feet away. He squeezed the trigger once, and that was all it took.

CHAPTER 46

BEIRUT, LEBANON

HURLEY stepped onto the roof, a bottle of Jack Daniel's in his hand, his thoughts already traveling back in time. The hotel was in a neighborhood called Bourj Hammoud. It was controlled by the Armenians, which was why Hurley had decided to stay here for the night. The Armenians were one of the few factions that had managed to stay neutral during the civil war. There had been a few shots fired between the Armenians and their Maronite neighbors, but no major battles.

It had been a strange day—the meeting with Kennedy, the briefing with Rapp before sending him off, and the analysis of the intercepts. There was nothing like stealing a man's fortune to get him riled up. Voices they hadn't tracked in years had popped up. Beirut was going to be a very target-rich environment. Before they could leave, though, they had to look the part. He dragged Richards to one of Zurich's secondhand clothing stores, where they purchased some ill-fitting suits and dress shirts, well-worn shoes, and some beat-up luggage. Hurley added some gray to his hair and both men skipped shaving. They boarded a flight for Paris and then on to Beirut, just two men in a sea of travelers.

They arrived as the sun was setting on the far end of the Mediterranean, feeling a mix of anticipation, anger, and apprehension. That's what Beirut did to Hurley. He'd spent time in the city before the civil war, back when it was a thriving mecca of Christians and Muslims living side by side, socializing, raising families, enjoying life, and for the most part getting along. Then the PLO began to radicalize the slums and demand a say in how things were run. The Maronites had no intention of sharing rule with these gypsies, and the battle lines were drawn. No one, not even Hurley, had thought the disagreement so egregious that it would plunge the city into a fifteen-year civil war, but it did. More than a million had fled, 250,000 were killed, hundreds of thousands of people were wounded and crippled, and the economy and much of central Beirut were laid to waste. That such a great city could be so thoroughly destroyed was enough to shake the faith of even the most optimistic.

At the airport there were a few signs that things were headed in the right direction. The part of the terminal that had been severely damaged during the Israeli shelling of 1982 was now torn down, and reconstruction was under way. Hurley and Richards trudged down the metal stairs with their fellow passengers. Tired and bored Lebanese militiamen flanked the travelers and directed them toward Immigration and Customs. The last time Hurley had been here, Immigration and Customs consisted of a single portly bureaucrat sitting behind a metal desk on the tarmac. His job had been less about border security than about collecting the bribes needed to enter the country. Now they filed into the airport, where there were posterboards announcing ambitious rebuilding plans.

They threaded through the Customs lines, trying their best to look tired and bored. Richards passed with barely a glance. He handed over his cash that they called a fee, but was more of a bribe, because it never saw its way into the Treasury. Hurley had to answer a few questions from the Customs official, but nothing that was too alarming. He thought he caught one of the supervisors standing behind the three Customs agents paying him a little too much attention, but that, after all, was his job. In the end it was nothing to worry about. The man did not intervene or follow them to baggage claim.

They collected their luggage and stood in line once again. This time they were both searched. Then, outside at the cab stand, Hurley slipped the man a twenty-dollar bill and told him in Arabic that he wanted to pick his own cab. For no reason other than the fact that it was random, Hurley chose the fourth cab in line. They took it to the under-renovation Intercontinental Hotel, where they went inside and bought a drink. This was also where Hurley persuaded the bartender to sell him the bottle of Jack Daniel's. From there, they found another cab, skirted the central business district, and had the man drop them off three blocks from the Mar Yousif Inn.

Hurley would have preferred to have had the safe house ready, but there was no getting around it. Not if he wanted to use someone he could absolutely trust. Besides, there was only so much he could control. Setting up a new base of operations was never easy, and was even more difficult in a town like this, with shifting battle lines.

Hurley looked out across the skyline. He couldn't swear, but there seemed to be quite a few more lights than there had been a few years earlier. Perhaps progress was being made. He heard some voices and stepped around the top of the blockhouse that encased the stairs. A few of the hotel workers were clustered around a folding table, sitting in plastic chairs. They waved to Hurley. He flashed them a smile and walked to the far edge. Beirut was like most densely packed cities, in that the inhabitants used roofs to try to escape the claustrophobic feeling of being shut in. There was another plastic chair in the corner where he was standing, but he didn't feel like sitting. He looked north, over the rooftops, at the ocean. Way out there on the horizon to the northwest he could make out the glow of the lights on Cyprus. Back to the south the airport was lit up, receiving its last few flights for the day.

A not-so-welcome memory started to bubble up. Hurley gripped the bottle tightly, held it to his lips, and took a swig of Jack with the hope that he could drown it out. After a minute he started up a heater and tried to remember the last time he'd been in the city. He wasn't counting his last trip two years earlier, as he had been in and out in less than a day. Hardly enough time to look up any of his old contacts. The city brought back so many memories. A few good, a lot bad.

He took another swig but it didn't work this time. His gaze was drawn to the west where the old embassy had stood. He'd been here that day—here being the Bourj Hammoud district. Hurley had met one of his contacts for coffee that morning, a man named Levon Petrosian, the Armenian crime boss who kept things working during the civil war. In addition to making sure the neighborhood had power, water, and food, Petrosian handled all of the gambling and prostitution, and of course collected a pretty penny in protection money. After their meeting, Hurley decided to take the crazy Armenian up on his offer to sample some of the merchandise. Hurley had been in bed with two women from the Armenian Highlands of Eastern Turkey when the explosion rocked the room.

His worst fears were realized when he'd scrambled onto the roof, still pulling on his pants. Bombs were becoming increasingly common back in 1983, but this one was much bigger than the average mortar round or RPG. The plume of debris and smoke was close enough to the embassy that Hurley was certain it had been the target. The only question was the amount of damage done. Hurley raced back to the bedroom to collect the rest of his stuff and then down to the street, where his driver was asleep behind the wheel of the company Jeep. Hurley bumped him out of the driver's seat, started the Jeep, and tore off down the street.

When he arrived and looked up at the seven-story building his heart was in his throat. The front entrance was gone. A gaping hole from the seventh floor all the way to the first. A big gash between the main part of the embassy and one of the wings. Strangely enough, the roof, for the most part, was intact. He remembered something about its being reinforced to handle all the communications gear they'd put up there. As the dust settled, the first of the survivors began to crawl out of the building. Hurley was still holding on to hope at that point.

It would be two full days before they grasped the extent of the damage. By then, the hope that Hurley had felt in those moments after watching the first survivor come out of the building was entirely gone, along with one of his best friends, Irene Kennedy's father, and sixty-two others. As was standard for the Lebanese civil war, the locals took the brunt of the blast, but in terms of American personnel, the CIA took the heaviest toll. Eight Agency employees were killed, and the Near East Section was decimated.

Stansfield had been associate deputy director of operations at the time, and he had rushed over to assess the damage. The guilt Hurley felt was overwhelming. He tried to resign, but Stansfield would hear none of it. He didn't care that Hurley had missed a one o'clock meeting at the embassy. There was some speculation about that. Was Islamic Jihad lucky in their timing, or did they have inside information that Langley's top people would be meeting at that time, and if so, some had spoken out loud that it was very convenient that Hurley missed the meeting. Hurley was placed under a microscope by a few higher-ups, but Stansfield covered for him.

His operative was meeting with Petrosian the Armenian, and the meeting had gone longer than anticipated. That was as much as anyone needed to know. The fact that he was in bed with two hookers while the van crashed through the gate was inconsequential. They had already lost enough good people, they didn't need to lose another because of his vices—vices that Stansfield was well aware of.

Hurley knew Stansfield was right, but that didn't mean he could simply ignore what had happened. He was an operational wreck for those next few months. Stansfield received a report that Muslim men were turning up dead in areas of the city that were known to be relatively peaceful, completely randomly and at all hours of the day. One man was shot while reading the paper on his small terrace, another was strangled in the bathroom of a public restroom, another killed leaving a nightclub. All three men had loose connections to Islamic Jihad. Stansfield called Hurley back to D.C. to ask him if he knew anything about the murders, and to his astonishment Hurley admitted to the killings.

Stansfield could not allow one of his oldest friends and best operatives to go running off half-cocked killing whomever he wanted, even if the targets were somewhat legitimate. As Hurley had pointed out, Islamic Jihad had declared war on the United States; he was simply obliging them by participating in the war. There was a bit of logic in his thinking, but Langley couldn't afford any more scrapes with the press and the politicians at the moment. The solution was easy. Things were heating up along the Afghanistan-Pakistan border, and Hurley knew the Russians better than anyone. So Stansfield shipped him off to Peshawar to help train and equip the mujahedeen.

And now, almost ten years later, here he was full circle. Right back in this stew of religious fascists who all fervently believed they, and they alone, knew what God wanted. Hurley had been trying to warn Langley for years that these Islamic wack jobs were the next big problem. He'd seen both fronts up close. Beirut and Afghanistan and the Afghanis made these guys look like pikers. Any culture that swaddles its women from head to toe and refuses a drop of booze while exporting opium around the globe is seriously screwed-up. Another of Hurley's rules was to be extremely distrustful of anyone who didn't drink. Afghanistan was an entire society that didn't drink, and it scared the piss out of him.

Hurley took a pull from the bottle and shook out another cigarette. He lit it, blew the smoke up into the ocean breeze, and thought about tomorrow. The safe house should be set up and equipped by then, and the backup would be ready by early afternoon. He'd have to see what kind of info the Agency guy had, and if it wasn't enough, he'd go pay Petrosian a call. Hurley had heard he owned more than two thousand apartment units in the neighborhood. That would generate a lot of income, but a guy like Petrosian could always use more money, and that was one thing that Hurley finally had a lot of.

What he didn't have was time. If they were going to save the Schnoz they would have to work fast. Sometimes working fast could be used to your advantage, but you had to mix it up, and they'd been moving at a pretty good clip for about a week. Sharif, Dorfman, and by now Ismael. They might as well stay on the attack for a few more days.

Hurley looked at the bottle of Tennessee whisky and wondered if he'd come back to Beirut to die. All the times he'd cheated death, all the men he'd killed over the years, all the gods, real or imagined, that he'd pissed off. If it was anyone's time it should be his. Looking skyward, he said, "Don't piss off the gods." He poured some of the whisky down his gullet and smiled. If it was his time, so be it.

CHAPTER 47

MARTYRS' SQUARE, BEIRUT

SUNDOWN was shortly after five in the evening and sunrise shortly after six in the morning. With limited power in the building, and no curtains on the windows, there wasn't much to do after sundown, so Sayyed had gone to bed early. Loyal Samir had scrounged up a mattress and a lantern and set up a room for him on the fifth floor away from all of the men and most of the noise. He'd checked on the two prisoners briefly to make sure they were following his orders. The businessman was faring much better than the spy. Sayyed had brought a doctor in to take a look at Cummins and the prognosis wasn't good. Due to the beatings, poor diet, and unsanitary conditions, the doctor feared he was suffering from liver failure.

The news upset Sayyed. He had been warning the guards for several weeks to lay off the prisoners. But they somehow couldn't get it through their thick heads that the two men were worthless to them if they were dead. Add to that the stress of the missing money and Ivanov coming to town and it was enough to make Sayyed's temper flare out of control. He gathered the men in the basement and told them he would execute the next man who dared lay a hand on either prisoner. He caught one of the men rolling his eyes at the order, and before the imbecile knew it Sayyed had the muzzle of his Markov pistol pressed firmly against his forehead. The others finally got the point.

Sayyed went to bed wondering if they would rebel or follow his orders. It was just another thing to add to his general discomfort. He did not sleep well. His dreams, vivid and bizarre, taunted and tortured him. He was running. He must have been on the beach, because no matter how fast he told himself to run, his legs plodded along as if they were stuck in deep sand. There was a dense fog, so thick that he could see no farther than the end of his hand. Jets were overhead, screeching and dropping deafening bombs in the distance. Bright flashes erupted through the marine layer, the noises of the big bombs muted by the moisture in the air. Why was he running toward the bombs? What was he running from? He woke up with a start, his heart pounding out of his chest, covered in sweat.

Sayyed looked around the office where he'd decided to spend the night. A soft moonlight spilled in from the blown-out window. There was a pile of garbage in the corner where Samir had swept the glass and debris. Scavengers had taken everything. The furniture, even the carpeting, had been pulled up, leaving only the bare concrete floor and the dried glue that had been used to hold the carpeting down. The whole thing was depressing. The geniuses in Damascus should all be forced to live like this for a night.

Sayyed decided to get some air. He pulled on his shirt but didn't bother to button it up. He climbed two flights to the roof and with a murmur greeted the two men standing watch. All was quiet across the street. He lit a cigarette and wondered what Ivanov was up to. The man was always plotting. Given the choice between making a fortune the honest way and stealing it from someone, he was convinced, Ivanov would prefer to steal it. He was a thief at heart. It was in no way a stretch to think of him plotting to kill Sharif, and then with the Turk out of the way, killing Dorfman and taking everything for himself.

Sayyed sighed. He wished he could skip ahead a day or two. Be done with this mess and go back to Damascus for a few weeks. His two girls were grown and married and had very little to do with him, and that was fine. He didn't particularly care for their husbands. Beyond that, he had never been around when they were growing up, so there was no real connection. His wife—they barely spoke. The women in life weren't the draw. Civilization was the draw. Running water, and functioning toilets, and sleeping in a clean bed without fear of two thousand pounds of steel and high explosives being dropped on your head. That's what he needed. A VCR and a stack of movies and some sleep. He needed to recharge.

If he could run, he would. Walk out of this hell-hole of a city and leave it all behind. He'd considered it many times as his pot of money grew with Herr Dorfman. Another year or two and he would have made it. He could have gone back to Damascus, retired, and used the money he had stashed away in Switzerland to invest in opportunities as Beirut stabilized. He could have lived like a wealthy sheik. All of those years of hard work gone in an instant. It was almost impossible to bear.

He finished his cigarette and looked at the stars. He did not like having to stay in one place like this, especially a place so primitive. The food was horrid and infrequent, the conditions ripe for illness, and he couldn't sleep, and if he couldn't sleep he would make mistakes. Mistakes were not something he could afford these next few days. He did not want to go back to the depressing room with the soiled mattress, but he had to, at least to close his eyes and rest.

Sayyed plodded down the steps and into the dark room. He took his shirt off, setting it on the floor, and then lay back down on the dirty mattress, trying to ignore the stench. The crux of the problem was the money, and it was a bigger problem than any of them realized. They were all lamenting their loss of personal wealth, but the dire situation lay in their inability to pay their people.

There were a few mentally unstable militants who would work for free, but the bulk of the foot soldiers would walk away. They were paid in cash every week, and payday was Thursday. They would be able to scrape together enough to get through this week, but then they would be bankrupt. The following week they had to pay their monthly bribes to the police, politicians, bureaucrats, and spies in the other camps. There would be hundreds if not thousands of hands extended, waiting for the money, and behind them families, waiting to put food on the table. If they did not rectify this situation quickly it could be a major disaster. The Maronites and the other factions would swoop in and pick up territory it had taken them years and thousands of men to gain.

Everything they had worked for would unravel. He would have to tell Damascus, and of course leave his personal loss out of it. They were likely to punish him by banishing him to Yamouk, the bleak Palestinian refugee camp on the outskirts of Damascus that was teeming with the pushy tribe in search of a permanent home. He heard footsteps down the hall and then some voices. They sounded as if they were going from room to room. Looking toward the open doorway, he saw the beam of a flashlight. Sayyed grabbed his pistol and sat up.

"He's up here somewhere," he heard a voice in the hallway say.

"Who is it?" Sayyed asked.

"It's me. I've been looking all over for you."

Sayyed recognized Radih's voice and lowered his gun. "I'm in here."

Radih appeared in the doorway. Three other men were behind him. "Assef, you are not going to believe the news I bring you." Radih clapped his hands together.

Sayyed looked for his watch, but couldn't find it. "What time is it?"

"Nearly two in the morning. You must get up. I have amazing news."

Sayyed sighed. He half rolled off the mattress, looking for his watch. He found it, strapped it on, and then grabbed his shirt. "It better be good. I need some sleep."

"You will not be disappointed."

Sayyed felt like crap. He needed water and then coffee and then some food, in that order, and then maybe he could think clearly. He motioned for Radih to get on with the story.

Radih told his men to leave and in a hushed voice said, "Do you remember an American who went by the name Bill Sherman?"

Did he remember him? The man had purportedly killed Sayyed's predecessor while he was enjoying his breakfast one spring morning. "Of course."

"My spies at the airport . . . one of them says he saw Sherman tonight."

"At the airport?"

"Yes. He came in on a flight from Paris, along with another man."

Sayyed was dubious. There had been rumors here and there that Sherman had been back to the city. In fact, anytime someone met his end at the hands of an assassin, Sherman's name somehow became attached. "How can you be so sure? It has been many years since anyone has seen him."

"My man says he has aged. His hair has gone gray, but the eyes"—Radih pointed to his own—

"he said they are those same eyes. Eyes of the Devil. He said he remembers him as a very nasty man with many vices."

Sayyed's lips felt unusually parched. He found the jug of water that Samir had left in the corner and took a drink. *Why would the Americans send Sherman to Beirut after all these years?* The most obvious answer was in the basement of this very building. They wanted their agent back. *But why send an assassin like Sherman?* The man was a harbinger of death, not a negotiator. Turning back to Radih, he asked, "Did your spy happen to know where he was headed?"

With a self-satisfied grin, Radih said, "I put out the word yesterday, after our meeting. I told everyone to be on the lookout for anything suspicious. My people know how to do their jobs. They followed him and the other man to the Intercontinental."

"And?"

"They had a drink at the bar, and he bought a bottle of Jack Daniel's from the bartender and then got into a cab, one of ours. He had the cabbie drop him off in front of a hotel on Daoura. After the cabbie was gone, they walked three blocks to a different hotel."

"Which one?"

"The Mar Yousif Inn."

"And he is there right now?"

"Yes. They got two rooms for one night. I just spoke to the manager. They are still there."

"Are you sure?" Sayyed asked skeptically. "The Bill Sherman I remember would never allow himself to be followed."

"My men are good. We have trained them to use radios. They have a system set up at the airport. When they see someone who might be a fat target they follow him and pass the word to me. We then swoop in and grab them. I have men heading to the area now. There's only one problem."

"What?"

"The hotel is in Bourj Hammoud."

Sayyed needed to wake up. Normally he would never ask such a stupid question. The Sherman he remembered was tight with the Armenians. This would have to be handled delicately. "If we get in a gun battle in Bourj Hammoud, we might not make it out alive."

Radih did not disagree. "We can wait and follow him. If he leaves the Bourj we can grab him."

They had been lucky enough to stumble across him. That luck would not hold with a man like Sherman. He would see them sooner rather than later, and then he would kill whoever it was who was watching him and disappear. "Tell your men to hold."

Radih seemed relieved. "And then what?"

"The chief of police owes me a favor. They can operate in Bourj Hammoud without too much trouble."

This time Radih shook his head. "I'm not so sure."

"Normally you would be correct, but there are some things that you are unaware of. Some influential Armenians owe the chief a few favors. As long as we aren't going in to take one of their own, we will be fine."

"If a single shot is fired . . ." Radih winced at the thought.

Sayyed finished it for him. "The entire neighborhood could erupt." Such was the reality of Beirut. The city was always one gun battle away from plunging back into chaos and civil war.

CHAPTER 48

WHEN he hit the midway point of the last run of stairs that led to the small lobby, Hurley noticed the man sitting in the chair with his back to the door. It was probably nothing, but then again Hurley had survived all these years by noticing the little things. If enough of them piled up, they usually led to trouble. There was a couch and three chairs. The man was in the chair the farthest to Hurley's left—the same seat he would have chosen if he was to keep an eye on any guests coming down. Hurley watched him intently as he crossed the red-tiled floor. The man slowly closed his eyes and went back to dozing. Rather than head straight out, Hurley stopped at the desk. No one was there. He looked through the open door of the small office and couldn't see anyone, but could hear a TV. Looking back over his shoulder, he checked to make sure the fat man in the chair was still in his position. He had his eyes closed again and appeared to be dozing. Hurley checked him off his list.

The pay phone was behind the man in a quaint, claustrophobic alcove. Rather than use it, Hurley decided to head outside and take in the lay of the land. When he reached the front door he paused to see if there were any goons loitering. If there were, he would head back up to the room, grab Richards, and they would head to the roof. They could make it two buildings in either direction by hopping from one roof to the next, and then use any of the adjoining apartment buildings to make their escape. The sidewalk in front of the hotel was empty, so he stepped outside, tapped out a Camel, and fired it up. He casually looked up and down the block. He counted eight cars that he had seen the night before and one new one, and it was only a small two-door hatchback. Nothing to be alarmed about.

Right or left? It was funny how often that's what it came down to—a flip of the coin. He chose left. It was slightly uphill, not that it mattered, but he remembered seeing a small market in that direction the night before and it had a pay phone out front. He flipped the butt of his heater into the street to join the menagerie of discarded brands and started moving. It was before eight and the street wasn't busy. It was empty, in fact. He saw two cars drive through the next intersection, moving from right to left, and then a man with a briefcase hustled across the street. Hurley couldn't remember if it was normal or abnormal for a city like Beirut to be so slow at this time. Every city had a different pulse. Some were bustling by seven, but most Mediterranean cities were a little slower-paced. Especially one that had endured as much trauma as this one.

There was a boy standing in front of the market. Hurley guessed him to be about eight. As Hurley approached, the boy held out a paper and started giving him his pitch. Hurley smiled at him. He didn't care where he was; you had to admire a kid who got his ass out of bed to sell something. He reached into his pocket to grab some money, and right about the time he had a firm grip on his wallet alarm bells started going off. There was movement to his left, from the market, two or three car engines turned over, and then there were footfalls. Hurley looked left, then right, and then noticed that the cute little kid was backpedaling to get out of the way.

Two men came out of the supermarket—big, burly guys in uniforms who stopped just out of his reach. Car tires were now squealing and engines were roaring as vehicles closed in from three directions. Hurley turned, with the idea of running back toward the hotel, but there were two more men hoofing it up the sidewalk. One of them had a big German shepherd on a leash. *That's new,* he thought, never having seen a police dog in the city. In less than five seconds he was surrounded by ten men and three sedans. Six of the men were wearing police uniforms and four were in civilian attire. The civilians had pistols drawn. They could be either part of a militia or detectives, or worse, Syrian intelligence officers. The uniformed police were wielding wooden truncheons.

Interesting, Hurley thought to himself. Not a single one of them attempted to lay a hand on him. Hurley calculated the odds while he slowly reached for his cigarettes. Even if he had had a gun, he wasn't sure he could have gotten himself out of this jam. They all looked nervous, which in itself told him something. Someone had prepped these guys. Told them to keep their distance, which was not standard operating procedure in this part of the world. Normally it was club first and ask questions later.

Hurley lit his cigarette with the steady hand of a brain surgeon. He greeted the men in Arabic and asked, "What seems to be the problem?"

"Good morning," announced a smiling man in a three-piece suit who appeared just beyond the phalanx of men. "We have been waiting for you, Mr. Sherman." He glanced ever so slightly at the two men behind Hurley and gave them a nod.

Hurley turned and blocked the first blow with his left hand, wrist to wrist, and then delivered a palm strike to the man's nose. He ripped the truncheon from the man's hand and ducked just in time to miss the blow from his partner. The man was out of position from swinging so hard and had left his ribs exposed, so Hurley rammed him with the truncheon and sent him to the ground. Just as he turned to face the others he was cracked across the head and then the back. He dropped to one knee and then to the ground as the batons and feet came crashing down. As they took the fight out of him, Hurley lay bleeding and hoping that Richards had enough time to run.

CHAPTER 49

RAPP rocked the clutch of the little silver Renault Clio and closed the gap between himself and the next car waiting to get through the checkpoint to Beirut proper. It was his third checkpoint since the Syrian border. The little 1.2-liter engine was about as big as the one on his dad's old John Deere riding mower. If he had to run from the authorities it would be a very short chase. He'd been in line now for about fifteen minutes, inching his way forward a few feet at a time. The car didn't have any air-conditioning so he had the windows rolled down.

Rapp slapped his hands on the steering wheel to the beat of some atrocious techno music that he'd picked up at the airport. The title of the album was *Euro Trash,* and he agreed. He would have preferred a little U2, or maybe some Bob Seger, but the idea here was to make them think he was French, not some American assassin on safari. Third in line now, he leaned out the window to get a better look at the teenager holding the AK-47 assault rifle. Rapp had no idea which faction he belonged to, but the kid seemed calm enough. The first checkpoints were manned by the Syrian army, and then as he neared the city the militias were in charge.

He'd found a pay phone at a gas station along the way and called in to check on things. The automated voice told him his room was ready and gave him the address and the location. Rapp wrote it down, memorized it while on the road, then crumpled it up and threw it out the window. The file told him to expect four checkpoints, counting the border. Each one would cost him between five and twenty dollars. So far whoever had put it together was right on the mark.

The line snaked ahead and Rapp yawned. It was finally catching up with him.

After sinking a hollow-tipped parabellum into Ismael's head, Rapp had steadily retreated, keeping his gun leveled at the woman, who was temporarily frozen with shock. Rapp wasn't going to shoot her and wasn't worried that she would shoot him. He kept his weapon raised to conceal his face and to deter her from looking too closely at him. People in general did not like to look down the barrel of a loaded gun. When the woman finally glanced down at the man who had threatened her life only moments before, Rapp turned and ran.

He didn't turn the corner because he did not want to head back down the street where Ismael had just fired the Uzi. Half the block was likely to be looking out their windows, and a few of them would be on the phone with the police. So he ran straight, at an all-out sprint, for two blocks, the gun at his side. Then he took a hard right turn and stopped. His breathing was heavy but under control. He holstered the pistol while he looked for a place to reverse his jacket. Twenty feet ahead on his right there was a stoop that would offer some concealment. Rapp ducked into the shadows, tore off his overcoat, and turned it inside out. He tossed the clear black-rimmed glasses to the ground and mussed up his slicked-back hair before emerging from the shadows wearing a khaki trench coat. He headed back to the corner he'd just rounded. The distinctly European police klaxon could be heard screeching in the distance.

Rapp calmly crossed the street, looking to his left. He could just barely make out the woman. She had been joined by three or four people. Rapp acted as if he didn't notice. After he cleared the intersection he picked up the pace, but not so much as to draw attention. He looked like a man out for a brisk walk. The Rhone was now only a block and a half in front of him. With each step the sirens grew in force, but Rapp wasn't worried. They would go to the body first and then they would check the damage caused by the Libyan's Uzi and then they would begin to look for a suspect.

Rapp reached the river, which at this point was fairly wide. He turned right and after looking up and down the block to make sure no one was watching, he casually slid his left hand between the folds of his jacket and grabbed the Beretta he'd used to kill Ismael. Rapp waited until he was in the shadows between two streetlights and then drew the gun. He flipped it casually a good twenty feet into the ice-cold water and kept moving. A block after that, he disposed of the second gun, then had to make his first big decision. Just on the other side of the river, one mile away, was Geneva International Airport. If he hustled, he might be able to catch the last flight out to Paris.

Airports made him nervous, though. There were always cameras and police, and if you were going to get on a plane you had to buy a ticket and show a passport, and that left a trail. His legends were to be cultivated and protected, not used for convenience' sake. So he turned back for the rental car and rehearsed what he would tell the police if they stopped him. Fortunately, the story was never needed. Police were flooding the area, but they were still headed to the crime scene. On his way back he didn't see a single police car heading out to look for suspects. When he climbed behind the wheel of the rental car he checked his stop-watch. Four minutes and thirty-seven seconds had elapsed since he'd taken refuge behind the mail-box. Not bad.

Once behind the wheel he had a lot of options. The primary plan was to cross the border into France and then drive to Lyon, but he was too pumped-up, and with the border crossing so close, they might be looking for a man of his general description. Again, there was no longer any hard evidence that could tie him to Ismael's death, but why push it?

Rapp wasn't sure he could calm his nerves for the border crossing. The reality of what he'd just been through was setting in. There was no queasiness or feeling of nausea. He was simply pumped, the feeling very similar to the way he felt after scoring a game-winning goal, but better. He cranked the music and headed back for Zurich. Greta was on his mind, but there wouldn't be time. He'd have to grab the first flight to Paris or Istanbul and then on to Damascus.

He made it to Zurich just before four, parked in the rental car lot, and tried to grab a few hours of sleep before things opened at six. It didn't work, though, and he sat there with his seat reclined, playing it over and over in his head until he had analyzed every second of what had happened with Ismael. Each mistake was noted and alternatives explored, but as his old high-school coach liked to say, "A win is a win. It doesn't matter how ugly it is."

Strip it all down and that's what it was. Rapp won and Ismael lost. As the sun started to rise, Rapp looked out from the concrete parking structure and realized that one day he might be in Ismael's shoes. He'd pretty much spent the rest of the morning thinking of ways to prevent himself from ending up with a fate similar to that of the Libyan intelligence officer. From Zurich to Istanbul, and then Damascus, and all the way down this hot, dusty road to Beirut, he played a game of chess with himself. What should Ismael have done, and how should he have reacted if Ismael had done something different?

Exhaustion was finally catching up. Rapp let out a long yawn and then the kid motioned him forward. Rapp greeted the kid in French. He couldn't have been more than sixteen. Rapp smiled while he tapped out the techno beat and chomped on his gum.

"What is your purpose?" the kid asked with a lack of enthusiasm you'd expect from someone who was expected to stand in the sun all day sucking on emissions and asking the same question over and over.

"Business."

"What kind of business?"

"Software."

The kid shook his head. "What's that?"

"Computer stuff." Rapp reached over and picked up the flashy color brochure they'd ordered from a French company. He showed the kid, who was by now bored with their conversation.

"I like your music."

"Really?" Rapp said, surprised. "Are you here every day?"

The kid nodded.

Rapp looked over at the kid's dusty boom box and then reached over and ejected the tape. He slid it into the case and said, "I've been listening to it for a week straight. Knock yourself out. I'll pick it up when I drive back out in a few days."

The kid was excited and lowered his rifle. "Thanks . . . for you . . . half price today." He flashed Rapp five fingers.

Rapp paid him, smiled, slipped the little car back into gear, and drove away. It took him another twenty minutes to find the safe house. Based on the stories he'd heard from Hurley, he was surprised that during that time he didn't run into any more armed men. As per his training, he did a normal drive-by and barely glanced at the building. All he wanted to do was go to sleep, but it had been drilled into him that these were the precautions that would save his life, so he continued past and then circled back, checking the next block in each direction.

It was a five-story apartment building among four-, five-, and six-story apartment buildings. Rapp was too tired to care if it had any architectural characteristics beyond a front and back door. He parked the car, grabbed his bag, and entered the building. He didn't have a gun on him, at least not yet, so there was pretty much only one thing to do. Climb the stairs. If it was a trap, he'd have to throw his bag at them and lie down and take a nap. No one was waiting for him when he got to the fifth floor. There were three doors on the left and three on the right. They had the two on the right toward the back. Or so he thought. After checking above each door he came up empty, so he checked the ones across the hall and found two keys. That was when he remembered he was supposed to enter from the back of the building.

That snapped him out of it a bit. That and the lesson that he might be Ismael someday. He told himself to slow down and stop rushing things. He checked his watch. It was two-eleven in the afternoon. He hadn't slept in more than a day, and the day before that only a few hours. He opened the door and closed and locked it behind him. He could barely keep his eyes open, but he still dug out the doorstop and wedged it under the door. Not bothering to check the rest of the place, he went into the bedroom and opened the closet. There on the floor was a suitcase that looked a lot like the one from Istanbul. Rapp placed it on the bed, opened it, and found three Beretta 92Fs with silencers and extra magazines. It was the same suitcase.

Rapp loaded one of the guns and put the suitcase away. With his last bit of strength, he stripped down to his boxers and climbed under the covers of the twin bed. He shoved the pistol under the pillow and wondered who the person was who went from city to city dropping off their tools of the trade. Would he ever get the chance to meet this mystery man or woman? Probably not. As Hurley liked to say, they were on a need-to-know basis and there wasn't a lot they needed to know. Rapp began to drift off to sleep even though he knew that Hurley and Richards would probably be there in a minute. He figured any sleep was better than none.

CHAPTER 50

THE bag they'd placed over his head offered a mix of putrid smells—feces, vomit, snot, and blood all mixed together with the sweat of all the men who had worn it before him. And it wasn't the perspiration of exertion, it was the ripe sweat of fear, an all-out assault on his olfactory system, designed to make him pliable to whoever it was who would walk through the door and begin asking questions. Hurley had no idea where he was, other than the fact that he was in a basement. He'd felt the stairs as they'd dragged him from the trunk of a car and into the building.

It was the second car he'd been in that morning. In the midst of his pummeling by the police he blurted out the only name that he thought might help. "Levon Petrosian! I am a friend of Petrosian!"

The clubbing and kicking stopped almost immediately, and then one of the men asked him what he'd said. Hurley could tell it was the portly one in the three-piece suit, even though he couldn't see him. The man ordered him cuffed and placed in the backseat of one of the cars. They were not gentle, but Hurley did not expect them to be, so it wasn't too bad. That was when they placed the first hood on his head. It wasn't too bad, really. It could have used a good cleaning, but at least it didn't smell like a bowl of shit.

He marked the time in the back of the car, counting the seconds and trying to make sense of the noises beyond the glass windows. The metal cuffs were biting into his skin. He twisted his wrists around and tried to see if he could get out of them, but it was no use. Twenty-seven seconds later, the car doors opened. Hurley couldn't be sure, but he thought two men got in the front seat and one man joined him in the back. He felt something hard jabbed into his ribs.

"Don't move, or I will kill you."

Hurley couldn't be sure if the object at his side was a gun or a truncheon. "Fuck you." The object was jabbed even harder into his side.

"You shouldn't talk to a policeman like that."

The voice came from the front seat. It was the older pudgeball. "Policeman," Hurley said with open disdain. "If you're cops, what am I being arrested for?"

"For striking a police officer. One of my men has a broken nose."

"You mean the one who was going to crack me over the back of the head with his stick? I have a great idea. Don't bullshit me, and I won't bullshit you."

"Striking a police officer is a very serious matter."

"Yeah . . . so is kidnapping, so why don't you just pull over and let me go and I'll make sure no one puts a price on your head."

"Are you threatening us?"

"Just telling you the truth. I make it a habit not to kill cops . . . that is, unless they are corrupt."

Hurley doubled over as the man next to him delivered a stinging blow with whatever it was that he was holding. Hurley recovered and said, "I can't wait to tell Petrosian about this . . . the first thing I'm going to do"—Hurley turned to his right as if he could actually see the man next to him—"is take that stick of yours and shove it up your ass. Although you'd probably like that, wouldn't you?" Hurley expected it this time and folded his arms up quickly, locking the object between his right biceps and forearm. Then he reeled his head back and smashed it in the general direction of the other man's head. They hit forehead to forehead, like two pool balls. A loud, resounding crack. Despite the pain that Hurley felt he started laughing wildly and kicking and thrashing.

That was when they decided to pull over and put him in the trunk. Not long after that, maybe ten minutes, they stopped, pulled him out of the trunk, and stripped him down to his birthday suit. Hurley endured this part without comment. He had a sinking feeling where this was all headed, and it was bleak, to say the least. He held out hope, though, that

Richards had been able to get away. They wasted no time tossing him into the trunk of a second car and speeding off. It was a bumpy ride, and it must have been an older car, because the fumes grew so strong that Hurley started to think he would suffocate. It occurred to him that that might be the best possible outcome. Fall asleep and die from carbon monoxide poisoning. He could skip all of the degradation and take his secrets with him.

Unfortunately, he had survived, and they had dragged him into this dank basement that smelled like an outhouse. They'd switched out the hood that the police had used and put this disgusting burlap bag on his head. Hurley took in shallow breaths through his mouth and focused his mind. Throwing up under this thing would be extremely unpleasant, but then again there was a really good chance that he was about to endure the most repugnant degradation the mind could imagine, so why worry?

The mind, Hurley knew, could take only so much before it simply opened up and let the secrets spill out. They said everyone eventually broke, but Hurley didn't think of himself as everyone. He was a mean, nasty man who might have lost a step, but he was still very much in control of his mind. Under the smelly hood he smiled at the challenge ahead of him. He went through the long, nasty list of the things they would do to him. He committed himself to fighting them every step of the way, and if he was lucky they'd either intentionally or accidentally kill him. And that was a victory he would take in a heartbeat.

Hurley sat there for at least an hour. He was bored, because he knew what they were doing, and he'd just as soon get on with it. Isolation was a standard interrogation/torture technique, and while it worked on most people it was useless on Hurley because of the simple fact that he really didn't like people all that much. There were a few here and there that he'd met over the years who could hold his interest, but most others were either boring or irritating.

There were noises on the other side of the door. Footsteps, some talking, but nothing he could make out, and then the door opened. Hurley tried to count the different steps. His best guess was three or four men. They spread out around him. Someone approached him from behind and Hurley resisted the impulse to flinch. The man grabbed the burlap bag and yanked it from his head. Hurley blinked several times and took a look around the room. An industrial lamp hung from the ceiling, a brown extension cord snaking its way to the door. Hurley looked at the three men he could see. Two were familiar.

"Gentlemen, there must be some misunderstanding here," Hurley announced in an easy tone. "I thought hostilities in Beirut were over."

The two men in front of Hurley shared a brief smile. The older one said, "Mr. Sherman, I have been looking forward to this for some time."

"So have I, Sayyed."

"So you know who I am?" Sayyed asked with a raised eyebrow.

"I sure do. You're the GSD goon here in Beirut."

"And you, Mr. Sherman, are a CIA assassin."

Hurley looked as if he had to think about that for a second, and then he nodded and said, "That would be correct. I kill people like you for a living. In fact, I killed your boss, Hisham."

Sayyed nodded. This was going to be very interesting. "It really was a shame that you weren't at the embassy that afternoon. We planned the entire operation with the hope that you would be there."

"Yeah . . . it was a real shame. Although I've tried to make up for it over the years by killing as many of you assholes as I can."

Sayyed gave him an affable smile. "It looks like your killing days have come to an end."

"Possibly." Hurley surveyed the dank room. "Things don't look so good, but I'm always up for a challenge."

"This is a challenge you will not win, and you know that."

"I'm afraid I don't. You see I'm a fucked-up guy. I'm not okay in the head, and I pretty much hate you limp dicks more than I love life, so this is gonna be a tough one."

"Really, Mr. Sherman, your false bravado is so American . . . so Hollywood."

Hurley winced at the word *Hollywood,* as if it pained him to be associated with the town. "No false bravado here, Sayyed. I am going to fuck with you until I take my last breath. I'm going to feed you so much disinformation, you won't know what to believe. You'll be killing your own people before it's all over. You won't sleep at night, and when you do you'll be dreaming of traitors around every corner. Spies in your own camp. This is going to be a blast."

"Really?"

"Yep." Hurley gave him a nod to confirm his conviction. "The two of us are going to take a little trip into the bowels of my sick mind, and trust me, you won't make it out unscathed."

"Ha," Sayyed laughed. This was a first. "Fine. I think we should begin our journey. Don't you?"

"Absolutely! The sooner the better . . . that's my motto."

"Why have you decided to come back to Beirut after all these years?"

"You know why I'm here."

"Let's not assume I know your motives."

Hurley smiled. "You have something I want."

"And what would that be?"

Hurley had thought about this while he had sat under the putrid hood. Ivanov was due to show up the day after tomorrow and he would be desperate. They were all desperate because Hurley himself had drained their little secret bank accounts. He just hoped they hadn't gotten their hands on Richards, and if they had, that he would be smart enough to leave Hamburg out of his interrogation. He needed to make this seem to be about exactly what it was without the money coming up. "I am here to negotiate the release of John Cummins."

"And why would I give him to you?"

Hurley tilted his head back and looked up at the ceiling. "Well, let's think about that. If you give him back to me, I won't kill you."

This elicited laughter from all, including Hurley.

Sayyed stopped laughing abruptly and snapped his fingers. He looked at one of his men and pointed at the door. The men left and came back a few seconds later wheeling the small stainless-steel cart. Sayyed took it from him and positioned it next to the subject. He smiled at Hurley and picked up the pliers, opening and closing them.

"Manicure?" Hurley asked.

"I like to call it Twenty Questions."

"You're so clever, Sayyed," Hurley said, his voice dripping with mock admiration. "Kind of like a game show. I can't wait to get started."

"Good. Let's start with your real name."

"Jack Mehoff," Hurley offered, straight-faced.

"Jack Mehoff," Sayyed repeated. "That is your real name?"

"Of course it isn't, you fucking moron. Jack Mehoff . . . jack me off. Come on, let's go. Off with the first fingernail. You win. I lose. Let's go."

Sayyed searched the subject's face for a sign of stress. He had never had a prisoner ask to have his fingernail torn off. His demeanor would change in a second, though. Sayyed chose the forefinger on the left hand and wedged the grip of the pliers in under the nail bed. "Last chance. Your first name?"

"Don't change the rules on me. Very confusing for your subjects. You said Twenty Questions. I blew the first one, come on, let's go," Hurley said with a smile.

Sayyed clamped down hard on the pliers and began to rock the nail back and forth.

"Oh, yeah," Hurley announced. "Let's get this party started."

Sayyed gave it one good yank and ripped the entire nail off.

"Holy Mary mother . . ." Hurley unleashed a string of swear words and then started laughing. "Damn, that stings. If that doesn't wake you up nothing will. This is great!" His laughing grew to the point where he couldn't control it. He was shaking so hard his eyes started to tear up. "Oh . . . I can't wait for the next one. This is fucking great."

Sayyed remained undeterred. "Your name?"

"Bill Donovan."

"Really?"

"Nope."

"Really, Mr. Sherman, what is the harm in your telling us your first name?"

"Probably nothing at this point, but it's my nature to fuck with guys like you."

"I will ask the question again." Sayyed stayed steady. "What is your real name?"

"Ulysses S. Grant."

"You are lying?"

"Of course, you fucking idiot. Don't you read history?"

Sayyed moved in for the second fingernail. He wedged the pliers under the nail bed, wiggled it again to make sure he had a good enough grip, and then looked into Hurley's eyes. He didn't like what he saw. It was the wild-eyed look of a crazy man.

"Do it. Come on," Hurley egged him on. "What

are you waiting for? You're not turning into a pussy on me, are you?"

Part of Sayyed knew he should stop and come back later when he could control the situation. The men were here, however, so he needed to pull this second nail, and then let this lunatic sit and stew for a while. Probably come back and use electricity. He tightened his grip and yanked the second nail free.

Hurley howled again with the laughter of a madman. The shrieking turned to cackles and then uncontrollable laughter. His eyes were filled with tears as he yelled, "Eighteen more to go! Heeee haw-www!"

Sayyed dropped the pliers on the cart. "That's right. We'll give you a little rest before we start with the others." He started for the door.

Hurley looked at the other man who was standing in front of him. "Is that you Abu . . . Abu Radih? I haven't seen you in years. I heard you have your own little terrorist group now . . . Fatah. Look at you . . . all grown-up," Hurley said admiringly.

Radih smiled and shook his head. He clearly thought the American insane.

Hurley tilted his head to the side as if trying to recall some distant memory. "I bet you weren't more than four feet tall when I used to fuck your mother. Did you tell your friends that she was a prostitute?" Hurley craned his head to look at the other two men. "His mom could suck cock better than any whore I ever met, and trust me, I've been with a lot of whores."

The smile left Radih's face in an instant. He

lashed out with his right fist, hitting Hurley in the mouth. Hurley's head rocked back from the blow, and then, before Radih could throw another punch, Sayyed grabbed him from behind.

"No," Sayyed ordered. "Do not let him get to you."

Hurley shook the sting and fog from his head and came up smiling. One of his top middle teeth had been knocked out and his mouth was filling with blood. "Look!" Hurley yelled, showing them the gap in his top row. "Look, you knocked my tooth out." Radih and Sayyed stopped struggling for a second, and that was when Hurley unleashed a gob of blood and the one busted tooth from his mouth. The bulk of it hit Radih in the face. With his arms tied behind his back and his legs taped to the chair, Hurley started bouncing the chair an inch at a time toward the two men, snapping his teeth and barking like a dog.

CHAPTER 51

MOSCOW, RUSSIA

IT was almost noon, and Ivanov was still in bed. He claimed he wasn't feeling well. Moaned something about the snow and the cold and the gray, depressing Moscow sky. Of course it had nothing to do with all of the vodka and wine and heavy foods he'd consumed until well past midnight. Shvets would have liked to throw him in a cold snowdrift and shock him back to the here and now. The young Russian didn't understand depression. He couldn't see how people allowed it to get so bad that they couldn't get out of bed, was unable to understand that the drinking and the sleeping were all intertwined like a big sheet wrapped around your body until you couldn't move. And then you started sinking. Stop the drinking, get out of bed, and work out. Have a purpose in life. It was not complicated.

Shvets crossed from one end of the parlor to the other, glancing at Alexei, who was one-half of his boss's favorite bodyguard duo. They were in a corner suite on the top floor of Hotel Baltschug. He looked out the big window across the frozen Moscow River at the Kremlin, Red Square, and St. Basil's Cathedral. Shvets had never understood why the Bolsheviks had let the cathedral stand. They were so anticzar, so antireligion, why let this one church remain while they destroyed so many others? The answer probably lay in their own doubts about what they were doing. The people had risen up and helped them grab power, but the people were a tough beast to tame. Shvets thought they probably feared it would bring about another revolution.

Frost had built up around the edges of the window. It was minus twenty degrees Celsius, and the wind was blowing, whipping up clouds of snow, but so what? That was February in Moscow. Only a weak man allows the weather to affect his mood. Shvets let out a long exhalation, his breath forming a fog on the window that froze within seconds. Ivanov was about to drag him down, take him under like some fool walking out onto the melting March ice of the Moscow River. These weren't the old days of deportation to a Siberian work camp, and executions against the back wall at Lubyanka, but the government was by no means just. The new regime was just more astute at PR. They could still be beaten senseless and be forced to sign false confessions of crimes against the state and whatever else they decided to trump up. Then they would be taken to the woods and shot, far away from the ears of the people and the new press.

Ivanov would of course try to save his vodka-soaked hide. That was his nature. He would blame anyone but himself, and since Shvets was the person most directly in the line of fire, the only person other than Ivanov who had actually met Herr Dorfman, he would be the scapegoat. Gripped with an unusual fear, Shvets had a sudden urge to flee. He paced from one end of the parlor and back, trying to calm himself, but he couldn't. The idea of running was suddenly in front of him, like a big flashing road sign warning the bridge is out. Turn now or crash.

But he had a wife and two boys—not that he saw them very much, or really loved them, or more precisely her. The boys were too young to judge. His wife, on the other hand, had been a mistake. She'd gotten fat and lazy, and Shvets spent as little time with her as possible. He could certainly live without them, but could he live with himself if anything happened to them? He wasn't sure about that one, so he set it aside. Starting over was the other problem. As Ivanov's top deputy, he was poised for lofty heights within the SVR, and like his boss, he could leverage that for personal gain in the not-so-distant future.

That was something he did not want to give up without a fight, but the rumors were starting, and by next week they would be undeniable. He had either to run or turn on Ivanov, go to SVR headquarters and ask for a face-to-face with Director Primakov. Even as he thought about it, he knew it would be far riskier than running. It was easy to trick himself into thinking they would reward him for doing the right thing, but the SVR was not all that different from the old KGB. You were rewarded for plotting, conspiring, and crushing your political and professional opponents, not for doing the right thing. If he turned on Ivanov in such a manner he would not be rewarded, he would be punished. Not right away, but eventually. They would send him away. No one would want to look at him, because he would be a reminder of their failures.

He didn't even consider going to the federal counterintelligence service. The FSK would jump at the chance to embarrass their flashy sister agency, especially if it meant taking down someone as big as Ivanov, but Shvets had no desire to be branded a traitor for the rest of his days. The men who turned against the security service had an extremely high occurrence of suicide.

Shvets was pragmatic to the core, but this sitting around could only spell disaster. Some type of action had to be taken. He turned away from the window and looked at Alexei, the thick-necked bodyguard. "Alexei, do you trust me?"

The bodyguard lifted his heavy head and looked at Shvets. He shrugged in the way a man shrugs when he finds a question not worth answering.

"Do you know what is going on with our boss?"

Another shrug.

"You know he's in trouble, yes?"

This time big Alexei nodded.

"He's in a great deal of trouble, and he doesn't want to admit it. He would prefer to drink himself silly and shut himself in with the hope that the problem will simply go away. The problem isn't going to go away. In fact, it is only going to get worse." Shvets was tempted to tell him what was going on, but wasn't prepared to go that far. "I need your help, Alexei. I need to get him out of bed and sober him up enough so that he can defend himself. Do you understand that?"

"Yes."

"Good," Shvets said, satisfied that he had gotten somewhere with the man. "Now don't shoot me or break my neck, but I'm going in there to wake him up."

Alexei pursed his big lips while he thought about that one. "He told me. No one. Including you."

"Your job is to protect him, right? Well, if he put a gun to his own head, would you try to stop him?"

"Yes."

"That's what he's doing right now. By getting drunk and sleeping the day away he's killing himself as surely as if he put a gun to his head and pulled the trigger. You need to help me save him."

"What do you want me to do?"

"Nothing. Just sit here . . . and don't hurt me." Shvets didn't wait for an answer. He went to the bedroom door, knocked twice, and then opened. The bed was huge, and with all the pillows and blankets and two prostitutes and poor light he couldn't tell what was what, so he went to the window and yanked open the heavy velvet drapes. Gray light poured into the room and Shvets heard Ivanov moan. He searched the tangled mess and still couldn't find the man's head.

"Sir," Shvets announced, "Director Primakov is here to see you."

A flurry of activity erupted from under the blankets. One or both of the girls screamed as Ivanov dug his way out, all elbows and knees. His red face appeared midway down the length of the bed. "What?" he asked, a mask of horror on his face. "You can't be serious."

"No, I am not, but if you don't get out of bed and do something about this situation, he will show up sooner than you think. Or maybe you would prefer Director Barannikov to show up with the FSK boys and drag you downtown."

Ivanov pulled his head back under the covers. "Go away."

"No, I will not. You have been pouting for three days now. We need to come up with a plan of action, or we are doomed."

"We are worse than doomed . . . We are fucked."

"Stop being such a baby."

"Be careful what you say to me, Nikolai, or I will get out of this bed and throw you out the window."

"Not a bad way to go when compared to what the FSK will do to me. Unfortunately, you have neither the strength nor the courage to throw me out the window, so it looks like I will be tortured in the basement of Lubyanka." He looked over at the bed, but there was no movement or reply. "Please, boss! I beg you to do something . . . anything. Defend yourself. Tell Director Primakov the money is gone."

"You are a fool. I will be put under an examination that I won't be able to withstand."

"Then place the blame on the dirty Palestinians. You know how Primakov hates them. Tell him they killed Sharif over a bad business deal and took all of the money. Blame the Americans, the Brits, the French, the Germans . . . I don't care. Just blame someone and start investigating. What you are doing . . ."

"What was that?" Ivanov snapped as he popped his head back out.

"Blame someone and start investigating."

"Before that . . . at the beginning."

"Blame the Arabs."

"You are right . . . Primakov does hate them. But my money . . . what about that?"

Shvets was pleased with his small victory. Now he needed to bait the hook. "I have some ideas about that as well." He started walking toward the double doors. "I suggest you get out of bed and shower. I will order an extremely late breakfast. We can discuss your finances over coffee and eggs."

CHAPTER 52

BEIRUT, LEBANON

RAPP was in his boxers, pistol at his side, staring at the door of the apartment and trying to decide what to do. It was dark and he had no idea how long he had slept. Whoever was trying to get into the apartment had picked the lock. Rapp raised the pistol and took aim. Either that or he had a key. He eased his finger off the trigger. Maybe it was a nosy landlady, or Hurley was testing him. No, it wouldn't be that. If they were still in training it would be something he'd gladly try, but not in the thick of it like this. For all he knew, Rapp might use it as an excuse to shoot him.

Rapp stayed in the hallway that led to the bedrooms so he could use the wall as cover. The door started to move and then stopped. The rubber stop he'd placed underneath it was doing its job. The door opened a crack and Rapp heard someone saying something, whispering as if they were talking to someone else. But then Rapp heard, "Hey . . . Open up," in English.

Part of the problem was that he had no idea how long he'd slept and consequently what time it was. He had awakened with a start as he heard some soft knocking on the door, followed by the sound of metal on metal, and now whoever was out there was talking to him and getting louder.

"Hey, shithead . . . Open the damn door. We've got big problems."

The contraction of *we have* was what caught his attention. It was not Hurley or Richards so the *we* thing threw another level of mystery into the equation.

"I know you're in there. Open this fucking door, so I don't have to break it down."

Rapp quietly crossed the room on the balls of his feet. The door was cracked about an inch. "Who is it?"

"Fucking Goldilocks. We've been compromised. Open the door. I need to get you the hell out of here."

Rapp's heart started trotting. *Goldilocks . . . compromised . . . What the hell was going on?* "What's the password?" Rapp heard the word *shit* followed by a heavy sigh.

"I'm not part of your merry little band. I don't know the password." There was a pause and then, "There's a leather case in the bedroom closet with a few handy things in it. You're probably holding one of the silenced Berettas right now. I'm the guy who put it there."

Rapp frowned. "Were you in Istanbul a week ago?"

There was a pause and then, "Yeah . . . was that you?"

"Nice little garden flat with alley access."

"Case was in an armoire."

"With a pillow and blanket on top," Rapp said.

"Bingo."

"Let me close the door first and then I'll let you in."

"Roger."

Rapp pushed the door closed and kicked the doorstop out of the way. With his pistol in his right hand he opened the door and then stepped back, holding the gun in a two-handed grip. The guy entered the room and closed the door behind him. He was wearing brown pants, brown shirt, and brown baseball hat. Where had Rapp seen that outfit before?

The visitor dropped the box he was carrying and raised his hands. "Kid, could you lower the gun. If I was a terrorist I would have blown the damn building up."

Looking over the iron sights of the Beretta, Rapp said, "A few more questions. What's going on?"

"You've been compromised. I was ordered by Washington to come get you."

"Who?"

"Irene."

Rapp lowered the gun. "Why?"

"Follow me," the man said as he picked up his box and started for the bedroom. "Stan and your other buddy were picked up at their hotel this morning."

"This morning?" Rapp asked, dumbfounded. "What time is it?"

"Almost six-thirty. They were grabbed by the cops and then handed over to those assholes from Islamic Jihad."

Rapp stopped moving. "Say that again."

"Don't stop moving, kid. They could be on their way here right now, and I don't think we want to be standing around talking when they show up." He opened the box and pulled out clothes that matched his. "Here . . . put these on. I'll grab your shit." He tossed the clothes on the bed and went to the closet, retrieving Rapp's suitcase as well as the beat-up leather case.

Rapp's mind was swimming upstream trying to process what he'd just learned. "But . . ."

The man turned on him, a frightened, wild look in his eyes. "No buts," he hissed. "No questions, no nothing. We need to get the fuck out of here, and I mean now."

Rapp nodded and began putting on his clothes. This stranger was right, of course. He quickly put on the brown uniform and stuffed his clothes in his suitcase, while the stranger wiped down the doorknobs. In just under two minutes they were out the door and on their way to the street. The stranger went out first and after casually looking up and down the street motioned for Rapp to follow. They threw the suitcase and empty box in the back of a simple white minivan, then left. Rapp glanced at his rental car and almost said something, but thought better of it. They had bigger problems.

CHAPTER 53

MUGHNIYAH refused to come to Martyrs' Square, so they had to go to him. Sayyed could hardly blame him. He couldn't wait for the standoff to end, and the hostages to be out of his care. He was tied to them like a mother to her breast-feeding brood. Still, there was something very exciting about the work that lay ahead. Bill Sherman was a once-in-a-lifetime experiment. The American intrigued and horrified him at the same time. Sayyed had participated in close to a hundred interrogations, and he'd never seen anything even close to what he'd witnessed today. The other man, the younger one, was fairly straightforward. A few threats, some punches and kicks, and one fingernail was all it took to get him talking. He'd gotten a name out of him. Several, actually. It was possible that they were both fake, but he didn't really care at this point.

The important thing was that the great and powerful America had once again failed. They had tried to interfere in the affairs of tiny Beirut and he had beaten them at their game yet again. And this one would hurt. Cummins was one thing, but Bill Sherman would have secrets to tell. Secrets that Moscow would have to pay for.

They were in the cellar of a bistro on General de Gaulle Boulevard—the west end of town, just a block from the ocean. The civil war followed the same patterns as any war, but on a much smaller scale. Two blocks either side of the Green Line were virtually destroyed, buildings blown to pieces from high-explosive artillery shells and mortar rounds. Nearly every building had the pockmarks of small-arms fire, but beyond the Green Line you could find a street devastated by the war, yet there would be one building untouched. That one would survive while six or eight in either direction fell made no sense, but it was an undeniable fact of war that some men, and some buildings, seemed to have an almost invisible shield around them. Farther away from the Green Line, entire neighborhoods had made it through the war with far better success, losing only a building or two from the random shelling. Mughniyah loved these buildings. He noted them and used them for his most important meetings.

This restaurant was that kind of lucky building. Sayyed had been initially irritated by all of the extra security measures. They were brought to three different locations and forced to switch cars before they arrived at the bistro. Mughniyah was the most paranoid of the group by a long shot. They found him in the back room with Badredeen. Plates of hummus, *ackawi,* roasted nuts, kibbeh, baba ghanouj, and spiced fish were waiting. After the last few days Sayyed could barely contain himself. He dug in, using the flatbread to scoop up the hummus and then some olives and cheese.

Mughniyah watched with interest as Sayyed devoured the food, and Radih sat sipping his water. He had heard of the deplorable conditions at Martyrs' Square. He'd spent the better part of his life living in abject poverty, so it wasn't that he was above slumming it with the men. And he despised the Maronites as much as, or more than, any of them. It was the American prisoners who kept him away. Those men would attract too much attention. The Americans would be looking for them, and if they got lucky—well, the building would be leveled with everyone in it.

"Radih," Mughniyah asked, "why aren't you eating?"

"I'm not hungry."

Mughniyah could tell there was something else bothering him, but he was extremely unsympathetic to the problems of others. He stabbed out his cigarette and asked, "Can we be sure he is the same Bill Sherman who escaped the embassy bombing in '83?"

Sayyed nodded while he washed some baba ghanouj down with a glass of water. "It's him."

"And did you learn anything from him today?"

"We should kill him," Radih said. "He is the

devil himself. We should not tempt fate a second time. Give me the word and I will kill him tonight."

Mughniyah had no idea what had precipitated such a drastic statement from a man who loved to barter for the lives of hostages. He turned to Sayyed. "And what do you think?"

"Mr. Sherman is an interesting man. A professional liar and provocateur, for certain, but he is also an extremely valuable asset."

"The man is a curse on all of us," Radih proclaimed. "I am telling you we should rid ourselves of lies and kill him tonight."

Thinking it would be a good idea to change the subject, Sayyed asked, "Where is Colonel Jalil?"

"He will not be joining us." Mughniyah turned and shared a knowing glance with Badredeen.

They had been conspiring. That was plain enough to Sayyed, and if it meant leaving the Iranian out, that was fine with him. Sayyed watched as Mughniyah's mood turned dark. He'd seen it before, and when he was sour like this he could be prone to violence. Like some fifteenth-century sultan, he could on a whim ask for someone's offensive head to be separated from the rest of his body. No hierarchy had ever been established for the group, but there was nonetheless a natural order to things. Mughniyah sat atop the food chain for the simple reason that he was the most ruthless among a group of men who were no strangers to violence.

The key, Sayyed had learned, was to think very carefully before answering him when he was in one of his exceptionally surly moods. "What do you have in mind, Mustapha?"

Before he could answer, Radih said for the third time, "I think we should kill him." He did not bother to look at the others. His voice was eerily devoid of his normal youthful passion. "I think the man is the Shaitan himself. We should take him out to the statue tonight and disembowel him. Leave him to a slow death. He can howl his lies at the moon. Let him be an example to the Americans and anyone else who wants to send their assassins to Beirut."

Sayyed held his breath. His eyes darted back and forth between the upstart and the lion. Radih was not a deeply religious man, and his proclamation that the prisoner was the devil was likely to give the duo from Islamic Jihad pause, but then again Mughniyah did not like being interrupted.

"Assef?" Mughniyah asked Sayyed.

Sayyed pulled in a quick breath and said, "I'm not sure I would go as far as to call the man Satan, but on the other hand there is undeniably something very wrong with Mr. Bill Sherman." Glancing at Radih he added, "I can appreciate why Abu might think that would be a good idea, but I'm afraid we would be destroying a very valuable commodity."

Mughniyah grinned knowingly. They were of the same mind.

"Before we decide on something so brash," Badredeen said in his easy tone, "we need to assess a few things. Such as our finances."

Mughniyah held out his hand and said, "We will get to that in a second, but first, I want to talk about Sherman . . . Why is he back after all these years?"

Sayyed straightened up. "He says he is here to kill us, but it is unwise to listen to much of anything that comes out of his mouth." He glanced at Radih and gave him a reassuring nod. What Sherman had said about the young man's mother did not have to be repeated. "His associate, though, is far more truthful, and he says they are here to negotiate the release of Agent Cummins."

Radih was rubbing his swollen knuckles. "I do not believe either of them."

"You don't think they are here to negotiate the release of Agent Cummins?" Mughniyah asked.

"I don't believe anything that comes out of their mouths."

Sayyed could see Mughniyah's legendary temper begin to simmer. "Do you understand the term *unintended consequences*?"

The young leader of Fatah shrugged as if he couldn't care less.

"How about luck . . . as in good or bad luck?"

Radih nodded this time.

"Well, let me explain to you why your mood is starting to upset me. Six months ago, you decided to kidnap an American businessman, who, as it turns out, is just that. He is not a spy. You kidnapped him without coming to us for approval. For that reason alone I could have you shot. That single kidnapping has set in motion a series of events. Agent Cummins was then sent to try to negotiate the release of this businessman. You decided to then grab Cummins rather than negotiate a fee and end it. Fortunately, or unfortunately, we found out that Mr. Cummins is a CIA spy."

"How could that be unfortunate?" Radih proclaimed more than asked.

Mughniyah sat back and gripped the armrests of his chair, almost as if he were trying to hold himself back. "I am in a rather bad mood tonight, so I suggest you keep your interruptions to a minimum, Abu, or I might lose control and snap your scrawny little neck." He let a moment pass, and when he was sure that he had the younger man's attention, he continued. "Where was I? Yes, as it turned out, Mr. Cummins was not who he said he was. He is in fact an American spy. Now, when we are a few days away from handing Cummins over to the Russian, the notorious Bill Sherman and another CIA lackey show up. Are you following me so far?"

Radih nodded.

"All of this was set in motion by one event. Your kidnapping of the businessman. These are what we would call unintended consequences. How many more unintended consequences are going to pop up? Are there any more Americans in the city, or on their way to the city? Will the four of us survive the week? These are the questions that we will not know the answers to until this thing plays itself out. Your heart is in the right place and you are eager, but you need to understand that your actions have consequences. Have I made myself clear?"

"Yes."

"Now the unfortunate thing is that the Americans appear to have learned their lesson after they let us ship their old station chief off to Tehran, so we could thoroughly interrogate him and then dismantle their network of spies. This time it appears they are going to try to get one of their own back. The only surprise is that they didn't try to do it sooner, but now that we have the legendary Mr. Sherman, I think the stakes have been raised considerably."

"How so?" Radih asked, trying not to sound confrontational.

"Mr. Sherman is a particularly nasty man, who no doubt has many nasty secrets bottled up in his sick little head. The CIA will not want those secrets to get out, so I am afraid they will try to get him back as well."

"So," Badredeen said, picking up the conversation, "we must move quickly and carefully to rid ourselves of all these Americans."

"And that is where the Russian comes in." Mughniyah stared at Sayyed. "Assef, when was the last time you heard from the Russian?"

Sayyed wiped the corners of his mouth. "Yesterday. I was not able to get hold of him today."

"Has he mentioned anything about Dorfman and the empty accounts?"

"No."

Mughniyah and Badredeen looked at each other and nodded in agreement. Badredeen spoke. "Don't you find his silence on the subject a bit strange?"

"I do."

"There are three possibilities." Badredeen held up one finger. "The first, the Russian has no idea our banker was murdered in his home on Sunday and that the very next morning, millions of dollars were emptied out of accounts that he himself helped us set up. Does anyone believe for a second that the Russian is that clueless?" When they were all done agreeing, Badredeen moved on to his second point. "The Russian, being the greedy man that he is, killed Dorfman and took all of the money for himself."

Mughniyah held up two fingers and said, "I am going with option two."

"What about option three?" Sayyed asked.

"Someone unknown to us killed Dorfman and stole the money. The only problem with this theory is that Dorfman was very secretive about his clients. The man had no social skill. He cared only for his dogs."

"Still . . . someone . . . an enemy could have found out." Sayyed tried to keep the options open.

"Let me ask you," Mughniyah said, leaning forward, "can you think of anyone you know who has a reputation for cheating people out of their money?"

"I don't want to be in the position of defending Ivanov, but I think we need more evidence before we settle on him as the thief."

"You didn't answer my question."

Sayyed nodded. "You are correct. Mikhail Ivanov is not exactly the most honest man I know."

"And let's not forget the little falling-out he had with our Turkish friend," Badredeen added.

Sayyed was the one who had passed on the information he'd picked up from Damascus. Hamdi

Sharif, the arms dealer whom they had worked with for close to a decade, had reportedly had a fight with Ivanov over a business deal. A month later, Sharif ended up assassinated on a park bench in front of his house. He had asked Ivanov about it, but of course the man had denied any connection.

Mughniyah placed his big hairy right hand on the table. He tapped a thick finger and said, "Moscow is a den of thieves. I warned all of you about this years ago. The collapse has turned it into a free-for-all where the most brutal simply take what they want."

Sayyed could not argue with what he had said. "So what do we do?"

"You say the Russian will be here Friday?"

"Yes."

"Good. We are going to have a little auction."

The word seemed to wake up Radih. "What kind of auction?"

"The kind where we sell the American spies to the highest bidder."

"What bidders?" Sayyed asked.

"Don't worry," Mughniyah cautioned. "Just make sure the Russian is here, and I'll take care of the rest."

"What about Damascus? I must report this missing money."

Mughniyah shook his head. "Not yet. Give me a few days and then you can tell them."

CHAPTER 54

RAPP stepped out into the hot afternoon sun and looked over the edge of the veranda. The narrow street that snaked its way up the hill was barely wide enough for a single car to pass. Down at the bottom, maybe a hundred yards away, he could see the Toyota pickup truck blocking the street. The houses on this little goat hill were all flat-roofed. Clotheslines were strung up and shirts and pants and other garments flapped in the breeze. Beneath him, in the tiny courtyard, three vehicles were packed in with no more than a few feet in between. The ten-foot wall had a ring of razor wire strung from one end to the other. He looked to his right and found a stack of green fiberglass crates. Stenciled on the side in black letters were a string of numbers and letters that he didn't understand, then a few that he did.

Each crate contained multiple M72 LAW antiarmor weapons. Next to those were a crate of rounds for an M203 grenade launcher that was leaning against the wall. Above that, affixed to the wall, was a hand-drawn laminated map that marked the distance and elevation to certain landmarks up to a mile away. Rapp was wondering what all this stuff was for when he heard the voice of the man who had pulled him out of the safe house the night before.

"We call this the sky box . . . not anymore really, but during the height of the war we would sit up here and watch it all unfold."

Rapp turned around to find Rob Ridley sipping on a bright red can of Coke. "Sky box?"

Ridley approached the edge of the balcony, pointed toward the ocean to the north, and then drew his hand south. "See that big, ugly scar that runs from the north to the south?"

"Yeah."

"That's the famous Green Line. We'd sit up here and watch them fight, like a football game. That's why we called it the sky box."

Rapp pointed to the stack of U.S. Army crates. "Looks like you guys did more than watch."

"That shit is more for self-defense, although I saw some badass snipers roll through here. That's the unwritten story about this little war . . . the snipers. They did most of the damage. We found that they were getting a little close." Hurley pointed up at the overhang. "They started sending rounds in here on a daily basis. We put up sandbags, and then after one of our guys got killed, we put in a request for a couple of those badasses from Fort Bragg. Two of them showed up five days later." Ridley pointed at the map on the wall. "They put that thing together. In six days they had thirty-one recorded kills, and that pretty much solved the problem. Kinda like bringing in an exterminator." Ridley laughed and then added, "That's classified, so don't go around telling that story to just anyone."

"How long have we had a presence up here?"

"You'd have to ask Stan that question. I was still in the Marine Corps when they blew our barracks up." Ridley pointed to the south. "Right over there. I showed up in '88. That was when we started rotating sniper teams through here. They loved it. In fact this is where the D Boys battle-tested the first Barrett .50 cal. He shot a guy just over seven thousand feet away."

"That's more than a mile."

"One-point-three and some change." Hurley looked off toward the Green Line. "Strange breed, those snipers. Pretty quiet lot . . . kept to themselves for the most part, but that night they got shitfaced and naked. I guess seven thousand feet is a pretty rare club. At any rate I think we've been up here since '85."

"I thought we pulled out," Rapp said.

"Langley never pulls out . . . or at least rarely. Shit, this little outpost is what stopped this thing from being a complete disaster. We knew everything Damascus was up to. We helped blow up supply convoys, target the occasional asshole who wandered too far away from his home turf. We even taught these guys how to use indirect fire and the other side knew we were here, too. That's why they sent those snipers after us."

"So this is where you're based?" Rapp asked, thinking it didn't make a lot of sense.

"No." Ridley shook his head. "Not for over a year. Things are too quiet around here now."

"So what exactly do you do for Langley?"

"I'm kind of here and there. I guess you could call me a floater."

Rapp had no idea what that meant and got the distinct impression that Ridley wasn't going to enlighten him any further. Rapp let out a yawn. His nights and days were upside-down. After their mad dash from the apartment, Ridley had filled in some of the blanks. The problem was that beyond the obvious fact that Hurley and Richards had been picked up, Ridley had very few details. Rapp had pressed him hard, wanting to know what Langley was doing to find them. Ridley had to admit not much of anything. Langley was sending a small six-man SOG team, and they were actively trying to collect any intel that would aid in a rescue.

Ridley worked his sources well past midnight, but every single one of them seemed to have conflicting information. Finally at 4:00 A.M. he sent Rapp to bed and told him to get some rest. He assured Rapp he'd been through more than a few of these abductions, and they tended to progress slowly, especially for the first few days. Rapp had a hard time falling asleep. He couldn't stop himself from imagining what Hurley and Richards were going through. As part of his training, he'd spent two days tied to a chair. Guys would come in randomly and smack him around. They even gave him some low-voltage shocks from a small engine battery. There was nothing remotely enjoyable about the experience, and Hurley had cautioned them that it paled in comparison to what they would go through at the hands of a sadist or a skilled interrogator. Finally, around sunrise, he had dozed off.

"Listen, I know what you're going through."

Rapp gave him a sideways glance. Ridley was a few inches shorter and a decade or so older. Rapp couldn't quite figure out if he was an optimist or a pessimist. He seemed to kind of float back and forth between the two.

"I've known Stan for six years. I'd do anything to try to save the guy. But we need to get some good intel before we can even consider lifting a finger."

Back in training, if someone had asked him to lay down his life to save Stan Hurley, he would have laughed at him, but now he wasn't so sure. "Any idea where they are?"

Ridley pointed east. "The other side of the big ugly scar. Indian country."

"You ever go over there?"

Ridley gave him a nervous laugh. "I try not to."

"So you've been?"

"Occasionally. It's nowhere near as bad as it was back when the shit was really flying." He searched Rapp's face, wondering what he was thinking. "It's still a nasty place for a stranger like you, kid."

Rapp nodded even though he really wasn't listening. "So it wouldn't be such a good idea to wander over there and start asking questions."

"That would be about the dumbest thing you could do, kid." Ridley could see the upstart wasn't listening to him. He reached out and grabbed his arm. "I've been to that little lake house down in southern Virginia. I've seen the way Stan takes badasses and grinds them up and spits out little pussies, so I'm guessing if you made it through his selection process you've got some serious skills. Am I right?"

Rapp looked at Ridley's grip until he released his arm. "What's your point?"

"I don't care how good you are. Going over to Indian country on your own is a suicide mission. We'll end up looking for three of you instead of two."

"Well . . . I'm not good at sitting around, so somebody better come up with a plan and come up with it quick."

The triple beep, beep, beep of a car horn caught their attention and they both looked to the base of the hill, where a three-car convoy had just pulled up to the roadblock.

"Finally," Ridley said.

"Who is it?"

"A local who knows more about this hellhole than anyone."

CHAPTER 55

MOSCOW, RUSSIA

SHVETS anxiously checked his watch. They'd been in there for more than an hour, and each passing tick of the clock only added to his apprehension. For starters, he didn't like sitting in the waiting room of Director Primakov's office on the top floor of SVR headquarters. Any trip to these lofty heights would test a man's nerves, but considering the events of the past few days, Shvets worried that he might be leaving the building in shackles. He doubted that Primakov knew about the missing money, or the other mistakes that were piling up. The SVR was an entrenched organization with thousands of operations, and Ivanov was regarded as a daring man who knew when to be ruthless and when to smile, and in the years between Stalin's violent mood swings and the collapse of the CCCP, that would have been more than enough. Now, he wasn't so sure.

This was a brave new world. The money grab was in full swing. Oligarchs were popping up and riding the wave of decentralization, but not without problems. The peasants were growing dissatisfied with what they saw as unbridled greed and corruption, and the one thing every Muscovite feared more than even a tyrant like Stalin was the rage of the mob. The mob was like some ancient god who needed regular sacrifices. The men in charge knew that, and in order to satisfy that mob and keep it from bubbling over into the streets, they would look for a few bodies to throw them. One or two public executions would go a long way toward calming the hordes.

It was Shvets's plan. After he'd forced some real food into Ivanov's gullet the previous afternoon, he began to sketch out their strategy. It would be centered on Primakov's distrust of Islamic Jihad and its sister organizations. The missing funds would be laid at their feet, along with the assassination of the banker. As Ivanov's devious brain began to work, he hit upon the idea of blaming them for Hamdi Sharif's murder as well. Shvets wasn't so sure. He was from the new generation. Ivanov was from the old, whose motto was, If you are going to lie, lie big.

The tricky part was this agent they were offering up. They had confirmed through one of their sources inside the CIA that John Cummins did in fact exist and that he had worked in Moscow before being stationed in Damascus. If Ivanov could deliver someone like that, Primakov might be willing to forget the missing funds. The only problem was coming up with the money to pay off the Palestinians. Ivanov would have to convince Primakov to give him the funds necessary to complete the transaction.

And then this morning Sayyed called and things became infinitely more interesting. He explained that he was now in possession of two more Americans, who had been sent to try to buy the release of Agent Cummins. One of the men was nothing more than an underling, but the other was the catch of a lifetime. When pressed, Sayyed refused to give details, saying he would only discuss the matter in person, when they arrived in Beirut. Still, there was no mention of Dorfman and the missing money.

Sayyed's continued silence over the missing funds had caused Ivanov to rethink the issue. What if Islamic Jihad and Fatah no longer feared him? What if they thought Russia too disorganized to care? There had been plenty of heated feuds between the various Palestinian factions over the years, and Sayyed was the man who had profited the most by peddling arms to all sides. What if that thug Mughniyah had decided to take what he wanted? Kill Dorfman, take all the money, solidify his position, and thumb his nose at Ivanov?

That thought had caused Ivanov to reach for the vodka, but Shvets had stopped him. He was scheduled to meet with Primakov in less than an hour, and he needed to be sober. The problem had become clear to Shvets as well. Why else would Sayyed stay quiet over the missing funds? If his money was gone as well, he would be demanding answers. The only logical reason for his silence was that they had taken the money and they were daring Ivanov to bring it up.

Ivanov had to assume they had every last shred of damning information that Dorfman had kept. All of the various accounts, and how Ivanov had bilked his own government out of millions on the arms shipments by playing the middleman with Sayyed. That information alone could sink him. Ivanov's hands were tied, at least for now. That was how Shvets had counseled him. Go along with this ruse. Go to Beirut and look the liars in their eyes, and then ask them where the money had gone. Bring a show of force that will make them think twice about stealing from you.

Ivanov liked the idea. As he walked into Primakov's office he turned and told Shvets to wait outside. Shvets knew his boss too well to think he was anything other than a duplicitous snake. As he nervously checked his watch, the minutes ticking by, he figured out what Ivanov was up to. He was in there right now, blaming him for the missing funds. He'd probably already ordered someone to begin creating a false trail between him and Dorfman. That way, when it really did blow up, Ivanov could step back and blame his inept deputy Shvets. Shvets didn't know if he was more upset with Ivanov or with himself for not seeing it sooner. He should have left him in bed and gone to Primakov and taken his chances.

When the door finally opened, Ivanov appeared with a stoic look on his face. He never broke stride as he headed for the elevator. As he walked past his deputy he snapped his fingers for him to follow. Shvets hopped to his feet and buttoned his jacket, hustling to catch up.

Once in the elevator, Shvets asked, "Well?"

"It was good. He understands what must be done."

Shvets started to ask another question, but Ivanov shook his head in a very curt way that told him this was not the place to talk. When they entered Ivanov's office less than a minute later, the director of Directorate S went straight for the vodka. Shvets did not try to stop him this time. It was approaching midafternoon, and he took it as a victory that he'd kept him sober this long. He waited for his boss to consume a few ounces.

When Ivanov looked relaxed enough, Shvets asked, "What did he say?"

Ivanov yanked at his tie. "He sees things our way. He knows the true character of those Palestinian carpet monkeys."

Shvets was used to his boss uttering racist slurs, so he paid them little attention. He also knew that his boss was paranoid enough in general, but especially today. He was worried his office was bugged. "So what is the plan?"

"We leave in the morning."

"Alone?" Shvets asked, honestly scared.

"No." Ivanov had a huge grin. "The director has been quite generous. He is sending along some Spetsnaz. One of the crack Vympel units."

Shvets wasn't sure if that was good or bad news.

The Vympel units specialized in assassination and sabotage, among other things. "Why a Vympel unit?"

"Because he's sending us with cash."

"How much?"

Ivanov smiled and held up five fingers.

"Really?" Shvets's surprise was evident on his face.

"Don't be so shocked. I have no doubt it will be counterfeit. Probably being printed as we speak."

Shvets had heard rumors about the old KGB printing presses that could turn out francs, deutsche marks, pounds, and dollars on demand. "Will they be able to tell?"

"If the Americans can't tell, how will the Palestinians be able to tell?"

Shvets wasn't so sure but he went along with it.

"Don't look so nervous." Ivanov came over and put an arm around Shvets's shoulders. "I told him how useful you have been to me. I have no doubt that when we return with these mystery Americans you will be given a nice promotion."

Shvets smiled, even though he didn't feel like it. The truth was, there was probably a better than even chance that he'd be given a dirty, dank cell.

CHAPTER 56

BEIRUT, LEBANON

ACCORDING to Ridley, it was very poor spycraft to meet a source at a safe house, but for this particular source they made exceptions. The reason was fairly straightforward. The source owned the house. Levon Petrosian had the complexion of someone who was born further north, but had lived long enough in the sun-baked city that his skin was deeply lined and had taken on the appearance of a permanent sunburn. His white hair had receded almost to the midpoint of his head, and he was a good fifty pounds overweight. He entered the house out of breath, a cigarette dangling from his lips, his four bodyguards moving in tandem, two in front and two behind. The bodyguards were young, big, and fit. Two looked like locals and two had Petrosian's northern complexion.

Petrosian walked over to Ridley, grabbed him by the shoulders, and kissed the American on both cheeks, and then, refusing to let go, he stared into Ridley's eyes and spoke to him. His face didn't so much as twitch. His eyes didn't blink. Only his lips moved. After the intense one-sided exchange, the Armenian gave Ridley one more hug and then his eyes lifted and settled on Rapp. He released Ridley and asked, "Is this the one?"

Ridley nodded.

Petrosian sized Rapp up and then announced, "I must shake your hand."

The man spoke perfect English, but with one of those clipped heavy Russian accents. Rapp couldn't come up with a single good reason why this man would want to shake his hand, but he stuck his right hand out as a polite reflex.

In a voice only the two of them could hear he said, "I have hated that Turkish pig Hamdi Sharif for almost twenty years. I want to thank you for putting a bullet in his black heart. When I heard he was dead I wept tears of joy."

Rapp's own heart began to beat a little faster. How in hell did this man know he had killed Sharif? Rapp tilted his head to the left so he could get a look at Ridley. The man shrugged his shoulders as if to say he was sorry. So much for secrecy.

"I am very sorry about Bill."

Rapp had to remind himself that to these people, Stan Hurley was Bill Sherman. "Thank you. Have you found any information that may help us?"

He winced as if disappointed in himself. "I'm not sure if it will help, but maybe. I confirmed that it was the police that picked our friend up in front of his hotel this morning. In fact it was the police chief, that pig Gabir Haddad."

"Haddad is not a bad man," Ridley said for Rapp's benefit. "Just extremely corrupt. He works with us sometimes."

"He works with anyone if they have enough money," Petrosian said.

"Levon, anything to drink?"

"No, thank you. My stomach is upset today."

"So this Haddad," Rapp said, "who gave him the order?"

"I am fairly certain it was your friends from Islamic Jihad, but I will know more later. I am having dinner with Haddad this evening."

"His idea or yours?" Ridley asked.

"His . . . He is afraid he has offended me, which he has, of course. He knows he cannot simply come into my neighborhood and grab my friends. It would have been nice if you had told me Bill was coming. All of this could have been avoided."

"I know . . . I already told you I was sorry. He was planning on seeing you today. He didn't want word getting out that he was back."

"And how did that work out for him?"

"I know . . . but just be careful with Haddad. We can't afford to lose you."

"I am always careful. It will be at a restaurant of my choosing, and I will make sure the street is blocked off. Trust me . . . he's the one who needs to be nervous."

"That's what worries me. What if he's desperate?"

"He has always been a desperate little man. He knows what he did this morning was wrong. He will be full of fear, and I will play on that fear to get every last piece of information from him."

"Any idea where they took him?" Rapp asked.

"That is the question, isn't it? Where did they take him?" Petrosian shuffled across the stone floor and out onto the veranda. "Beirut is not a small city. It is not like your New York or Chicago, but it is not small. Have you figured out how they found him?"

"No," Ridley said. "He flew in last night shortly after nine. That's all we know."

"I have talked to the people at the hotel, and I am satisfied that they did not know who he was. Somebody must have spotted him at the airport. From the old days. He made a big enough impression in certain circles, and those little Palestinian rats do all the dirty work at the airport. Baggage and fueling . . . cleaning the planes and the terminal. They treat it like their own little syndicate," Petrosian said with contempt. "I have heard rumors that some of the cab drivers are involved in a kidnapping ring."

"Would they have any pull with Haddad?" Ridley asked, thinking of the police chief.

"No," Petrosian answered as he flicked a long ash over the edge and onto the cars below. "That would have to be someone much higher up. My guess is the same people who grabbed your other man . . . the Schnoz . . . Isn't that what you call him?"

"Yes. You mean Islamic Jihad?"

"Correct . . . with the help of a few others."

"Anything else?"

"Little things here and there." Petrosian paused and chewed on his lip for a moment. "Have you heard about this standoff at Martyrs' Square?"

"I heard a little something yesterday, but not much."

"It is a funny thing," Petrosian said while looking off into the distance.

"What are you talking about?" Rapp asked.

Ridley pointed to the north. "Follow the scar to the sea . . . one block short, you can see an open area. That's Martyrs' Square."

"Before the war it was a beautiful place. Full of life," Petrosian said in a sad voice.

"It was the scene of some of the heaviest fighting during the war," Ridley added. "The buildings are all empty shells now."

"Now that the cease-fire has held, certain groups have gotten the idea that it is time to grab land while they still can. The Maronites started earlier in the week and they began occupying the buildings along the east side of the square. The Muslims got word and started moving their people into a building on the west side."

Rapp looked at the spit of land. He guessed it was around two miles away. "Does that mean a fight is brewing?"

"Part of me wishes they would all just kill each other so the rest of us can pick up the pieces and get back to where we were before this mess started, but I know that this is not the answer. We need the peace to hold."

"And how does this Martyrs' Square situation figure into our other problem?"

"It might not, but then again manpower is an issue."

"Manpower?" Rapp asked, not understanding.

"These groups are like any organization. They have limited resources. They have to collect garbage, collect taxes, man their roadblocks, punish those who aren't behaving . . . the list goes on and on. The point is, if they are forced to hold the west end of Martyrs' Square they will be weak in other places."

Rapp wondered how he could use that to his advantage. As the sun moved across the afternoon sky he got the sinking feeling that they were losing an opportunity. That if they didn't act, didn't do something bold and do it soon, Richards and Hurley would share the same fate as Bill Buckley.

CHAPTER 57

HURLEY had lost track of time. After the fingernail incident, they'd left him alone. Turned off the light and shut the door. He sat in the chair, his arms duct-taped to the armrests and his ankles to the two front legs. His chest and shoulders were also taped to the chair back. Big loops of silver tape, as if he were a mummy. For the first few hours he tried to catalogue everything he'd seen, said, and heard. Abu Radih was what he'd expected—a thin-skinned overwrought child in a man's body. If he was lucky, he could provoke the man into killing him. That was the first priority. He had to enrage the man to the point where he defied the orders of the others. Go down fighting. He dozed off thinking of his own death. What a beautiful death it would be if he could pull it off. Exercise his will over a free man. Inflict enough mental pain on Radih to get him to do something he himself knew was wrong.

The thought brought a smile to his swollen lips, and then he let his chin rest on his chest and went to sleep. He awoke some time later. It could have been an hour, three hours, or half a day, and what did it really matter? The stink in the room was horrendous, but it was far better than the hood. He needed to go to the bathroom, so he whizzed right there, letting it splash over the seat of the chair onto the concrete floor. That helped him relax a little bit, but his fingers were starting to really sting, so he started talking to God to take his mind off the pain.

Hurley had no illusions about his potential for sainthood. He pretty much knew where he was headed when it was over, and yes, he did believe in the man upstairs and the man downstairs. He'd seen too much nasty shit in his life to think for a second that there wasn't both good and evil in this world. Where he fit into that paradigm was a little more complicated. One of his favorite aphorisms involved sending Boy Scouts after bad men. Good people needed men like Hurley even if they couldn't bring themselves to admit it. Maybe God would take pity on him. Maybe he wouldn't.

Hurley bowed his head and asked for forgiveness for any of the innocent people he'd killed over the years, but that was as far as he was willing to go. The assholes, he would not apologize for. He then nodded off to sleep again. He awoke later to the sounds of a man screaming. He knew instantly that it was Richards. What they were doing to him, Hurley could only imagine. The screams came and went, rising and falling like waves crashing into the rocks. And then Hurley could tell by the steady rhythm what they were doing. They were electrocuting him and they weren't bothering to ask questions. They were just trying to wear him down. Listening to the pain of one of his own men was the most difficult thing of all.

Hurley bowed his head again and asked God for the strength to kill these men. It went like this for four or five cycles. He tried not to obsess over the time. When he was awake, he tried to prepare himself for what would come next. With an almost endless string of awful possibilities, there was one in particular that had him worried, and when the door finally opened, it was as if his captors had read his mind.

A man entered, plugged in the cord for the light, and there in the doorway was a bloodied and battered Richards. Two men were at his sides, holding him up. His wrists were bound in front of him with duct tape. The red marks on his chest confirmed what they had been doing, although it wasn't all. Richards's face was beaten and swollen—one of his eyes completely shut.

Sayyed entered the room, a man following him with a chair similar to the one Hurley was in. He showed the man where to place it and said to Hurley, "How are you feeling today?"

"Great!" Hurley said with enthusiasm. "You guys really do a nice job of making people feel comfortable."

"Yes." Sayyed smiled. "I'm sure you would show us the same hospitality if we were in your country."

"Slightly better," Hurley said, flashing the new gap in his teeth. "You know how competitive we Americans are. We didn't put a man on the moon by making our women walk around in sheets all day and blowing ourselves up."

"We all know that was faked."

"Sure it was," Hurley said agreeably as they placed Richards in the other chair. One of the men produced a knife so he could cut Richards's duct tape. Hurley wanted that knife, and in Arabic asked, "Where's my buddy Radih? Either of you boys ever get a blow job from his mom?" Hurley then launched into an invective-filled description of the sex acts that Radih's mom used to perform for him.

Sayyed would never admit it, but this American's descriptive abilities were in a league of their own. In fact, the descriptions were so detailed that even he wondered for a second if it could be true.

Hurley read the unsure looks on the faces of the two goons and said, "You really didn't know Radih's mother was a whore? You should try her sometime. She's getting a little up there in age . . . not quite as tight a fit, if you know what I mean." Hurley winked at them as if they were of the same mind.

"That will be enough," Sayyed said. He ordered the men to finish taping Richards's wrists to the chair. When they were finished he told them they could wait outside.

Hurley smiled at them and waited until they were at the door and then shouted, "Don't forget to ask Radih about his mother. Dirtiest piece of ass I've ever had."

The door closed with a click. Sayyed placed his hands on his hips and let out an exasperated sigh.

"It's true," Hurley said, punctuating his words with an emphatic nod. "The woman was a sex machine. She should have paid me."

Doctrine told Sayyed he should ignore the comments, but he felt that he needed to say something. "You are a very interesting man, Mr. Sherman. You must be very unsure of yourself."

"Why do you say that, Colonel?"

"It is so obvious. Do I really have to say it?"

"Well, unless I've learned how to read minds since we last saw each other, I suggest you spit it out."

"You are afraid you won't be able to stand up to my methods, so you are trying to enrage my colleague to the point where he kills you."

Hurley screwed on a confused look. "Colonel, you give me way too much credit. I'm not that smart. I'm just a horny bastard who's slept with a ton of prostitutes . . . one of whom just happens to be Radih's mom."

Sayyed laughed at him. "You are an unusual man."

"What do I have to do to get you guys to take me seriously? I'm going to lie to you about a lot of shit, but I am dead serious about Radih's mom, and I'm not knocking the woman, she was amazing. And besides, you can't blame a woman for trying to put some food on the table. Can you?"

Sayyed thought about that for a second and simply shook his head. It was time to take charge again. He wheeled his little cart over and checked his instruments. When he was ready he broke open some smelling salts and stuck them under the other American's nose. Richards snorted and opened his eyes. Turning back to the foul-mouthed older one, he said, "Your friend, Mr. Richards, was kind enough to give us his name."

"Never heard of him."

"Yes . . . well, let's see if we can jog your memory. This is what we are going to do." Sayyed picked up the tin snips and said, "I will ask you a question. If you refuse to answer or lie I will cut off one of his fingers."

"Cool." Hurley straightened up as much as the tape would allow. "I'd like to see you cut one off right now. Go ahead . . . let's get started."

"Mr. Sherman, what is your real name?"

"Come on, cut his finger off. Cut his wrist off . . . that would be really awesome."

Richards was awake now, a panicked look in his eyes. "What the hell?"

Sayyed said, "He has already told us your name, but I want to hear you say it."

"Fine . . . William Tecumseh Sherman. Are you happy now? Can we go home?"

"No. That is not the name he gave us."

"I think I'd know my own name."

"Last chance." Sayyed placed the tin snips around the first knuckle on Richards's left hand.

"William Tecumseh Sherman."

"Wrong answer." Sayyed pushed the two red handles together and there was a quick snip and the pinky fell to the dirty floor. Richards started screaming, and Sayyed quickly moved the snips over to Hurley's pinky. "Your turn," he yelled. "Name?"

Hurley had already turned his head away, as if he couldn't bear to watch what was going on. He started to move his lips and mumbled a name.

"Louder . . . I can't hear you."

Hurley slowly turned his head, made eye contact with Sayyed, and then looked down at his pinky. The distance was about right. He pretended he was starting to cry while again mumbling, and when Sayyed moved just a touch closer, offering up his good ear so he could hear better, Hurley lunged forward, tilting his head to the right. He caught the top third of the man's left ear between his teeth and clamped down with all of his strength, grinding and chewing and growling and then yanking his head back.

Sayyed screamed and broke free, his hand clamped around his bloody ear. He stumbled away and then turned to look at his subject. What he saw horrified him. Bill Sherman had a chunk of his ear hanging half out of his mouth. The insane American smiled at him and then started chewing on the ear, crunching it like a potato chip.

CHAPTER 58

RAPP looked out across the city. Night had fallen and that scar known as the Green Line now looked like a wide, formidable river, a black swath of darkness that cut the city in half. But travel two blocks in either direction and there were signs of life. Buildings lit up with inhabitants, traffic moving about the city, horns blaring, and under-powered engines revving—all the normal sights and sounds of a city. But not in that desolate corridor. Only twice in the last hour had he seen a car dare cross no-man's-land. It appeared the cease-fire was activated as they usually are, by segregating the various factions. He could not see the east-west streets to the north, and it was likely that more cars had crossed in that sector, but not enough to change what was obvious. This was literally a city torn asunder.

The problem as Rapp saw it was fundamental

geography. He was on this side and they were on the other side—the *they* being Hurley and Richards. The only way to save them was to go over there, but Ridley had explained to him that going over there was a very bad idea. Going over there would result in his being captured, tortured, and then killed, in that order.

Rapp's response to Ridley was, "So you're pretty much admitting that Stan and Bob are going to be tortured and killed."

"I'm admitting no such thing."

"The hell you're not," Rapp said, his frustration finally boiling over.

Ridley shot back, "I know you're the new wonder boy, so this might be hard for you to understand, but there are things that are going on that you have not been read in on."

"Like what?"

"Things that are way above your pay grade, rookie." Ridley caught his mistake and tried to temper his words by adding, "Listen, I don't make the rules. There are certain protocols that I have to follow. Langley tells me who I can share things with. If you're not on that list my hands are tied."

"Like Petrosian, for instance. I'm sure you cleared that with Langley. You telling a foreign national that I was the man who killed Sharif." Rapp watched as Ridley looked away. "Are you fucking kidding me? There's no way in hell you got approval from Irene to give him that information."

Ridley sighed. "We need Petrosian on this one, and the man does not trust strangers, so I gave him a little piece of information that I knew would please him. He hated Hamdi Sharif more than any person on the planet. It goes back to the beginning of the civil war here. They were both arms dealers and they agreed not to sell weapons to Fatah. Petrosian lived here, and he felt that a militarized Fatah would only prolong the fighting. About six months into the war he found out that Sharif had broken their agreement and was selling weapons to the radical Palestinians. Petrosian was right. It prolonged the war, destroyed the city, killed thousands more, and Sharif became a very wealthy man. Petrosian vowed to kill him, but Sharif never set foot in the city again."

"Fine . . . so you used what I did for your own benefit, which means you owe me. I deserve to know what in hell is going on." Rapp could see Ridley was at least thinking about it, so he pressed him a little harder. "That could have just as easily been me that got picked up. I deserve to know what Langley is doing to try to get them back."

"They're working on different levels. Signal intercepts, applying pressure where they can, calling in favors . . ."

"What in hell does all that mean?"

"It's complicated, is what it's supposed to mean, and on top of that, Stan, your friend Bobby, and you aren't even supposed to exist. How the fuck do you expect them to go to the State Department with that one . . . Excuse me," he said in a falsetto, "two of our black ops guys, who don't actually exist, were kidnapped in Beirut. Could you help us get them back?"

"Bullshit."

"Bullshit . . . what in hell is that supposed to mean?"

"It means it's bullshit. If you think the State Department is the answer to our problems, if Langley thinks they're our solution, we're fucked."

"I didn't say they were the only game. I told you it's complicated. And what the hell would you know? You're a damn rookie."

"A rookie who's smart enough to know this is bullshit," Rapp yelled. "You know what the solution is . . . you just don't want to say it because you"—Rapp pointed at him—"and all of the other pussies back at Langley don't have the balls to follow through on it."

"Please, enlighten me, boy wonder. What's the solution?"

"We do what the Russians did."

"What the Russians did?" Ridley mocked him.

"Yeah . . . back in the mideighties . . . after four of their diplomats were kidnapped."

Ridley's gaze narrowed. "Where'd you hear that story?"

"Stan."

"For Christ's sake," Ridley muttered, obviously not happy that Hurley had told Rapp the story.

"Two diplomats and two KGB guys get snatched by one of the Palestinian factions. One of them happens to be the KGB's station chief here in Beirut. The Russians know what happened to the CIA's station chief when he got kidnapped, because they paid for the information that the Iranians sucked out of him. They don't want to see all of their operations exposed, so they send in a joint force of Spetsnaz and KGB goons and they start whacking people."

Ridley was shaking his head. "That's not the answer."

"Really . . . since you appear to know the story, tell me how it ended."

Ridley shook his head. "Nope."

"One was killed and the three were released," Rapp said. "And how many Russians were kidnapped after that?"

"Zero," Ridley reluctantly admitted.

"That's right, and how many Americans?"

Ridley shrugged. "Not zero."

"So what's the lesson to be learned?"

"We're not the Russians."

"That's your answer."

"Listen . . . I know you're frustrated. *I'm* frustrated, but I am telling you this is way above both of us. There are a lot of really important people who want this cease-fire to last. They will never allow us to go around shooting people like the Russians did."

"But the Palestinians can keep kidnapping *our* people?" Rapp waited for Ridley to give him an answer that wasn't coming anytime soon. "Like I said . . . this is bullshit."

That had been more than three hours ago. Rapp and Ridley had not exchanged words since then. Rapp had dumped his anger into studying maps of West Beirut, reading the intelligence reports, and trying to come up with some way to prevent this disaster from following the course of the previous hostage negotiations. Anyone who didn't understand where this was headed was either deluding himself by ignoring history or just too stupid to connect the dots. Out of this frustration came the realization of what it would all mean to his own future.

He'd spent years thinking of little more than how he would make the other side hurt, and now after all of his training, right when he was getting started, it would be derailed. Hurley and Richards would end up telling them everything they knew about him. His career would be over. The anger welled up inside him, and as he looked out across the city, he could feel himself drifting further and further away from the people pulling the strings in D.C. Their half measures and dithering disgusted him. It was like Hurley had told them on the drive down from Hamburg: "We got soft in the eighties and let these assholes get away with way too much shit." Apparently Washington still hadn't learned its lesson.

Ridley joined him on the veranda. He was holding two beers. He set one in front of Rapp and took a swig out of the other.

Rapp eyed the beer and then said, "I'm not in the mood."

"Shut up and drink. And listen for a change. I've been doing some thinking. This thing isn't going to end well. Cummins was bad enough . . . Stan . . . the shit that guy has in his brain . . . the stuff he's seen over the years." Ridley shuddered at the thought of the enemy getting their hands on all that information. "I can't even begin to calculate the damage." He paused, took a swig of beer, and shook his head. "Someone needs to do something and you seem like just the kind of crazy asshole that would volunteer for a mission like this, although it's actually not a mission. There's nothing official about it. In fact, I'm going to get so pissed tonight that I pass out. And then when I wake up in the morning, and you're not here, I'll call Langley and tell them you've gone AWOL."

"And where will I be?" Rapp asked.

"Petrosian will be here in one hour. He has arranged to take you over to the other side. The police chief, no less, is taking you."

Rapp was surprised. "The same asshole who snatched Stan?"

"One and the same."

"Can I trust him?"

"Absolutely."

"How?"

"Because this time he has given Petrosian his word that nothing will happen to you."

"And I should be impressed by that?"

"Yes, you should. The chief will drop you off at a small hotel a few blocks west of Nijmeh Square, and then you're on your own. My advice is you spread some cash around, telling the hotel manager and the vendors that you would like to meet with Colonel Assef Sayyed. They will claim they've never heard of him, but they all know who he is. They will tell him you are looking for him and he will have someone collect you before the day is out. Then it will go one of two ways." Ridley took another drink and organized his thoughts. "He will either sit down and negotiate with you, in which case Petrosian has agreed to bankroll you to the tune of one million dollars."

"You're kidding me."

"No, he is a man who likes to show his gratitude, and besides, you just eliminated one of his top competitors. He's bound to pick up a few more contracts."

"Will a million do it?"

"Doubtful, but it will let them know we are serious, and they all know Petrosian is not a man to be fucked with."

"So if it's not enough money . . ."

Ridley waved him off. "I'm going to be working on getting more."

"Langley?"

"Maybe, but we have some other options. I just need to see if I can pull it off."

Rapp thought about the money that Hurley had taken from the Swiss bank accounts. He almost told Ridley but decided to keep it to himself for now. "That's option one. What's option two?"

"They throw you in the dungeon and they torture you and eventually kill you."

"But I'm a rookie, so how much harm can I really do." It was a statement, not a question.

"Something like that. A pawn for a bishop." Ridley shrugged. "Maybe you even get lucky and take a few of them down with you." Ridley drained his beer and looked to the west. "There's one last thing. The story about the Russians."

"Yeah."

"Stan didn't tell you the whole thing. The Russians . . . they wiped out a couple of families . . . women and children included. Fucking butchers." Ridley shook his head, trying to get rid of the bad memories. "We're not the Russians. We don't kill women and children. At least not intentionally. Never forget that."

CHAPTER 59

SAYYED held the small mirror in his hand, turned his head to the right and checked his bandage, carefully fingering the edges. The morning sunlight came through the window of his room, providing ample light. There was no hope of reattaching the jagged hunk of cartilage and skin—at least that's what the doctor had told him, although Sayyed suspected that the man was not well versed on the most recent medical advances. When all of this was over, which he hoped would be very soon, he would have to go to Paris and see if there was a plastic surgeon who could do something about the nub that was now his ear.

Growing his hair out would help, but Sayyed did not want to live the rest of his years with such a permanent reminder of his time spent with Bill Sherman. That was still the only name he had to go on. The other man, Mr. Richards, had told them he did not know his boss's real name. As to whether he was telling the truth, Sayyed would only know that after a few more sessions, and depending on how the bidding went, he might not get that opportunity.

One thing was certain: Mr. Sherman's sanity was no longer up for discussion. In the nearly twenty years that Sayyed had been doing this, he had never encountered anyone close to this animal. The man was clearly insane. How else could you explain biting off someone's ear and then chewing it? The all-too-fresh memory caused Sayyed to shudder. He'd never experienced anything so strange in his life. The pain had been bad, excruciating at the time, but it had faded. The image, though, of another person chewing on his ear had only grown stronger. He did not like it one bit, and it made him all the more anxious to get through this day and be done with this Bill Sherman or whatever his real name was.

Sayyed finished buttoning the fresh white shirt that Ali had fetched for him and then put on his suit coat. He heard footsteps coming down the hall and turned to see Radih standing in the open doorway.

"You wanted to see me?"

"Yes. How are our neighbors across the street?"

"Nothing new. We estimate they have between thirty and fifty men."

"And us?"

"Thirty-two."

Sayyed nodded, and thought the number enough to handle a problem should one arise. Changing subjects, he said, "You have heard about this new American? The one who is staying at the Shady Cedar?"

Radih nodded. "Two of my men have been following him this morning." He held up a two-way radio. "They have sent me regular updates. They say the man is a fool."

"A fool?" Sayyed said, finding the word an interesting choice.

"He is wandering around the streets, asking merchants for information about kidnapped Americans and mentioning your name. He's handing out money and telling people where he is staying. Telling them he is here to negotiate their release."

Sayyed was not surprised that his name was being mentioned. Chief Haddad had told him everything. The fact that Petrosian was sticking his nose into their business did not surprise him. He had known when he sent the chief into the Bourj to grab the two Americans that there would be repercussions. That was why he had to pay Haddad such an outrageous sum.

Sayyed could tell something was bothering Radih, so he asked, "What is wrong?"

"I am worried that some other faction will grab him. In fact, I will be amazed if he makes it to lunch, and if someone else gets him . . ." He made a pained expression and a clicking noise.

"It could complicate our negotiations."

"Yes."

Haddad had told Sayyed that the new American was young, inexperienced, and very nervous. Radih was right. If one of the other factions grabbed him, they would try to ransom him, which would make things more complicated, especially if he wanted to complete the entire transaction today. There was another angle that he had just considered, but could not share with the others. If the Americans were serious about bidding, they were likely to drive the price far beyond what he was hoping to get. In the end it was unlikely that Mughniyah and Badredeen would agree to hand them back to the U.S. government, but it was worth a try. The smart thing to do was to take this new variable out of play and see what the Americans were willing to offer. "Why don't you pick him up, but be very careful. You know how sneaky the Americans can be. Take him someplace first and strip him down. Make sure he isn't carrying any tracking devices. Then bring him here and show him the rabid dog in the basement . . . find out how serious they are about making an offer."

"You are not seriously considering handing them back to the Americans?"

Maybe not, but Sayyed was at a minimum willing to consider his options. America was a very wealthy country. Maybe they could make up all of their lost funds and then some. Sayyed could put himself back on the road to a life of opulence. Knowing how unhinged Radih was about the American, Sayyed knew he would have to keep these thoughts to himself. "No, I am not, but I would like to see if the Americans can help drive the price up a bit."

Radih stared at him for a moment and said, "You should let me kill him. Remove all temptation."

Can I trust Radih with these prisoners today? was the question Sayyed asked himself yet again. It would be nice if he could convince Mughniyah to come keep an eye on things, but he wanted to be part of the negotiations at the airport. Sayyed understood his colleague's anger, but he could not understand his persistence. The man simply did not understand what was at stake here today. He supposed a great deal of it was due to his youth. He could crawl back to Sabra and Shatila and rely on his black market trades and the payoffs he received from all of the impoverished refugees. He had many years ahead of him and many opportunities to rebuild his wealth and he did not have to answer to Damascus for missing funds. Still, none of these points would matter to him. His judgment was clouded by his hatred. Normally, he would chastise Radih or humiliate him, but not this time. They just needed to get through today and then things would return to normal. He decided on a more mature approach. Not wanting to argue with him, he said, "I understand your anger, but you are better than this, Abu."

Radih shook his head. "I do not think so. My heart is filled with nothing but hatred for this man. I will not sleep until I have killed him."

"And that is understandable, but you must take comfort in the fact he will die a thousand deaths at the hands of whoever buys him today. He will experience more pain than we can even begin to imagine."

"None of that matters to me. I must kill him with my own hand."

A compromise occurred to Sayyed, one that he would never have to honor, but one that might be enough to keep Radih from ruining their chances of refilling their coffers. "I promise you, Abu, that whoever buys him today, I will make the transaction contingent on the other party agreeing that when they are done with Mr. Sherman you will be given the honor of killing him." Sayyed watched the Palestinian turn this idea over in his hate-filled mind. He could see that he was not quite convinced, so he said, "And I will allow you to spend some time with him today, so he can be taught a proper lesson before he leaves."

A thin smile creased Radih's lips and he said, "I would like that very much."

"Good," Sayyed said, placing his hand on his shoulder. "Now go get this other American, and make sure no one is following you. Bring him back here and we will see what he has to say, and then I will give you some time to take out your frustrations on Mr. Sherman."

CHAPTER 60

RAPP sat on the edge of the hotel room's bed, tapping his foot. It was ten-oh-nine in the morning, and he was having a hell of a time trying to calm his nerves. All he'd brought along was a small duffel bag that Ridley had helped him pack. Petrosian had come back to the safe house after his dinner with the police chief to go over the plan. He was not optimistic that Rapp would succeed, but agreed that doing nothing was a worse alternative. So, shortly before midnight, Rapp was shuttled from Petrosian's armor-plated sedan to the Beirut police chief's four-door Peugeot. Rapp was not thrilled about the idea at first, but when Petrosian explained that the chief was eager to make amends for his lack of judgment the day before, Rapp went along with it. Petrosian also knew that the chief would tell the right people that another CIA man had shown up and was looking to negotiate the release of his colleagues.

They made it through the checkpoint fine, but Rapp had to resist the urge to shoot the smug little turd of a police chief and both of his men. It would have sent a nice message, but ultimately the wrong one, considering his final objectives. And besides, he had a role to play, so as they neared the hotel Rapp fired off one anxious, paranoid question after another. The chief did his best to calm his guest, but Rapp played the inconsolable nervous wreck better than he could have hoped.

They reached the Shady Cedar Hotel at twenty minutes past midnight. Ridley had handpicked the hotel because it was smack dab in the middle of Indian country. All three men escorted Rapp into the lobby. The chief asked to have a private word with the manager, and the two men disappeared behind the closed door of the small office behind the reception desk. The other two policemen stood chain-smoking by the door, while Rapp stood at the front desk and did his best to look nervous as hell, which was no easy thing considering the fact that he really wanted to kick down the door and pistol-whip the double-dealing police chief.

After five minutes Chief Haddad appeared, stroking his mustache and assuring Rapp that everything was taken care of. The little kiss-ass hotel manager joined in, telling Rapp that all would be fine. Rapp got the distinct impression that all would not be fine, and that both of these men would look to make money by turning him in to Islamic Jihad, but that was the point of the whole crazy exercise. So Rapp anxiously shuffled his feet and kept rubbing his neck as if he was a wreck.

Pointing toward the door, Rapp asked, "Can't one of your men stay the night?"

"I'm afraid that is not possible. Besides, you will be safe here."

Rapp acted even more worried, but truth be told, he didn't have a worry in the world. He could sleep in peace and then in the morning he could begin to ask around for information. The idea that the chief wouldn't tell the very people who had asked him to grab Hurley was ludicrous, but Rapp played dumb.

The elevator was out of order, so he took the stairs to the fourth floor. He closed and locked the door to the room and wedged the rubber doorstop into the small gap at the bottom. Next he opened the curtains to see what kind of exit the window might provide. It was a good twenty-five feet to the street. Ridley had sent him off with a grab bag of things, including a thirty-foot coil of rope. Rapp tied one end to the foot of the bed and left the rest of it coiled by the window. Then he took out his silenced Beretta and Motorola radio. He set the gun on the nightstand and keyed the transmit button on the radio.

Ridley's voice came over the radio a few seconds later. Rapp told him he'd made it to the hotel and was in his room. The radios weren't secure, so they kept the conversation vague and short. Rapp confirmed that he would check in at eight and then every two hours after that. If he missed any of the check-ins, Ridley should assume Rapp had made contact. After that, it was anyone's guess how things would turn out. Rapp brushed his teeth and lay down on the bed with his clothes on. He didn't expect to sleep, but if he did, all the better.

He lay there in the dark with his eyes closed, going over all of his options. In his mind's eye he could see how things were going to proceed, and if he had any chance at all of making it back alive, he would have to stay calm and seize the opportunity if and when it presented itself. *When* it presented itself, he amended. Petrosian had said it himself. The Fatah and Islamic Jihad factions had grown thin during the cease-fire. Men were leaving their ranks and finding jobs. It was very possible that they would make a mistake. It was simply up to Rapp to see it coming and make his daring move.

Rapp did fall asleep. He had no idea when he had dozed off, or for how long, but it was enough to recharge his battery. He checked in with Ridley at the appointed hour, and then, not wanting to lose his nerve, he left the hotel and proceeded directly to Maarad Street a few blocks away. The vendors were manning their tents, selling all kinds of produce and food. Rapp worked his way up and down both sides of the street, speaking English and playing down his French when he had to speak it. He continued to play the role of the dolt. Almost to a man, people shunned him as soon as he asked about Colonel Sayyed. There was one man, though, who had opened up. He was selling electronics, small radios, tape players, and two-way radios like Rapp's Motorola.

Rapp stepped into his small tent and said hello. There was a polite exchange and then Rapp asked him, "Do you know anything about the two Americans who were picked up a few days ago?"

The man pointed to two radios and loudly asked Rapp, "Which one do you like better?" And then in a much quieter voice he said, "Yes, I know of the Americans." He then stuck out his hand for cash.

Rapp peeled off seven one-hundred-dollar bills. The man pocketed the bills and picked up a small alarm clock radio. He began to explain its various features. In between lauding the various components he lowered his voice and said, "There is a rumor that the Americans are being held in the basement of an old building on the west side of Martyrs' Square."

Before Rapp could ask another question the man was stuffing the alarm clock in a bag and sending him off. That was when Rapp noticed the two guys with stern faces and distinctive bulges under their jackets. He went straight back to the hotel. He wanted to pass on this nugget of information before he was picked up. As he reached the street that the hotel was on, he turned left, which was the wrong way. He took two steps, and then, acting as if he'd just realized his mistake, he turned left again and saw the two men halfway down the block just standing there, staring at him. Rapp kept moving so as to not let them know that he was onto them. It was not lost on him that the two men following him had made no effort to conceal their interest.

Rapp hustled up the next block, and when he entered the hotel he noticed a new manager behind the desk, who gave him a very unpleasant look. Rapp supposed the man thought someone might blow up the hotel just because of his presence. As he climbed the stairs to the fourth floor he realized you could hardly blame the guy. He was like some saloonkeeper in one of those old western movies where the troublemakers were all gunning for the new sheriff.

When Rapp got up to the room he sat on the edge of the bed and collected his thoughts, trying to prioritize the various bits and pieces. The vendor was the only real highlight, and even that might be worthless. Was it a wild rumor or was it fact? Rapp knew that unless he had a chance to talk to the man he would never be able to figure it out. The two men trailing him had him worried. Were they on their way up to his room right now, preparing to kick his door down and drag him off?

Rapp thumbed the transmit button and said, "Curly, this is Moe, over." The Three Stooges monikers was Ridley's idea.

"I'm here, Moe, what's up?"

"I just got back from the market. Two guys tailed me back to the hotel."

"Not a surprise. How was the market?"

"Pretty much treated me like a leper . . . just like you said."

"Yeah . . . bad part of town. They haven't seen a gringo around there in some time. I'm sure you were a big hit."

"I did pick up one piece of information." Rapp paused, trying to figure out the best way to pass it along without giving too much away on an open channel. "Remember last night . . . when our Armenian friend talked to us about the manpower issue."

There was a slight delay and then, "Yep . . . I remember."

"He referenced a local standoff . . . a land grab . . . kind of a standoff at the OK Corral."

"I'm with you."

"There was one vendor . . . cagey fellow. Told me on one side of the corral, the guys are keeping some things in the basement."

"I think I copy. Can you give me more on the source?"

"He sold electronics. Boom boxes, small radios, clocks, that kind of stuff."

Ridley asked for a description of the man and his stall and Rapp gave it to him. Then Ridley said, "I'll pass this on to the American and see what he's heard. Anything else?"

"No," Rapp said as he crossed over to the window and pulled back the curtain. The two men who had followed him had taken up positions directly across the street. "Those guys I mentioned have decided to camp out in front of the hotel."

"Not a surprise. You sure you still want to do this?"

Rapp had just been asking himself the same question. But like his high-school lacrosse coach used to say, you can't score unless you shoot. "I'm fine," Rapp said into the small radio. "If I don't check in at noon, you'll know I'm either dead or in the middle of negotiations."

"Let's hope it's the latter."

"Roger that. Over and out." Rapp took off his khaki sport coat and went into the bathroom to splash some cold water on his face. He patted the drops of water with a towel and looked at himself in the dusty, cracked mirror. Rapp eyed his fractured reflection; his thick head of black hair, the beginnings of a beard, his bronzed olive skin and his eyes so dark that they were almost black. He could walk among the enemy without getting so much as a suspicious glance, but that would all change if he didn't do something. Very carefully he patted his hair and then, using his index finger, he probed a little deeper. He could barely feel the small section of metal. Ridley had taken a flexible fourteen-inch bandsaw blade and cut it down to a neat little three-inch piece. An eighth of an inch thick and only a half inch wide, the black metal section was then threaded into his dark head of black hair.

Rapp played Ridley's words over again in his head. "We know from debriefings that these things follow a certain pattern. It usually starts with a whack across the back of the head, but not always. You're then tossed in either the backseat or the trunk, taken somewhere and stripped naked, and then moved one or two more times. There's a good chance you'll never be in the same building as them. Then again . . . they might be two doors down and you'll never know they're there unless you get free."

Rapp stared at his reflection and questioned his sanity. "Are you fucking nuts?" Rapp couldn't remember if he'd ever talked to himself out loud like this in the mirror. Maybe drunk, but never sober. It all flashed before him in that moment. He could slip out the back door and find his way back to the other side of town. Like Ridley had told him last night, "If you get cold feet, no one will judge you." Except for himself, of course. Rapp did not want to live the rest of his life that way. This wasn't like making a mistake in the heat of battle. This would be making a conscious decision to run from the field of battle. And not just to run, but to desert two of his fellow soldiers and leave them for dead. Rapp knew himself well enough to understand that a failure of this magnitude would haunt him for the rest of his days.

He pushed himself away from the mirror before he lost the courage. He checked the window again. They were still down there and had possibly been joined by another guy who was standing at the far end of the block. Rapp looked over at his gun, which was on the night table. It had been suggested that, to complete his performance, he should leave the gun in the room, but he didn't like that idea. He'd rather walk out of the hotel buck-naked than leave the gun. He could explain it away as a precaution. Everyone else in this town walked around with a gun, so why shouldn't he? The radio was the only other thing to decide on. He chose to bring it with him. If he didn't get picked up right away, he might need to call Ridley with an update. As a precaution, he changed the channel and turned it off.

Rapp quickly scrawled a note and left it on the small desk in the corner, then put his sport coat back on and checked all the pockets. Everything was where it should be. Lifting the back of his jacket, he wedged the Beretta into his waistband and gathered his sunglasses, the map, and a large wad of cash and headed for the door. He hesitated for a split second, then told himself not to think.

"I'd rather go down swinging," he muttered as he shut the door. If he survived this little ordeal he'd have to ask Lewis if talking to yourself was a symptom of losing your mind.

Rapp moved quickly down the four flights of stairs to the lobby. There was a new man behind the front desk and he looked nervous as all hell, which Rapp took as a sign that someone had talked to him. This was it. Showtime. Rapp continued out the front door into the blazing daylight and held his map above his head to block the sun while he looked up and down the street. Looking out from behind the sunglasses, he pretended not to notice the duo from Islamic Jihad. With his face buried in the map, he turned to the right and started heading east as if he was going back to the market.

Within half a block, Rapp's nervous system began sending his brain alarms, each more frantic than the previous one. Now he was talking to himself again, but this time it was in his brain. The conscious, here-and-now, higher-functioning part was talking to the ingrained lower-functioning part like a jockey talks to a thoroughbred as it's being led into the starting gate. *Easy*, he repeated to himself over and over. It took every ounce of control to override his training and millions of years of basic survival instincts that were embedded like code into the human brain. Up ahead, Rapp recognized a black car that was parked across the street. Earlier in the morning the car had been empty. Rapp ignored the man behind the wheel and turned down a narrow side street. Just thirty paces ahead a rough-looking man was stationed in front of a shop. His left leg was straight and firmly planted on the pavement and the other bent up behind him and placed against the side of the building. His big frame was resting against the wall while he took a long drag off his cigarette. The man had dusty black pants and a white dress shirt with sweat-stained armpits, and there was something vaguely familiar about him. Rapp wondered if he had been in one of the photos Ridley had shown him.

The street was otherwise empty. The survivors of the bloody civil war could smell trouble, and they had wisely decided to stay indoors until the morning's sideshow was concluded. Rapp heard the men behind him, their thick shoes pounding out their progress and pace on the sidewalk. Suddenly a car engine revved, and the pace of his pursuers quickened. With every step Rapp could feel them closing in from behind. His brain ran through options and avenues of escape and he denied each one, willing himself to stay the course like a deranged ship's captain headed for the shoals at full speed.

They were close now. Rapp could feel them. The big fellow up ahead threw his cigarette to the

ground and pushed himself away from the building. He smiled at Rapp and produced a leather truncheon from his back pocket. It was at that moment
Rapp realized who the man was. Rapp dropped the
map in feigned surprise and turned to flee. The two
men were exactly where he expected them to be,
guns drawn, one pointed at Rapp's head, the other
at his chest.

The sedan skidded to a stop just to his right,
the trunk and front passenger door swinging open.
Rapp knew what was next. He closed his eyes and
clenched his jaw as the truncheon cracked him
across the back of the head. Rapp stumbled forward, his sunglasses clattering to the pavement. He
fell into the arms of the two men with pistols. He
let his legs go limp, and the men struggled with his
weight. He felt the arms of the big man wrap around
his chest and yank him upright. His 9mm Beretta
was pulled from the back of his waistband and he
was dragged the short distance to the car's trunk.
Rapp landed headfirst with a thud. The rest of his
body was folded in on top of him, and then the
trunk was slammed shut.

The engine roared and the rear tires bit through
a layer of sand and dirt until they found asphalt.
Rapp was thrown back as the vehicle shot away. He
slowly cracked open his eyes, and as expected, found
himself enveloped in darkness. His head was throbbing a bit from the blow, but not too badly. There
was no fear on his face or doubt in his mind, though.
Just a smile on his lips as he thought of his childhood
friend Cal Berkley and his pet snake. Cal's pride and

joy was his pet boa constrictor, Buckeye. When they were bored during the hot summer months they'd go over to Cal's house and watch him feed rats to Buckeye. Well, one day Cal came home from school to find Buckeye dead, with a hole in the side of his body and a bloody white rat still alive in the tank. Apparently, Buckeye had gotten lazy and swallowed the rat before it was dead. Once inside, the rat had then chewed its way out.

Rapp couldn't help but smile at the thought of doing the same thing to these assholes. This was either going to be the most spectacular success of his life, or the end of it. Fear and debate no longer had a place in his thoughts. There was no turning back. No more hand-wringing. This was all about deception and action. The game had started. He was descending into the belly of the beast. The only question was, would he be able to eat his way out?

CHAPTER 61

THE Aeroflot Tupolev Tu-154 was cleared for
landing on Beirut International Airport's
only operating runway. Ivanov's bullish attitude
was back. Primakov was backing him all the way on
this little excursion. These Palestinian dogs thought
they had everything figured out, but as usual Ivanov was three steps ahead of them. Ivanov blamed
himself for just one mistake during this entire mess.
Why hadn't he thought of killing Dorfman first? All
of that money could have been his. How could he
have missed such an opportunity? Ivanov supposed
he had been blind out of necessity. In his world a
talented banker who knew how to skirt laws and
hide money was absolutely essential. That was another problem he now had to deal with. Where was
he going to find another man with those capabili-
ties? He would have to fly to Hamburg soon after he
delivered the Americans to Primakov. He would sit

down with Dorfman's boss, Herr Koenig, and make him see that certain reparations were in order.

Shvets had come up with that idea. Get Koenig to authorize a few loans to shell companies that were in Ivanov's name and were run out of Switzerland. Loans that would never be repaid. Shvets explained that a bank of this size wrote off more than a hundred million dollars a year in bad loans. If handled the right way, he could bleed Herr Koenig out of several million dollars a year. This opened up a whole new avenue of possibilities for Ivanov. He could apply the same principle with a few of the new bankers in Moscow. In only a few years he could have all his money back and then some. That Shvets was a smart boy. Maybe too smart.

Ivanov watched Shvets exit the cockpit and close the door. As his deputy sat in the aisle seat next to him, he noted the way Shvets glanced at his glass of vodka, barely able to hide his contempt.

"We will be on the ground in less than a minute," Shvets announced while he fastened his seat belt.

"Good. I am eager to get this over with and get back to Moscow."

Shvets wondered what kind of man wished to be gone from a place before he'd arrived.

Glancing out the window, Ivanov asked, "Do you think we could persuade Herr Koenig to visit us in Moscow early next week?"

"Doubtful," Shvets said with a shake of his head.

"Well, try, and if he won't come to us then I will go to him. As always, though, I would like to try to do this the civilized way first. Two businessmen exploring an opportunity."

"In some countries they call it a shakedown."

Ivanov drained his glass and gave Shvets an unhappy frown.

Shvets realized the sulking Ivanov was gone and the ruthless one was back. "Sorry."

Ivanov did not reply at first. He had picked up on the man's growing insolence over the past year, but it seemed to have grown exponentially over the past week. Maybe it was time to replace him. The question was with whom. The private sector was exploding with opportunity, and the SVR no longer had the pick of the litter. He decided he shouldn't give up on him so easily. A good lesson or two might restore the proper attitude, and if that didn't work, he'd think about having him shot. Cutting him free would be foolish. Shvets knew too many of his secrets.

The plane landed on the relatively short runway and braked hard. While they taxied to the designated area, Shvets leaned over and asked, "What is our plan if the bidding goes over five million dollars?"

Ivanov laughed. "It won't."

"How can you be so sure?"

"Because I am smarter than these dogs."

Shvets was intrigued. "What have you been up to, sir?"

"Let's just say I made a few calls to my friends in Tehran and Baghdad."

"And?"

"They have agreed that it would be foolish to pay for something that I am willing to give them for free."

Shvets was dubious. "Are you sure you can trust them?"

The plane stopped in front of an old, rusty hangar. The doors were open and light streamed into the interior from the holes in the roof. Sayyed stepped from the shadows and waved at the plane. Ivanov laughed at the sight of him. "There are two things you need to know to understand the Middle East. The first is that they all hate the Jews. The second is that they have nothing but contempt for the Palestinians."

CHAPTER 62

IT couldn't have been more than five minutes. The trunk opened and they were on him. Rapp couldn't tell how many, but it was more than two and fewer than five. They punched, grabbed, and pulled, finally yanking him from the space and throwing him to the floor. Rapp tried to block the blows as best he could, but they were coming from too many directions, and besides, the goal was not to show them how skilled he was at fighting, it was to play possum. To that end, Rapp started screaming and begging them to stop. The ass-kicking did stop, but only because they began stripping him.

When they were done, Rapp lay on the hard, dusty floor, whimpering. As best he could tell, they were in some type of bombed-out building. All of his clothes and possessions were thrown into the trunk of the car that he had just been yanked from. The vehicle started up again, and then the driver floored the gas and sprayed Rapp with loose gravel. The four men who were standing around him all started laughing.

A fifth man walked into the circle. Rapp recognized him as the one who had been leaning against the building. He was a senior member of Fatah. "Why are you doing this? I have been authorized by my government to negotiate with you."

Radih squatted on his haunches. He held out Rapp's Beretta. "Why do you need this to negotiate?"

Rapp shrugged. "This is a dangerous town . . . I don't know."

Radih slapped him hard across the face. "I think you are a liar."

"Sorry."

"Shut up!"

"But the money . . ."

Radih slapped him again and Rapp started to whimper.

"I'm just a messenger."

"And what do you have to offer?"

"Money. Lots of it."

"How much?"

"A million dollars."

Radih roared with laughter. "I think it will cost you a lot more than that."

"Maybe I can get more money?" Rapp said hopefully.

"And maybe we will sell you to the Russians with the others."

"I can get you the money."

"I don't care about the money. And besides, you do not seem like you would fetch a very good price." The other men nodded and laughed. Radih was suddenly curious about this man. He had to be very low-level. "Why were you chosen to negotiate their release?"

Rapp shrugged and didn't answer.

Radih slapped him and one of the other men kicked his legs and screamed, "Answer him."

"I volunteered. Please don't hit me."

"And why would anyone volunteer for something like this?"

Rapp spoke softly into the floor.

"Speak up!"

"I said I am related to one of the men."

"Related? To who?"

"Stan Hurley."

"We don't have a hostage named Stan Hurley."

"Yes, you do. Hurley is his real name. You probably know him as Bill Sherman. That's why I volunteered. Please don't hurt me," Rapp pleaded. "I mean you no harm, I just want to get these men released. I promise we will not bother you again—"

"How are you related to this Stan Hurley?"

"He's my dad."

Radih could hardly believe his luck. He might not be able to kill Bill Sherman, but Sayyed had said nothing about his son. Radih stood. "Let's go," he announced to his men. "Tape his wrists and toss him in the trunk."

Rapp was as passive as he could be while they wound the duct tape quickly around his wrists. He counted ten times and noted that they didn't bother to tape his ankles.

"I can make you guys rich," Rapp pleaded as they tossed him in the trunk of a different car. The trunk was slammed shut and then they were off. He had no idea where they were to begin with, so the twenty-odd-minute drive that they went on through the city was unnecessary. Just before they stopped, however, things became noticeably quieter. Almost as if they were in the country. When the trunk popped again, Rapp was hit with a blast of sunlight. He glimpsed a building that looked like it was slated for demolition. Two big men yanked him roughly from the trunk. Rapp's bare feet hit the rough ground and he realized they were in an alley. The buildings on each side were riddled with pockmarks, and not one of them had a window. Two blocks away he caught a glimpse of blue. Before he could take in anything else he was rushed into the building and down a flight of stairs. He was immediately hit by the smell of raw sewage. He almost gagged, and this time it wasn't for effect.

The hallway was ten feet wide with rooms on each side. They were all missing doors except three rooms at the midpoint on the right. He noted the two guards with bandannas tied around their faces. They were the first men who had tried to conceal their faces, and then Rapp realized it was the smell. The men who had him by the arms yelled ahead to the guards to open the first door. They removed the padlock from the latch and swung the door open.

With a good enough head start Rapp thought he might be able to bust the latch off.

"Please," Rapp pleaded with the men. "I'm only an analyst. I can't do this. Please give me my clothes back and let me call Washington. I'll get you your money."

They tossed Rapp into the room like a rag doll. He tumbled to the floor, begging them to listen to him. Then the door was closed, and he was again enveloped in darkness. Rapp began to whimper, softly at first and then a little louder. For some strange reason, this room smelled better than the hallway, almost as if it had been cleaned with bleach. He recalled the landscape in the alley and remembered the thin strip of blue on the horizon only a few blocks away. It was the sea for certain, and with all of the bombed-out buildings it fit the general description of Martyrs' Square. The merchant must have been right. Rapp rolled onto his side and started digging through his thick hair. The fact that they hadn't covered his head with a hood worried him. He found the small blade and placed one end in his teeth. He set the blade against the top edge of the tape and began slowly moving his hands back and forth.

CHAPTER 63

THE stairs at the tail of the Russian plane were lowered and Sayyed watched the soldiers in black fatigues file down the steps. He counted thirty. All heavily armed. All Russian special forces. Sayyed had no doubt they were intended as both a show of force and an insult.

Sayyed raised the radio to his lips and said, "You were right."

Mughniyah's voice came back, "How many men?"

"Thirty Spetsnaz. Heavily armed."

There was a long pause and then, "I will be there in five minutes."

Sayyed attached the radio to his belt and watched as the elite Russian soldiers spread out to cover the area. Finally, Shvets appeared and then Ivanov. Both men were in suits and wearing sunglasses to protect their delicate Moscow eyes. As they approached, Ivanov yelled at Sayyed from across the tarmac. The big Russian threw out his arms and walked the final ten paces as if it had been far too long since they had last seen each other.

Sayyed was not going to be a rude host, so he held out his arms as well, and despite his misgivings, he greeted Ivanov with a smile. As much as he distrusted the man, there was something likable about him.

"Assef, my friend, how are you?" Ivanov practically picked the Syrian up in his arms.

"I am well. Thank you for coming."

Ivanov pushed the Syrian intelligence officer away and held him at arm's length. "What happened to your ear?"

Sayyed gently touched the bandage and said, "Oh, nothing. Just a little accident."

"Other than that you are well?"

"Yes."

Ivanov peered over the top of his sunglasses at the hangar and the surrounding landscape—the bombed-out hangar, an airliner with only one wing, and another with no engines. "I see Beirut hasn't changed much."

"Things are getting better." Sayyed pointed back toward the construction equipment at the main terminal. "We thought privacy would be best for this meeting." He motioned toward the hangar, saying, "I promise it will be worth your effort."

"Yes, but what is this nonsense? I have to compete for my information like some rancher bidding on heads of cattle?"

They started walking toward the shade of the hangar. Sayyed followed the script that Mughniyah had given him. "Yes . . . well, if it was up to me it would only be you. But I am not the only one with a voice in this."

"Mughniyah?" Ivanov asked.

"Yes."

"I have warned you. He is in love with the religious zealots in Iran, and we both know they will never be the answer to a lasting peace in Beirut."

"I know . . . I know," Sayyed said, patting Ivanov's arm as they entered the hangar, "but there is only so much I can do."

"And you have been a staunch supporter. Do not think that has gone unnoticed." Ivanov took off his sunglasses. "Now, where are these Americans that we are all so interested in?"

Sayyed pointed to their left. In the shadowy recesses of the hangar next to a rusty, broken-down truck, a man wearing a black hood sat in a single chair.

"But I thought there would be three?"

"There are," Sayyed said. "Think of this one as a sample."

Ivanov was not happy. "I have flown all this way and you play games with me. I do not like this, Assef."

"No games," Sayyed lied. "Security is very important. One of these Americans is such a big fish that we must be extra careful."

"What is his name?"

"I cannot say just yet."

"Why?"

"We must wait for the others."

Ivanov looked around the empty space. Shvets and the Spetsnaz commander had wisely stopped twenty feet away to give them some privacy. Where were the representatives from Iran and Iraq? Turning back to Sayyed, he asked that exact question.

"They will be here any minute."

Ivanov checked his watch and huffed. His instincts told him something else was going on here. "I do not like this. I do not like this one bit. I am on time. I have important business to attend to back in Moscow."

"I am sorry, Mikhail."

"Sorry will not work." Ivanov leaned in close so he was eye to eye with Sayyed. "When you come to Moscow, I treat you like a prince. I come here, and we meet in this." He waved his hand around the dilapidated space.

"Mikhail, I am sorry. We do not have your resources."

"And that is something you would be wise to remember. I do not deserve to be treated like this."

"I am sorry," Sayyed could only say again.

"If you are so sorry, you will stop playing games with me and tell me who this big fish is. And if you do not want to stop playing games, then I will be forced to start playing them as well. Maybe I will get on my plane and fly back to Moscow. You can conduct your little auction without me."

"Mikhail, I am—"

"Don't say it again. If you are truly sorry you

will tell me who the mystery American is. If not, I am done playing games and I will leave."

Mughniyah had specifically told him not to divulge that information until he was there, but Sayyed was growing weary of the man's paranoia. He did not trust Ivanov, but he couldn't see what harm could be caused by telling him about Bill Sherman. "I will give you a sneak peek, but you have to play dumb when Mughniyah gets here." Turning, Sayyed said, "Follow me." As they walked over to a folding table, he said, "This American is rumored to have been heavily involved in some of the CIA's most sensitive operations. Including operations directed at your country." There were three files on the table. Sayyed picked up one and handed it to Ivanov.

Ivanov had been preparing himself for this for the past twenty-four hours. He had expected to see the man in person, but in a way it would be easier for him to downplay his reaction this way. He opened the file, looked at the Polaroid photo of the American spy, and nearly gasped. Ivanov hid his emotions and tilted his head as if he were trying to place the face, even though he knew with absolute certainty who the man was. He and Stan Hurley had tangled back in Berlin a long time ago. Hurley had become such a problem that he had sent two of his best men to kill him one night. Neither came back. Their bodies were found floating in the Spree River the next day. The day after that, Hurley marched into Ivanov's office in broad daylight and put a gun to his head. Hurley explained the rules to him that morning, rules that Ivanov already knew, but had nonetheless ignored. The Americans and Russians were not supposed to kill each other. It was all part of the new détente of the Cold War, the easing of tensions in the early seventies brought about by Nixon and Brezhnev. The American then gagged him, blindfolded him, tied him up, and pilfered his files.

When Hurley was done, he loosened the ropes on Ivanov's wrists a bit and whispered in his ear, "You should be able to wiggle your way out of these in a few minutes. By then I'll be gone, and you'll be faced with two options. You can scream your head off and try to chase me. If you do that your bosses and everyone else back in Moscow will know that you let an American waltz into your office in the middle of the day, tie you up, and steal your files. You will be an embarrassment to the KGB, and we both know how much the KGB likes to be embarrassed. Your other option . . . well, let's just say I hope you're smart enough to figure it out."

Ivanov was smart enough, and he had never told a soul about that day. He coughed into his hand and turned to Sayyed. "I have heard of this man. What else can you tell me about him?"

Sayyed thought it best to not be too forthright on this point. Telling him that the American was the toughest, craziest man he'd ever encountered would not be good for the negotiations. Fortunately, he was saved by the sounds of approaching vehicles.

CHAPTER 64

HURLEY dangled in the air from a hook that was tied to his wrists. His toes hovered only a few inches from the floor. His shoulders ached like nothing he had ever experienced. This had been his punishment for taking a bite out of Sayyed. They also decided to tape his mouth shut, but he thought that had more to do with silencing his insults than with their fear of being bitten. The only nice thing to come of it was that they'd left him alone. Not that hanging by your wrists a few inches off the ground was a nice thing, but it was certainly preferable to having your fingernails ripped out and being electrocuted.

There was a noise at the door. A second later it opened and the light turned on. Hurley blinked a few times before he could see it was Radih. The Fatah leader crossed over and exhaled cigarette smoke into Hurley's face. Hurley inhaled the smoke and thought he might apologize for all the nasty things he'd said about Radih's mother if only the man would offer him a heater.

Radih reached up and tore the tape off the American's mouth. "I have a surprise for you."

"We gonna try the rubber hose today?"

"No, something much better."

"Great," Hurley said with feigned enthusiasm. "I can't wait. Hey . . . about that stuff I said about your mom—"

Before Hurley could get the rest of it out, Radih smashed his fist into Hurley's stomach. "I have had enough of your lies. I am going to make you feel more pain than you have ever imagined."

"Good," Hurley coughed. "I hope you kill me, because Mughniyah will kill you for it. Nothing could make me happier than making sure you went down with me."

"Don't worry. I'm not going to kill you," Radih said, smiling. "But I am going to kill your son."

Hurley laughed. "What the fuck are you talking about?"

Radih turned to his men. "Get him."

"My son?" Hurley asked. "You must be off your rocker, unless you mean one of your bastard brothers I fathered with your mother."

"Yes . . . keep talking. We will see how tough you are in a moment."

The two men returned, each with one arm looped under Rapp's armpits. Rapp was shuffling along trying to keep up and blabbing incessantly about the money he could get them.

Rapp saw Hurley and yelled, "Dad. Don't worry, we're going to get out of this. Washington is going to pay for your release."

Hurley looked at Rapp and said, "What the fuck are you talking about? Have you lost your mind?"

Radih was finally having some fun. "This is beautiful. You are right. I can't kill you, but I can kill your son. A big American fuck-you." Radih snapped his fingers and pointed at the floor. "Bring him here." The men dumped Rapp on the ground at Radih's feet. "I will handle him," he said as he drew the American's silenced Beretta from his waistband. "Hold the father's head and make sure his eyes are open."

The two men left Rapp and took up positions on the right and left side of Hurley. They grabbed his head and dug their thumbs into the skin just under his eyebrows and pulled up.

"Make him look," Radih commanded as he grabbed a fistful of Rapp's hair. "Over here."

"Why are you doing this?" Rapp wailed in a panicked voice. "Our government will pay you."

Radih bent over and said, "They will pay for him, you idiot. You are worthless." He straightened and looked at Hurley. "Are there any other lies you'd like to spew about my mother?"

Hurley didn't offer a reply.

"How does a man of your considerable though twisted talents sire such a stupid child?"

Rapp looked up, only half listening to the insults. His focus was on a beautiful 9mm suppressed Beretta. Radih kept waving the gun back and forth, sticking it in Hurley's face and then pointing it at Rapp's head. Rapp followed it like a tennis volley. Radih's finger was on the trigger and the red dot above his thumb told Rapp that the safety was off and the gun was hot. The man settled into a rhythm with his insults. He was now saying something about Rapp's mother, the woman he presumed to have slept with Hurley. The Palestinian stuck the tip of the suppressor under Hurley's nose and ordered him to beg for his son's life. As Hurley started to speak, the gun began its slow-motion arc back to Rapp.

Rapp made his move. He'd sawed most of the way through the tape around his wrists while he was back in the holding cell. Now, not sure the tape would break, he went for a two-handed grab around the barrel of the gun. His hands clamped down on the steel while the gun was still swinging Rapp's way. Rapp stood, driving the gun straight up so a misfire wouldn't bury itself in Hurley's chest. At the top, he pivoted to his left, bringing the gun up and over the top of his head, before pulling it back down on the other side, effectively putting Radih in an arm bar. In this position the Palestinian couldn't move unless he let go of the gun. Rapp delivered a quick knee strike to Radih's face, and a bullet spat harmlessly into the cinder-block wall.

Having dazed him, Rapp ripped the gun free. He swung the pistol back, cracking Radih across the forehead with the heavy metal grip. The blow sent him to the floor. Rapp tried to wrench his wrists free of the remaining duct tape but it caught. The other two men were finally starting to move. Hurley, realizing that one of the men might yell for help, started screaming at the top of his lungs as if he were being beaten. Rapp took a step back to get a better angle and yanked again, but the last bit of tape held, so he flipped the gun up in the air and caught the grip with both hands. The man on his left was no more than four feet away when he fired the gun twice, hitting him both times in the chest. The man collapsed at Rapp's feet.

Rapp swung the gun around on the other man, who was caught between the door and Hurley. He was never going to make it, so he stopped and put his hands up in the air.

"Shoot him," Hurley ordered in a raspy voice.

Rapp squeezed the trigger and buried a bullet in the man's forehead.

"Get me down . . . quick," Hurley hissed.

"What about him?" Rapp asked, pointing the gun at Radih, who was showing signs of life.

"Get me down first."

Rapp ripped through the last bit of tape while he ran over to the wall and untied the makeshift pulley. Hurley dropped the short distance to the floor, landing on his feet. He wavered for a second and then caught his balance.

"Give me that gun," Hurley ordered, "and check the right thigh pocket of that second one you shot. He should have a knife."

Rapp placed the gun in Hurley's hands and went off to search for the knife.

Hurley walked over to Radih, whose arms were starting to flop around as if he was waking up from a deep sleep. Hurley stomped on his stomach, and the Palestinian's eyes popped open. Hurley bent over and pressed the suppressor against Radih's chest. Looking into his eyes, he said, "You should have killed me when you had the chance, you piece of shit." Hurley pulled the trigger.

CHAPTER 65

TWO of the sedans pulled into the hangar and three more stopped just outside. All of the doors opened at roughly the same time and a dozen well-armed men fanned out, creating a barrier at the door, effectively sealing Ivanov off from his Spetsnaz escort.

Ivanov looked at the commander with extreme disappointment.

Mughniyah approached with a confident grin on his face. Four of his bodyguards trailed a few paces back. "Mikhail, welcome to Beirut."

"I would hardly call this a welcome."

"You will have to excuse all of this, but I am not in a good mood today."

"And why is that?"

"Because I just found out that you have been scheming behind my back yet again."

"What are you talking about?"

"You will notice that our Iraqi and Iranian friends are not here."

"Why?" Sayyed asked, alarmed by the news.

"Because I found out that Mikhail had made a deal with them. Didn't you, Mikhail?"

Ivanov tried to laugh the question away as if it was a harmless maneuver.

Mughniyah turned his attention back to Sayyed and said, "He set the ceiling at five million. The others were going to bow out and let him win."

"What did you do with them?" Sayyed asked.

"For the moment they are my guests. I will decide if I am going to kill them later."

Ivanov clasped his hands together and laughed. Mughniyah was proving to be much smarter than he had given him credit for. "You have outsmarted me, Imad. That does not happen very often. Would you like me to leave, or would you like to discuss business? Negotiate some terms, perhaps?"

"I will negotiate nothing with you. I am going to name a price and you are going to pay it."

"Really?" Ivanov said. "And what if I decide I don't like your price?"

"Then we will have a big problem."

Ivanov nodded as if he found the game amusing.

"Before we get to that, though, I need you to return all of the money you took from our Swiss bank accounts."

"Money that I took!" Ivanov's eyes nearly bulged out of his head. "I did no such thing."

"I think you did."

"As a matter of fact I want my money back from *you*."

"Your money?"

"Yes, my money." Ivanov's face was blazing red. "The money that you took. You don't think I suspected you at once? You never liked Sharif. You did nothing but complain about his prices. You called him a rat and a traitor to the cause for charging his inflated prices."

"I did not kill Sharif," Mughniyah denied flatly.

"And why should I believe you?"

"Because I am a man of honor. Someone who fights for what he believes in . . . not a thief like you."

"Honor! This is beautiful. You, of all people, speak of honor. Imad Mughniyah, the hijacker of civilian airliners, the kidnapper of professors, the man who shells entire neighborhoods filled with women and children. You speak of honor. That is laughable." Ivanov literally spat the last word at his accuser.

Mughniyah reached for his gun, but the Spetsnaz commander beat him to the draw and pointed the barrel of his Markov pistol at the side of Mughniyah's head. All of a sudden it appeared as if everyone had a gun. Slides were being racked and hammers cocked.

"Enough," Sayyed shouted. "Your disdain for each other has blinded your judgment."

"And you are a fool," Mughniyah yelled.

Sayyed approached him, and in a voice loud enough for only Mughniyah to hear said, "And you are broke. How are you going to pay all of your men next week and the week after that? Get control of your hot temper and let me handle this." Speaking to the group, he then said, "Everyone, lower your weapons." He motioned with his hands and repeated himself two more times until finally all of the weapons were either holstered or pointed in a safe direction.

"I know that Imad did not steal the money, and I do not think that Mikhail did so either."

"How can you know?" Mughniyah angrily asked.

"Tell me. Why would he come here today if he had stolen our money?"

While Mughniyah pondered that question, Shvets stepped forward. "I can assure you that my boss had nothing to do with the stolen funds. I visited Herr Dorfman's boss in Hamburg last week. More than fifty million dollars was stolen. It appears we were not the only targets." Shvets wanted to get out of here with his life, so he quickly added, "We are following several leads, including one that the money was stolen by an organized crime element out of Prague."

"And I can promise you," Ivanov added quickly, "that when we find these people, we will get our money back, and we will punish the people who took it."

"Thank you," Sayyed said. "Right now, we have something very important to negotiate. We have three Americans. John Cummins, who served four years in Moscow and the last four in Damascus, another relatively young man by the name of Robert Richards, and the infamous Bill Sherman." Sayyed grabbed the file off the table and handed it to Ivanov, giving him a second to study the photo again. "Now, how much would your government be willing to pay for these three men?"

Ivanov unconsciously licked his lips. A prize like Stan Hurley would virtually guarantee him the directorship. Primakov was getting old and lacked the ruthless animal instinct that it took to run the SVR. He could control the interrogation and filter what information he passed on. The thought of keeping that asshole Hurley in the basement of one of his secure sites like some exotic animal was almost too much to take. He reminded himself that this was still a negotiation and his funds were not unlimited. "I am confident that my government would pay five million dollars for these three."

"That is not enough," Mughniyah complained before anyone had had a chance to absorb the offer.

Thus started the back and forth, with Ivanov coming up three million in his price. They were stuck there for a few minutes while Mughniyah kept saying that he would only accept an offer of sixteen million. Ivanov, as well as Sayyed, tried to explain to him that the issues of the stolen money and the value of the American spies had nothing to do with each other. Ivanov raised his offer to ten and was prepared to walk away when Mughniyah finally countered at fourteen. Thirty seconds later they had agreed on twelve, and everyone breathed a sigh of relief, no one more so than Sayyed.

They were only halfway done, though. Mughniyah wanted all the money in their possession before they would turn the men over, and Ivanov wasn't going to release a red cent until he laid eyes on Stan Hurley.

Sayyed broke the stalemate by saying, "You need to call Moscow, correct?"

"Yes."

"Why don't I retrieve the prisoners? They are not far from here. You can make the arrangements to have the money transferred, and when we get back we can complete the transaction."

Ivanov, who wanted to get as far away from this horrible place and these horrible people as quickly as possible, leaped at the chance to expedite his departure. "That is a wonderful idea." Turning to Shvets, he said, "Nikolai, go with Assef and bring the prisoners back here."

The last thing Shvets wanted to do was leave the relative security of this hangar and drive into downtown Beirut. He considered asking if he could bring a few of the Spetsnaz with him, but he knew the request would be denied. As he followed Sayyed and his men to their car, he wondered how much longer he could continue to work for Ivanov.

CHAPTER 66

RAPP found the knife, dug it out of the man's pants, and crossed the room. He took his gun back from Hurley and stuck it under his armpit while he cut the tape from Hurley's wrists.

The tape peeled free and Hurley said, "Give me the gun."

Rapp held out the knife. "Get your own."

Hurley grumbled and took the knife.

"There are two guys in the hallway." Rapp started dragging one of the bodies across the room and placed it by the wall with the door. "I'll open the door, you try to sound like Radih. Yell for them to get in here and I'll pop 'em."

When the bodies were piled out of sight, Rapp placed his hand on the door handle. Hurley stood behind him. Rapp nodded and yanked the door open. Hurley muttered something about a mess and ordered the two guards to get in there. Unfortunately, only one appeared. Rapp shot him in the back of the head while pulling the door open farther and swinging his left arm around, searching for the second man. The tip of the suppressor ended up less than a foot from the man's face. Rapp squeezed the trigger and shot him in the nose, pink mist exploding out into the hallway. Stepping over the body, he looked left and right. The hallway was empty.

Rapp dragged the guard into the room. Hurley was already stripping the first guard of his pants, shirt, and boots. Rapp did the same with the second guard and told Hurley to grab the man's bandanna. When Rapp found the radio he asked Hurley, "Do you know where we are?"

"No."

"I think I might. What about Bobby and Cummins?"

"Bobby should be here, but I think they took Cummins to the airport. They're trying to auction off our asses."

"We'll get Bobby in a second, but I need to call Ridley first." Rapp dialed in the right frequency and hit the transmit button. All he got was static.

"Bad reception down here," Hurley told him. "We'll have to get out of the basement."

"All right . . ." Rapp looked around the room. "I assume Bobby is naked, too."

"Yeah . . . Let's grab him some clothes."

Rapp scavenged up a set while Hurley collected two ammo pouches with eight extra AK-47 magazines. When they had everything, they tied the bandannas around their faces and Rapp checked the hallway. It was still empty, so they ducked out, closing the door behind them and locking it. The next door over was padlocked, so Rapp shot the lock off with his Beretta. Hurley opened the door and froze. There, dangling from the hook in the middle of the room, with a rope wrapped around his neck, was Richards.

"Motherfuckers," was all Hurley could manage to say.

Rapp considered checking for a pulse, but Richards's skin was chalk white. He'd been dead for hours. "Should we bring him with us?"

"No." Hurley shook his head.

Rapp closed the door to Richards's cell and told himself he would process it later. They ran down the back hallway, but when they got near the stairs they heard some voices. Hurley started making hand gestures, but Rapp waved him off, pulling him back away from the stairs.

Whispering in his ear, Rapp said, "I have an idea." Rapp handed him the two-way radio. "Try Ridley again. Tell him I think we're at Martyrs' Square. I'm gonna run down to the front of the building and see if I can start a little something." Rapp started to move, but Hurley grabbed him.

"What are you talking about?"

"Just wait here. If I'm right, you're gonna hear a shitload of gunfire in about a half minute. Then we'll make our break." Rapp pointed at the radio. "Just try to raise Ridley. I'll be right back."

Rapp tore off down the hallway, slowing when

he was fifteen feet from the stairs at the front of the building. He stopped and listened for a moment, but heard nothing. Then there was the sound of a foot scraping along the floor and a faint voice. Rapp couldn't tell if it was coming from the first floor or farther up. He considered going back to Hurley. He could use his silenced Beretta to take out whoever was at the back of the building and then try to make a run for it. Fundamentally, though, there was a problem. They were on the wrong side of town and severely outgunned. They needed a diversion to get out of here.

"Full speed ahead," he muttered to himself as he started up the stairs, his silenced pistol in his left hand and the AK-47 in the right. Midway up the steps he got his first glimpse of a small lobby off to the left, maybe fifteen by fifteen feet. Rapp counted two heads and then three. The main entrance was sandbagged, as were the windows on each side, although they'd left two holes in the sandbags to fire from—exactly what Rapp was looking for.

When he hit the landing he noticed two more men lying on the floor. One was standing, looking out one hole in the sandbags, watching the street, and two more were sitting in folding chairs, playing a board game. Rapp walked straight for the man who was on his feet. He kept his pace casual and started shaking his head as if he was going to tell them just how crappy things were downstairs. One of the men started bitching in Arabic. The best Rapp could figure was that the man was telling him he had another hour before he had to pull a watch in the toilet. Rapp laughed and then raised the suppressed Beretta. He had had eighteen shots to start with and was down to twelve.

The guy who was standing got it first, a nice little shot from ten feet right in the left eye. The two guys playing the board game—one got it in the back of the head and the other in his open mouth. Rapp never stopped moving. It was another nice thing Hurley had taught him. When you have the advantage, close with the enemy. He was no more than eight feet away when he shot the two nappers. The first one was clean, but with the second guy, he was off a bit on the first shot, so he had to fire one more to put him out of his misery.

Six shots left. Rapp glanced to his left. The hallway had been barricaded with scraps of broken office furniture. The stairs going up were empty. He walked over to the little one-by-one-foot hole in the sandbags and looked across the street. Sure enough, about two hundred feet away was a similar building. This had to be Martyrs' Square. Rapp slung his AK-47 over his right shoulder, stuffed the Beretta in his waistband, and picked up the dead lookout's AK-47. He gripped the rifle firmly, flipped the selector switch to full automatic, and sighted at the building across the street. He didn't want to kill anyone over there, but he did want to make sure he got their attention, so he chose a position on the second floor and let it rip. The bullets shredded the afternoon calm, thudding into the sandbags across the street and then the building itself as it climbed.

Rapp emptied the entire magazine and dropped the weapon.

Without hesitating, he moved to the peephole on the other side of the front door and took aim with the other AK-47. This time he sprayed the entire building down, firing in controlled bursts. Twenty or so rounds into the magazine, the building across the street erupted in gunfire. Rapp hauled ass down the stairs as he heard bullets smacking into the building and gunfire being returned.

Hurley was standing at the other end, waiting for him. "What in hell did you just do?"

"I gave the big FU to Washington and got us a little diversion." Rapp looked up the stairs. The men were gone. "Come on. Let's get the hell out of here."

They climbed up the stairs, and when they reached the landing a heavyset guy in green fatigues came running down from the floor above and started ordering them to the upper floors to return fire. Hurley pointed out the back door with his rifle, and when the man looked in that direction, he deftly stuck a knife through his carotid artery. Blood came cascading out, pulsating through his fingers.

Hurley followed Rapp out the back door just as a sedan skidded to a stop between two piles of rubble. The two men in the front seat jumped out of the car, yelling and asking what was going on. Rapp couldn't hear them over the gunfire, and since they weren't pointing a gun at him he wasn't in any rush to kill them. All he wanted was their car. Two more men exited the rear of the car, one Caucasian and the other Middle Eastern. Both looked vaguely familiar, which made Rapp think he'd seen them in some of the photos Ridley had shown him.

Hurley said, "Merry fucking Christmas," and then shot the two men in front.

Rapp raised the Beretta and took aim at the fair-skinned guy on the left.

Hurley yelled, "Don't kill the little Commie. Crack him over the head and stuff him in the trunk. I've got the other one."

Rapp and Hurley rushed the two men, their weapons leveled.

Hurley swung the butt end of his rifle and cracked Sayyed across the temple. As the Syrian dropped to his knees, Hurley said, "Sayyed, old buddy. I can't wait to play Twenty Questions with you."

EPILOGUE

ZURICH, SWITZERLAND, FOUR DAYS LATER

THOMAS Stansfield sat on the park bench and looked up at the Rietberg Museum. He loved Zurich—the lake, the unique pace, the beauty of the mountains, but most important the safety it afforded a man of his profession. This city, and the small country it was part of, had managed to stay out of World War II, even with war raging just beyond its borders in every direction. And in the years after that, it had continued to offer respite for Cold Warriors like himself and the man he was about to meet, a place where they could lower their guard, not completely, but enough to enjoy life a little, and occasionally meet face-to-face to discuss mutually beneficial opportunities, or in this instance, conclude vital transactions.

Stansfield saw the two black sedans enter the park and glanced at his watch. The meeting would start on time, which was a nice surprise. The man he was meeting was notoriously late. Stansfield watched the sedans stop thirty feet behind the two vehicles in his entourage. Every detail had been agreed to in advance so as to not make either party unduly skittish. Two men in dark overcoats and sunglasses exited the first car. They looked like Eastern European versions of the two men who were standing a respectful thirty feet behind the CIA's deputy director of operations.

A man with unusually large ears and puffy eyes exited the second car and buttoned his blue, double-breasted suit coat. One of the men approached with a wool overcoat, but the older man waved him off, which brought the hint of a smile to Stansfield's face. He had spent six years in Moscow. To a Russian, forty degrees in Zurich this time of year would feel like summer. Yevgeny Primakov motioned for his men to stay by the car and walked over to the bench.

Stansfield did not stand and Primakov did not expect him to. Neither were handshakes offered. These were two men whose entire jobs revolved around seeing through other people's deceptions.

"Did you bring my man?" Stansfield asked.

"Yes. Did you bring mine?"

"That was not part of the agreement."

"It should have been," Primakov said gruffly.

"There would have been a slight problem there, Yevgeny."

"What?"

Stansfield turned so he could face him. "My man wants to come back to America. Your man." Stansfield shook his head. "He doesn't want to go back to Russia. What does that tell you?"

"How can I know that? You have not allowed me to talk to him."

Stansfield pulled a manila envelope from inside his jacket. "I gave you the highlights on the phone. His boss, one of your deputies, has stolen more than twenty million dollars from Mother Russia and her fine citizens. That money is currently sitting in various accounts around the world. How do you think Deputy Shvets would be treated if I were to hand him over to you?"

Primakov did not answer the question.

"Yevgeny, you do realize I could have given this to the White House? They would have shared it with your president when the time was right, and you would have been put under suspicion along with that thug Ivanov."

Primakov couldn't bring himself to say thank you, so he asked, "Why the courtesy?"

"Because I don't like my people being kidnapped and treated like a science experiment. You did bring Mr. Cummins?"

"Yes." Primakov stuck out his hand for the envelope.

"Not until I see my man."

Primakov motioned to his men, and they opened the back door of the first car. The bodyguard had to help Cummins out of the sedan. He was incredibly thin, but it was him. Stansfield looked over his shoulder and snapped his fingers. One of his bodyguards took off at a trot to help with the transfer.

"The package."

Stansfield handed it to Primakov, who immediately tore it open. He flipped through the twenty-odd pages and asked, "And how do I know this isn't all made up?"

"Check it yourself. The access codes are all there. The money is still in the accounts, although trust me, I thought about using it for a few of our more creative programs."

Primakov considered that for a moment. He finally managed to say, "Thank you."

"You're welcome," Stansfield said as he stood. "Just do me a favor, Yevgeny. Let's stick to the old rules. You stay away from my guys, and I'll stay away from yours."

Stansfield walked away with his other bodyguard close behind. He stopped at the first sedan to check on the Schnoz, and then got into the backseat of the second car. The bodyguard closed the door and then went around the other side and climbed in the backseat. As soon as they were out of the park the bodyguard took off his sunglasses and asked, "Did he buy it, sir?"

Stansfield looked over at Mitch Rapp and said, "One hundred percent."

Rapp looked out the window, thinking that Hurley had truly lived up to his reputation as the biggest SOB on the block. It had been pure evil genius to pay Ivanov's money back into his accounts and have Shvets inform on him. "So what's going to happen to Ivanov?"

Stansfield looked down and straightened his tie. "I think Mikhail Ivanov is going to spend the next few months being thoroughly interrogated by the SVR's goon squad."

"And then what?"

"He won't be able to deny the money, will he?"

"No."

Stansfield nodded. "You're a smart kid. Fill in the blanks."

"Couldn't happen to a nicer guy." Rapp shrugged as if he didn't care. "What about Sayyed?"

"Some questions are better off not asked."

Rapp frowned. He didn't like not knowing.

"Listen," Stansfield said, "I can't release a guy like Sayyed. He'll just go back and torture more of our people." Stansfield shook his head. "The man will get what he deserves."

"Sir, I hope you know I don't give a crap what happens to him."

"Good."

"What about Shvets?"

"Shvets will be fine as long as he continues to cooperate. In a few years we'll cut him loose and let him start a life of his own."

They drove in silence for a while, and then Rapp finally asked, "Sir, why did you want me to come along for this? Being your bodyguard is not exactly my area of expertise."

Stansfield had been wondering when the rookie was going to get around to asking the question. He grinned to himself and asked Rapp, "You think Stan Hurley is a son of a bitch?"

"The biggest one I've ever met, sir."

Stansfield laughed. "Now you know he's not big on compliments?"

Rapp nodded.

"Well, he had some pretty amazing things to say about you when you got back from Beirut. Ridley as well. Irene has been telling me for close to two years that she thought you might have the goods, and I guess you proved to all of us last week that you most certainly do."

"Thank you, sir."

"So I guess I wanted to have a closer look at you . . . and show you that despite what you may have thought in Beirut, I will go to great lengths to get my people back."

Rapp nodded. He supposed Ridley had passed on his blistering critique. "I know that now, sir."

"Good. Now I think you should take a week off. You've earned it. I don't care where you go as long as it's west of here. Seven days from now report to Stan. I've got something else I want you two to work on."

Rapp was tempted to ask, but decided he didn't want it weighing on him while he was trying to recharge.

"Any idea where you're going to go?" Stansfield asked. "In case we need to get hold of you?"

Rapp looked at the snow-capped mountains and thought of Greta. With a smile on his face he said, "I think I'm going to stay right here in Zurich."

ATRIA BOOKS
PROUDLY PRESENTS

KILL SHOT

VINCE FLYNN

Turn the page for a preview of
Kill Shot...

PARIS, FRANCE

RAPP secured the gray nylon rope to a cast-iron vent stack and walked to the edge of the roof. He glanced at the balcony two floors below and then looked out across the City of Light. Sunrise was a few hours off and the din of the late-night revelers had faded to a trickle. It was that rare moment of relative inactivity that even a city as vibrant as Paris endured once each day. Every city had it's own unique feel, and Rapp had learned to pay attention to their ebb and flow, their natural rhythms. They had their similarities just like people. For all of the hang-ups about individuality, few understood that for the most part people were extremely similar. They slept, woke, ate, worked, ate some more, worked some more, ate again, watched TV, and then went to sleep again. It was the basic drumbeat of people the world over. The macro overview of how people met their basic needs.

All men had their unique attributes, and they often manifested themselves in habits—habits that Rapp had learned to exploit. As a general rule, the best time to strike was this witching hour, between dusk and dawn, when the overwhelming majority of the human race was asleep, or trying to sleep. The physiological reasons were obvious. If it took world-class athletes hours to warm up before a major event, how would a man defend himself when yanked from deep sleep? Rapp could not always choose the appointed hour, and occasionally a target's habits created an opening that was so painfully obvious, he simply couldn't ignore the opportunity.

Three weeks earlier Rapp had been in Athens. His target walked the same bustling sidewalk every morning from his apartment to his office. Rapp had considered shooting him on the sidewalk, as there was plenty of cover and distractions. It wouldn't have been difficult, but witnesses were always a concern. That, and the off chance that a police officer could always stumble by at the wrong moment. As he studied his target he noticed another habit. After arriving at work, the man had one more cup of coffee and then went down the hall with his newspaper and took a prolonged visit to the men's room.

Other than catching someone asleep, the next best thing was catching them with their pants down. On the fourth day, Rapp waited in the middle of three stalls and at the appointed hour his target sat down on his right. Rapp stood on the toilet seat, leaned over the divider, called out the man's name, and then after their eyes met, he smiled and sent a single 9mm hollow-tipped round through the top of the man's head. He fired one more round into the man's brainpan for good measure and calmly left the building. Thirty minutes later he was on a ferry slicing through the warm morning air of the Aegean Sea, headed for the island of Crete.

Most of the kills had been like that. Unsuspecting fools who thought themselves safe after years of the United States doing little or nothing to pursue them for their involvement in various terrorist attacks. Rapp's singular goal was to take the fight to these men. Bleed them until they began to have doubts. Until they lay awake at night wondering if they were next. It was the only thing that made sense to him. Inaction was what had emboldened these men to continue with their plots to attack innocent civilians. The belief that they were secure to continue to wage their war of terror, had given them a smug confidence. Rapp was single-handedly replacing that confidence with genuine fear.

By now they were aware that something was wrong. Too many men had been shot in the head in the last year for it to be a coincidence. Rapp's handler had reported the rumors. Most suspected that the Israelis had resurrected one of their hit teams, and that was fine with Rapp—the more disinformation the better. He was not looking for credit. In spite of his hot streak, tonight would be it for a while. The powers that be in Virginia were getting nervous. Too many people were talking. Too many foreign intelligence agencies were allocating assets to look into this rash of deaths among the world's most notorious terrorists and their network of financiers and arms dealers. Rapp was to return stateside for some rest and relaxation when he finished this one. At least that's what Rapp's handler had told him. Even after a quick year, however, he knew how things worked. Rest and relaxation meant that they wanted to observe him. Make sure some part of his psyche hadn't wandered down a dark corridor never to return. The thought brought a smile to Rapp's face. Killing these assholes was the most therapeutic thing he'd ever done in his life. It was better than a lifetime of psychotherapy.

He placed his hand over his left ear and focused on the tiny transmitter that was relaying the sounds of the luxury hotel suite two floors below. Just like the night before, and the night before that, he could hear the portly Libyan wheezing and snorting. The man was a three-pack-a-day chain smoker. If Rapp could only chase him up a flight of stairs he might be able to accomplish his task.

Rapp followed a delivery van as it quietly passed beneath on the Quai Voltaire. Something was bothering him, but he couldn't place it. He scanned the street for the slightest evidence that something was out of place and then turned his attention to the tree-lined walking paths that bordered the Seine River. They too were empty. All was as it should be, but still something was gnawing at him. Maybe things had been too easy as of late; one kill after another, city after city, and not so much as a single close call. The law of averages told him that sooner or later something would go wrong, and he would end up in a jam that might land him in a foreign jail or possibly cost him his life. Those two thoughts were always in the back of his mind, and depending on what country he was in, he wasn't sure which would be his preference.

There was little room for fear and doubt in what he did. There should be caution and a keen eye to detail, but fear and doubt could incapacitate. He could stand up here all night thinking up excuses not to proceed. Stan Hurley, the tough SOB who had trained him, had warned him about the pitfalls of paralysis by analysis. Rap thought about the stern warning that Hurley had given him and decided it was more than likely his handler's anxiety. She had warned him that if the slightest thing didn't seem right, he was to abort the mission. An American could not be caught doing this kind of dirty work in Paris. Not ever, and especially not now, given the current political climate.

In the big picture, the target was a link. Another name to cross off his list, but to Rapp it was always more personal than the big picture. He wanted to make every last one of these men pay for what they'd done. Each kill would grow more difficult— more dangerous—and it didn't bother Rapp in the least. He welcomed the challenge. In fact, he took sincere joy in the fact that these assholes were looking over their shoulder each day and going to sleep every night wondering who was hunting them.

Rapp asked himself one more time if he should be concerned that the Libyan was traveling without security. There was a good chance that the man found security in his position as his country's oil minister. As an important member of the diplomatic community, he probably thought himself above the dirty games of terrorists and assassins. *Well,* Rapp thought to himself, *once a terrorist always a terrorist.* Dress him up in a suit and tie and put him up in a thousand-dollar-a-night suite in Paris, and he was still a terrorist.

Rapp scanned the street and listened to the Libyan snoring like a pig. After a half-minute he made up his mind. The man would not see another sunrise. Rapp began to move in an efficient almost robotic way as he went over his gear one last time. His silenced Beretta was secured in a shoulder holster under his right arm; two extra magazines were safely tucked away under his left arm; a double-edged, four-inch combat knife was sheathed at the small of his back; and a smaller 9mm pistol was strapped to his right ankle. These were merely the offensive weapons he'd brought along. There was a small med kit, a radio that was tuned into the hotel's security channel, flex cuffs, and a perfectly forged set of documents that said he was a Palestinian recently immigrated from Amman, Jordan. And then there was the bulletproof vest. Wearing it was one of several things that had been beaten into him during his seemingly never-ending training.

Rapp flipped up the collar on his black trench coat and pulled a thin black balaclava over his face. He hefted the coil of climbing rope, looked over the edge of the building, and said to himself, "Two shots to the head." It was a bit redundant, but that was the point, and the essence of what this entire exercise was about.

Rapp gently let the rope play its way out and then swung both legs over the lip of the roof. In one smooth move he hopped off the ledge and spun 180 degrees. His gloved hands clamped onto the rope and slowed his descent until he had one foot on the railing of the balcony. Holding firmly to the rope he gently stepped down onto the small black iron grating. He was careful to keep himself off to one side despite the fact that the blackout drapes were pulled. Dropping to a knee he took the rope and brought it around the railing so it would be available should he need to make a quick exit. He had disabled the lock on the balcony door when he'd planted the listening device two days earlier. If there was time he would retrieve the device, but it was nothing special. Rapp always made sure to use devices that couldn't be traced back to one of the high-end manufacturers that Langley used.

He had the layout of the suite memorized. It was one big room with a sitting area on the left and king-size platform bed on the other. Rapp listened to the noises on the other side of the doors. The prostitute was more than likely there, but Rapp couldn't hear her over the obnoxious snorting and wheezing the Libyan was making. Everything was as it should be. Rapp drew his Beretta and slowly began to place pressure on the brass door handle with his gloved hand. He moved it from the three o'clock position down to five, and then it released without so much as a click.

Rapp pulled the door toward him and swung it flat against the side of the building. He placed his free hand on the seam of the blackout curtains and pushed through in a low crouch, his pistol up and sweeping from left to right. It was six steps from the balcony to where his target was sleeping. The bed was up so high that the platform had a step that wrapped around three sides. A massive, gaudy mirror served as the headboard. The elevation put the target at nearly chest height for the six-foot-one Rapp. With the tip of the silencer only four feet from the Libyan's head, Rapp stole a quick glance in hopes that he could locate the prostitute. The best he could do was get a sense that she was somewhere on the other side, buried under a jumble of pillows and blankets. He would never shoot her, but he might have to pistol-whip her in the event she woke up and started screaming.

Rapp moved a half step closer and leveled his weapon. He aimed the orange dot of his front sight on the bridge of the man's nose, and then brought into position the two dots from the rear. The pressure was already on the trigger, and without so much as the tiniest flash of hesitation, Rapp squeezed the trigger and sent a bullet into the man's head. The suppressor jumped one inch, fell back in line, and Rapp fired the second shot.

Rapp looked down at the Libyan. The second shot had enlarged the dime-sized hole by half. Death was instantaneous, which meant that the snoring had stopped. In the new silence of the room, Rapp's eyes darted to the jumbled pile on the far side of the bed, and after three seconds of no movement he dropped to his knee and reached around the back of the nightstand. The fingertips of his right hand had just found what he was looking for when he felt the floor beneath him tremble. The vibration was intense enough that Rapp knew it could only be caused by one thing. He withdrew his hand, leaving the listening device where it was, and rose enough so that he could look over the bed to the hotel room's door.

There, in the thin strip of light under the door, Rapp saw one shadow pass and then another. He cursed to himself, and was about to make a break toward the balcony when the door crashed open flooding the suite with a band of light. As Rapp began to drop, he saw the distinct black barrel of a submachine gun, and then a bright muzzle flash. While he took cover behind the bed and its heavy platform, he heard the distinctive spit of bullets leaving the end of a suppressor.

The mirror above the bed shattered with a crash and then bullets began thudding into the walls. Rapp tried to count the shots, but quickly realized that a second and third gun had joined the fight. He took a look at the balcony, a mere six steps away, and fought the urge to bolt. With this much lead flying, he would never make it. Plaster was raining down on him, and he could hear bullets impacting the mattress just a few inches above his head. Rapp pressed himself to the floor taking cover behind the carpeted platform that elevated the bed. His only avenue of escape was cut off, and he was cornered and outgunned. As the hail of bullets continued around him, he was reminded of something his trainer Stan Hurley had once said. It took Rapp a half-second before he realized it was his only chance. Grabbing a spare magazine from under his left arm, he focused on the area past the foot of the bed and waited for his chance.